"I *am* a natural disaster."

Minh's human face ~~~~~~~~~~~~~~~~~~~~~. Her hands slipped through ~~~~~~~~~~~~~~~~~~~ heavy pause, she sigh~~~~~~~~~~~~~~~~~~~~~~~~~~~ his will get bloody. ~~~~~~~~~~~~~~~~~~~~~~~~~ an anyone could an~~~~~~~~~~~~~~~~~~~~~ blood is spilled? ~~~~~~~~~~~~~~~~~~~~~~ te?"

"I don't ~~~~~~~~~~~~~~~~~~~ess that Paige could feel ~~~~~~~~~~~~~~~~ 's find out."

MARCUS PELEGRIMAS's SKINNERS

"Pelegrimas has done the impossible—come up with a fresh and exciting twist on vampire lore."

Ed Gorman, bestselling co-author of
Dean Koontz's Frankenstein: City of Night

"An amazing talent!"

Robert J. Randisi

"Bram Stoker reinvigorated Gothic horror in the late 19th century . . . Pelegrimas [has] the potential to do the same thing here in the 21st century. . . . His storytelling style is utterly readable, his characters are unconventional and endearing, his wry sense of humor priceless."

Paul Goat Allen

"Fans of Jim Butcher and Laurell K. Hamilton will definitely want a bite of this!"

Jonathan Maberry,
Bram Stoker Award-winning author of *Patient Zero*

By Marcus Pelegrimas

Skinners
BLOOD BLADE
HOWLING LEGION
TEETH OF BEASTS
VAMPIRE UPRISING
THE BREAKING

ATTENTION: ORGANIZATIONS AND CORPORATIONS
Most Harper Voyager paperbacks are available at special quantity discounts for bulk purchases for sales promotions, premiums, or fund raising. For information, please call or write:

**Special Markets Department, HarperCollins Publishers,
10 East 53rd Street, New York, New York 10022-5299.
Telephone: (212) 207-7528.   Fax: (212) 207-7222.**

The Breaking
SKINNERS

MARCUS PELEGRIMAS

HARPER Voyager
An Imprint of HarperCollinsPublishers

This is a work of fiction. Names, characters, places, and incidents are products of the author's imagination or are used fictitiously and are not to be construed as real. Any resemblance to actual events, locales, organizations, or persons, living or dead, is entirely coincidental.

HARPER Voyager

An Imprint of HarperCollins*Publishers*
10 East 53rd Street
New York, New York 10022-5299

Copyright © 2011 by Marcus Pelegrimas
Excerpt from *Extinction Agenda* copyright © 2011 by Marcus Pelegrimas
Cover art by Larry Rostant
ISBN 978-0-06-198634-5
www.harpervoyagerbooks.com

All rights reserved. No part of this book may be used or reproduced in any manner whatsoever without written permission, except in the case of brief quotations embodied in critical articles and reviews. For more information, address Harper Voyager, an Imprint of HarperCollins Publishers.

First Harper Voyager mass market printing: June 2011

Harper Voyager and) is a trademark of HCP LLC.

Printed in the U.S.A.

10 9 8 7 6 5 4 3 2 1

If you purchased this book without a cover, you should be aware that this book is stolen property. It was reported as "unsold and destroyed" to the publisher, and neither the author nor the publisher has received any payment for this "stripped book."

The Breaking

Prologue

Smoky Hill River, Kansas
Fifteen miles west of Cedar Bluff State Park

It had been just over three weeks since the Nymar declared war on all Skinners. They'd targeted the hunters they knew, burnt them from their homes and coaxed them into open combat. Apart from thinning the Skinner ranks, they'd introduced the Shadow Spore into the modern world and blamed the Skinners for the deaths of dozens of police officers in a crossfire spanning most of the United States. Things settled down a bit after authorities stumbled upon a Skinner raid in Denver and arrested a man believed to be one of the main perpetrators in all of those cop killings. That man was Cole Warnecki, and ever since he was put behind bars, a spokesman for the police had shown up in several random interviews declaring the carnage over.

That spokesman's narrow, smiling face had been broadcast on every major network, assuring the country that blood was no longer being spilled and the authorities had everything well in hand. Even the few humans who recognized Kawosa's face were unable to resist being drawn in by the calming words spoken by one known as the First Deceiver. Some Skinners, however, couldn't be pacified like the rest of the viewing public. For them, just keeping their heads above water was a struggle. Even if they knew Cole Warnecki had been framed by the Nymar, the hunt never stopped.

The stomping grounds of the Skinner known as Jessup were in the mountain ranges of Montana, but the territory he protected branched out to cover several states in each direction. The last year had been filled with commotion that put too many Skinners into the ground. Since then he'd done his part to pick up the slack by hitting the road and keeping his eyes open for anything that might need killing. Upon arriving in Ness City, Jessup only had to spark a conversation in a few local diners to hear stories about a pack of wolves that were known to fly, bark at the moon, run like the wind, and bite through solid steel. Even after making allowances for excited exaggeration, Jessup was confident he'd found something worth his time. At the very least, he could add a few Half Breed pelts and teeth to his collection. Most of the attacks supposedly happened north of town in the flatlands on either side of the Smoky Hill River, so the Skinner tipped his hat to the ones who'd told the stories, paid for his meat loaf, climbed into his Ford F150 and headed north.

The scars on his hands started to burn after less than an hour of driving. Three miles down the road, when the trail started to cool, Jessup pulled to a stop and climbed down from the driver's seat before he lost it completely. Most werewolves didn't bother with roads, and he knew that chasing after the things on four wheels didn't do a lick of good anyway. A pack of werewolves could outrun, outmaneuver, and overturn any vehicle falling short of a tank. More than likely they'd already sniffed him out anyway, and were circling in close enough to take their first run at him.

As soon as his boots touched the ground, Jessup walked around the truck and pulled down the tailgate. His field kit was kept in a green canvas duffel bag covered in stenciled lettering and dirt picked up from opposite ends of the globe. Pockets were stitched into the inside walls to carry items he'd either need quickly or didn't want to mix with the rest of his supplies. He pulled out an old mayonnaise jar filled with a thick black jelly that became even murkier when he shook it up. After filling his lungs with a generous portion of air that smelled of burnt leaves, he held his breath and twisted open the jar. Even after bracing himself for the stench, Jessup had to force back his gag reflex once the pungent

Skinners: The Breaking

aroma of blood, spoiled meat, and shapeshifter pheromones drifted into his nostrils.

Although the basic ingredients were the same, every Skinner had their own twist on the recipe for werewolf bait. Jessup's included a few additions to hit the creatures' sense of hunger as well as their instinctual attraction to certain substances. Not wasting time with cleanliness, he dipped his fingers into the jar and spattered the potent concoction on the tall grass around him while walking slowly away from the road and whistling to himself.

After all the bickering and haggling he'd been forced to endure with other Skinners who squabbled about how to fight the same battle, Jessup was now on his own, savoring the simple pleasures of the hunt. Old man Lancroft might have been crazy, but as far as Jessup was concerned, he did have a point when he'd written about Skinners losing their way. Nobody was sure who'd sent out the journals to everyone on MEG's e-mail list, but Lancroft's words made Jessup eager to strike out on his own and make whatever difference he could. On a more basic level, it just felt good to have the sun on his face, a weapon in his hands, and less bitching in his ears.

Before long a keening howl drifted through the air. He placed a hand on the brim of his beaten cowboy hat, shifted it toward the back of his head and waited.

The howl came again. This time it was joined by other animal voices that were just a bit too high-pitched to be the ones he was after. Another clearer, almost musical howl rolled in from the east. Once it made itself known, the others stopped quicker than steam choked off by a closed valve. Jessup remained still. His six-foot-four-inch frame blended in with its surroundings like another tree trunk that had been halved by a tornado from a rough summer. His eyes narrowed and a barely audible breath passed from between chapped lips. The only other sound he created came from the clatter of long, gnarled fangs fastened to thin cords dangling from his beaten leather vest. Slowly, he bent down to slip a hand into one of the pockets of his Army surplus fatigues. Digging out a tube of pepper spray from the pants pocket, he set it on the ground and marked the spot with a knife that he flung into the dirt.

The first set of howls had come from the northwest and weren't made by Half Breeds. Whatever they were, more of the shaggy figures had circled around him to the south and southeast. The more musical howl was silent now, but he couldn't worry about that one at the moment. The burning in his scars remained at a simmer as several animals stalked toward him. They were bigger than dogs or wolves, yet too narrow at the shoulders to be small bears or even wild pigs. In his years of hunting, Jessup had been fooled by both kinds of animals, and that wasn't going to change now. The reaction in his scars hadn't worsened, because they weren't shapeshifters. That was the final piece to solve the identity of his mystery guests.

"Damn Shunkaws," he muttered. "Ain't seen these things for a good long time. Fits the bill from those stories, though. Should've guessed it."

As he grumbled to himself, Jessup reached for the stainless steel .45 caliber pistol holstered beneath his vest. The handgun had been put together using pieces of other weapons he'd bought or confiscated throughout the years. "First the Chupes spring up near every damn lake I find, and now a pack of Shunkaws roaming the plains. What's next? The lizard men gonna march on Tallahassee?"

Jessup spotted five of the creatures fanning out to flank him. Their arched backs were marked by a distinctive ridge of bone protruding from a patchy coat of hardened fur that moved like a single piece of armor. He patted his pockets, touching three extra magazines for the .45 and a holdout revolver loaded with five .48 caliber rounds that he'd packed himself. Each of those rounds could punch a hole through a car. Shunkaws weren't that tough to put down, but he was more concerned with the beast that sent a wave of heat through his scars along with a wailing howl to stop the pack cold.

It took some mental gymnastics, but Jessup managed to think back to what might attract the Shunkaws even better than the mixture he carried for Half Breeds. Their noses picked up sweet scents more than anything else, which was partially why they were drawn to children or anyone else who frequently had ice cream, chocolate, or jelly smeared on them. Fortunately, he'd picked up some Peanut M&Ms along with a spicy beef stick at the last gas station. He tore open the bag of candy, emptied it into his mouth and chewed them. It took a great amount of restraint to keep from swallowing the glob of chocolaty goodness before spitting it out in smaller, marble-sized chunks into the grass.

A chorus of scratchy, panting breaths drifted through the air, followed by the crunching of large paws against dried earth. As the pack drew closer, Jessup backed away and prepared to meet it. Soon he would see the faces of the beasts at the front of the group. Squat, long heads were accented by wide brows that looked like shelves made of bark. Their eyes were disturbingly human, with uniformly dark green pupils on fields of white. But what set them apart from any other canine were their short snouts and peculiar teeth. Although there were several smaller molars set along the backs of their jaws, most of the damage was done by two large teeth: one on the upper jaw and another on the lower, angled into a point and curved toward their throats. The shape added a grating sound to their breaths and a rasp to their howl, which Jessup heard when he caught the eye of the pack's leader.

The wailing howl of the thing that had set his scars to burning snaked across the plains like smoke on a breeze. It was definitely closer.

"Come on," Jessup said. "Come to me, you ugly bastards."

There was some debate as to whether Shunkaws could understand human language. Right now, Jessup simply wanted to catch the creatures' attention before he had an even bigger threat to worry about. When the leader of the closer group of animals nodded toward his followers to get them to back away, Jessup fired a round from his .45 that caught the Shunkaw squarely in the face. Its head snapped to one side as a small amount of blood and flecks of bone sprayed from the wound. Its skeletal structure was too dense to be punctured so easily, but the alpha was definitely put off his game as the others swarmed the Skinner to extract some payback.

The gun in Jessup's right hand barked again and again while he reached for a finely tooled shoulder harness with his left. A hatchet hung there from a loop of braided leather where it could be drawn with a quick forward swipe. Slightly larger than a tomahawk, the weapon was carved from one piece of wood, stained with several layers of varnish mixed from an old Skinner formula, and adorned with teeth of various sizes that had been embedded into the wood like an insect that had been absorbed into amber. Thorns in its handle bit into Jessup's palms, starting a trickle of blood that awakened the bond between the weapon and the man who wielded it.

When the next beast reached him, Jessup snarled, "That's it! Soup's on." Sidestepping half a second before the first Shunkaw got a chance to clamp its jaws around his leg, he fired a round into the top of its head that drove its chin into the dirt. He followed that up by burying the hatchet blade into its skull. Crafted from supernatural materials, the hatchet cut a lot deeper than the .45's bullets. The Shunkaw clawed at the ground and let out a shuddering gasp. Jessup willed the hatchet blade to become thinner so he could more easily pull it from where it had been lodged and swing at the next incoming beast.

One Shunkaw charged at him just ahead of another. Both creatures set their wide, vacant eyes upon him and opened their mouths in preparation for their meal. The first one ducked beneath Jessup's swing and the second caught three bullets from the .45 in its head and neck. Its head wobbled from the impact of rounds that thumped against dense bone and became lodged in thick, leathery muscle. Even as Jessup kicked at the yelping Shunkaw, he looked around for the other one. Only four of the five were accounted for, which meant the last one could be sneaking around to bring him down from whatever open angle it could find. He fired more shots at the alpha, willed his hatchet blade to form something closer to a pickaxe and then buried it into the chest of the first creature to spring forward in an attempt to bring him down.

Something moved near his leg, and as Jessup turned toward it, he found a Shunkaw with its belly pressed against the ground so it could scurry forward to snap at his ankle. The Skinner was barely quick enough to kick the Shunkaw's chin before its two angled front teeth were introduced to his flesh. The alpha collected himself enough then to let out a grating snarl that was quickly mimicked by the surviving members of the pack. The fifth Shunkaw had done its job and flanked him, so Jessup crouched down as he spun around to swing his weapon at the creature. But instead of another narrow, buck-toothed canine face, he found the sleek visage of a Full Blood.

There was no mistaking it. The burning in his scars had flared up so badly that he felt as if his hands were pressed against the glowing surface of a stove. Thickly matted fur lay flat against the creature's trim body. Large pointed ears extended straight back as if it was running with enough power to generate a breeze. One glance at its markings and coat told Jessup it wasn't any of the Full Bloods from the area. The teeth it showed while curling back its lips were bony icicles glistening with saliva flowing from torn, bloody gums. Curved claws dug into the soil as crystalline hazel eyes silently challenged the Skinner to make his next move.

The Shunkaw that had gotten behind Jessup lay on its side, half of its chest peeled open and its eyes fixed upon the oblivion to which it had been sent. Although Jessup had seen plenty of wounds in his days, he was astounded by the one that had opened up that creature. It was so clean and wide that it could very well have been made by a helicopter rotor.

"Easy, now," he said while reaching under his vest for the holdout pistol. Despite the high caliber weapon and body armor sewn into the vest he wore, he couldn't help but feel exposed. The .48 would only piss a Full Blood off, and no amount of tanned Half Breed skins could withstand the frenzied assault that would follow.

The alpha Shunkaw growled at his last remaining follower, prompting that one to lunge at the Full Blood in a flurry of teeth and claws. It was all Jessup could do to clear a path, which played directly into the alpha's plan. The wounded Shunkaw hopped to one side, waited for the Skinner to stop moving, then clamped down on his left shin.

Jessup cried out in pain as the creature's two large teeth pierced his skin, dug through the meat below it and hit bone. From there, the Shunkaw used his teeth to their full potential and dragged its head down along Jessup's leg to try and strip the meat from his bone like cheese being cut away from a block. Before that could happen, Jessup unleashed a flurry of attacks. The pain had already been washed away by numbness that claimed his leg below the knee, but he still dropped to one knee. When his hatchet made contact with the Shunkaw's neck, its head was nearly removed from its shoulders. Jessup grabbed it by one ear, pulled so its teeth came up and out of him, and then finished the job he'd started with another hacking blow from his weapon. The Shunkaw's head dangled from his fist when Jessup rolled over to face not one, but two Full Bloods.

The one he'd already spotted had ripped apart the last of the Shunkaws and had its snout buried inside the ravaged chest cavity. Blood poured from its mouth to spatter upon its silver fur. The second Full Blood stood just behind that one. Its dark brown coat bristled and the corner of one crystalline blue-gray eye twitched as a powerful wind swept across the grassy plain. It stalked forward, keeping the other werewolf in check with a warning growl emanating from the back of his throat.

Jessup tried standing up. He couldn't even make it halfway before a fresh wave of agony took his breath away. He didn't want to look at his leg. The wound was bad, and knowing more than that wouldn't do him any good. Acting on nothing more than primitive instinct, he lifted the Shunkaw's severed head and tossed it at the werewolf's feet.

The Full Blood with the brown coat was nearly double the size of the silver one. Scars lay just beneath the fur of its shoulder and cut a nasty groove down one cheek like cracks hewn into the side of a mountain. Its lips quivered while its nose twitched to pull in Jessup's scent.

"I heard of you," Jessup said. "Burkis, ain't it?"

Expelling its breath with a powerful snuff, the Full Blood furrowed its brow and examined him with renewed interest.

"That's right," Jessup said. "Ain't no place you can hide from us no more. Did that friend of yours set these things loose? Just like he sicced them Half Breeds on Kansas City?" Since that didn't get a reaction from the Full Blood, he tightened his grip on the holdout pistol. "It don't matter how many Half Breeds you make or how many other beasties you dig up. We'll find them and bury them just like I found these child-stealing bastards!"

Skinners: The Breaking

The smaller Full Blood looked at the larger one expectantly.

One second, Burkis was on four legs, and the next he'd stretched into a form with a slender torso and limbs that grew into fully realized arms and legs. Front paws became hands, one of which slapped the gun from Jessup's hand. "You didn't find us, Skinner," the Full Blood snarled. "We found you."

"Okay. So, now what?"

"Now, you'll keep an eye on this one," Burkis said as he pointed a clawed finger at the other Full Blood.

"I beg your pardon?"

"You heard me," the werewolf snarled in a voice that caused birds to scatter from trees a mile away. "Keep her alive and keep her away from the others of my kind."

"Why would I do that?"

Burkis lowered his head to glare at Jessup in a way that made the Skinner clench. "The Breaking is coming, and her life could make the difference between only some of you feeling its wrath or your entire species being lost amid a torrent of snapping bones."

Chapter One

Toronto, Ontario
Canada

It had been a long drive from Rochester. Despite the fact that Paige had made longer trips in a much crappier car, she felt every mile as if each one had knuckles to rap against her temples. She missed the rattling comfort of the Chevy Cavalier that had served her so well before sputtering its last breath. What little solace she could gain from the two-door Hyundai she'd rented had been eroded by the company she'd been forced to keep.

"Are we there yet?" Rico groaned. When he saw the death glare Paige shot him, he flashed an expanse of blocky teeth. "Just kidding."

"Wasn't funny three hours ago and it ain't funny now."

"Why didn't the nymphs teleport us to where we needed to go?" asked the young Skinner who'd passed off a fake ID well enough to sign the car's rental agreement. "Are the Mounties cracking down on tittie bars on Canadian soil?"

"I already told you. After the Nymar set us up to take the fall for all those cops that were killed, the nymphs want to keep their distance from us for a while," Paige explained.

The man in the passenger seat wore a thick biker's jacket wrapped around a solid muscular frame. After several days of hopping from one cheap motel to another, Rico's face had become overgrown with the promising start of a graying beard. It was the best opportunity short of surgery to separate himself from the pictures that had been making the rounds on the national news networks after the legal trouble started. Rico was no stranger to scraping the law the wrong way. Even though the last several weeks had been filled with enough running and hiding to make the Skinners feel more like prey than hunters, he hadn't missed a wink of sleep.

Paige sat in a relaxed posture behind the wheel, with one elbow propped against the window frame so she could keep the tips of her fingers pressed against her forehead. Whenever the car skidded on a patch of wet pavement, she corrected with an instinctive tilt of the wheel or pump of the brakes. "Is there a reason you decided to bring up the nymphs again?"

"Yeah," the man in the backseat replied. He extended one finger to point at a billboard on the side of the road that read: TURN RIGHT FOR ANDREA'S CHAMPAGNE ROOM. LIVE DANCING AND BUFFET.

When Paige looked at the other Skinner, using the rearview mirror, she found a man in his late twenties with light olive skin, a large nose, and hair cut into a flat top that could be found on any soldier after his first day of boot camp. He'd been fidgety ever since she picked him up at a safe house in a wooded section of New York's Wayne County. The nervousness was easy enough to explain, since all Skinners had either been burned out of their homes by Nymar or placed on the Most Wanted lists by local and federal authorities. "What makes you think that's a nymph bar?" Paige asked.

"The buffet. We could stop in and check. Or maybe you could call Tristan. She'd be able to tell us where to go for—"

"Oh she'll tell us where to go, all right. Besides, it's too late to need any help with transport. The Nymar we're after is in Toronto, and we've been in Toronto for fifteen minutes."

"What about gettin' home?" Rico asked. "You tellin' me we gotta drive all the way back to St. Louis from here?"

"We'll figure something out."

"Just like you figured out with Cole?"

Paige's foot slammed against the brake pedal, putting the car into a skid that made a stomach-wrenching sound of rubber brushing against pavement that still glistened with rain. They were on a section of the Gardiner Expressway that looked down on a row of squat gray buildings to the left and had a view of an ornate structure with tall towers topped with small green domes on the right. Several cars honked at her, which did nothing to prevent her from coming to a stop on the side of the road.

Her hair had been clipped into a pointed bob the previous summer, and although she tried to maintain the style in the following months, it had grown out into a simpler shape that was only slightly longer along the sides than it was in back. Anger filled her brown eyes, and the nostrils of her subtly bent nose flared as she asked, "Just what the fuck was that supposed to mean?"

"You heard me, Bloodhound. You were at that warehouse in Denver when the shit went down with the Nymar and those dead cops. Or, I should say you were there at the end when you were flown in via helicopter like a goddamn rock star."

"Yeah," the guy in the backseat chimed in. "What's the deal with that?"

Paige jabbed a finger at the younger man as if she meant to shatter the car's rear window. "You don't get to talk to me like that. In fact, do yourself a favor and stop talking altogether."

When the guy prepared to defend himself, Rico waved at him and said, "Best listen to her, Steve. You weren't there."

As she shifted her eyes toward Rico, a hint of pain could be seen amidst the ever-present fierceness. "Any reason you decided to spring this on me now after we've been in the car all this time?"

"I was hoping you'd tell me on yer own. After all we been through, it's the least you could do."

"It's between me and Cole," she said while cranking the steering wheel so she could reenter the flow of eastbound traffic. "And when are we supposed to talk? We've been on the run, living off of beef jerky and coffee for two weeks."

"Then we had that split after nearly getting pinched by those cops in Bismarck," Rico chuckled fondly.

"We've been hiding in ditches and laying low in basements until we got into New York. Ever since then we've had that one tagging along."

Responding to the scarred hand being waved back at him from the driver's seat, Steve grunted. "You can trust me. I'm a damn Skinner too."

"So you keep saying," she told him. "You may have plenty of people vouching for you and a good record in MEG's files, but you still need to earn your stripes with me, And it's funny to hear you so concerned about Cole, Rico. Last time I checked, you hadn't even gone to look in on him."

"When did you check?"

"Does it matter?"

Suddenly, Rico became concerned with adjusting the vent so warm air from the heater was hitting his face at precisely the right angle. "All right, you got me. I ain't exactly eager to walk into another prison. Odds are about fifty-fifty of me not walkin' out again. Besides, after you left to back Gerald's play when he moved to Chicago, you stopped bein' me and Ned's partner. You never checked in on us until you needed help in St. Louis."

Paige shook her head while weaving between cars on the sloppy expressway. "Are you trying to come off like you stood by Ned no matter what? You expect me to forget about you going rogue in the Badlands or doing work for the mob?"

"Allegedly," Rico corrected as he snapped an uneasy glare over his shoulder. He shifted in his seat and focused on the road in front of him. Despite being only a few hours away from New York, he could feel a difference in his surroundings. It wasn't exactly foreign soil, but Canada had a calmness to it that struck a Skinner like the tranquil look in a deer's eyes when it had no clue how many rifles were pointed at its head. "Maybe me and Ned weren't exactly sentimental, but that still don't mean you get a pass on what happened in Denver."

The bulk of the city was behind them, leaving a wide open expanse of concrete to fill the windshield. The evening rush hour was over, but just barely. Rain that had fallen weeks ago remained pooled on the side of the road, illuminated by the dimming rays of the sun and streetlights that were too weak to cast more than a glow before night fully took hold. Paige scanned the signs marking the upcoming exits and allowed herself to settle into her seat. "What happened in Denver is what needed to happen. I'll see to it that it gets explained to Cole, but I don't need to explain it to anyone else."

"The hell you don't. I'm the only one of us that trusts you anymore. The only way for that to change is for you to come clean because you sure as hell can't survive in this fight alone."

"So when you talk about the other Skinners, are you referring to the ones like Abel and Selina who joined up with Hope and Tara to set us all up for this fall? Yeah, I really want to make sure they don't think badly of me."

She didn't have to look over at Rico to know he was glaring at her. "Some of 'em double-crossed us," he said sternly, "but there are plenty out there just trying to stay alive. We lost some good people when Liam and those Mongrels hit Lancroft's place. Even if there are fewer of us now, the ones that are still on the right side of the fence can pull together like never before. We can finally open our eyes to all the shit we've been missing and start fighting to win for a change."

"You'd better not tell me I wasn't fighting to win."

"I know you've still got your eyes on the prize, girl. That's why I came all the way up north with you even after you refuse to tell me everything I need to know. We're all in this together. Ain't that right, Steve?"

The younger man nodded. "That's right. We're in this together."

Paige took some comfort from that, even though she wasn't exactly sure why. "That's not the only reason you're here right now," she said to Rico. "You're keeping tabs on me to make sure I don't step any further out of line."

"Could be."

After rounding a bend on the expressway, Paige turned to look at the big man so she could study him when she asked, "And what happens if I do anything else you don't agree with? Are you going to take me out?"

Rico's hand lay casually on his hip. It was close to the Sig Sauer holstered under his arm, but he hadn't made a move to pull the .45 from its resting place. "You're worked up," he sighed. "We been through too much for you to believe shit like that."

"We have been through a lot. The Nymar have risen up from a pain in our asses, skipped over being a thorn in our sides, and become the stake in our collective chest. As ironic as that is, it means we've all got to be careful." Now that she'd turned onto the Don Valley Parkway and was headed north, she paid closer attention to the street signs and cars around her. "I don't know," she grumbled. "Is that even irony?"

"I think so." After scratching his roughly stubbled chin, Rico asked, "Is that irony, Steve?"

"Nope. That's just a bad play on words."

"Look, Bloodhound, I get that everything's been flipped upside down. I was there when it happened. We been on the run for over a month, hiding, laying low, and living day to day. But that don't cut it no more. It's time to stop hiding from the shit storm and start dealing with it."

"Amen to that."

"And if we're gonna deal with it, we need to deal the right way."

Paige cut him short by holding up a hand to show him one of her scarred palms. "And that means me telling you everything I know, including who those guys were that brought me to Denver in that helicopter. Am I right?"

"That'd be a good start."

"Too bad we're almost at our exit," she said with a crooked grin and half a sideways glance. "If you would've asked me about this earlier, I might have had some time to get into the whole story."

"We got time," Rico growled. "After you take the next exit, we need to get onto Queen Street and head into the Upper Beaches area." Seeing the way she raised her eyebrows, he added, "I can do research too, you know. What makes you think this Cobb guy is even there?"

"Before he was taken away, Cole told Prophet how to intercept some of the e-mail the Nymar have been using to communicate with each other. Prophet got a few hits, he sent them to some techie guys, MEG helped out a little more, and finally we got our little fingers into the Nymar Web ring. Remember those bloodsuckers you flushed out of Cedar Rapids?"

"Oh yeah. They talked a big game but didn't have anything to back it up. Ran like a bunch of bitches."

"Damn right they did," Paige said. "Ran straight to me. After some colorful questioning techniques, they told me some more about the guy running the Nymar communication network. He's supposed to be based here in Canada, and even if he's not in the house where we're headed, there should be someone in the area to point us in the right direction. Hope wasn't the only double-seeded Nymar working on that uprising. I'm thinking one of the others will be guarding this place."

"Could be Cobb38 is double-seeded too," Steve offered.

"You really think so?" Paige asked. "Leading a bunch of Nymar on the street is one thing. Those double-seeded bloodsuckers are usually too hungry to do anything on a scale like this."

"We'll find out soon enough," Rico said. "There should be a computer setup or at least the remains of one in a Nymar safe house. Did you pay close enough attention to Cole when he was around to learn some of those geek skills of his?"

Paige pulled in a breath, blinked heavily a few times and nodded once.

"Good," Rico said. "That's our exit." Waiting until she was committed to making the turn, he added, "That means you've got some time to explain yourself where Denver is concerned. Before you flip me any more of that shit about only explaining to Cole, you gotta remember that you left me, Prophet, and all them Amriany out there to fend for ourselves too. Me and the Gypsies don't exactly see eye-to-eye, but they held their own that night."

"Remember Officer Stanze?"

"The cop from Kansas City? Yeah."

"Before Liam tried to tear that city down, he found a Half Breed carcass and started asking around about it. He even tried to sell it online. I was the one who bought it, but there were other people who took notice of the auction. Once werewolves of all shapes and sizes started charging down metropolitan streets, those people put some very important pieces together. One of them was in that helicopter."

"Another cop?"

"Not quite."

Although that eased Rico's nerves a bit, it didn't help much. "What, then? A fed?"

"No. I'm going to Kenilworth Avenue, right?"

"That's right. Tell me who those guys are."

"They're the ones that have been keeping all of this from boiling over into something a hell of a lot worse than it is."

"All of what?" Rico asked. "You mean the crap that the Nymar pulled? Coming from someone whose home was burnt down by those vampire motherfuckers, it's hard to believe you're saying this shit hasn't already boiled way the hell over."

"Skinners have been going through hell," Paige told him, "but we signed up for it." She drove down a section of Queen Street that was lined on both sides with two-story storefronts ranging from small restaurants and bars to specialty shops and a few little apartment buildings. Traffic was getting worse, but she held her own thanks to a Chicago driving attitude that shifted between persistent and crazy. "It's not just the casualties we need to worry about anymore," she continued. "Everything from Misonyk and Henry's first rampage in Chicago to the vampires running amok a few months ago is out there for the whole damn world to see."

"Yeah, I've noticed that. The news and God only knows how many websites have been packed full of bullshit about dog attacks and vampires. Most of it's either dried up on its own or been pushed aside for bigger news."

"Like the Mud Flu," Paige said. "And that was one of ours too. Somehow, we were still able to set up shop in Lancroft's place and try to deal with the Nymar."

"Great job we did of that."

"Could have been worse if we had more pressure from the real world. It took the Nymar to bring all of that down on us. Stanze was on to something other than the Half Breed he found. His department and the cops in a few other cities started coming to him for advice on their own wild dog attacks. Pretty soon he was approached by someone else looking for answers. I went to him for help while you, Cole, and Prophet were in Denver. That's when Stanze introduced me to the guys who found him."

"All right, then," Rico grunted. "How'd you wind up in that helicopter?"

"Tell ya what. Why don't I pull over, order some coffee and doughnuts, and we can talk about it some more?" Kenilworth Avenue was the next intersection she found, so Paige turned left and pulled over. "I know why not. We came here to find out who's been pushing the goddamn Nymar to wipe us out." She killed the engine and her headlights, pulled the keys from the ignition, and drew a pistol from the holster clipped to her hip. The Beretta PX4 Storm Compact strayed from Rico's mandate that all Skinners carry .45s, but the handgun fit nicely in her grip and the 9mm rounds packed a solid punch. When she needed more than one punch, all she had to do was draw the second PX4 from the holster strapped around her shoulder. She pulled out the magazine, checking not only that it was full, but that it contained rounds treated with the antidote used to poison Nymar spore.

"You gotta make this right," Rico told her. "Not just with me, but with the others too. There's a hell of a lot brewin' ever since Skinners were all hung out to dry as cop killers. We gotta pull together and turn this thing around before it buries us all. Them Mongrels that attacked the Lancroft place ain't been seen for a while. Neither has the Full Blood that was leading them or the one that became your buddy so recently."

"Mr. Burkis is a long way from a buddy. As for Liam, he could be anywhere. If there was more hours in the day, I could take time to hunt them down."

"You won't need to hunt them," Steve reminded her. "They can find us whenever the hell they want."

"Good," she said as she slapped the magazine into the Beretta, then chambered the first round. "I've still got some of that ammo dipped in the Blood Blade fragments that should put a real crimp in their day."

"Hopefully it'll work better than the Nymar rounds do against Shadow Spore," Steve said from the backseat. "Did Daniels come up with anything that works on them?"

"Not yet."

"Then we could be walking into a whole lot of trouble by waving guns around loaded with bullets that won't even do the job."

"They'll do the job," she assured him. "Just keep firing until their hearts are turned into paste."

"Any way I can talk you out of this? I know some guys that might be up for this job. They're workin' on some angles of their own right now, organizing the Skinners that can make a difference in this fight, but they still might be able to pitch in here."

"I'm not interested in working with more strangers," Paige snapped as she turned toward Steve. "You said I needed to put this right and that's what I want to do. I found you. Prophet is already back chasing fugitives. Those Amriany disappeared on their own. That leaves Cole, and he's the only one that I owe a goddamn thing to anymore. We didn't cause these problems. We didn't create these monsters and we sure as hell didn't set them loose. We're doing our best, but if people can't defend themselves every now and then, something's bound to pick them off."

Rico's features were like folds in an elephant's hide. When they shifted, it was just to another version of ugly. Paige had known him long enough to recognize the hint of a grin hidden under all of those unattractive layers, but she wasn't about to answer back with one of her own. Reaching around to grab the Mossberg Model 535 Tactical 12-gauge shotgun he'd stowed on the floor of the seat behind him, he said, "You might get along with these friends of mine better than you think."

Every other house on Kenilworth Avenue seemed to be a duplex. For each little single family home on the clean, tree-lined street, there was another that looked as if it had been built with one wall butting against a mirror. Paige's destination was one of the duplexes just north of the intersection at Kenilworth and Norway Avenue. It was a tan run-down structure with two sets of screen doors that had taken equal amounts of abuse from owners and elements alike. By the time she, Steve, and Rico had made their way up the street

Skinners: The Breaking

to get a look at the place, the sky had dimmed to a mix of dark purples and blues. Cars rolled through the residential neighborhood, but the drivers were more concerned with getting home than taking notice of anyone ambling along the sidewalk.

Paige had her hands stuffed into the pockets of a dark green jacket made of heavy canvas. It was baggy enough to allow her to move freely without getting snagged on the underlying layers consisting of a tactical vest over a dark gray T-shirt. The storerooms beneath Jonah Lancroft's home in Philadelphia had provided her with plenty of Half Breed skins to use as lining for the vest that took a lot of punishment from almost anything, even if it wasn't treated using Rico's tanning techniques. The harness zipped around the skins, providing her with more protection than any conventional body armor.

Striding beside her, Rico kept his arms hanging at his sides as if he was walking down an Old West boardwalk with the intention of facing his doom at sundown. His jacket was the sort of battered garment that would have been worn with pride by any self-respecting biker. Several dozen Half Breeds had died to either create or patch up that jacket over the years and it still wasn't complete. Strips of canvas were stitched in to fill the remaining gaps, and leather cords were laced up both sides so he could expand or tighten the jacket as the occasion demanded. For the moment, it was loose enough to accommodate his shoulder holster and the bulk of extra shotgun shells stuffed into his pocket. It wasn't long enough, however, to do much to hide the Mossberg.

Steve carried three guns, all .45s, holstered beneath a baggy raincoat. Although he didn't seem to handle the weapons with much expertise, he assured both Skinners that he knew how to make them sing. That was good enough for Paige, especially since he'd survived the last few weeks, when so many Skinners had been picked off by Nymar who blended into the darkness and moved faster than the now outdated variety of vampire. "How many are inside?" he asked.

"Don't know."

Looking at the front of the house, Rico glanced back and

forth between both front doors at the top of a single, narrow set of stairs leading up from the sidewalk. "Do you even know which side it's on?"

"I figured we'd each take one," she replied. "Shouldn't be long before we figure out which is which."

"Good plan," Rico grunted.

"Thanks."

"I was being sarcastic."

"I know." Facing the corner where she'd parked the car, Paige casually reached for the Beretta holstered at her hip. "If you've got a preference, tell me now."

The house wasn't much to look at, but was well-maintained. Despite the fact that the outside was weather-beaten and battered, the simple curtains in the windows were clean and drawn shut tightly enough to keep the inside tucked away and out of sight. There wasn't a single feature to differentiate one half from the other. Even the windows on both sides were dark in the exact same way. "I'll take the right," he said with a shrug.

"You'll also take the new guy." After glancing back and forth to make certain the sidewalk in front of the house and its closest neighbors was empty, Paige held her pistol in a two-handed grip with the barrel pointed at the ground and added, "Either of you needs help, just yell. Remember, we're looking for any Nymar and a computer setup."

"I was listening during the ride over," Steve whined. "I know what you're looking for."

"Good. Then let's find it."

Chapter Two

Paige approached the door on the left, placed her shoulder against the wall and leaned to try and look through the window. There was a small gap between the frame and the edge of the curtain, which wasn't enough for her to see much of anything inside other than a few lights deeper within the place. Once Rico approached his door, she stepped over and opened hers with a straight kick that slammed her heel a few inches below the knob. It gave way with the crackle of splintering wood and the creak of an old dead bolt being dislodged from its housing.

The room was almost pitch-black, illuminated only by the scant bit of light spilling out from a short hallway that led to the back rooms. Her eyes had adjusted quickly enough to make out the blocky shapes of furniture in her path and a television set on a stand to her left. Bundles lay on the floor in a way that let her picture the homeowner casually dropping them while heading deeper into the house. Raising her Beretta to sight along the top of its barrel, she stepped over the bundles and waited for someone to answer the simultaneous break-ins. The response came in the form of one of those bundles reaching up to grab her.

"Son of a bitch!" she snapped.

Rather than fight the thick fingers wrapped around her ankle, Paige moved her free leg out to the side and planted it to steady her balance. She maintained a grip on the Beretta while staring down at the face of a Nymar that almost completely blended in with the shadows filling the living room. Even when the vampire opened its mouth to hiss at her, she could see only the faint reflection of dim light off fangs.

In the months since they'd put the Skinners in the sights of every law enforcement agency in America, the Nymar had been learning to use the gifts given to them by the Shadow Spore. These included claws that could draw blood through hollow feeding tubes and tendrils directly beneath their skin that could expand in darkness and contract in light to give them natural camouflage both in the shadows and among humans. Because the Shadow Spore was a strain unknown to modern hunters until a few months ago, it was immune to the antidote used to kill Nymar, and didn't trigger the itch in the Skinners' scars that served as an early warning system.

In the near dark, Paige couldn't make out what the rest of the Nymar's body was doing. When it swept her legs from beneath her and she fell to the floor, she fired two shots directly into its face. Her antidote rounds didn't react to the vampire's blood, but they did punch a few messy holes through its skull, which were instantly plugged by oily black tendrils. She knew that even if its brain was blown completely through the back of its head, the spore could maintain enough control to keep the body moving. It was quite a sight.

Paige swung her back leg around to kick it in the face. Her foot pounded against the Nymar's chin, snapping its head to one side with a sickening wet crunch. Now that her eyes had adjusted well enough to make out the vampire's figure, she was able to slam her heel into its stomach to force the air from its lungs. It was still camouflaged too well for her to tell if the Nymar was male or female. Blackened skin was wrapped around a bare torso that had curves slight enough to be an athletic version of either gender. The impact forced the Nymar away, giving Paige a chance to jump to her feet and look down the hall toward the sound of approaching footsteps.

Two more figures stomped out of one of the other rooms. Because of the sudden light when the door opened, Paige couldn't tell whether they were human or if their tendrils had merely become too thin for her to see. Fortunately, they

Skinners: The Breaking

removed the guesswork by snarling at her, revealing sets of fangs extending from their upper and lower jaws. One pumped a shell into a sawed-off shotgun, while the other sighted along the top of a semiautomatic pistol.

Dropping to one knee to present a smaller target, Paige fired. She couldn't rely on the antidote rounds or the brute power of ballistics, so she compensated by hitting each of them with no fewer than five shots each. The extended magazine in her Beretta had three shots left, which she fired into the Nymar on the floor as it sunk its claws into her leg.

When she tried to pull her ankle from its grasp, she only succeeded in dragging the wounded Nymar an inch or two closer. Its facial features and body structure were that of a male. The Beretta had claimed one of his eyes, along with a sizable chunk of his temple, but those wounds were already filled with tendrils resembling fresh tar that had been poured into a pothole. Paige kicked and pulled, but still couldn't free herself before the Nymar reached out with its other hand to drag her down again. She hit the floor on her hip, and the Nymar crawled like a scurrying millipede and was able to dig into her right arm with his claws. Those sharpened nails could shred through most nonmetallic materials, but weren't strong enough to do more than scrape against the hardened exterior of her arm.

In the months following an injury involving an experimental substance she'd injected into herself, Paige hadn't been able to regain full use of her arm. Through a rigid exercise routine, she improved her mobility to somewhere close to normal, but the accident had left the limb feeling like a slab of concrete wrapped in warm silk. As uncomfortable as that was for her, it was even more so to anyone who got that arm smashed into their face. After pulling it free from the vampire's grasp, she did just that to the Nymar. Deciding not to waste any more bullets, she pulled her knee close to her body, and with her heel pointed at the Nymar's chest, placed her other foot on top of the wooden baton holstered at the side of her boot. The upper end of that weapon was rounded, but the lower end was sharpened into a point that punched through leather with ease as she pushed it down with her foot.

The petrified wood ripped from its holster to emerge several inches past the sole of her boot. Snapping both legs forward, Paige drove the weapon into the Nymar's chest and then twisted her feet. He screamed and tried to pull away as she stood up while keeping the weapon lodged within his breast plate. After slamming the Beretta against the Nymar's temple, she shifted her weight so most of it drove the weapon farther down, until it hit what she guessed was either the Nymar's backbone or the floor beneath him. Her hands flew through the motions of reloading the Beretta and pulled back the slide just in time to fire at the two Nymar who'd recovered from her first salvo.

More gunshots thumped next door, meaning Rico and Steve were either making progress or getting hammered by superior weaponry. Either way, Paige knew she couldn't do much about it. She lifted the boot with the shredded holster, dropped it down to force the weapon back up into its leather case, and walked toward the hallway while firing three quick shots at the Nymar, who had regrouped and moved into another room. As they recoiled, she drew the second Beretta and rushed them. Accustomed to being feared based solely on their appearance, the Nymar were surprised when she charged into the room after them and placed a gun barrel against each of their chests. She pulled her triggers several times, doing enough damage to turn their hearts into paste and send them to the floor. She would have liked to make sure they weren't about to get up but instead continued down the hall to get a look into the rooms branching off of it.

She entered a bedroom with two beds and a clock radio on the floor near an outlet. A particle board entertainment center bore a cheap CD player and a few selections of whiny, wannabe punk rock.A bathroom across the hall contained only a toilet, sink, tub, and a collection of threadbare towels hanging on old metal racks.

At the end of the hall a second bedroom had been converted into an office, complete with a dusty desk and cabinets that reached up to a water-stained ceiling. A computer, printer, modem, and several notebooks lay on the desk, and beneath it were some larger components. One of those was obviously a computer tower, but the others resembled what

Cole had once described to her as servers for use in setting up or maintaining Internet sites.

The tech guys from MEG had told her how to try and squeeze what she wanted out of the equipment. Stu, who answered phones for Branch 40 and knew his way around just about any kind of electronics, had explained how to look for hidden files, search for e-mail logs, and transfer vital data onto a flash drive. Since time was a factor, Paige holstered the pistols so she could dig into her pocket for the flash drive—a thumb-sized hunk of blue plastic.

"Come on," she muttered while going through the series of typed commands and mouse clicks she'd memorized. Though she knew she couldn't get everything she wanted from the computer in such a short amount of time, she hoped to get at least one piece of halfway decent information that she hadn't already gotten from another source. As long as the fighting next door continued, she figured she could push her luck by digging a little deeper.

"Now this is more like it," she said while shifting her attention to the sort of information that fell more within her comfort zone. The notebooks stacked on the desk were logs of messages that needed to be sent and had been received. There were dates, names, and locations. Even if some of them had been faked or encrypted, she had plenty of gaming geeks on her speed dial who would love the chance to crack a real vampire code. In fact, she might be able to retire if she set up a bidding war at the MEG offices.

After gathering up the books and shoving them into a plastic grocery bag she'd found on the floor, Paige checked the computer. The shooting next door had stopped. From the other half of the duplex she heard several heavy thumps and a very familiar if muffled voice. Rico was wrapping up.

The transfer of files was done: not surprising, since she barely knew the basics about what to look for and had probably missed lots of them. A quick glance into the next room told her that only one of the Nymar was still moving. Some commotion came from outside and the cops were surely on their way. She clicked on the icon for the main computer interface, opened the Documents folder, looked at a short list of users and found one marked CP01-99. She grinned and clicked on that, having already found a reference to it in one of the sites the Nymar had created on ChatterPages.com.

Most of the files were labeled with gobbledygook involving random letters and nonsequential numbers. Just as Paige was about to back out to copy the entire folder to her flash drive, she found one labeled in plain English. It was called *Skinner contact list*.

Her first thought was that the file was speculation on locations of people she already knew, but something in her gut forced her to tap the mouse key one more time and bring up the document. It was a list of names. Most of them were Skinners she'd either heard of or briefly talked to over the years. Some were familiar, thanks to the time she'd spent in Philadelphia helping to dole out Jonah Lancroft's belongings to hunters who swarmed in from different parts of the country to claim their portion of the loot.

One of those names was Bobby Ferguson, a Skinner who had decided to jump the fence and join up with Hope during the recent Nymar attacks on local police. Selina was on the list as well, a Philadelphia Skinner high on Paige's own list of suspected traitors. After picking out one more name, Paige transferred the files to her flash drive, yanked it from the port and stuffed it into her pocket.

"Hey, Bloodhound!" Rico shouted from the living room. "You through?"

"Yeah." Rather than waste her ammunition, Paige took out some aggression by stepping back and delivering a straight kick to the computer tower, which toppled over so she could bust it with her baton.

Paige jogged down the hall, drew her pistol and popped a few more rounds into the chest of the one surviving Nymar. She knew that one was finished when the spore attached to its heart tried to suck every last bit of moisture from its host. The moment that process got rolling, the Nymar's body started to dry up into a flaky mess of ashy skin particles, until it resembled the others she'd left behind.

Outside, Rico and Steve were waiting for her. "What'd you find in there?" Rico asked.

"I'm pretty sure that was the place we were after. No

Cobb, though. That is, unless he was one of those idiots who tried to charge me when I walked in."

"Were they Stripes?" he asked, using his own term for Shadow Spore that had more or less become accepted among the Skinners.

"Yep. What did you find?" she said to the younger man.

"Not a lot," Steve replied.

"Just shooting up the neighbors, huh? No wonder everyone hates Americans."

"There were a few Stripes playing cards and one feeding off a trashy lookin' redhead," Rico told her. "They were armed to the teeth, but weren't quick enough to put us down." When they got to the car and piled in, Rico couldn't have looked more grateful. "Them guys obviously weren't guarding much of anything. You sure you can trust what you found?"

"We'll see about that when I get it all deciphered," she said while rolling her window down to fill her lungs with a few long breaths. "I don't know if I did the technical stuff perfectly, but I got some pretty interesting files."

"How interesting?"

"Most were in code or marked by gibberish, but a few were plain as day. One was labeled 'Skinner Contacts.'"

"Did you get a chance to look it over?"

After rounding another corner, Paige came to a stop well away from the duplex that had been shot up. "Yeah," she said quietly. "I did. Even saw a name on there I recognized."

"You should be the one answering questions," Steve replied. "We found records that said you were the one working with traitors."

Rico's arms came up as if they'd been spring-loaded. The Mossberg's wide, menacing barrel looked at her like a soulless, unblinking eye. "That's right," he grunted. "What do ya got to say about that?"

"We have to get out of here," Steve said urgently. "Right now."

Although she was reluctant to take her eyes off of him, Paige knew the guy in the backseat was right. They had to get moving.

"Go on," Rico said with every bit of the urgency she was feeling. "Get the hell away from here. And if I even think you're trying to do something cute, I'll blow a hole through you, your door, and anyone driving by."

Paige's experience with the shotgun made her absolutely certain he wasn't bluffing. Sirens wailed in the distance. People stared from their windows. A few even walked outside to look down the street. Although Rico's shotgun now rested across his lap, it was still pointed at her. Stopping at a red light, she turned to look into the eyes of the man beside her. "Who are those friends you mentioned? The ones who you said might like my style."

When Rico's eyes drifted to the backseat, Steve shrugged and said, "You should tell us about them."

"They're students of Jonah Lancroft," Paige said. "They study his journals. Some even talked to him over the course of the last few years. It's pretty interesting stuff. There's some shit in those notes about shapeshifters that I've never heard before."

"Like what?" Steve asked as he leaned forward. "What did the notes say?"

Paige ignored the younger Skinner and said to Rico, "You stood with me and Cole when that Mud Flu was getting people killed. If we didn't do anything about it, more would have died. Daniels told me that disease could have gotten worse over time. Thousands could have been killed and that was all Lancroft's doing."

"He wouldn't have let it get that far," Rico assured her. "He was a smart man."

"Do you seriously regret putting Lancroft down like the sick animal he was?"

"I thought we were doing the right thing at the time, but he was the purest Skinner we've ever had," Rico said in a voice fueled by indignant fire. "There's something to be said for taking extreme measures to fight an extreme problem. After what happened in Kansas City, the Half Breed problem was out of control. We couldn't have done anything more than just run around killing however many of those things we could find. What about the ones we couldn't find? What about the ones the Full Bloods created to replace the dead Half Breeds?"

"It's the same problem as before," she insisted. "It's a balance we've stricken. Skinners and Half Breeds. Us and Nymar. They do their thing and we do ours. It's a shitty way to live for us, but we're part of the ecosystem."

Rico let out a single grunting laugh. "Green light." After Paige slammed her foot on the gas and sent Steve flopping back into his seat, the big man said, "You can't seriously believe that tree hugging bullshit you were spouting."

"What else is there?"

"Lancroft devoted his life to figuring out how those things work," he said, as if he'd been waiting for months to deliver those words. "Shapeshifters, Nymar, even shit we don't know about. He tore them down, looked inside and wrote what he found so we could all learn from it."

"Then how come we all thought he was dead until we found him in Philly? How come the only legacy he left behind was a collapsed insane asylum and Henry? You'd think such a great man would be more of a presence or leave something a little better for the rest of us."

"He did. We just weren't the ones to get it."

When he heard that, Steve leaned forward again. Paige noticed, however, that he was cautious not to get close enough to draw much attention.

She drove for another few blocks, retracing her steps to the expressway that had brought her to Cobb's neighborhood. Only after they'd gone a few more miles did she feel comfortable enough to let her shoulders come down from around her ears. The fact that Rico still had his shotgun pointed at her was a threat that was beyond her control for the moment, and she took a small amount of comfort from that. Once she had a chance to do something or make a move, she'd go back to worrying.

"What did Lancroft leave behind?" she asked.

"From what I've heard, it's some good stuff. It'd be stupid of me to tell you more."

"You should tell us," Steve said. "We're supposed to be on the same side."

"But we're not," Rico snapped. "There's always been more'n one way of doing things. Hell, it ain't like there's anything better than legend for us to go by, and even that's just a buncha crap. All that separates legend from Internet rumor is what the words are written on."

"You're not sure she can be trusted," Steve guessed.

"No. I'm not." After watching the road for a few seconds, Rico said, "I've made plenty of mistakes. Turning my back on a partner ain't one of 'em."

Paige swerved around a few of the slower cars, then took a poignant glance at the shotgun across his lap. "You're sure about that?"

"Heh. Point taken. This ain't my first choice, just like you keep saying about flying off to leave Cole to rot in Denver."

Steve gripped the back of Rico's seat as Paige took a corner fast enough to slide him against the door. "That's not good enough," he said.

"What the fuck do you know about any of this?" she asked. "I don't even know who the hell you are."

"I'm one of you!" Steve replied. "And I've heard about what happened, just like everyone else."

That hit Paige deeply, but didn't erase the scowl from her face.

"Rico can vouch for me."

"It's like I told ya," Rico said. "I've known Steve here for a little while and he's proven to be on the right side of the fence. We just need to make sure we're all in that same spot. There's a lot of changing going on these days, and it's the sort of thing Jonah Lancroft saw comin' from a mile away. Some of us are willing to do what's gotta be done and some aren't. Lancroft made it his business to reach out to those of us that are suited for the task."

"And when did he make this offer to you?" she scoffed. "Before or after you came along with me and Cole to put him down?"

Behind them, lights flashed from atop police cars that sped toward the duplexes the Skinners had blasted apart. Rico barely acknowledged the commotion as he shifted in his seat and said, "I was contacted after I put the word out that the old man was dead."

"Which old man are you talking about? Lancroft or Ned?" Paige asked, knowing how close Rico had been to the older Skinner who lived in St. Louis. "You remember

Skinners: The Breaking 33

Ned, don't you? He was the guy who owned the house that you live in when you're not on the run. He's the guy who taught you how to read those runes that have been cropping up more and more lately. He's also the guy that Lancroft killed during that whole Mud Flu outbreak."

"That doesn't matter," Steve insisted. "There are bigger things at stake. First of all, you should tell us where to find these men who follow Dr. Lancroft so closely."

Paige turned to look at him. Her eyes lingered on him even when it bordered on being a detriment to her driving. She'd been uncertain about the other Skinner several times before, but had always put her fears to rest one way or another.

Rico nodded and adjusted the shotgun so it was sure to kill Paige even if it went off by accident. "They're based out of Louisville," Rico said. "That's all I know right now. I been looking into these guys ever since I started digging into the shit that Ned was into. They're barely organized, but with all that's happened lately, they've been pulling together real quick."

"Speaking of our last business with Ned," Paige said, "you seem to glaze right over the Mud Flu thing. Did you forget that Lancroft made that to infect people so they'd be attacked by Nymar and shapeshifters?"

"And when they were attacked, the flu killed those bloodsuckers *and* the shapeshifters," Rico said. "Extreme actions for hard times. That's what created Skinners in the first place. We step up when everybody else backs down or when they just don't bother to look at what's out there gunning for us. Lancroft's got plenty of good ideas, and unlike every other loudmouth politician or cop out there, he's got the means to back it up. Since the newest crop of Half Breeds can eat the Mud Flu for lunch and we don't even know if Full Bloods were affected at all, we could use some good ideas right about now. You've always been the one to take the right action no matter what anyone else thought. Your only problem is that you don't always know what the right thing is."

Paige felt a knot form in her stomach. It only grew when she looked into the rearview mirror at Steve. "I always thought the same thing about you, Rico," she said earnestly.

"The Skinners as we know 'em are done," Rico continued. "The Nymar saw to that, and they could never have done so much damage if we hadn't all been too preoccupied or just too damn short-sighted to prevent it from happening."

"So what's the plan from here?"

"We have to solve this problem right now," Steve said.

"You're right," Rico replied.

Paige agreed with him as well, which brought three problems to mind. For one thing, she'd never agreed so many times in a row with anybody. The second problem was that Rico wasn't the kind of guy who took direct orders from anyone without at least attempting to buck against them or grumble about it. And yet, Steve was able to order him around with more ease than Ned ever could. Considering how highly Rico thought of Ned, that was saying a lot. The third problem was in the rearview mirror. For some reason, the harder she thought about those other problems, the hazier Steve's reflection became.

"We've got options," Rico said. "Lancroft's followers have been keeping tabs on Full Blood movements for a while now. They even know about at least two more that have come to North America since the Mud Flu was wiped out."

"You think Dr. Lancroft's cult is capable of so much?" Steve asked.

"Don't talk about them like they're a joke," Rico snarled as he twisted around to stare into the backseat. "They're doing important work. Work that needs to get done before it's too damn late. A lot of blood's about to be spilled. The Full Bloods have always been happy to roam their territories, keep out of sight and do their thing without kicking up enough dust to be noticed. Liam changed that when he attacked Kansas City. He put a storm in motion, and the others like him are set to take advantage of it. We'll need all the help we can get once the shit really starts to hit the fan."

"After the siege of Kansas City, the Mud Flu, and everything else," Paige said, "you still don't think the shit's hit the fan?"

"Honey," he grunted, knowing all too well how a nickname like that would grate on her, "it ain't even started to stink yet."

Skinners: The Breaking 35

Driving north on the expressway, Paige casually watched the side of the road for anything that might be useful. A stalled car or some debris could make a big enough boom when she hit it. Even a large pothole in the right spot could jostle her passenger enough to give her the opening she was looking for. Instead, all she saw was evenly spaced traffic and clear road. Damn Canadians and their fully functional infrastructure. "So why do you have the shotgun pointed at me again, Rico?" she asked.

"He saw the same thing you did," Steve replied. "Tell him what you saw."

"I found a list of Skinner contacts being used by the Nymar," Paige said.

"I really wish you hadn't seen that list, Bloodhound. I wanted to make sure you'd be on board with this before doing something drastic. Once you saw my name, though, I didn't have much choice."

She glanced over to him and said, "I didn't see your name on the list, Rico. Just Jory, some of the Philly Skinners, and some others I didn't recognize."

Rico was stunned.

"You did see his name," Steve told her. "Just like we found yours in an e-mail that explained how you betrayed all Skinners to the men flying that helicopter that brought you to Denver."

Paige watched the road, still looking for anything that could be put to use.

Steve moved so he was looking at her like the proverbial devil sitting on Rico's shoulder. "Tell us about those people who flew in that helicopter."

"They helped me once," she said. "They're not exactly on my Christmas list."

"Are they with the government?"

"No."

"Cops?" Rico asked.

"Getting colder," Paige sighed.

Steve placed a hand on Rico's shoulder and said, "She's trying to manipulate us."

When Rico's fingers tightened around the Mossberg, Paige thought she could hear the shotgun bend within his angry grasp. "Cut the bullshit and tell me everything, Bloodhound."

The expressway was clear and straight enough for her to see she wasn't going to get the break she'd been hoping for. There was always the chance of making a move that was sudden enough to get the drop on the big man in the passenger seat, but she'd worked with him for too long to expect his trigger finger to let her live through something like that. In an earlier time of her life, when she'd first been introduced to the darkness that crept in around society's edges, Paige might have welcomed an opportunity to roll those dice and risk going out in a quick blaze of shotgun fire. Things might have become even darker, but she'd found something else to cling to. As much as it had torn her up to leave that something behind back in Denver, she wasn't about to forget it anytime soon. In fact, it was a rare moment that she wasn't thinking about him.

"You have to tell us about the group," Steve said. "You can trust us."

"It's got some military ties, but it's privately run," she said. "They've also got friends in the press. And before you ask, yes. They do have some important jobs for me to do in exchange for the protection they can offer."

"Protection?"

Paige shook her head solemnly. "I'm not saying another word." When Rico placed the shotgun to his shoulder and pointed it at her cheek, he braced his arms and legs as if the kick of the Mossberg and the turbulence that would follow once the car was without its driver were both as inevitable as the rain.

Looking at her in the mirror, Steve said, "He'll shoot you, Paige."

She saw the image waver once more, so she looked away from it and to the familiar face beside her. "I know you would, but never based on so little. We've been through worse, including when you finally agreed to help Gerald train me."

When Rico let out a breath, a fond smile accompanied it. "Gerald knew his way around the sticks, but we could always take him in a fistfight. Remember the look on his face when you knocked him on his ass that time?"

"Yes."

The expressway cleared out along a stretch that curved sharply to the left. It glistened with a thick layer of water tainted by a mix of oil and any number of fluids dripping from the hundreds of cars using the road on a daily basis.

"So you must be one of these guys that Rico's talking about, right, Steve?" she asked while glancing back and forth between the mirror and the road. "I figure that has to be the case since you seem to be so familiar with Lancroft."

"I never said that."

"No, but you called him *Doctor* Lancroft. The only one I've ever heard call him that was Henry. Henry's dead, and if you're not one of Lancroft's followers, maybe you were around him for a long time for some other reason?"

"I . . . am one of his followers," Steve admitted.

Although Paige believed that implicitly, she held onto her underlying train of thought. "And what about you, Rico? You must have known this guy for years to let him boss you around that way."

"I—"

"He has," Steve interrupted.

Rico nodded. "Yeah, I have."

"Funny how you never mentioned him." Gripping the steering wheel, Paige added, "It's also funny how both of us go along with whatever this asshole says as long as he tells us to. He doesn't ask. He doesn't request. He orders us, Rico. Last time I checked, neither one of us takes orders too well." As she said that, she looked into the rearview mirror. She wouldn't have taken her eyes off it even if that meant slamming into the back end of a bus. That way, she was sure to see any more flickers in Steve's reflection. Fortunately, it didn't take long before she saw that very thing.

"She's trying to talk her way out of this so she can kill you!" Steve said. "You have to shoot her!"

"See?" Paige mused with a calmness that came from finally taking back the reins, even if those reins were connected to a team of rabid, stampeding horses. "Not even orders. He tells you things and you believe them." Meeting Steve's gaze in the mirror, she asked, "Is that why Lancroft had to lock you up in a cage two levels beneath his home in

Philly and throw away the key? You're just too slippery for him to risk—"

"You have to kill her!" Although Steve was the one who started that statement, it was Kawosa who finished it. The shapeshifter had been in Lancroft's custody possibly longer than anyone or anything else, which pushed his confinement past the two hundred year mark. After being busted out by a group of Full Bloods and Mongrels, Kawosa had demonstrated his talents on more than one occasion. All Paige had been able to find out about him was that he was known as the First Deceiver, and possibly was the mold from which all shapeshifters were cast. Even knowing that, however, she'd still been taken in by his oily words. All of which raced through her mind as she looked over to see the commitment in Rico's eyes. He had to kill her.

She flicked the switch to unlock the car door and cranked the steering wheel hard to the left. The vehicle had already been moving that way to follow the curve of the expressway, but her sudden movement pitched it into a swerving fishtail.

"What in the—" was all Rico could say before being thrown against his door.

Paige already had her door open as the car lost its last bit of control. Before she had a chance to think any better of it, she leaned to the left, forced the door open the rest of the way, and twisted her body around as she tumbled outside. Behind her the Mossberg let out a furious roar that spat buckshot, ripping several burning wounds along her hip and leg. But any pain from that was quickly washed away by her impact against the pavement.

Ever since she'd been wounded, Paige had seesawed between wanting to push through the affliction that hardened the muscles in her arm into a rigid, unfeeling mass or hack it off at the shoulder. Diligent exercise and base-level stubbornness had allowed her to regain most of her mobility, but it wasn't until now that she was grateful for what had happened. In fact, she was praying that her near-petrified limb was as unyielding as the rest of her.

She hit the expressway on her side, just as she'd planned.

Her arm smashed against the pavement first, just as she'd hoped.

Skinners: The Breaking

There was no way to plan for the pain that followed, and all she could do was hope it didn't stop too soon. A sharp bout of numbness after jumping from a moving car was most definitely not a good thing.

Horns wailed around her. The screeching of nearby tires came from the car she'd just left as well as from several others that had to swerve to avoid it. Engines roared from every direction, giving her more than enough incentive to roll toward the narrow median of the expressway. Unfortunately, momentum was still making it damn near impossible to steer her body.

Using her wounded limb as a narrow sled, she kicked at the ground and resisted the urge to reach out with her good hand to slow her progress into traffic. She made a fist, gnashed her teeth and allowed herself to cry out as the uppermost layers of her arm were stripped away. Finally, her leg slapped against the ground and she came to a halt.

Several yards ahead, metal wrapped around a cement divider as the rental car found a guardrail at the edge of the expressway. So much for that deposit. Sparks were still flying when Kawosa exploded from the back window. His arms were held in front of his face and his skinny, ragged body came through the bent opening as if he'd been catapulted toward the street. Either she had convinced herself to see through the mask or Kawosa was no longer wearing it, because he now had the slender build of a short man with long, raven-black hair, clad in filthy rawhide leggings and a beaded necklace flapping around his neck. After shifting into the body of a gangly coyote, he hopped onto the guardrail and skittered along its uneven surface back in the direction from which they'd driven.

Too stunned to try standing up just yet, Paige dragged herself toward the middle of the expressway. A narrow oasis beckoned as glaring headlights washed over her. She closed her eyes, lowered her head and let out a vicious groan as a Grim Reaper on four bald tires rolled straight at her. The car blared its horn, swerved to the right and screeched a few inches from her feet. The continued sound of its horn was added to the honking chorus around her as she moved on. No time to be thankful.

The median was barely wider than Paige's torso. It was a long speed bump running along the center of the expressway, dotted with the occasional cement divider. She rolled onto her side, reached for the Beretta at her hip and came up empty. The gun and holster must have been peeled away somewhere during her tumble. At least the weapon had provided some much needed cushioning for the fall. She shifted her search toward the shoulder holster. That one was still there, but it was torn up pretty badly. She drew the pistol and aimed it at the car wreck while pulling herself up to her feet.

Even with the healing serum flowing through her veins, she was hurting. The body armor she'd worn to raid Cobb's house had come in more useful now than when she'd been wading through a room full of angry Nymar. Much of the tactical vest had been shredded, exposing the Half Breed hide underneath. That left the hardened shell of the vest itself, which did its job nicely by preventing her skin from being peeled away. Since there was no sign of Rico yet, she took a quick peek at her right arm. Immediately, she wished she hadn't.

It had been a while since that arm was normal. She'd been injured some time ago, but being able to move it normally and feel a full range of sensation through it was just a fond memory. Her most recent gamble had worked in that her arm withstood the punishment of her fall. Like the tactical vest, the outer layers were stripped away, revealing the true extent of the injury she'd received in Kansas City. Flesh had been frozen into a hardened shell that looked more like a crude sketch of human anatomy instead of the real thing. Blood was caked onto it like an old stain made by cheap, flaking red paint, and when she flexed her arm tentatively, the veins barely shifted within the mess. Paige couldn't bear to look at it any longer. She didn't even want to know how much of her arm was being preserved by the healing serum and how much was simply kept in its petrified state by whatever toxins were still inside of her.

Another car horn, followed by a familiar voice snarling viciously at the twisted metal around him, was all she needed to get back on the proper track. Her legs hurt but were still moving and supporting her weight. Because of the healing serum produced within her bloodstream, the pain filling her entire body ignited her resolve, instead of crippling her like it would a normal person. When she hobbled into the next lane to take advantage of a small opening between approaching cars, she only glanced occasionally to either side. Compared to what she'd left behind, oncoming traffic was the least of her worries.

The expressway was slick beneath her boots, but not slippery. That worked in her favor by getting the cars to slow down as they rounded the bend to avoid the same sort of crash that she had purposely endured. By the time she neared the guardrail on the opposite side of the road from the wrecked rental car, she heard a bellowing voice roll toward her from the other side of the expressway.

"Where do you think yer goin', Bloodhound?"

She might have to kill him, she realized. It was simple survival now.

Paige hobbled backward until she felt her legs bump against the rail. A glance behind her showed how long a drop awaited if she decided to jump, and even if she did make it, Rico wouldn't need many guesses to figure out where she'd gone. Ignoring the horns and engines of the cars that passed between them, she focused on the heap of wreckage. Some voices came from a few passing cars, but the angry and concerned ones alike were silenced when she raised her Beretta to sight along the top of its barrel.

She fired the moment she spotted Rico, but there was too much twisted metal in front of him for a bullet to find a clean path. He seemed to be as dazed as she was. Although he didn't have a petrified arm to protect him, the jacket stitched together from Half Breed skins had done a fine job of seeing him through the crash. Judging by the awkward way he dropped and shuffled behind the car, however, his legs weren't in very good shape.

"This ain't how I wanted it to go!" he shouted.

She replied by squeezing off one more careful shot that sparked against the side of the rental car.

Rico's voice was calmer when he said, "I'll chalk it up to nerves if you cut this shit out right now. Don't make me hunt you!"

She fired again, punching another few holes into the

wrecked car. Her grouping was solid, and it wouldn't be long before she hit pay dirt. All she knew was that she couldn't let him get away. She just couldn't. There was no other reason than that. Once she peeled away her logic to that point, Paige realized it was shallower than the puddles on the expressway. Turning her head to give herself a moment to think, she found herself looking into a narrow, angular face that still dripped with the water kicked up during his escape from the rental car.

"You have to kill him," Kawosa said in a voice that had somehow been wiped away before. "You're all alone and can only worry about surviving now."

Even as she looked at the creature that had spoken those words, the sight of him began to fade. He wasn't disappearing, she reminded herself. He'd told her she was alone and she believed him, just like she must have when she first started shooting. Something about his words was impossible to dispute. Instead of trying to figure out why that was, she pointed her gun at him.

"No," he said. "You can't shoot me."

Realizing it was true, she lowered her Beretta. Kawosa started to say something else, but she drew the machete from her boot and swung at him before he could get his words out. The edge that had been treated with the metallic varnish infused with fragments from the Blood Blade would have sliced through Kawosa's skinny neck like butter if he hadn't been so quick to lean away. Instead, it grazed the side of his head and cut a straight line up toward one eye. The blade didn't come anywhere close to blinding him, but it did send a quick spray of blood to the ground. By the time the drops hit her boot, Kawosa had shifted into his animal form and bounded away. Since she'd acted quickly enough to sidestep his lies, she figured he wouldn't be returning to try again anytime soon.

Suddenly, Rico stood up from behind his cover. He'd ditched the shotgun in favor of the Sig Sauer that had been his trusted companion for the last several years. There was no more talking to be done. The instant he caught sight of her, he squeezed his trigger to unleash a steady current of lead that ripped across the expressway, chipped at a few passing cars, and hissed progressively closer to the spot where Paige was standing.

She waited until he ran along the shoulder to try and get a better angle on her, then fired until her rounds finally punched through the layers of steel protecting the rental car's gas tank. It caused a spark that ignited the fuel and set off an explosion that shoved the car sideways several feet against the glistening pavement. It wasn't the grand finale sort of explosion she'd been promised by all those movies and cop shows, but it was good enough to force Rico to dive for cover before he was blown over the guardrail behind him.

Paige knew he wasn't down for the count. She also knew she couldn't move at more than half speed as she turned and hobbled along the side of the road. More cars were either gawking at the flaming wreck or slowing to ease past it. Drivers shouted at each other, her, and possibly Rico, but she couldn't bother with any of that. It took all of her focus to block them out while tearing off a piece of her shirt and crouching down to dab at the blood on the pavement. Praying she wasn't just cleaning up her own mess, she let out a relieved breath when she found something that was even better than what she'd hoped to collect. She couldn't be absolutely certain, but the little piece of rounded flesh looked like an earlobe. It was still warm after being cut from Kawosa's head, so she wrapped it up and tucked it safely into a pocket. From there, she resumed moving along the shoulder of the expressway toward a spot where the slope of the ground rose up to meet the guardrail. Her arm hung at her side, throbbing with more pain than she'd felt since it was first poisoned. She needed to get more healing serum. She needed to get somewhere safe enough to make a phone call. But more than either of those things, she just needed to get the hell away from Rico.

"Screw it," she grunted as she grabbed onto the rail and swung her legs over.

Motorists shouted for her to stop. They told her help was on the way.

Paige couldn't stop.

There was no help on its way.

Chapter Three

Colorado State Penitentiary
Canon City, Colorado
Three weeks ago

Nine cops were dead, and those were only the ones that had been killed in Denver on the night that Cole, Rico, Prophet, and the Amriany shot their way through a warehouse being used by the Nymar. Across the country, more cops had died in similar raids or were murdered in silence and left with Skinner weapons in their bodies. It didn't take long for those crimes to be tied together and pinned onto what was quickly labeled a cell of home-grown terrorists. Thanks to the news coverage focused on the blood-soaked Denver warehouse, Cole's capture was heralded as the death of that cell.

Riding away from the warehouse that night in a SWAT van had been one of the most terrifying moments of his thirty-four years on this planet. That was no small thing, considering all the horrific things he'd seen in those years. First there was the speedy ascension of dancing reality shows to the top of the ratings, followed by the slow death of old fashioned rock 'n' roll. Once he got his first look at a real werewolf, his world had gotten even worse.

Training to be a Skinner was a painful process where he was ground into someone cold enough to drive a sharpened piece of wood into another living thing, occasionally interrupted by those very same living things trying to rip his head off. After that he'd seen shapeshifters of all flavors, as well as vampires, nymphs, and even a Chupacabra. Somehow, those creatures had been easier to handle than the scalding glares of the cops who rode with him in the van that night.

They all wanted to kill him.

If the stories were to be believed—and there was no good reason for the cops not to believe them—they had every right to kill him in the most gruesome way possible.

But by some miracle, he had been shackled to his seat and driven straight to the nearest jail cell. Apart from several choice words snarled at him through many sets of gritted teeth, he arrived without incident.

He was processed and thrown into a cage.

After standing in front of a judge barely long enough to feel the courtroom beneath his state-issued canvas shoes, he was given a jumpsuit and thrown into a smaller cell.

There were no visits from lawyers, no questions from the authorities. Just hours upon hours of solitude, within three stark gray walls and a set of iron bars, during which he was made aware of one simple fact: cop killers lived on borrowed time. But he was no cop killer. He'd been smacked around by Full Bloods, shot, hit with blunt sticks, cut with all manner of blades, and bitten by vampires.

That last part was what stuck with him the most.

Cole's time as a Skinner had been extensive enough for his body to produce the healing serum on its own. That stuff had seen him through most of the punishment heaped upon him in the days following his capture. It was also supposed to help make sure he wasn't infected when a Nymar tried to seed him. The antidote he'd been given after he was bitten should have done the same thing. He had found out the hard way, however, that neither the serum nor the antidote did much of anything against Shadow Spore. He'd been seeded by one of those striped bastards, and the process of getting the spore out of him was something he relived in brutal detail everytime he closed his eyes and allowed himself to lapse into unconsciousness.

The spore was gone, but something remained inside of him.

It cinched around his insides, constricting until he thought he would burst, tightening until he prayed for something vital inside his body to rupture and be done with it. He had plenty of time to think about that lovely image when he was carted off to the cage that would be his home.

Colorado State Penitentiary looked like one of the buildings at a college campus. It was several stories tall, had a well-maintained lawn, was coated in clean stone and labeled by stern metal letters that looked as if they'd been typewritten upon the front of the structure. Hedges and sidewalks marked the perimeter of a large parking lot. Unlike those buildings of higher learning, this one was filled with 756 beds encased in fortified steel and occupied by violent offenders who required attention known as Security Level 5. It was a maximum security facility that could be the last bit of earthly hell he would know before being sent to the real deal at the end of a rusty shiv or a broken fork smuggled out of the cafeteria by one of his criminally disturbed neighbors.

Cole was processed for what felt to him like the hundredth time, given yet another jumpsuit to wear, and shoved down one of many drab hallways that had filled his most recent days. When he attempted to look up at the walkways above him or at any of the cells on either side, his head was viciously turned forward and he was warned to keep his eyes on the floor. If he attempted to glance at the bars to his left, he was shoved forward, with the accompanying clatter of the chains secured to his wrists and ankles. By now, he'd forgotten what it was like to move his arms or legs without the extra weight of cuffs around them. The rattle of stainless steel links were as familiar to him as the strained wheezing of his own breath.

But even after all the shocks his system had taken lately, none of them compared to the one he got when he saw the inside of his cell.

"This is it?" he asked.

"What did you expect? A hotel suite?"

"That's a hospital bed."

"Right, and you're going to lay down on it."

Cole studied the bed carefully, as if that was enough to make it change into something else. The walls were con-

Skinners: The Breaking

crete, and covered with chipped, light green paint. He'd been locked up once in a holding cell with a toilet that wasn't much more than a curved metal shelf with plumbing sticking out of the wall. One of those may have been installed in the farthest wall of this cell at one time, but all that remained was a patch of cracked wall and some pipes cut and sealed with cement.

"Is this for some sort of examination?" Cole asked.

"Lie down."

There was no way to get out of the prison and nowhere to run, even if he did make it that far, so he climbed onto the bed and stretched out.

Someone in medical scrubs walked into the cell, accompanied by more guards. Cole could hear every scrape of her paper-covered sneakers against the floor and every lid she popped off needles attached to IV tubes before she cleaned them off.

"How many other prisoners are in here?" he asked.

"Don't worry about it," a guard replied while strapping him to the table. The man resembled the others who had brought him this far. Similar uniform, similar body armor, similar helmet, similar boots, similar hate-filled eyes.

"What is this?" Cole asked. Panic flooded through his body as he started to wonder if Colorado administered its death penalty through lethal injection. Come to think of it, he didn't even know if Colorado had the death penalty. "Don't I get a lawyer? A phone call? At least tell me what's in this goddamn needle!"

If an explanation was given, Cole didn't hear it. Once the drugs were pumped from the IV bag into his arm, he didn't see or hear anything either.

Cole dreamt in a cold torrent of slush that filled his head and leaked out in a series of thrashing muscle spasms and incoherent screams.

He didn't feel like he was falling or lying down. Instead, he was just suspended inside himself with only disembodied voices to fill his days.

Days, or maybe weeks.

Could have been years.

Whatever length of time it was ended abruptly when his consciousness started turning end over end. Although he couldn't see the walls of his dark cell, he knew they were spinning around him. The steady, thumping rhythms that had been his only source of reference sped up and then slowed down.

Memories drifted away.

Sounds came closer while falling back at the same time.

There was a pressure that seemed more real than anything else in his world.

Something wailed and beeped.

Beeping. Just like the first games his dad had bought for his old Atari 2600. Clumsy tones that were the best those early programmers could do and were music to his adolescent ears. Beeping. Squawking. Digitized warbles that eventually became something close to voices. By the time he was in college, his games had acquired real voices and music. That had been a true landmark for a kid who so rarely went outside.

The pressure still came from somewhere, and the voices were getting clearer. If he focused hard enough, he might be able to make out what they said.

"Somebody get in here!"

More pressure, along with a pinch. He was no longer spinning. His head was wrapped in something cool and soft.

"Back away, motherfucker!"

That was definitely not from any game Cole had grown up with. Neither was the snarling hiss that was close enough to send a few drops of bitter venom over his lip and into the stubble that had claimed his chin.

Consciousness exploded in a surge of adrenaline that snapped his eyes wide open so he could see a Nymar's head poking up from the collar of a standard guard uniform. It was a round clean-shaven face with no telltale black markings. Even without seeing the tendrils moving beneath the man's skin, the two sets of fangs extending from his upper jaw gave him away. One set were the feeders that slid down over the normal canine teeth, and the others were a curved, slender pair that fit along the inner edges of the first set. Venom dripped from the curved fangs as the vampire hissed

Skinners: The Breaking 49

at the guards. At least, he assumed there were more guards, since he couldn't lift his head enough to see.

Cole switched immediately into survival mode. He tried to sit up, but the Nymar pressed him right back down again using the hand that was already clamped around his throat to dig sharpened nails into his flesh. That explained the pressure and pinching he'd dreamt about. The real guards were shouting their threats, but the man with the round face didn't pay them any mind. He simply looked down at Cole, lowered his face to within a few inches of his and snarled, "Tara sends her best."

Tara was one of Paige's friends dating back more than eleven years. During a nightmare that had laid the foundation of Paige becoming a Skinner, Tara was turned into a Nymar. More than that, she'd been double-seeded. Two spores were attached to her heart, making her stronger, hungrier, and more vicious as a reward for surviving the process. Perhaps this was payback for him killing the Nymar that had created her. At the moment he could only be concerned with drawing his next breath.

He saw a slender arm wrapped around the Nymar's throat. Although the medical tech wasn't strong enough to choke a vampire, she was able to jab a needle into his neck and push the plunger. When the toxin went into him, the Nymar only tightened his grip. Cole grabbed his wrist with both hands and fought to sit up. This time he was stopped by a fiery pain that blazed over the entire front of his torso. "Son of a bitch!" he grunted.

The Nymar grinned wider and pressed until his fingernails broke the skin of Cole's neck. Using his free hand to grab the medical tech, he pulled her closer and bit into her jugular.

"Why isn't he dead yet?" one of the guards asked.

"Sh-Shadow Spore," Cole said. While the Nymar was feeding, his attention was too divided to keep Cole down. "Antidote doesn't work on them," he wheezed.

The guards were still baffled, so Cole took matters into his own hands by managing to sit up and drive his arms forward with enough power to snap the restraints around his chest.

Without the tendrils that had been left behind, he wouldn't have had the strength to do it. Now, with their innate power and a hunger that had gotten worse over his time in custody, he was able to grab the reinforced collar of the Nymar's uniform and pull him away from the tech. Rather than drag the Nymar straight back, he eased its mouth away and then wrapped his other arm around its forehead to try and lift its feeding fangs out of the tech without tearing her flesh. Once the Nymar felt himself being separated from his meal, a thicker set of fangs emerged from his lower jaw to try and sink into her for good. If those were allowed to puncture the tech's skin, Cole knew he might as well let him drink. The alternative would be to rip the Nymar off while taking most of her neck along with him.

"Somebody *do something!*" he shouted.

Blood sprayed from the tech's opened vein. The Nymar's hiss took on a deeper, almost demonic tone as his eyes became solid black orbs. Cole pulled back with all of his weight, forcing the Nymar away from the tech so she could hit the floor in a heap. The Nymar was quick to pull away from him, but now that the hostage was clear, guards surged into the room to turn confusion into chaos.

Cole found himself wanting to dive into that chaos and ride it out until it was over. That's what Skinners did. Even though he'd managed to break his restraints, there was something stabbing him in the stomach that turned every movement into a lesson in agony. When he reached down to try and pull out the blade that had impaled him, the only thing he found was a bloodstain that was quickly spreading across the front of his hospital gown. Desperately, he ripped the material away until he could see fresh stitches marking an incision that had been cut from his chest all the way down to within eight inches of his groin.

"We know where you are, Skinner!" the Nymar raged. "We'll know where all of you are! We'll find you!"

Guards had surrounded the Nymar on all sides. Before he could spout any more threats, all of the guards pulled the triggers of the shotguns they carried. Cole's ears exploded with the combined thunder of all of those weapons, followed by a high-pitched ringing that filled his brain. The pain fill-

Skinners: The Breaking 51

ing his wounded belly dropped him back down onto the bed. By the time the scent of burnt gunpowder hit the back of his throat, he was being held down again and jabbed with more needles. This time, however, the darkness didn't come.

Two more gunshots thumped through the roar filling Cole's head. When he spoke, his own voice was the only thing that didn't sound like it was three hundred miles away.

"What happened to me?" he shouted.

Although the guards who approached him seemed to hear what he'd asked, they didn't reply. Through the bed and floor, Cole could feel the impact of more scuffling, which quickly subsided. Two guards dragged the Nymar away, and the only way he identified the bloody mess as such was from the uniform wrapped around the pulpy remains infused with severed, twitching tendrils.

"What's happening?" Cole demanded.

But all he got from the remaining guards was a shotgun barrel pointed at him as another one tried to refasten the restraints. Since the padded leather belts had been pulled from their moorings, two guards stood watch over him with their shotguns constantly at the ready.

The tech was alive, but had to be carried out due to all the venom pumped into her system through the Nymar's fangs. There was no way of telling how the vampire had gotten into the prison, but some of the venom spat into someone's eyes could have given him enough control over that person to do the trick. By the time most of the mess was cleaned up, the blaring whine in Cole's ears had decreased to an annoying ring.

Someone entered the room. He was dressed in a cheap brown suit that wasn't cut well enough to hide the gun holstered under his left arm. Tall, athletically built, and pale, he had the look of an ex-cop or soldier who had been busted down to desk detail. "Is he still awake?" the man asked one of the guards.

"Yes," Cole replied. "He is. What the hell did you do to him?"

The man spoke to the guard posted at the door in a clipped whisper. He then turned to Cole, smiled in condescendingly lukewarm fashion and approached the guard who stood closest to the bed. "You've been entrusted to this facility by your friend, Paige Strobel."

"She told me to go with you guys back in Denver, so I did."

"You didn't have much choice, now did you?"

"There were choices," Cole assured him. "I could have left like the others who got away from that warehouse."

"How many others?"

Cole took no small amount of comfort from that question, since it meant that Rico, Prophet, and the Amriany had made it away from there. Changing the subject quickly enough for him to hear gears grinding, he asked, "What did you do to me?"

"We tried to do you a favor, Mr. Warnecki, and had a look at those tendrils that remain inside of you after the Nymar spore attached itself to your heart."

It was a constant act of willpower for Cole to not dwell on the memory of when that thing was inside of him. Like a presence that never grew tired of trying to break his sanity, those thoughts lingered and whispered no matter how he tried to shut them out. The spore had been removed. He could only remind himself of that. He didn't need to remind himself of what had been left behind. The constant pain of his body being garroted from the inside did that well enough.

"You cut me open?" he asked. No matter how obvious it had become, he still couldn't quite wrap his mind around it.

"Nothing worse than what was already done to you when the spore was removed," the man replied. "And much more sterile."

"If anything's gonna kill me, infection is the least of my worries."

"But that's all that separates a human from a Nymar. A very aggressive infection. Also, as we've discovered over the last two weeks, very stubborn."

"Two *weeks*?"

The man nodded. "We didn't exactly want you to wake up yet, but at least that murderer didn't get to you before your stitches healed. I suppose we've got a more traditional kind of medicine to thank for that, huh? I think you've been in this game long enough to be of some use to us while you're awake. Excellent."

Cole sat up again, ignoring the pain that came from it. "Paige wouldn't have signed on for this."

"That doesn't matter. She was kind enough to hand you over under the implication that we would do what we could to get those tendrils out of you. In return, we could study what was happening to you and why you were able to be seeded when something like that should be impossible."

"So . . . you're a Skinner?"

The man merely smiled curtly and walked forward to peel the gown away from Cole's body so he could get a look at the fresh scar. With a few inquisitive prods of his finger against the incision, he brought Cole's focus right back to where he wanted it to be. "The tendrils can't be removed," he said, as if he was talking about a mole on Cole's leg. "We opened you up . . . several times and from several angles. You're quite a healer, by the way. Those tendrils are wrapped around your major organs. Stomach, kidneys, and of course the intestines. Those are the nasty ones. We managed to remove a few sections here and there, but the rest are wrapped around you so tightly in spots that they've cut you. The only thing keeping you from bleeding out is that the tendrils also hold you together. That is, until they get hungry.

"You see, like any simple organism, these things develop ways of communicating. Theirs is to cinch in tighter to provoke an anger response that leads to pain and eventually to the conclusion that you need to feed them. Either that or they just tighten as some sort of reflex. I won't be certain about that until we do some more studying. Of course, we may have to stop feeding them as a way to gauge how their reactions change. Since we seem to have a problem putting you back under, it's best to keep you from gathering so much strength anyway. Surely you understand."

"I want to talk to Paige."

"I bet you do. She was never informed of your real location. Even the press believes you're still being held in Canon City before being moved to Indiana."

"You mean I'm not?"

"Close," the man replied, "but not close enough for you to hear all the commotion."

"She'll find me," Cole said with absolute certainty.

"Will she?" The man pondered that for a moment and then stepped back. "Thanks to our intruder today, I'm tightening security around here. It should be interesting to find out how close she or anyone else can get to you." Looking to a guard, he said, "After his incision is redressed, take him to G7 and institute every level of containment."

Chapter Four

Cole was escorted down a corridor that took him past an entire section of empty cells to a small freight elevator. Beside it was a booth sealed behind safety glass sandwiched between two metal grates. The floor beneath his feet was dark red. Beyond that, it was gray. The walls deeper within the building were the same colors, all of which had been painted recently enough for fumes to still waft through the air. Without any other prisoners behind the bars of those cells, it seemed almost comical to be going through the motions of being in official custody. Every step of the way his senses absorbed his surroundings to look for any opening that might present itself. He was weaponless, exposed, wounded, surrounded by guards who knew way too much about what he was, and abandoned by the people who were supposed to help him. And just when his prospects couldn't get any better, the pain in his guts crept back in.

Due to the open layout of the corridor, he could see the bare cement of the two floors beneath him. His best guess was that he was in an abandoned jail or possibly even an old department store. When he was shoved into the freight elevator, Cole wasn't allowed to turn back around to face the door. Instead, his head was pressed against the wall and pinned there by a baton jammed against the back of his neck. "So," he grunted while turning so his mouth wasn't scraping against the wall, "I take it that saving someone from getting fed upon doesn't count for anything?"

"That thing would have killed you too if we hadn't come in," one of the guards said. "That makes us even."

"What about a phone call? Do I still get one of those? It's been a while, but I've never been allowed to make a phone call."

"That's a privilege," one of the guards said. "Not a right. You lost all of your privileges."

"So now I'm really in trouble, huh?"

The elevator was slow, which made it easier for Cole to figure out they were headed up. When he was turned around, he spotted the number 3 illuminated above the doors. "What's G7?" he asked. When he didn't get a response, he added, "Did I sink someone's battleship?"

A rough hand slapped against the back of his head to force it down until his chin knocked against the top of his chest. More hands shoved Cole forward as one of the guards stayed behind to press a series of buttons just beyond the elevator doors.

The concrete floor was clean, cold, and gray. Unlike the rest of the prison, Cole could feel eyes upon him from every angle, and when he tried to get a look at who was watching him, his head was viciously turned back toward the floor.

Growing nervous as well as cautious, the guards plodded methodically down the corridor. That gave Cole some time to test his limits in much the same way he'd been taught to constantly move his arms in the event of being tied up with rope. He could turn his head a fraction of an inch in either direction so long as the movement looked like a natural sway. Shifting his eyes in their sockets all the way to one side allowed him to catch a glimpse of the bottom edges of more cells. Some had pairs of feet wrapped in standard-issue canvas slip-ons standing just behind the bars. Others were stained with what could have been vomit, spilled lunch, or dried blood. When he caught sight of markings etched into the bars, Cole realized his captors weren't just Skinner wannabes.

The markings weren't anything as simple as manufacturer stamps or graffiti left behind by a prisoner. They were carved very carefully into the iron with too much precision to have been put there by tools that could be smuggled into a cell. Cole's suspicions were confirmed when he noticed

Skinners: The Breaking

the same markings etched into every bar he passed. They were runes. He'd seen enough of the blocky, arcane shapes on Lancroft's walls and above the doorways in Ned's house to recognize the Skinner symbols anywhere. He didn't know what they said, but it meant there was a lot more going on here than he'd suspected.

One guard hurried to get to one of the cells farther along the line. Although Cole didn't hear the rattle of keys or the movement of machinery, he could hear the creak of metal hinges grating against each other. After several more paces he was pulled to a stop, turned to the right and shown a set of bars set directly into the floor. An opening three bars wide had been created when a door, only slightly bigger than one built for a dog, was unlocked.

"Get in," the guard said.

Cole planted his feet and told him, "No."

"Get in."

"Not until you tell me what's going on. Are you guys Skinners or not?"

The silence was thick enough to let him know they weren't strangers to that term.

He forced his head up, turned around and was taken aback by the presence of four guards instead of the two who had brought him to the third floor. "I've seen cells like this before. They were in Jonah Lancroft's basement. You know who he is, don't you?"

Slapping the end of a baton against Cole's chest, the guard shoved him toward the cell. "Shut up and get moving."

Cole grabbed the stick and moved it aside. "You do know who he is. What about the guy in the suit? I bet he knows plenty."

"Get into that cell. This is your last warning." Now that the other guards were closing ranks around him, the man with the baton was rediscovering his courage. His partners brandished weapons ranging from bats to shotguns.

Cole clenched his fists and tried to draw on whatever strength he could pull from the tendrils inside him. Without a spore at their base, and now blood to replenish what they'd burned up earlier, however, the tendrils were nothing more than remnants that constricted or relaxed out of hunger-driven reflex. "This is a mistake. I know what these runes are. I don't belong in this cage."

"That's what they all say." Placing the end of the baton once more against Cole's upper body, the guard said, "Now get in."

"I want to see the warden. I want to see someone in charge! At least bring me the suit guy! Anyone who can tell me why I'm being moved to this place."

Before Cole could hit his stride, he was jabbed by something sharp that poked through the front of his jumpsuit to dig into his flesh. The point had emerged from the end of the guard's baton with a creaking sound that he knew all too well. His suspicions were confirmed when he saw the trickle of blood dripping from between the guard's fingers.

"You are Skinners," he said.

The guard held the pointed end of the baton in place. It had barely pierced Cole's skin, but wouldn't need much of a push to dig deeper. "You need to stop throwing that word around. Especially after all the damage you've caused."

"I didn't kill any of those cops."

"I'm not talking about that. You and the bitch from Chicago practically gave the Nymar the keys to the kingdom. You let them set up shop in one city, allowed a pack of Mongrels to dig into another, and then you killed the one man who had a chance of changing things for the better. If it was up to me, you would've been dead about two minutes after we snuck you out of the state pen."

"Why didn't you do it, then?"

"Because we follow rules. We respect the chain of command. You won't be going anywhere. It may even do me some good to see what happens to you after you've been locked in here for a year or two."

"Sounds like a shorter sentence than I would've gotten at a real trial."

"We'll see how happy you are about it once the testing starts. On your knees."

Cole had seen a similar little door leading into a cell beneath the Lancroft house in Philadelphia. His guess had been that the small entrance was created to force a prisoner to crawl if they wanted to get in or out. It wasn't his area of expertise, but there had to be psychological as well as practical reasons for putting a prisoner into such a compromising position while passing through the bars. "I'll get in once you back up," he said. "I don't know how, but I seem to have gotten a little paranoid over the last few weeks."

Reluctantly, the guard with the weapon took a step back. As he did, the other guards fanned out on either side of him to form a half circle that Cole would have to break if he intended on going anywhere other than the cell. Since the other guards were armed and he had no quick way of telling how many of them had supernatural tricks up their sleeves, he dropped to his hands and knees and backed into the cell. Every inch of floor he scooted across felt like a bad idea. Unfortunately, his only other choice was to attempt getting killed or beaten into unconsciousness, so he would probably just wake up in that cell anyway.

Fighting now would be pointless.

Dying, even more so.

The guards stepped forward, pushed the door closed and turned a key in a lock that was so well-maintained it didn't even make the sound of metal moving against metal. After that, the guard closest to the bars reached up to touch the wall. Cole knew he was tracing his finger along some of the runes, just as Rico and Ned had done to activate or deactivate the power within the symbols. Since he didn't know which runes were being touched or what direction the guard's fingers were moving, he didn't have a shot at deactivating them himself. Plus, there was the fact that he would need longer arms and a few more joints to reach that section of the wall.

"What about that phone call?" Cole asked as he stood up to face the men in uniform.

The guard with the sharpened club in his bloody hand held the weapon up and willed the spiked end to sink down until it was a simple baton. "I'll get right on that."

"You'd better, or my lawyer will hear about it."

Either missing or ignoring Cole's sarcasm, the guard said, "The system doesn't apply to us, Mr. Warnecki. We make our own, and if we're not careful, ours will be the only system left."

"Real philosophical," Cole grunted. "Can we discuss it further over some food? Maybe some water?"

Leaning forward until his face was almost touching the bars, the guard said, "I'm surprised you're hungry at all, you Nymar piece of shit. If I were you, I'd stop whining before we bring some of those cops' buddies in here. They won't care where you're being held or what's going on here as long as they get a chance to tear you apart with their bare hands."

"I didn't kill those—"

He was cut off by the sharp clang of a baton against the bars. "I saw what you are. Shut your goddamn mouth and pray we don't kill you just to cut down on the bloodsucker population."

Having heard that tone of voice and even similar words from Skinners he knew all too well, Cole realized there was nothing he could do or say at that moment to make any progress. So, rather than waste his breath, he backed up until his shoulders bumped against the smooth cement wall and slid down to sit on the floor. His arms came to a rest upon his knees, and his eyes focused on the guard as though he was staring at him through a sniper's scope.

The guard had no smart remarks or threats to give. He stepped away from the bars and headed back to the elevator. In a matter of seconds all footsteps were washed out by the rattle of the elevator door and the rumble of machinery that took the car to another floor.

A simple glance to either side was enough for him to see the bunk bed frame with a mattress that was about half an inch thick on one side of the cement room, and a squat metal cylinder that smelled too bad to be anything other than a toilet on the other. The cell across the hall was identical, but contained a skinny little guy who sucked air in through his mouth as if he was trying to consume as much as humanly possible before someone else in the room beat him to his share.

"What's your name?" the inmate across from him asked.

"Whoever you are," Cole said, "just leave me alone. I'm sick of introducing myself. I'm sick of this damn place and I'm sick of this whole fucking world."

"I hear that, bud."

Another guard walked down the hall and slowed down just long enough to throw Cole a threadbare towel that was presumably too weak to support his weight if he tried to hang himself and a set of paper-thin stained sheets. "You be good, Lambert," he said while shooting a quick glance at the cell across from Cole's. He then turned and walked away while talking to one of his coworkers on a small handheld radio.

Going for the most cover he could get, Cole chose the bottom bunk and started flipping his sheets over the lumpy mattress. He waited for any number of comments regarding the living situation or his space on the inmate sexual pecking order, but all he heard was the steady rasp of Lambert's breath. Something about the way the skinny guy stared at him from across the hall made Cole less than anxious to turn his back on him. The guy might have been barely wide enough to make a dent in his rumpled jumpsuit, but his eyes were sharper and more alert than some of the inhuman predators topping the Skinner watch list. "So," Cole said. "Lambert, is it?"

"Yeah," the other guy breathed.

"You prefer to go by any other name?"

"What the fuck's that supposed to mean?"

Cole nodded slowly to himself. Here it comes.

Rather than try to sidestep the confrontation until it snuck back to bite him when the inmates were within easier reach of each other, Cole grabbed his bars and met the glare coming from the occupant of the other cell. "Just making conversation, okay?"

"So you want to talk now, huh?"

"You don't want any part of it," Cole said, "that's fine."

Lambert pressed his face against the bars as if he meant to shove his head through them. He looked to be a few inches shorter than Cole and would have seemed even smaller if his thick, spiky clump of black hair had been shaved. Wiry fingers curled into fists and then stretched out again to waggle at the end of hands that looked more like knotted collections of veins and faded tattoos. He watched Cole intently while rubbing his bottom lip against the edges of his teeth. "You're damn right it's fine," he said. "Why so nervous?"

Since Cole couldn't think of an appropriately tough or funny response, he kept quiet.

A scowl eased across Lambert's face in the same way a piece of bad pork might work its way through his bowels. Judging by the smell coming from the direction of his cell, it seemed to Cole that might have been the case not long before his arrival. Scraggly eyebrows flicked upward and an appraising moan gurgled from the back of Lambert's throat. "What's that on your neck?" he asked. "Some kinda tribal? Ain't from no gang I ever seen."

Cole looked down, spotted the traces of black stretching from the base of his throat, and pulled up the collar of his jumpsuit to cover more of it. The Nymar tendrils were common among vampires that had an active spore inside them. Black filaments stretched out and made themselves at home within their host's chests, but Cole's spore was gone. Although the markings weren't moving beneath his skin, they were still more visible now than they'd been a few days ago. "It's nothing," he said. "Just left over from a bad night."

"I hear that," Lambert chuckled while unbuttoning his jumpsuit.

Despite the distance and bars between them, Cole stepped away from the front of his cell. "Uhh, what are you doing?"

The other prisoner grinned widely while continuing to undress. He unbuttoned and peeled away the front of his jumpsuit to reveal a pale sunken chest covered in stringy black hair. Opening the jumpsuit farther, Lambert displayed a set of ribs that looked more like a xylophone covered in skin that had been transplanted from a fish's belly. "Take a gander at that," he said.

As much as Cole wanted to resist, he took the gander that had been offered. On Lambert's ribs, written in a flowing script accented with ladybugs and lip marks, were the words, *Sweet Sarah Sunshine.*

Lambert nodded and waggled his eyebrows as if he'd just shown Cole the lost pieces of an ancient text. "Wanna hear about a bad night? I met this lady when I was baked off my ass. I smoked so much weed and drank so much Jim Beam that I got convinced a bunch of blinkin' streetlights were transmitting code to me. Seriously."

"That sounds a bit more than just being drunk," Cole said.

"All I can tell you is it was fuckin' weird. Anyway, I met her that fuckin' weird night and we got along real nice. Gave her a ride home."

"Sounds like you were in great shape to drive."

"Oh yeah. I went between not knowin' where I was headed and not knowin' where I came from. Could've been worse, though. I've driven when I didn't know either. Anyhoo, I made it to her place and she repaid me with the best head I ever got."

"That's not something I'd expect to hear from a guy in maximum security prison," Cole mused as he inched closer to the bars so he could get a better look at Lambert's tattoo. The lettering was done to look like it had been written in ribbon held up by the ladybugs. After what he'd just heard, he had a pretty good idea why the lip marks were there.

Suddenly, Lambert pulled his jumpsuit back up. "Why wouldn't you expect to hear that from me?" he asked indignantly. "You think just because I'm locked up, I want some dude to suck my dick instead of a woman?"

"No. I meant I didn't think I'd ever hear a maximum security prisoner say the word 'anyhoo.'"

When Lambert laughed, he followed it up with a dry, hacking cough that rocked his entire upper body. He let his hands fall away from his jumpsuit as he headed back to his bunk and sat on the edge of the mattress. "That bitch went down on me right there in my car in front of her apartment building. Hot damn, she was good."

Cole gave him a moment to reflect while pressing his cheek against his bars. Keeping Lambert inside his peripheral vision, he surveyed as much as he could of the area beyond his cell. There wasn't much to see. Directly in front of him was the walkway that led all the way down the row to the elevator. From what he could see, the other cells had the same look as his and Lambert's. Something might have been moving in one of the other nearby cages, but the one next to Lambert was definitely empty. Guards were posted at the end of the hall with the elevator, and the opposite end led straight into a solid concrete wall.

"Damn, she could work some magic with that tongue of hers," Lambert continued. "I knew she'd be able to make my dick sing. I could read it on her face, hear it in her head, that she loved givin' head. At least I could tell she was good at it anyway."

"What? Oh yeah. Sweet Sarah." Cole looked between his feet. There was something on the concrete that looked as if a shadow had dripped from the ceiling to stain the floor. When he wasn't able to rub away the dusty grime caked onto the floor, he licked his thumb and tried again. This time he managed to confirm that the stain was another marking taken from the same runic alphabet as the ones etched into the bars. "Sounds like that wasn't such a bad night."

"Hell no. The bad night came later. I was still buzzin' after that bj in the car when I took her out for a night on the town." Lambert's sunken features brightened as he said, "Big thick burger with all the toppings. Ice cream shakes at a drive-in. Snuck into a movie."

Cole felt a warm rumble in his stomach, and his fingers scraped against the floor a little harder. "Sounds classic."

"It was, man. It really was. We topped it off with her blowin' me again in the alley next to a tattoo shop."

So much for classic.

"Does your cell have markings on the floor?" Cole asked.

"Uh-huh. Walls and ceiling too. Ain't very good reading, though."

"Do you know what they mean?"

"Probably left by someone that was here before." Lambert craned his neck to look above him and all around. "I think maybe this prison's been here a long time. At least the building has. Dunno if it was a prison the whole time. Think these marks are some kind of writing. Could just be graffiti for all I know. Some of these gangs tag with dragons and others use Chinese letters. I bet that guard with the stick put some of them there. Or maybe Waylon. They mean something to him. Touches them every time he opens or closes the door."

Cole had revealed half of the symbol on the floor by now.

He hadn't learned enough to decipher it completely, but it was definitely similar to the ones carved into the wall on the main floor of Lancroft's house. He ran his fingers along the rune but didn't get his hopes up. As suspected, nothing happened. Most of the runes were put down like a circuit designed for protection or defense, and only a few were activators. If he had time, he might be able to remember enough to figure something out. He winced at the notion that he might have all the time he could ever want. Anxious to distract himself, he asked, "Who's Waylon?"

"Dude who runs G7."

Cole nodded, pulled himself up from where he'd been squatting, and grunted at the pain of his insides shifting within the constricting tendrils wrapped around them. His stitched incision wasn't exactly tickling either. "Serious looking guy who dresses like a high school principal?"

"That's the one. Usually carries a clipboard. Anyway, this gal with the sweet mouth I was tellin' you about was wearin' a tight little skirt," Lambert mused. "Know what I did after I blew my load?"

"Nope."

"I set her up on some boxes, stepped up and . . . What are you doin' over there?"

Cole had stood up and walked over to the wall on the left side of his cell. The solid sheet of rock was smooth and covered with runes that were so faded they could barely be seen. Scratches marred the wall's surface, but the runes were either too deeply imprinted to be broken or simply unable to be interrupted by something as ordinary as a set of claws or sharpened piece of metal. He thought about the symbols he'd seen in Henry's room at the Lancroft Reformatory, which had remained intact even after a werewolf scratched at them. Plus, there was no reason to think any activators would be inside the cell with a prisoner. More than likely, the runes were meant to seal the cell, strengthen it, or whatever the hell else a witch doctor might do to keep his subjects in line.

Since Lambert had drifted away from Memory Lane for a moment, Cole tried to steer him back on course by asking, "Did you tell Sweet Lips you loved her?"

"Nah. I hiked up that skirt, pulled them hot little panties aside and ate her out right then and there."

Nodding while forcing half a smile onto his face, Cole said, "Nice one."

"It sure was. She didn't even need to ask me to go downtown or nothin'. That's how I knew it was love. You got anyone like that on the outside?"

Even if he'd known the guy well enough, he truly didn't want to talk about Paige. Just thinking of the last time he'd seen her caused him to twitch. She insisted he hand himself over to the authorities so they could help him. Apparently, the plan had been for those men to try and remove the Nymar tendrils, but that went real bad real quick, and Paige was nowhere to be found. Perhaps she truly didn't know what had happened, but that didn't make him feel much better.

Anxious to divert his attention, if only for a moment, Cole leaned against a wall, crossed his arms over his chest and asked, "So you and Sweet Lips had some breath mints and lived happily ever after?"

"Even better, man. I took her by the hand and led her into that tattoo shop. She said somethin' somewhere along the line about likin' ladybugs, so I got them inked on me. And since I already kissed her in all the right spots, I thought I'd commemorate that too."

Cole realized that his guess about the lip marks hadn't been exactly right, but it was close enough.

"That's some good work on your neck," Lambert said.

Cole took another look down at the markings. They were the same as last time and still hadn't moved. That was a little bit of good news.

"You got any ink on yer ribs?"

"No," Cole replied. "At least, not since the last time I checked."

"Ha! Gettin' inked there ain't easy, I can tell you that much. The buzz I was on lasted for about the first five minutes or so and then it was just me and that prick with the electric needle in his hand. I got it done, blazed through a chunk of credit I had on my Visa, and then went out to show my new lady with the magic mouth. Know what she said?"

A slight young man in hospital scrubs approached the pair

of guards at the far end of the hall without a word of acknowledgment and then stepped into the elevator. "What did she say?" Cole asked.

"She told me that Sarah ain't spelled with an H. You ever hear of that? All that hell I went through, all that ink I got drilled into me, all that lickin' I did outside the shop, and she tells me I spelled Sarah the wrong way. I demanded that bitch show me her driver's license just to make sure she wasn't giving me a hard time."

"Yeah?"

"Yeah!" Tracing his hands along the ribbon lettering, Lambert finally slapped his ribs and winced as though the ink was still fresh. "She was right. Damnedest thing I ever saw. Sara. Right there in black and white. No H."

"Did you try to get the tattoo fixed?"

"Nah. I stole the bitch's purse and ran like hell." Grinning from ear-to-ear as he situated his jumpsuit and sealed it up, he added, "Made it all the way to the mountains."

"Is that how you wound up here?"

"Hell no! I was dragged away after reading the minds of some rich folks in Aspen."

"Were they thinking anything interesting?"

"Don't recall," Lambert said with a shrug.

"More weed and Jim Beam?"

"Nah. I just don't remember. This night, though," he said, while patting the side where his Sweet Sarah Sunshine resided, "is one I won't never forget. I dream about those lips of hers. So what about you? What's your story?"

"I killed a building full of vampires in Denver. They framed me for killing cops and made sure I was caught for it."

Lambert's eyes grew wide. "Seriously? Now that sounds like a helluva good day!"

"Not really, but maybe you should put a good word in for me at my parole hearing."

"Parole hearing?" Lambert grunted. "What's that? Nobody on this floor gets to see the outside again unless it's by an act of God. Come to think of it," he added while rolling his eyes up to look at the low ceiling, "maybe that's what the G in G7 stands for."

"How long have you been here?"

"Can't remember. The more mind readin' I try to do, the more of my own crap up here gets wiped clean," the other prisoner said while tapping his forehead.

"That sucks."

Footsteps slapped against the concrete floor outside of the cell, announcing the arrival of Waylon and one other guard. He looked inside at Cole, scribbled a few notes onto his clipboard and said, "On your knees and approach the bars."

After the guard opened the cell door, Cole was allowed to crawl through. Before he was clear of the bars, a foot slammed between his shoulders and pinned him to the floor. Waylon tugged at the collar of Cole's jumpsuit so he could see the tendril markings and then stepped back while saying, "You're getting a roommate."

Cole tried to lift himself up, but was forced back down again so harshly that his face cracked against the floor. Looking up with blood trickling from his nose and lip, he asked, "Am I supposed to shine his shoes while I'm down here?"

Lambert chuckled.

Waylon scribbled.

The guard motioned to someone farther down the hall while drawing a stun gun from his belt. More interesting than that, Cole spotted a bulky figure in the cell beside his. The prisoner there barely made a sound as he moved his wide, leathery body away from the bars and out of sight.

The elevator door rattled open and two more guards escorted another prisoner down the hall. He was Cole's height, had lighter skin, dark eyes, and about a quarter of his teeth. Instead of the jumpsuits worn by Cole and Lambert, he wore light gray sweatpants and a white T-shirt that was missing its sleeves. The tattoos on his arms, knuckles, and neck looked as if they'd been smeared on with a toothpick after his skin was sliced away and then steamed back into place.

"Put him through his paces," Waylon said as Cole was forced to back into his cell. "And remember what happens. I'll want to know everything."

The stocky prisoner knew the drill of getting into Cole's cell, but wasn't happy about it. He dropped to his knees and lowered his head only as long as it took for him to crawl

Skinners: The Breaking

through the low opening. When he looked up again, he glared at Cole as looking at the man who'd molested his baby sister. Climbing back to his feet, the prisoner tugged at the bottom of his shirt and hiked up his pants. "Anything I should know about him?" he asked.

Waylon checked his notes. "Just that he needs to be kept alive. Other than that . . . put him through his paces."

"This isn't right," Cole said. "I didn't hurt any of those cops. I already told that to everyone that had ahold of me since that night. Jesus Christ, when is someone gonna check the security cameras at that warehouse? There were cameras! There was a damn news helicopter! Someone will—"

His cellmate drove his shin into his groin, forcing Cole to buckle as all of the breath was swept from his lungs and expelled through his gaping mouth. It would take a second or two for the pain to really sink in, so he rushed the bigger prisoner and slammed his shoulder into the guy's chest and pushed him against the bars. Waylon and all of the guards walked away amidst the knocking of hard soles upon a harder floor.

When Cole felt an elbow drop onto his back, he rammed his shoulder once again into the slab of beef that was his new cellmate. He kept his head down and delivered short hooking punches to the other man's ribs as if chopping down a tree from two angles. The prisoner weathered the storm while twisting his body to wedge an arm between Cole's shoulder and his own chest. As soon as Cole was shoved back, he delivered an uppercut that knocked the back of the other man's head against the bars. The prisoner barely even twitched before driving an elbow into Cole's face.

Not only did that elbow hit him like a club, but Cole's groin now felt like it had been hit by a flaming jackhammer. Two hooking punches barely caught the other prisoner's attention. A sharp jab to the nose took the smile off the other man's face, but only until the prisoner thumped his fist against a portion of Cole's jumpsuit that was already soaked through with blood. The moment those knuckles hit his incision, Cole was done. The prisoner shoved him toward the toilet and walked over to lay his bulky frame on the freshly made bottom bunk.

Since Cole could barely move, he sat on the toilet and prayed for death.

"Hey, friend," Lambert said from across the hall. "I didn't catch your name."

"Cole."

"You got some balls, Cole."

"Yeah. Too bad they're up near the back of my throat right now."

Both of the other inmates laughed at that one.

Chapter Five

The next two days passed in a blur. At least, Cole thought it was two days. Since he wasn't let out of his cell once in that amount of time, he had to use the movements of the rest of the prison as his only gauge. Meals were served. Lights were shut off and turned back on again. Also, his psychotic cellmate only stopped pounding his face into pulp right before lunch and for a few hours after dinner.

Cole had taken to calling him Chop, simply because letters spelling the words PORK CHOP were tattooed onto his fingers just below the knuckles of each hand. And the only reason he got such good looks at those tattoos was because they were flying at him nonstop for what he guessed was two days. Chop never let up unless he needed to use the toilet, get something to drink, or eat some food off the trays that were slid into the cell by guards who were all too eager to move along. By the time day three rolled around, Cole wondered if he was simply being beaten to death as penance for what he was supposed to have done to those cops in Denver. Judging by the disgusted looks he was getting from the guards, he could very well have been getting off light.

"Step aside, asshole," Chop said. "I gotta take a piss." He and Cole were both bloodied and battered from their near-constant brawling. Both men could handle themselves, but neither was about to concede. Even more important, Cole's incision was healing thanks to his enhanced system and his willingness to let the rest of his body take a beating just to divert Chop's fists from that spot. Even so, it was only a matter of time before Chop tore him wide open. Judging by the interest with which Waylon scribbled his notes, that might well have been what the man in the suit was hoping to see.

When Chop moved over to the toilet and tended to his business, Cole looked over at Lambert. So far the skinnier inmate had been content to remain on his bunk like a rodent seeking refuge in the narrowest crevice of a cave. The sound of a steady liquid stream hitting dented metal filled the cell, accompanied by a contented sigh from the man directing the flow. Cole rushed at Chop from behind and almost got an arm around the man's thick neck before the inmate spun around to intercept him. His leaky penis was still hanging over the top of his sweats as Chop once again introduced his tattooed fist to Cole's face.

"Took ya long enough to try that," Chop mused before lunging forward to get a grip on Cole's jumpsuit so he could toss him into the metal frame of the bunk bed.

Cole bounced off the bed and landed in a sideways stance. The plan had been to outlast the constant assault and defend himself until Chop was either called off or convinced that he'd met his match, and Paige's training had been good enough to get him this far. Now, after days of spitting blood and sleeping with one eye open, he was starting to rethink that plan. The healing serum in his body was wearing thin, and the Nymar tendrils had faded into lines beneath his flesh that gave him occasional jolts of strength along with a constant ache running all the way down to his core.

If the spore was still inside him, Cole knew he could have thrown Chop through a wall or maybe even pulled the cell door from its hinges. With only the torn tendrils left behind, those were no longer options. He wasn't Nymar. He was just sick and tired of being locked up and knocked around. The pain that cinched around his innards tightened, forcing a hardened scowl onto his face. When Chop punched him in the stomach, his fist thumped against a thick mess of scar tissue. Cole pulled away from the other man's grip and delivered a quick blow to his ribs. His fist landed in the same spot

Skinners: The Breaking

he'd been hitting ever since the beatings first started, putting one of Paige's lessons into action. If someone's weakness couldn't be found, make one.

Chop kept fighting, but Cole remained one step ahead. By the time he swept Chop's legs out from under him to drop him straight to the floor, he could hear Lambert hollering joyously from the other cell.

"Put me through my paces?" Cole snarled as he straddled Chop's chest and clamped a hand around his throat. "What's that supposed to mean? Tell me!"

"You're dead, you piece of shit," Chop grunted as he struggled to pry Cole's hand away from his neck. "If it ain't me, it'll be someone else that does it. You stop now and I'll let you live long enough to suck my dick."

After driving his knee into the tempting target still dangling from the front of Chop's pants, Cole placed his hand flat on the prisoner's face. As good as it was to be on the winning end for a change, it felt as if his organs were going to rupture like pieces of wet sausage being sliced by lengths of garrote wire.

"Get off him!" a guard shouted from outside the cell.

Lambert stood so his body was plastered against the bars and shouted, "Chop started it!"

"Both of you move to opposite sides of the cell!"

After finally managing to pry Cole's hand away from his windpipe, Chop sank his teeth deeply into his wrist. The wet crunch was the last incentive Cole needed to do what he'd been trying to avoid for so long.

He'd done it once already, but that was back in Denver when he thought he might be under Nymar influence. Now, with the only Nymar in the vicinity having been turned into a pile of ashen skin flakes in a trash bag somewhere, Cole knew he was acting purely out of frustration, anger, and hunger.

"What the fuck are you doin'?" Chop grunted as Cole dropped his face down to bite into his shoulder. Teeth shredded Chop's flesh and burrowed down even farther in search of what lay beneath the filthy tattooed layers.

"He's a biter!" one of the guards shouted. "Get this door open!"

The man who responded to that was the same one who'd ordered Lambert to step aside. Waylon's profile was barely recognizable from the edge of Cole's vision as he moved in behind the other guards and gazed into the cell over their shoulders. "Everybody move back," he said. "Make sure there's a video feed rolling on this and remove anyone not approved for G7 cases from the surveillance rooms. *Now!*"

Feet scrambled and bodies moved. That was all Cole could make out, since he wasn't about to stop what he was doing. Chop struggled beneath him and pounded his fists against his ribs and shoulders. When he hit the side of Cole's head, he only forced him to twist his face and rip off a sizable portion of skin. Chop screamed and grabbed hold of Cole's hair, pulling him up and away from the coaster-sized hole within inches of his throat.

If he had fangs, the job would have been so much easier. The fact that he even thought that made Cole realize just how far he'd fallen. He was a Skinner. He had the scars and nightmares to prove it. Although the skills he'd been taught had served him well so far, it was the cinching pain inside that spurred him into drinking another human's blood. What sickened him even more was the fact that allowing that blood to flow down his throat brought him more relief than he'd felt in recent memory. The tendrils wrapped around his innards relaxed. The pain subsided. The healing serum kicked in. He started to get dizzy with the joy of no longer feeling like all of his organs were being pinched between the coils of a spring. Even with the coppery taste of Chop's blood coating the back of his throat, he couldn't help but smile as the cell door was opened and the guards crawled inside. The wound on Chop's neck glistened like a freshly cut piece of raw meat that had been plastered to his skin.

"Is he dead?" Waylon asked.

The guards grabbed Cole, shoved the sparking end of a stun gun into his side and cuffed him. "Could be. Want me to check?"

"No. Take him to Medical ASAP."

Waylon stood just outside the cell as Cole was slammed up against the bars. He jotted on his clipboard and asked, "What made you do that?"

"Didn't have a choice," Cole wheezed. "He wouldn't stop swinging at me when I asked him nicely to stop."

"Hold him steady," Waylon said to the other two guards. Once Cole was straightened up and both arms were secured behind his back, Waylon reached into a pocket to remove a bundle of cotton swabs wrapped in a plastic baggie. "I saw you drink his blood. What made you do that?"

When the swab was rubbed against his chin, Cole squirmed away but wasn't quick enough to prevent the sample from being taken. Now that the pain had subsided, he felt like he could withstand whatever punishment was about to be heaped upon him. He stared defiantly at the guards and kept his mouth shut.

"You're not a host to the vampire growth," Waylon said. "Do those tendril fragments somehow give you an innate need to feed or was this just to make your discomfort subside? Do those tendrils help you in some way like they do for the Nymar? Your scars and blood samples mark you as a Skinner. Are you truly being turned or is this possibly a by-product of the Mud Flu?"

Rather than say anything that could possibly be of any help to anyone, Cole asked, "Who the hell are *you*?"

"Answer me first and things can go a lot smoother for you. Otherwise, you'll be quarantined and I'll just deduce the answers myself. If you fill in some of the blanks of my research, you'll spare someone else the time and discomfort of being imprisoned."

"Spare who?"

"Whoever is brought to us next," Waylon replied. "Perhaps someone you know. Perhaps a stranger. Either way, you would have kept that person from going through the same ordeal you now face." Squinting as if he was trying to get a closer look at whatever lay behind Cole's eyes, Waylon added, "I can make it worth your while. You're in a great deal of trouble with the law."

"Isn't that why I'm here? Aren't you guys connected to the goddamn law?"

Once Chop was dragged from the cell and lifted to his feet, Cole was tossed back inside so his face skidded along the floor.

Waylon watched with the same amount of interest he might give to an ant farm. He handed a small digital recorder to the closest guard. "If he starts talking, record it with this."

"What about him?" the guard asked as he nodded toward the cell across from Cole's.

Fixing Lambert with a cold stare, Waylon replied, "He's still under observation. Observe him. As for you," he said to Cole, "you're in our custody on a temporary basis. Whether you're handed back to the authorities as a cop killer or allowed to slip through the cracks after you're reported as having killed yourself while in custody is up to you."

"That motherfucker tore my fucking throat out!" Chop roared.

Waylon, as well as the rest of the guards, locked everything back up to how it was supposed to be and left Cole with the cuffs around his wrists. The sound of the elevator doors opening mixed with the crackle of a stun gun. After that, Chop didn't have anything else to say.

"Jesus," Cole groaned once the hallway was clear. "This is the strangest life I've ever known."

"The great James Morrison of the even greater Doors," Lambert said. "Great music. Genius lyrics."

"You listen to the Doors?"

"What? You think I'm just some token Mexican who only digs Santana?"

"Didn't even know you were Mexican."

"I've got true soul, man. All music flows through me."

After Cole lowered himself onto his bunk and curled into an aching ball, he was serenaded by an off-key rendition of "L.A. Woman." Without Chop in his cell to terrorize him, he closed his eyes and enjoyed the concert.

Chapter Six

Canadian-U.S. border
Ten miles west of Niagara Falls

After renting a cheap room in Toronto and resting there overnight with her Beretta grafted into her hand, Paige was more nervous about crossing the border than she was about stealing the car she'd used to do it. In that time, she'd cleaned up her arm well enough to find less damage than she'd been expecting. The muscle tissue was scraped and gouged, but was still solid enough to function. A few injections of healing serum from the kit strapped around her ankle did a good enough job to get her on the right track. She wasn't one hundred percent, but could barely remember what that felt like anymore.

The vehicle she'd stolen was a little blue Toyota Tercel missing a taillight, several loops of electrical cord holding the rear bumper in place. The shabby exterior matched an engine that rattled noisily under the hood in what could very well be its last hurrah. Whoever the previous owner was, they were probably glad to be rid of the heap and collect the insurance. When she pulled up to the border crossing station, Paige was concerned that she might not be able to get the car moving again. An even bigger concern was that her friend in uniform had already met with the same lying little prick who had turned Rico against her.

"Hey, Mike, it's me again," she said with a tired smile.

Wearing his fifty-plus years on a face that was weather-beaten and scarred by three jagged grooves running all the way down his left cheekbone, Mike smiled and waved away the other Border Patrol officer who started to approach the car. "Back so soon? Usually you guys spend a little more time to get to know a place."

"Things went better than normal," Paige told him. "Just headed home."

"Where's Rico?"

Mike wouldn't have made a great spy. That much was certain. On the few occasions she'd needed to get into Canada, he'd been extremely helpful in either waving her through or arranging for one of his friends to let another Skinner pass somewhere else along the border. He'd made several calls to help Gerald into the Great White North, and was the one to grease the wheels for Cole to reenter the States after Gerald and Brad were killed. None of those things made it any easier for her to tighten her grip around the Beretta hidden beneath the flap of her jacket.

"He had to stay behind," she told him, while praying that he didn't know anything more than a retired trucker and ex-Marine who'd been jumped by a Yeti in the Adirondacks should know. "Cleanup stuff. You know the drill."

Mike let out a tired breath and nodded as if he was simply praising the fact that Mondays were indeed the worst. "Yeah. I hear that. Should I expect him soon?"

"Not sure." Before his experienced eyes picked up on something that might delay her any further, she faced forward and set her sights on the gate that blocked her progress. "Should I just go ahead, then?"

Mike's hand slapped flat against the top of the car just above her head.

He looked over his shoulder at his partner and another car that had just pulled up to the station.

He started leaning in to the window.

If he got much closer or asked too many more questions about Rico, she would have to assume he was either tainted by Kawosa or aligned with the Skinners who had rallied under Lancroft's flag. And if that was the case, she figured

Skinners: The Breaking

she might as well shoot her buddy Mike and drive straight through the barricade. What's the worst that could happen? The law might try to hunt her down?

In a fierce whisper he asked, "Is this trip connected to those policemen that were killed?"

"Maybe," she replied as her thumb flicked off the Beretta's safety. "But you've got to know we don't kill innocents."

"Can you tell me where Rico is?"

Paige shifted her eyes to look at him and angled her gun barrel so she would be sure to hit him if she started firing through the car door. "I could," she said, "but then I'd have to kill you."

After a few seconds Mike nodded and gave her a quick little wink. "Gotchya. Walked right into that one, didn't I?"

"Just about."

He smacked the car again as if he was swatting a football player's shoulder pad. "If I see him, I'll let him know you came by. You have a safe trip and keep up the good work."

Paige waved graciously and drove beneath the barricade that was lifted and then lowered behind her before the next car in line could slip through. She sped down the road without seeing any of the beautiful scenery around her. The terrain looked as if it had been painted as an ode to approaching winter, which normally would have put her in a very good place. Now, she saw the falling leaves and brown grass as more death heaped onto an already rotting world. Cole would tell her to lighten up when she got like this, but she stopped thinking about him before her mood any worse.

After pulling off to a spot marked as a scenic overlook, she dug her phone from her pocket to dial a number she'd memorized instead of programming it into the phone's memory. The Beretta was kept on her lap, with her free hand resting upon its grip. Just when she thought she wasn't going to get an answer over the phone, a connection was made and a crisp voice made itself known with a simple, monosyllabic greeting.

"I need to talk to Adderson," she said.

The person who'd answered sounded like a dispatcher from any number of taped 911 calls. He was quick, sharp, and had less personality than a discount greeting card. "He's not available. Who is this?"

"Paige Strobel. I know he's available. Put me through to him now."

"One moment."

There was a series of electronic crackles, a few short buzzes, and then half a muted ring tone. Paige knew she was being recorded, but for once she was talking to people who had more right to be paranoid than she did.

"This is Adderson," said an even sharper voice than the one that had answered the call.

"Where's Cole? I need to know right now, dammit."

"Paige?"

"You know it's me. If you're trying to trace the call, don't bother. I had a friend of mine wire this phone good enough to screw you up for a while." That wasn't exactly a bluff, but she wasn't entirely convinced that Prophet knew what he was doing. The bounty hunter had access to some good equipment through his employer, and swore it would do the job as advertised. She took very little at face value anymore and would be moving along soon enough anyway. "Things are even shittier than before, and I don't want to leave my partner in a lurch. It was bad enough handing him over in Denver."

"He's safer where he is than on the outside," Adderson replied. "Already, some of the local police units have lessened their searches for you and your people."

"I want to see him. You said you'd keep tabs on him, and I want to know where he is."

"Where are you?"

"New York," Paige replied, figuring the equipment at the other man's disposal would be good enough to find out that much anyway. "The last I heard, he was already being hauled off to a maximum security prison."

"That's right."

"Just because you put that crap on TV about him getting held up in a trial is just a smokescreen, that doesn't mean you guys can just lock him up wherever you like and keep him there. He's supposed to be getting medical attention."

"He's getting the best care we can give him, Paige. Didn't Bob tell you how we operate?"

Bob Stanze was a great cop. He was the only cop who'd tried to do something about the encroaching werewolf presence before they swarmed Kansas City. After that he'd been one of the few to survive the Full Blood siege without trying to pass it off as an urban riot that took place while a pack of wild dogs were prowling the streets.

"I went to Bob for help in tracking those Nymar in Denver before those cops were killed," Paige said. "He told me you guys would also be able to help with what happened to Cole."

"A lot of those Denver cops are alive because of what you and your partners did."

"And some died. Plenty more were killed across the country. I'm starting to think we could've done just as well without you."

"The IRD is in its infancy," Adderson explained. "Like any agency, it's not going to hit its stride right away. Considering what we've got to work with, I'd say we're doing pretty well. We'd be doing even better if you were more forthcoming about the rest of the Skinners throughout the country."

"You convinced me to hand over my partner and you still want me to help you recruit? You've got some set of brass under that expensive suit. Until I hear something solid about Cole, you can consider me one hell of a potential problem who's really good at fading away when the heat's on."

The man at the other end of the line sighed. "Cole was supposed to be held at one of our facilities in Boulder where he would be given a preliminary hearing to keep the Justice Department off our backs. After that, as far as any official documentation goes, he was transferred to the Colorado State Penitentiary in Canon City. That was supposed to buy us some time to do what we could before anyone pressed too hard for a trial or an interview with the prisoner."

"And?"

"And . . . he was transferred."

"That wasn't part of the deal," she snapped.

"Maybe I should remind you that *none* of this has gone according to the original plan," Adderson said in a voice that sounded like a steel cable on the verge of snapping. "The Skinners in that warehouse were *all* to be remanded to our custody so we could take some of the heat off of both you and us. We would do our best to help your partner, and the others would be approached with a deal that would be mutually beneficial if completed properly. Even though the others fled the scene of a crime, we have done our best to see to it that your partner gets the attention he needs."

"You forgot the part where you promised I'd be able to see him once things settled down. That was the only way I agreed to throw in with you guys at all, and you'd better not fucking back out on that now."

Shifting into a tone that reeked of federal authority, Adderson said, "You were in no position to threaten me when Officer Stanze brought you to us, and you're in no better position now."

"That's where we differ. See, my whole life is sliding into hell. When someone doesn't have anything else to lose, the last thing you want to do is set them off. You know what would make me feel better?"

"Talking to Cole?"

"Now there's the smart guy Bob promised me."

The tapping she heard at the other end of the line wasn't a keyboard. Judging by the frustration in Adderson's voice, it was most likely a pen being bounced off a desk or even the crackling of knuckles. "I'll be candid with you, Paige. Things simply never settled down long enough for us to get you in to see him. Now that he's been . . . diverted, that situation is worse."

"Where has he been diverted to?" she asked.

"Actually, although one member of the IRD checked Cole out of Canon City, he was taken away by someone not under my jurisdiction."

"So . . . Cole's just gone?"

"He can't be far," Adderson assured her. "Our people are watching the roads and have a great number of contacts in that area. That's why it was so vital for us to make our move in Denver as opposed to—"

Paige interrupted in a voice that was sharp enough to snip an iron post in half. "Is it possible the real cops took him from one prison and transferred him through the system?"

"We're checking on that."

"Yeah? Well you'd better not be waiting for our trouble with the cops to blow over. By the time that happens, Cole could be a stain on an electric chair. What do you know about what happened to him?"

"We had visual confirmation that Cole was taken into Canon City. He was put into Maximum Security Holding and was under constant surveillance. After we sent someone in to deliver the message from you, he was moved."

"Where to?" The long silence she got was enough to answer her question. "You seriously don't know, do you?"

When Adderson failed to respond to that, Paige gritted her teeth and prepared to unleash as many kinds of hell as she could summon. Before she could spit her first piece of brimstone, another car rolled to a stop several yards away. It was stuffed with two adults in the front seats and several bouncing little ankle biters in the back. The driver pushed open his door and staggered out, looking as if he was ready to take a dive over the guardrail just to earn a few moments of peace.

Turning her head away from that car, she said, "You guys are supposed to know what you're doing! The only reason I agreed to let Bob set me up with you is because you had the resources to start getting this fucking mess cleaned up."

"We're a privately owned organization operating outside the parameters of several official agencies. Right now, it's taking everything we've got to keep from being noticed."

"Don't give me that bullshit!" Paige snarled. "With all the contacts you've made and the resources you've got, there's no way you could work outside *every* government agency. Someone's gotta know about you."

After a pause, Adderson calmly replied, "Highly ranked officials in the Army and Marine Corps are aware of us, but not in an official capacity. Perhaps it would also make you feel better knowing that one of our men in that SWAT van with Cole kept him from being shot by angry officers who lost their friends that night. And before you spout off again, I realize you Skinners had nothing to do with actually killing those men and women. You want to know what we've been doing? The IRD has been stretched almost beyond our limits just keeping the truth about all of this from being spread across the Internet. Do you have any idea how difficult it is to create plausible deniability regarding monsters that are showing up on everything from conspiracy blogs to national news sites?"

"Actually, yes. I do."

"Your friend Cole did some good work with those doctored videos and pictures he circulated after the Kansas City riots. Those got a lot of people willing to write these instances off as a bad hoax in troubled times. But there's more to it now. You people simply do not know how to lay low. It's bad enough that my agency was forced to show itself once the Nymar started targeting innocent people and police officers. With all the attention being aimed at you, it's that much harder for us to keep our heads out of the sights."

"You've got ties to the government. Doesn't that make anything easier?"

The sound Adderson made was barely recognizable as a laugh. "We have some funding and equipment from the military and many members with federal or state law enforcement duties. If anything, that makes things a whole lot more difficult. And before you consider threatening me with becoming a squeakier wheel, let me remind you that if you were on your own, none of you would have gotten away from that warehouse."

Paige knew he had a point, but there was no way she was about to give him that much slack. "Is that how you'd react if one of your men disappeared?"

"We haven't abandoned Cole. We're still trying to find out what's going on in Colorado."

"I want to go there. Send a chopper for me."

After a short pause he asked, "After all of that spiteful talk, you want us to be the ones to pick you up? What's wrong? Is there a search being conducted with your name attached to it?"

"Cole's been alone too long as it is. At the very least, I need to try and get another message to him."

"If that were possible, we—"

"Just take me there," she snapped. "If you've got men in Boulder, then take me to them. I can help track Cole down."

"No. Our people are placed strategically and cannot be

exposed just to ease your mind about your partner. I promised we'd take him out of Denver before he was brought down by police snipers, and we did. I promised we'd put him in a facility where the IRD has a presence, and we did."

"What about the other promise you made about getting Cole medical attention? Do you people even really have doctors that know their way around Nymar spore?"

"Of course we do. There were some initial studies done by one of our doctors." Adderson lowered his voice until she could barely hear it over the phone. "We think the medical team is where we were infiltrated. Cole was in their care when he was taken. One of them was under my microscope about a day before Cole disappeared from Canon City."

"Who is it?"

Surprisingly, Adderson replied, "His name is Hal Waylon. Run that by your sources, and if you find anything, let me know. As long as we get proof that he's been sanctioned, we don't care who does the deed."

"If sanctioning is the same as jamming a shotgun up his ass and pulling a trigger, I'm in." When Paige looked over at the other car, she found two sets of little eyes staring at her from the backseat. She wasn't certain she'd been loud enough for them to hear her, but the harried dad stretching his legs suddenly seemed ready to climb back into his kidmobile just to get away from there.

"Which brings us to ground we've already covered." Adderson sighed. "As soon as I get an update on where Cole is, I'll let you know. Now, would you like me to arrange a pickup? It would be helpful for us to know if we might encounter any hostility when we arrive."

Paige ground her teeth, suddenly thinking of reasons to refuse the offer. She needed to move faster than her stolen car could take her, but if Cole had gone missing while in Adderson's care, then perhaps it wasn't such a great idea to climb into another one of those choppers. Also, she had a few more tactical options available when she wasn't hindered by any sort of authority looking over her shoulder. Even worse, the last thing she needed was to lead Kawosa to a pseudomilitary group that was armed to the teeth and had enough access to arrange tricky ways to bamboozle the citizens of a major country. She still didn't know where the shapeshifter had gone after scampering away from that expressway. "I got some hostility, all right," she told Adderson. "I've been saving it up for a special occasion and I think I know where to send it."

"We can pick it up if you like."

She'd never wanted to hit someone so badly in her life, and that included the day when she couldn't get away from a boy band radio marathon while being stuck in a cab during rush hour. "Forget it. Call me when you find out anything. I'll make my own way."

Adderson's valiant attempt to get the last word in was cut short by a decisive poke from Paige's thumb. Once she'd hung up on him, she dialed another number and opened her window to get a better look at the road leading up to the crescent-shaped little parking area. The cool air helped calm her down, right until the point that she was reminded of how Cole used to hang his head out the window like a dog just to feel a breeze on his face. She allowed herself a quick sad smile while watching for any sign that she was being followed. Rico wasn't dead, which meant he would be coming after her with all he had if he still believed he had to kill her. Since she doubted that Kawosa had planted that stuff about a Skinner splinter group, she wasn't sure if she should trust him anyhow. That was a tough fact to wrap her mind around, but would have been dangerous for her to take lightly.

"Midwestern Ectological Group, Branch 40," chirped a fresh voice that Paige had never heard before.

"Can I talk to Stu?"

"He's in the field. Someone else can help you, though."

"No. Put me through to him. Take this number down." After Paige rattled off her identification number, the girl at the other end of the phone wrote it down, asked someone else what to do with it, looked it up and then made a quick connection that resulted in a transfer to another phone line.

"Paige? Where have you been? Wait, is this really you?"

"Yeah, Stu, it's me."

"Prove it."

She drew a breath and brought the phone so close to her mouth that she almost ate it. "I already gave my number to the stupid little dimwit you got answering the phones, and if you make me give it out again, I'll drive to wherever you are and tattoo it onto your face with a piece of broken glass."

"Whoa! That's you, all right. Sorry about that, but we've had some changes on this end. And please don't start making comments about my end. I'm kinda in mixed company here."

Not everyone at MEG knew about Skinners. Most of the organization just chased ghosts and investigated paranormal claims, but the core members were more than happy to provide a communication structure for those who knew where to find the occasional genuine Bigfoot lair. Stu was not only eager to be Paige and Cole's primary contact, but able to back up that trust with results.

"Have you heard anything from Cole?" he asked.

"I was just going to ask the same thing."

"If we had, don't you think we would have called?"

"Yes," she said earnestly. "What about Rico? Have you heard anything from him?"

"Yeah. Just a little while ago. Sounds like you two got separated. Want me to connect you to him?"

"No. Calling him right now may be dangerous. You know how it is."

"Yeah," Stu said, even though he was too far removed to know how anything was.

"Do you know anyone who can pick me up?"

"Any Skinners, you mean?"

"No," she replied, without worrying whether it was too quick. Rico still hadn't tracked her down, but that was as comforting as a fuse taking just a little longer than expected to reach the dynamite. "I was thinking more along the lines of one of the MEG branches. You guys have to have an office somewhere in New York, right?"

"Our closest branch is in South Jersey. There's another bunch of guys covering the East Coast paranormal scene better than us. I could make a call. They don't know about you, but they'd probably be willing to help you out as a favor to us."

Paige was going to accept the offer when she thought better of it. Calling the MEG guys was sketchy enough.

They were still only observers and phone operators. Bringing anyone else into this mess was just cruel.

"Paige? You still there?"

"Yeah, Stu. I'm just thinking."

"Let me call the Jersey branch. Don't you know someone out that way?"

"It's all right." Wanting desperately to put him on another track, she asked, "What are you doing in the field? Usually the only time you're away from the office is to play in one of those *Sniper Ranger* tournaments."

"One of our investigators got shoved off a patio. He swears it was a poltergeist that did it, but the guy once tripped over a bump in the sidewalk and broke his wrist. Whatever the reason, I'm taking his place. I love talking to you guys, but going out on real investigations beats the snot out of staring at a computer screen all day."

"Congrats."

"Thanks. Everything all right, Paige? You sound upset."

She fired back with: "Maybe it's the whole fugitive thing. Or it could have something to do with Cole being in prison. That kind of stuff tends to put a damper on things."

"Okay, fair enough. Dumb question. Just trying to help."

There was no way for Stu to help. She felt like an idiot for even thinking MEG could be of any use in this situation, especially when they were purposely kept as far removed from Skinner business as possible. "Do me a favor. Try to find out what you can about Cole. Run a search on Colorado State Penitentiary. Google his name. I don't care. If you find anything, let me know before anyone else."

"I can do that, definitely."

"I'm serious about that last part. No matter who else calls or asks, even Rico, I want to know first."

"He's your partner," Stu replied. "I can respect that."

"Okay. Thanks." Paige hung up and faced the stretch of road leading back to I-190. Her ears had picked up the crunch of approaching tires on gravel. Moments before the car came into view, her hand was already wrapped around the Beretta and preparing to empty its entire magazine through her window. She didn't relax until she was certain that the old woman driving the late model Dodge wasn't one of Rico's contacts.

After the Dodge pulled to a stop, the old woman killed the engine and reached for her passenger seat. When she turned back around, she was holding a little sandwich that she nibbled on while gazing out her windshield.

There was one more number Paige wanted to dial, but she wasn't going to do so while standing still. Her nerves were jangling so badly that she thought it might feel better to run all the way back to Chicago. She backed out of her spot, headed for the interstate, and began tapping out her next call.

Prophet wasn't answering his phone. Screening his calls was one of several precautions the bounty hunter was taking after escaping Denver the night the SWAT teams took Cole away. Deciding against leaving a message, she hung up.

Her car was barely up to full speed when her phone rang with Prophet's caller ID notification lighting up her screen. "Walter," she said without wasting time on a greeting, "when was the last time you saw those Gypsies?"

"Number one," Prophet replied, "they don't like it when we call them Gypsies. It's insulting, but only when it comes from an outsider. Maybe a racist thing. I kind of lose track, but the proper name is Amriany, and that's what they like to hear. They carry a lot of guns, so you might wanna keep that in mind."

"Yeah, yeah. Have you seen them lately?"

"Number two," Prophet continued calmly, "I haven't seen them since Denver."

"Can you get ahold of them?"

"Maybe. Why?"

"I'm in a jam. Rico and I went after the Nymar communication hub in Toronto. We got some leads, but Kawosa turned him against me."

Suddenly, Paige felt like her stomach had imploded. If Kawosa had somehow tracked the bounty hunter down, she could very well be making the same mistake where Prophet was concerned. If he'd already taken Rico's side, he could call the big man and send him to her. Unfortunately, it was too late to worry about all that. She needed to trust someone, and if Walter wasn't trustworthy, things were even worse than she'd imagined. "I need help, Prophet, and I don't know who else to turn to. You said the Amriany had serious funding and transportation. Is there any way you could convince them to get me to Denver? It'll take too long for me to drive, and I'm not about to surrender my weapons to make it through an airport security check."

"Don't you know any other pilots? What about the guy who smuggled Cole out of Canada after Gerald and Brad were killed?"

That man was a Skinner, and she hadn't spoken to him more than a handful of times in her life. Considering what had happened with Rico and the fact that Kawosa could be turning any number of the others against her, going outside the Skinners made the most sense. "He's not available," she said. "It's got to be the Amriany."

Prophet sighed heavily. "I can make some calls. Even if I can get them to pick you up, I can't guarantee they'll just drop you off wherever you want."

"Thanks, Walter. Tell them I don't expect a free ride, but I've got to get away from here. Tell them—"

"I'll think of something," he cut in. "Just let me get to calling before you talk me out of it."

Chapter Seven

Cole sat with his back against the side wall of his cell. He was close enough to the bars to reach out and scrape his fingers against them without having to extend his arm more than an inch or two from his body. The grating of his thumbnail against the iron was a sound that reached all the way down to the base of his skull to twang his nerves like banjo strings. After a few hours he barely even heard it anymore.

The guards filed in like a marching band. Instead of tubas and drums, however, they carried shotguns and riot shields. When he got a look at that, he jumped to his feet.

The guard who stepped forward was one of those who had been watching him since he woke up on that hospital bed. "You know the drill," he said. "Stand back."

"What drill?"

"To visit another section of the prison. It's the same every time."

"I've barely been out of this room," Cole said.

When the guard approached, he looked into the cell to find nothing but bloodstains on the floor, a rumpled bed, the squat cylindrical toilet, and a wadded napkin stained with sour gravy that was the only remnant from lunch. "Turn around, get on your knees, clasp your hands behind your back and stick them between the bars."

Cole did as he was ordered. Once his hands were extended

between the bars, he felt a pair of lightweight cuffs cinched around his wrists. Unlike the cuffs that had been used so far, these were lighter and scraped uncomfortably against his skin. Twisting his hands within the restraints, he could feel the warm flow of blood start.

"Don't fidget so much," the guard said. "You'll only hurt yourself. Now get on your hands and knees."

No matter how badly he wanted to get outside his cell, Cole hated crawling for the privilege. He assumed the position, clenched his fists and planned three different ways to defend himself from an attack that might be launched when he was vulnerable. The most threatening thing he heard was the brushing of fingers against a wall followed by the creak of hinges.

"Crawl through," the guard said. "Backward. That's your only warning. Try to come through any other way and I'll cave your head in."

Cole found the opening by tapping his feet against the bars and backed through as quickly as possible. Once he was outside, he choked back the desire to jump to his feet, and instead asked, "Can I get up now?"

"Slowly."

The guard gripped the short length of steel links between Cole's wrists and stood behind him. When Cole tried to move in a way the guard didn't like, he felt the sting of the sharpened cuffs against his wrists.

"Are these cuffs standard issue?"

"No," the guard replied. "We don't answer to anyone when it comes to how we do things. Kind of like you guys, huh?" To make his point, the guard pulled up on the cuffs to send a jolt of pain all the way up through Cole's arms. "You want me to tighten them, just keep on talking."

Cole looked over to the cell where Lambert was held. The skinny man held up one arm to show him a wrist that had a thick scar encircling his entire wrist. The look in his eyes was a friendly reminder to do what he was told before the guard made good on his threat. When Cole looked at the cells he passed on his way to the elevator, he expected that his head would be shoved down, as it had been upon his arrival. But the guards didn't seem interested in averting his eyes, so he took the opportunity to catch a fleeting glimpse of a collection of specimens from what might have been in a Skinner's field guide.

Half Breeds paced in two of the cells on one side of the corridor, while a Nymar in a straitjacket sat on the toilet in another. The cell directly beside Cole's was inhabited by a tall man wearing a standard-issue jumpsuit. He filled out the garment with a solid, muscular build. Unlike the bodybuilders one would expect to find in a prison, this one's skin was pale yellow, segmented by rings that sectioned his flesh into narrow strips, and covered in bumps that resembled chunks of gravel embedded beneath his flesh. He crossed his arms, flexed the gill flaps along the bridge of his nose, his translucent lids blinking open to reveal solid yellow eyes.

The elevator doors slid open and Cole was shoved inside, to find Waylon already waiting with clipboard in hand.

"Evening, boss," Cole said in an accent he'd lifted straight out of *Cool Hand Luke*.

After the doors slid shut, Waylon replied, "It's afternoon."

"Really? What day?"

"Two, since you were brought here."

"Is that all?"

Waylon nodded while scribbling a few notes onto his clipboard. "Maybe."

"Do I get my phone call yet?"

"No." Punctuating his note with a loud tap that would have snapped the tip off of a lesser writing implement, Waylon pressed the button at the end of his steel gray pen and dropped it into the breast pocket of a crisp, dark blue shirt. "A woman has been making inquiries at the Canon City facility about you. Is she your partner?"

The rigors of the last few days had chiseled Cole's expression into solid rock as he said, "Maybe she's an ambitious lawyer."

"It's too late for that, Mr. Warnecki. After the commotion that was stirred up by the deaths of all those police officers, we were certain to throw them a sacrificial lamb right away."

"So you have control of the media too? Good luck with that."

"Not control," Waylon said. "Someone had to stand trial,

to answer for your crimes, someone who was connected to all those murders. We gave them another Skinner who was apprehended at a similar fracas in Texas, so now you and I have all the time in the world together."

"Oh shit," Cole grunted. "Is this some sort of weird conjugal visit? Even if I swung that way, I'd rather go without than see what's under that suit."

After a quick nod from Waylon, one of the two guards in the elevator slammed the butt of his shotgun into Cole's ribs. As soon as his knees hit the floor, the second guard cracked his knee against his face.

"I'd suggest you cooperate," Waylon warned. "The tests that lie ahead may be rigorous, but we could always get some answers from you in the form of an autopsy." Only then did Waylon press a button on the wall panel.

Cole looked up at the guard who stood closest to the short column of buttons. He was another familiar face that had been shoving him around since he woke up strapped to a bed. The key he clutched between calloused fingers was fitted into the slot next to the DOOR OPEN switch.

"Mr. Warnecki," Waylon said while leading the way out of the elevator, "you should know that we're not keeping you here for trivial reasons. Things have begun that need to be dealt with, and in order to do that, certain answers must be found. First among them is how the new strain of Nymar infections interact with humans. Since we're already intimately familiar with Skinners, seeing how the newest Nymar spore interacts with you provides a unique opportunity."

Cole was dragged to his feet and pulled along behind the man in the suit. "I'll bet it does," he said, while struggling to carry his own weight. "And what did you learn from telling that thick-necked asshole to beat me to a pulp in my cell?"

Without levity or malice, Waylon said, "We needed to test the limits of your recuperative abilities and how they were affected by those tendrils. It turns out they help you more than you may know."

"Did you even try to remove them when you cut me open?"

"Of course we did. What better way to study them? If we could have gotten them as well as the organs to which they were attached without ruining the specimens, you wouldn't have even woken up from the anesthesia. Once we get into the next room, do yourself a favor and don't give me a reason to rethink that decision." Retrieving the pen from his pocket and tapping its button, he asked, "Who might be looking for you?"

"How am I supposed to know that?"

Flipping the pen around his first two fingers, Waylon said, "You know how your partners operate. You know their contacts. Tell me the details."

"If you're so intimately familiar with Skinners, you should already know that."

Waylon flipped the pen around again. "Your partner's name is Paige Strobel. Does she have any official contacts in Colorado or know of any *other* Skinners in the vicinity?"

"Yes."

He smiled approvingly, flipped the pen and asked, "Who?"

"Me."

Waylon nodded, flipped the pen around to grip it at the end with the button and then jabbed its tip into Cole's chest. The strike came too quickly for Cole to do anything about it, and although it was a shallow wound, the pen scraped against bone with a pain that felt as if a cattle prod had connected with the inside of his body.

When he reflexively tried to defend himself, Cole was grabbed by a guard on either side. The pen was not only still in him, but was being twisted and driven in deeper by Waylon's hand.

"Does she have any *other* contacts?" Waylon asked.

Cole struggled against the guards, but knew he wouldn't be able to break loose from their grip. The lightweight cuffs were used to pull his arms up behind his back until they felt about to snap in two places, and the sharpened interior of the cuffs chewed viciously into his wrists.

"Answer this question and the rest of today's exercises will be easier," Waylon said. Without changing a single aspect of his emotionless face, he pulled out the pen and formed a fist around it before driving his knuckles into Cole's jaw. The pen added a nice bit of sting to the punch that Cole felt all the way back in the space where his wisdom teeth had been. Instead of asking another question, Waylon waited for Cole to meet his eyes again and then snapped another punch into the same spot. "You had your chance," he said. "Remember that."

Once the doors were open, the guards shoved Cole through them and into what felt like a whole other world. Compared to Canon City, the freshly painted hall and sparkling tile floors seemed like luxury hotel accommodations. Some normal people shuffled through a normal door at the end of the hall. No scars on their hands. No runes etched into the frame. The guards tightened their grip as if they too had to brace for their reentry into the mundane.

The door at the end of the hall opened into something that reminded Cole of a large, drab break room. There were a few metal tables and small stools welded to the floor, and several spots where more tables and stools had obviously been removed. There were a few vending machines along one wall, but only one was plugged in. As long as he wanted a bottle of overpriced water, he was in luck. A television was bracketed to the ceiling in one corner, and no less than half a dozen surveillance cameras were hanging from different spots along the room's upper perimeter. The moment he stepped inside, all of those cameras shifted to point at him. He counted six guards already in the room. Four men and two women dressed in full riot gear had fanned out to surround him, and the two who brought him from his cell were absorbed into the pack. Two of the guards had shotguns, but the other four carried AK-47s and were positioned so if they all decided to fire on him at once, the collateral damage would be kept to a minimum.

"We've already tested your pain tolerance and ability to heal," Waylon said as Cole was shoved down onto a stool. "Now I'd like to see how your modification affects other functions."

"Modification?" Cole grunted. "You make it sound like a cool bionic arm or something."

Waylon let out a stifled snort, which was probably meant to be a laugh. "Bring in the weapons."

That didn't seem like a good thing. His entire body tensed as a guard entered the room to set a small metal case on the table. Then the guard moved around to grab his cuffs.

"What is that?" Cole asked.

Skinners: The Breaking

The cuffs were removed, causing all of the guards to raise their weapons to their shoulders. Small devices were taped to his neck and chest, and when they were all in place, a tech dressed in scrubs walked over to a set of machines behind the guards. The machines were flipped on, giving off the same electronic noises Cole had heard when he woke on a hospital bed.

"I want you to open the case, Cole," Waylon said. "And I also want to remind you that nobody knows you're here. Even if they realize you're missing, no police agency in this country would give a damn if we delivered your body to them in pieces. More importantly, I want you to know that my guards are under strict orders to shoot to maim. There's no easy out for you. In fact, if you misuse what's inside that case in any way, I'll see to it that the first dozen bullets hit below your waist. After that, the testing will still commence. Got it?"

Cole nodded while rubbing his tender wrists. He reached out, flipped the latches on the case and opened it. Inside, there were two rounded wooden stakes. The points had been whittled down until smooth, and the handles were studded with small, sharp thorns stained with blood. Grabbing one of the stakes, he jumped to his feet and demanded, "Tell me where you got these!"

"Sit down, Mr. Warnecki."

"Let's see your hands."

One of the guards took half a step forward. "He told you to sit down!"

Waylon stepped up but didn't enter the circle formed by his firing squad. Holding up a palm, he showed Cole a palm that was marked by the neatest row of scars he'd ever seen. Unlike the random patterns of most Skinner weapons, the thorns in whatever weapon he'd crafted were just as orderly as the notes he scribbled on his clipboard. "Satisfied? Now sit down."

Cole looked at the stakes from every angle, which was all he needed to deduce one simple fact. "These don't belong to you." Glancing around at the guards, he added, "And I'd bet they don't belong to any of you. Nobody working in a place like this would be far away from their weapon. So whose body did you steal these from?"

"I want you to shift that weapon's shape, Cole," Waylon said.

"Not until you tell me where you got them."

"Sit down, then hold the weapons properly and shift their shape."

Cole made sure his fingers fit between the thorns. The blood staining its grip was old and blackened. "Did you kill someone to get this? Answer me or—"

One of the guards to Cole's left fired a single shot from his AK-47. The round tore through the meat in Cole's calf, knocking that leg out from under him and sending him straight down to the stool. His tailbone cracked against the uncushioned seat and his chest knocked against the edge of the table. Before he could slide to the floor, another guard rushed over to him, lifted him onto the stool and then slammed the flat side of his shotgun stock against the back of Cole's head. The jarring impact knocked his face against the table, but wasn't hard enough to keep him there.

Waylon reached into an interior jacket pocket to produce a small syringe that was about half the size of a pencil. "Cooperate and I'll administer this serum to you."

Recognizing the fluid in that syringe almost immediately, Cole gripped the table and nodded. Even with his body's ability to produce the serum, the bleeding from his flesh wound would soon cause him to pass out. Since he didn't want to be at the mercy of these men, he dropped the stakes and allowed two guards to restrain him while the serum was administered. The moment he experienced the cool, familiar rush of it through his leg, he felt better. The tech knelt down to pinch the wound together as both the shotgun and AK barrels were jammed against Cole's head. The wound itched as it sealed, but that sensation was almost completely lost beneath the comforting light-headedness that followed. Whether that came from the serum or the blood he'd lost, Cole was grateful for the breather.

Following the tech as best he could, he grunted, "That's better than the stuff we mix at home."

"Of course," Waylon said. "Now can we continue?"

Cole sat up, took hold of the stakes and couldn't help but

stare at the flakes of dried blood that fell from the thorns onto his skin.

"You know what to do," Waylon prodded. "Do it."

Gazing defiantly into the eyes of the guard who'd shot him, Cole clenched his fist around the weapon and drove the spikes into his palms. Oddly enough, he could actually tell the difference between those and the thorns on his own weapon.

"Now shift its shape," Waylon commanded.

If he was holding his own spear, it would have been easy. He'd bonded with that weapon to the point that it felt more like a piece of his own body. But the stakes were foreign to him. When he willed the pointed end to curl, it barely twitched.

Waylon looked over to the wall behind Cole, which was dominated by a large window. "Are you getting this?"

He was answered by a few sharp taps from the other side of the thick window.

"Is that all you can do, Cole?"

In another part of the converted visitors' lounge, machines chirped the rhythm of his heartbeat and whatever other vital signs were being measured by the components stuck to his neck and chest.

"How are you feeling?" the tech asked.

"Tired," Cole replied.

"Are you having chest pains? Any pressure from the tendrils?"

Hearing someone refer to vampire fragments inside of him as if they were nothing more than kidney stones was strange. Then again, it wasn't much stranger than the fact that everyone was more concerned about a stick changing shape than the bullet wound in his leg, which had almost healed. Cole reminded himself to get that recipe.

He shook his head and then winced.

"You are, aren't you?" the tech asked.

Lowering his eyes, Cole nodded and let out a breath he'd been prolonging for the better part of a minute.

Waylon jotted down a note and said, "You can do better than that, Cole. Make that weapon into something you could use."

Those words caused all of the guards to tense.

Cole kept his head hanging low, mostly as a way to try and make himself look weaker than he truly was. Just because there wasn't a way to keep Waylon from recording his data didn't mean he couldn't screw with that data as much as possible. When he focused on the floor and the lower portion of the room, he spotted more of the Skinner runes etched into the walls. Whether they were protections or some sort of ward, he couldn't tell. Seeing those symbols gave him an idea, however, which involved playing along with Waylon's little experiment just enough to make him seem like a worthwhile experiment.

"Can you hear him?" the tech asked. "You need to reshape that weapon."

Cole grunted and lifted his head, hoping he wasn't overdoing the theatrics. "Yeah. Just give me a moment."

Reshaping his own weapon had become a reflex, but it was one that had to be trained. Cole drew on that experience as he willed the stakes in his hands into a new shape. After several moments of strained silence, sweat began to trickle down his forehead. More perspiration came when he thought he might not be able to get the stakes to change shape at all. But then the varnish worked into the stake did its thing. The Nymar blood infused into the mixture bonded with Cole's blood, allowing a bridge to form between his mental commands and the components in the varnish that had been taken from a shapeshifter.

The stake began to creak. The sharpened end stretched outward into a finer, narrower point.

"Very good," Waylon said as his pen scratched furiously on his clipboard. "The data we collect today will help more Skinners than you know, Mr. Warnecki."

When Cole shifted his hands, he worked both thumbs to grind the stakes against his palms as much as possible. The thorns were still embedded in his flesh, and they tugged at his skin while scraping against tender, exposed meat.

"His heart rate is escalating," the tech reported. "More than normal."

That came as no surprise to Cole. Even though the stakes continued to sharpen and eventually curve into hooks, he wasn't feeling the results he was after. And the less he felt in that regard, the longer he'd be locked away inside a building that had probably been shut down and crossed off of any list maintained by the Department of Corrections or anyone else who kept track of large buildings. He clenched his eyes shut, focused harder, and zeroed in on nothing but the image of what he wanted the weapon to do.

Still, nothing more than what Waylon had asked for.

"Good," the man with the clipboard said. "Now shift them back."

Sweat rolled down Cole's face. He'd only managed to find one chink in the prison's armor, and it was looking like he couldn't exploit it. As soon as that thought rolled through his mind, he could hear the heart monitor whine into overdrive.

"We might want to slow this down," the tech said.

Waylon's voice was cool and crisp. "Is he going into arrest?"

"Not yet."

"Then keep going. If anything ruptures, we can revive him. Cole, keep those weapons touching the table or I'll have you shot."

None of those words sank in. Cole's entire world had devolved into one task. And when that task drifted further out of reach, he thought of an image that centered him and steered him back on course. More important, it made him want to fight even harder to climb out of the pit into which he'd sunk.

"Bring it back to where it was, Cole." That wasn't a request from Waylon. It was a demand backed up by a squad of gunmen.

What he'd tried to do was simple in theory, but wound up being a lot harder than he'd anticipated. One of the thorns waggled within his palm, and when he focused harder, it waggled even more. The stakes shrank back down and straightened out. The thorns remained wedged in his palm, but the waggling one felt more like a loose tooth on the verge of popping out. He gripped both weapons tightly, driving every thorn deeper, and concentrated for one more push.

Doing his best to cover what he was doing, he kept his fingers wrapped around the weapons as that one loose thorn burrowed in at a new angle. With a little more shifting within his bloody fingers, the stake's handle pushed against the heel of his palm. His fingers tightened to the point of trembling, which rattled the weapon's handle against the table.

Obviously speaking to someone via an earpiece or phone, Waylon said, "Yes, I can see the differences in the process. Focus on the tendrils."

Cole couldn't feel anything from the tendrils, but he couldn't feel much from the rest of his body either, thanks to the pain of varnished wood slowly sliding into his hand. Only a small part of his attention was centered on returning the stakes to their normal form, since that was the easiest part of the process. His body strained to put enough willpower behind his command to not only peel away a section of the handle, but to divert that one loose thorn into his palm as far as it could go. Somewhere along the line the jagged sliver began slicing into more delicate tissue and touched a nerve that caused him to sit bolt upright and throw his head back.

When the tech moved in behind him, Cole swiveled around and swung his arm as if he meant to shove the man back. That prompted all of the guards to move in with their guns pointed at his head.

"Just get away from me!" he shouted.

"Put the stakes down!" one of the guards said. That sentiment was echoed by more and more of the armed guards while Waylon simply stood back and watched.

Cole slammed the stakes against the table, driving the sliver even farther up into his hand. There was still one obstacle left, and the only solution he could come up with was going to hurt. A lot.

Uncurling the fingers of his left hand, he allowed that stake to fall from his grasp. "Come here, asshole," he said while standing up and holding the weapon in his right hand out, as if offering it to Waylon. "Come take it for yourself."

Waylon scowled at him like a disappointed parent. "Someone bring those weapons to me."

A guard with a shotgun stepped forward. Her stern face might have been pretty beneath the helmet she wore, but there was nothing that made Cole think she would hesitate to pull a trigger. "Hand it over," she said.

Cole made sure to hold the stake so neither end was pointed at her. His arm was low and at waist level when he said, "Take it."

"Drop it."

Since he could just about feel the tension in all of those trigger fingers, he grabbed the table with his free hand and used his other to pound the stake against it like a gavel. Not only did the loose thorn dig even farther up into his palm, but all the others gouged him as well. "Come and get it!"

"Take it from him," Waylon said.

Another guard handed his weapon to the woman with the shotgun and clamped a powerful hand around Cole's wrist. Just to be sure he got what he was after, Cole showed the guard a sweaty grin when he whispered, "Sure takes a lot of backup for you to take a stick away from a wounded man. Your mom must be real proud of you. How about I ask her the next time I'm—"

Taking hold of the stake, the guard pulled it loose in a powerful motion followed by a twist to scrape the thorns as much as possible against Cole's bloody palm. He let out a pained grunt to cover the sound of snapping wood and slumped forward to rest his head and chest against the table. When he placed his hands flat on the tabletop, he slid them across the smooth surface to leave crimson trails and smear the blood on his skin.

"What are the readings?" Waylon asked.

The tech nervously rattled off some numbers.

"How's his leg?"

The guard who'd already gotten his hands dirty moved in to restrain Cole while the tech checked the bullet wound.

"It went right through the meat," the tech confirmed. "Looks like that serum we put together does work faster than the original formula."

"Great. That means we can continue."

"I really don't think that's a good idea."

"Why? We can always patch him up if things get too bad. I just want to make sure he hasn't sprouted fangs."

"I haven't," Cole said. "Can't you see that much for yourself?"

"They retract," Waylon said, as if explaining a simple sketch to a child. "They also respond to external stimulus such as perceived threats or sources of food."

"Haven't you starved me enough and thrown enough goddamn threats at me to spark what you needed?"

Waylon smiled and then shrugged. "Maybe. But perhaps the process of turning you into a Nymar hasn't been halted. Perhaps it's merely been slowed." As he continued to talk, guards surrounded Cole and another one moved in behind him with something that looked like an upended gurney. "Perhaps something else is happening, but we know the Nymar organism evolves quickly in response to the unique situations of its host. Since we've got you here and you resisted the drugs to put you back under again, we'll run our experiments while you're awake."

"When did I refuse anesthesia?" Cole asked while he was stood up and strapped into the gurney. "Seriously! I'll take whatever painkillers you've got."

"Relax, Cole. This should only take another hour or two." Once Waylon's subject was completely tied down and surrounded by armed guards, he said, "Get the drills."

A door opened at the back of the room and something was wheeled out. Cole spent the short amount of time preparing himself to stay awake and keep his fists clenched tightly enough to keep his palms secure. When he caught his first glimpse of the little handheld drills on the cart that was wheeled to his table, keeping his fists clenched wasn't much of a concern. The motor of the first drill sounded like a smaller version of a hydraulic tool used to remove bolts from a car's wheel.

"Someone get him a towel," Waylon said.

Cole needed his hands to remain dirty until he got back to his cell. If that wasn't allowed to happen and his palms were examined too carefully, all of the pain he'd suffered would count for squat.

When the tech stepped up to his side holding one of the prison's threadbare towels, Waylon said, "Good, now stuff it in his mouth."

As the tech pushed the towel in, he made sure he was still

able to see Cole's teeth. The drill gouged into his shoulder smoothly, but squealed when it hit bone. Agony shot through Cole's entire body and he nearly bit all the way through the towel as he screamed into it. Waylon looked pleased as his subject thrashed against his restraints and the machines recorded every moment of Cole's ordeal.

Chapter Eight

Eighteen hours later
Sixty-five miles northeast of Atoka, Oklahoma

Paige hadn't been eager to make the call to Prophet regarding the Amriany, but it proved to be a gamble worth taking. Not only had the European hunters agreed to extract her within hours after she contacted them, but they'd flown into a private strip at Buffalo-Niagara International Airport and took off before the engines of their Gulfstream G200 had a chance to cool.

The inside of the jet looked like a smaller version of the waiting room Paige had haunted while waiting for the Amriany to arrive. It was sparsely furnished, smelled of stale cigarette smoke, and vibrated with the hum of engines. Three of the ten seats in the cabin were occupied. She sat near one of the windows, angling her chair so she could watch the other passengers. Two of them had worked with Cole, Rico, and Prophet in Denver. The third was a short man plagued by a constant twitch in his right eye. His olive-colored skin was deeply tanned and marred by scars of all shapes and sizes, some of which were deep enough to interrupt the flow of a short, curly beard. The largest scar ran along his left cheek and down his chin. If Cole had been there, Paige thought, he'd make a comment about how the bush on the scarred man's face would have looked more natural between the Gypsy's legs. She laughed quietly, reminding herself to call the Amriany by their proper name.

"What is so funny?" the man with the bush on his face asked.

Paige shook her head. "Nothing. Just trying to pop my ears. We took off so fast that I barely had a chance to grab onto something."

"You said you were in a hurry."

"Right, but I didn't expect you guys to come so quickly."

"If you could have waited, you should have said something," the man said impatiently. "There is a lot to do and we don't need to waste time picking up Americans who are too cheap to pay for a goddamn ticket."

Before the man could get any more riled up, he was shoved back into his seat by a firm hand that slapped his shoulder several times. The woman attached to that hand kept her short brown hair beneath a leather skullcap. Her pointy nose dominated an otherwise fragile-looking face. "We're still on schedule, Milosh," she said. "Paige will prove to be worth the diversion."

"She'd better," Milosh scowled through his beard. From there, he pulled a long blade from a scabbard at his waist and began polishing the gleaming steel with a cloth that reeked of oils smelling vaguely like the varnish used for Skinner weapons.

"Hi, Nadya," Paige said in the cheeriest voice she could manage. "Prophet sends his best."

The woman had a face that was pretty, but rough around the edges. Reflexively touching the spot where she'd been wounded during the ill-fated raid on the Nymar warehouse in Denver, Nadya sat down in the seat directly across from her and said, "We're sorry about what happened to Cole. That was an unfortunate sacrifice, but it allowed most of us to escape."

"He didn't get brought in just to save you," Paige said. "There's more to it than that."

"And he wasn't the only one to sacrifice," Milosh pointed out. "Tobar was captured as well."

An athletic man wearing a tactical vest and brown fatigues stood up from a seat at the other end of the cabin. His vest looked to be the same make and design as the shell

Paige used for body armor, but was modified by strands of silver woven into black mesh. Despite the graying hair on his head, his face still had a youthful smoothness that would get him carded at casinos for years to come.

The smooth-faced Gunari might have been one of the Amriany who had joined forces with the Skinners in Denver, but the fire in his eyes still reflected generations of mistrust between the two groups of hunters. Sometimes tradition was a real bitch. "We had to flee from that bloodbath," he said to Paige, "but not before we saw you step out of a fancy helicopter. Tell me, did the Skinners win another lottery thanks to that psychic you work with?"

"No," she replied. "Prophet's been busy doing other stuff, like trying to stay out of jail and divert any attention that might come our way thanks to warrants issued after all of that Nymar business. Speaking of that, since he's covering your asses too, maybe you should call him by name instead of 'that psychic.' Okay?"

Gunari nodded. "He was also supposed to find information from those Nymar about their communication network and pass it along to us in exchange for us helping you Skinners survive that massacre. We haven't gotten anything from him or you."

"And," Milosh grunted, "if you think we're gonna let you go so you can screw us over, you're fucking wrong."

"I told you I've got information you can use," Paige said. "You can make a copy when you drop me off in Denver."

"Not good enough," Milosh grunted.

She extended her arm, flipped up one finger and panned it slowly back and forth so all of the Amriany could see it. "I'll e-mail the rest to you. Until then, kiss my ass. Good enough now? My partner's in a maximum security prison so the rest of you could get away. If I don't hear from him soon, it means he's probably dead and I made the worst mistake of my life. Prophet brokered an information exchange to repay you for this ride. You don't like it? Either drop me at the next airport or hand me a parachute."

"Cole can handle himself," Nadya said. "I saw him wade through the worst moments in that warehouse." Her voice trailed off as memories of that night flooded through her mind. Just when it seemed she might become lost in those images, she blinked them away. "If anything, the men in that prison should fear him. Since Tobar is also locked in a cage somewhere, we're all working toward the same thing."

"Are we?" Paige asked. "Why do you want that Nymar communication network so badly? I haven't heard anything about an uprising overseas, so the network probably only covers the U.S. and Canada."

"You know nothing about what the Nymar do in our country," Tobar replied. "And you know nothing about reports of any policemen that may have been hurt or killed by those leeches."

Unfortunately, Paige knew that she truly didn't know about those things, so she slid right into the next topic. "The Nymar communicate through a site on ChatterPages.com run by someone named Cobb38. I got some stuff from their computers but haven't had a chance to look through it yet. The computer was barely guarded by a bunch of Stripes like the ones we found at the warehouse. You know. The Nymar with those black markings?"

"We know," Milosh said. "We've been trying to find a simpler way to kill them since that day."

"And?"

"And we would not tell you shit even if we found it."

"So you didn't come up with anything either," Paige said. "Seems like we're all the same kind of worthless."

Even though Milosh looked as if he was ready to use the knife in his hands, Gunari and Nadya shared a quick sideways glance before laughing. Their camaraderie struck a nerve with Paige. It hadn't been so long ago that she had the same sort of connection to a partner, but it had been a while since things were easy enough for her and Cole to relax and enjoy a moment together. Thinking back to one moment in particular brought a fraction of a smile to her face. Before it was noticed, she asked, "Any chance of you telling me where we're going?"

"Oklahoma," Gunari replied.

"Where the wind comes sweepin' down the plain." When she didn't get a reaction from that, Paige added, "Wavin' wheat can sure smell sweet?"

Surprisingly enough, it was Milosh who said, "And the

wind comes right behind the rain. Rodgers and Hammerstein. Geniuses."

"I don't know if I'd push them into genius territory, but you're in the right ballpark. I knew we'd find some common ground before too long. So what's in Oklahoma besides wheat, wind, and rain?"

"Werewolves," Nadya said. "The same one that was in Kansas City and at least one other."

All of the humor in Paige's voice dried up when she heard that. "How can you be sure? Did someone see them?"

"We got a sample of its fur."

"Nadya!"

"Hush, Milosh!" she snapped as if scolding a dog. And, much like a pup that had just sniffed the wrong piece of carpeting, he backed down. Nadya drew one of her blades and removed a sharpening stone from a kit strapped to the back of the seat in front of her. "We can take you to Denver, but not until this other matter is settled."

"Cole's in a lot of trouble," Paige said. "He needs help now."

"And so does Tobar," Gunari snapped. "Yet we let him stay where he is because we know he can fend for himself. If not, then he is surely already dead. I've seen enough of Cole to know he should be given that same sort of respect. Since we thought you might not want to share your information right away, we expect a favor in return for picking you up on such short notice."

Paige reached into her pocket to remove the little plastic flash drive. "If you've got a laptop or something, you can download a copy right now."

Although all three of the Amriany sat up and took notice of what was in her hand, none of them made a move to take it. "Can you guarantee what's on there will be enough to make up for dragging us into the legal troubles with your police that will follow anyone helping such a group of wanted criminals like yourselves?" Gunari asked.

"If they were *my* police, they wouldn't want to drag me over the coals so badly," Paige said frankly. "But this information is all I've got. You're right, though that if there are Full Bloods gathering somewhere, we need to see what they're doing."

Rather than take the flash drive from her, Gunari reached

into one of the overhead compartments for a computer. He handed the notebook device to Nadya and said, "Download a copy." To Paige, he added, "You're welcome to watch if you want to make sure it is done properly."

"Cole's the one who'd know if you were trying to put one over on me. If it takes too long, I'll just rip it out of there and smash that computer to bits."

Gunari grinned at her and nodded. "And if you prove to be someone we can work with this easily, we may be able to extend our hand to you in the future."

"And I don't mind lending a hand with you guys for whatever you need, especially since we seem to be working toward the same thing. Your partner is in the same tight spot as mine. He may even be locked up by the same group."

"They are both in prison," Gunari said. "Isn't that what you mean?"

"They are both in buildings called prisons, but they're not in the system."

Milosh leaned forward in his seat as if to mirror Paige's confidence. "What do you know of Tobar?"

"Have you seen any videos of him online or on the news?"

"No," Nadya replied.

"Have you been able to contact him?"

"No."

"Which means he's disappeared just like Cole. I'm trying to find out something about where he wound up after he was pulled out of Denver. At the very least," Paige added as she shifted to look at each of the Amriany in turn, "I should be able to check if both of them are alive, dead, or presumed something else."

Gunari pointed a critical stare at Paige and asked, "How do you know this?"

"I've got contacts. Isn't that what you like about me?"

"Americans," Milosh grunted. "Always talk in circles, but never saying anything."

Looking out her window, Paige said, "Prophet told me about what you guys did in Denver, so I don't have any problem with doing what I can to find your partner. In the meantime, you can tell me how you're so sure about that Full Blood in Oklahoma."

The speakers mounted in the cabin over their heads crackled, and a feminine voice with a sharp, eastern European accent was transmitted through them. "Is that Drina?" Paige asked, pointing up to the closest speaker.

"We'll be landing in five minutes," Nadya said. "Buckle up."

Paige tugged on the strap of her seat belt to show that she'd never unbuckled it.

"How quickly can you find out about Tobar?" Gunari asked.

"Depends on how long it takes to finish up this Oklahoma business. By the way," Paige said, cocking her head to one side, "what was this business again?"

Nadya fixed her eyes on Paige, but before she could say anything, Milosh snarled something at her in their native tongue. After tersely responding to him, she looked back to Paige and said, "We need to be more trusting of each other. There is no cause for bad feelings between you and I, other than the rivalry that has existed between Skinners and Amriany for generations."

As the plane dipped into a landing pattern, Paige felt something in her gut that came from more than just a change of altitude. The Amriany all stared at her expectantly before casting their eyes at each other as if they didn't know whether to open up to her or gang up to make certain she never got up from her seat.

"We have Dikh Chakano," Nadya declared. "Far Seers. All they need is a piece of a shapeshifter and they can find them."

"They need more than that," Milosh was quick to say.

"Really?" Paige scoffed. "Because I was about to piece together and steal an entire Gypsy ritual with just that last sentence."

Milosh wagged a blade at her and asked, "You know what my people call an ignorant savage? 'Skinner.' See how that word rolls off my tongue like a kernel of shit someone slipped into my soup? When your people speak of us as superstitious fortune-tellers and thieves, 'Gypsy' sounds much the same way. If we are to start respecting each other, we can stop spitting these words at each other this way."

"Fair enough. So what's the Gypsy method for spotting Full Bloods?"

In a strange way, the word did sound different that time.

Tossing a dismissive wave in Milosh's direction, Nadya continued, "We have been collecting samples of as many shapeshifters as we could from this country, just as we've done for our own. With all that's happened here recently, there's a lot more for us to collect."

"Yeah, the fur's really been flying."

If Cole was there, he might have laughed at that. This audience wasn't nearly as kind.

"More fur will fly in the place we're going. Since it seems there are already at least two Full Bloods, a pack of Mongrels, and Half Breeds there as well, we may already be too late."

Now, Paige hoped it was the Amriany who were attempting to pull a cheap laugh out of her. "There are that many shapeshifters in one spot?"

"At least. Possibly more. Our Dikh Chakano was almost knocked from his seat by the amount of power coming from this spot on his map. We got your message while we were in the air, and if you hadn't already proven to be a valuable fighter, we wouldn't have wasted the time to get you."

"And what if I'd refused to help in a fight as lopsided as this one?" Paige asked.

Nadya was quick to reply, "Then we would have taken your weapons and put them to good use."

Another indecipherable announcement was broadcast through the speakers, but Paige didn't need a translation. The jet was approaching ground level. She could tell by the lightness in her stomach and the crackle in her ears. "You're certain the Full Blood that attacked Kansas City is here?"

Gunari nodded. "The sample I bought was collected from a tower where most of the fighting took place during that siege. The seller was trying to make money by auctioning the patch of fur online."

Dreading the answer she would get, Paige asked, "Was he a police officer?"

"No. Just some idiot trying to cash in. At least some stupid people can be useful."

Paige showed him a friendly smile, enhanced with a hint of relief. "Finally we're speaking the same language."

Chapter Nine

The plane touched down at Atoka Municipal Airport on a strip of concrete that barely seemed long enough to accommodate it. After tires screeched against concrete, the Gulfstream came to a stop that nearly sent every one of its passengers into the nose cone. As soon as it rolled off the strip and completed a quick 180-degree turn, the engines cooled off and the door popped open.

Gunari stormed the stairs that swung down from the side door as if the war he wanted to join was ten feet in front of him, carrying a duffel bag of supplies, weapons, and ammunition in each hand. Drina had been one of the pilots, which meant this was the first time Paige saw her. Her long, dark blond hair was pulled back and held in place with a black baseball cap. After looking Paige over with a set of striking green eyes, she slung a FAMAS assault rifle over her shoulder and headed down the stairs. Nadya came out next, with Paige following close behind. Milosh made no effort to hide the fact that he was keeping an eye on the Skinner as he brought up the rear.

Gunari's briefing had been quick and concise. According to the Amriany Far Seers, shapeshifters were converging in or around the small town of Atoka, Oklahoma. One of them was supposedly confirmed to be Liam, which meant he was probably after something. Although Gunari didn't know what that something was, he didn't want a Full Blood as dangerous Liam to get it. Despite many years of disagreement that existed between the two groups, Paige assumed any Skinner would agree with that line of reasoning. Other than the Full Blood, there were Mongrels and Half Breeds circling the city. Since the Amriany Far Seer hadn't been completely clear on that point, Paige decided to take that with a grain of salt.

"There's something wrong with your plan," she pointed out. "The slowest of those creatures can run from one state to another in less time than it took your plane to land. How do you know they're still here?"

"We'll soon find out," Gunari said. "Get into the car."

Idling next to a row of shacks next to the airstrip was an SUV that looked as if it had been sitting there through the last dozen dust storms that whipped across the Oklahoma landscape. The Amriany piled in, and Paige made sure she was the last to get inside. If things went too badly, she would gladly take her chances with gravity by jumping out of another moving vehicle.

"You guys really have your stuff together," she said. "Private jets. Cars at every airfield."

"What's the matter?" Milosh scoffed. "You don't know how to call ahead for a car?"

"Sure. It's the jet that I have a little trouble with. Must be some deep pockets back home."

"Don't worry about our money, Skinner," he replied in a way that harkened back to their earlier conversation about kernels. "Be more concerned with making yourself useful. Otherwise, you'll be watching that jet take off from the ground as it leaves you here when this is through."

"If we make it through, you mean."

Milosh smirked and nodded. "Right."

Before they made their first turn onto West Liberty Road, Paige could feel the heat in her scars become even worse. She'd started feeling it when the jet was still on its way down, but now it was an intense, stabbing reminder that Full Bloods were nearby. Out her window she could see only a low building with a wide garage door and an empty parking lot. Turning to look at the other side of the street, she spotted a group of dark shapes rushing at the SUV like a fleet of pickup trucks barreling through an intersection.

Drina was behind the wheel of the SUV and she steered hard toward the incoming shapes while gunning the engine. "Hold on!" she screamed.

All Paige could do was jam both feet against the floorboards and wedge her arms against the door and ceiling. The impacts against the SUV came in a flurry of solid thumps that knocked the vehicle off half of its tires and flipped it onto its side. The Amriany shouted back and forth at each other in their native language while they and Paige tried to find the fastest way out.

Milosh and Nadya were in the backseat with her. He climbed up to stand on an armrest so he could reach up and shove open his passenger door. After sticking his head out for all of a second, he pulled it in again before it would have been lopped off by a set of claws that sliced through the air like a set of conjoined filleting knives.

Swearing under his breath, Milosh pulled a 9mm from a holster clipped to his belt and fired as he climbed up and out of the SUV's side door. All around her, Paige could hear glass shattering and metal groaning as it was bent and peeled apart. Since she was on the bottom of the pile and had to wait her turn to escape, she busied herself by pulling the gnarled wood of her right-handed weapon from the holster on her boot and willing it to shift into its bladed form. It grew into a roughly formed machete by the time her left hand had found her Beretta. She fired reflexively at the claws that raked through the roof, which had been turned into a thin metal wall only a few inches away from her shoulder. The metal came away to reveal the snarling face of a Half Breed.

It wasn't one of the normal creatures she'd been hunting for so many years. This was one of the newer beasts that had emerged since the werewolves were forced to either evolve or be wiped off the face of the earth by Lancroft's Mud Flu. Its fur was thicker and more like the wiry coat of a Full Blood. Even though her bullets snapped its head back and chipped away at its solid body, they were barely enough to force the creature away from the SUV. She continued firing, however, until she scored enough head shots to put it down. Before she could get too excited about that, another

Skinners: The Breaking

Half Breed stalked toward the opening the other had made. Its eyes narrowed into angry slits, and a long, wide snout opened wide to reveal a set of curved tusks that stretched out from its upper and lower jaws.

As soon as that werewolf came at her, Paige snapped her right arm forward to drive the tip of her machete into its face. Her weapon only glanced along the Half Breed's face after it twisted its head away, and instead sank an inch or so into its shoulder. The creature snapped its jaws in a desperate attempt to rip her apart, but with a bit of good timing and a strong pull on the machete's handle, Paige steered its face toward a jagged section of torn roof. When one set of tusks punched through the metal and became stuck there, she placed the barrel of her pistol against its forehead and was about to squeeze her trigger when the Half Breed surprised her again.

The creature pulled away from the shredded roof, leaving its two tusks embedded there after a sharp tug that was strong enough to jerk the machete from Paige's hand. The thorns in the weapon's grip opened her palm even farther as it was taken away from her when the Half Breed hopped away from the overturned SUV.

Paige quickly reloaded the Beretta and sent round after round into the Half Breed's chest and head. Although the bullets didn't kill the creature, they forced it back far enough to let her climb out through the roof. Every time the Beretta bucked against her palm, agony ran up through her savaged right hand. In an almost perverse way, the pain excited her. It was the most she'd felt in that hand since before it had been nearly petrified by the batch of prototype ink she'd injected in Kansas City.

"Where is the young one?" a vaguely familiar voice bellowed.

Realizing it came from the Half Breed responsible for her cars, and the intense heat she felt from them, Paige launched herself at it. Without breaking stride, she holstered the gun, reached out to grab onto the machete that protruded from its cheek and used her momentum to drive it in even farther. After sinking it several more inches, she dropped down so all of her weight pulled the machete like a lever. As tough as the creature may have been, the Half Breed couldn't out-muscle a weapon infused with fragments of a Blood Blade that cleaved all the way through its skull.

Paige landed in a seated position, rolled to one side and pulled her weapon free of the mutilated remains of the werewolf's head. The Half Breed flopped onto its chest amid a tangle of limbs that suddenly had all the strength of wet knotted rope. She jumped to her feet and took quick stock of her situation. There were no fewer than eight werewolves swarming over the SUV. They scattered as a pair of thick hands covered in black fur clamped around the SUV and pulled it down onto all four wheels with the ease of a child correcting an overturned go-cart.

The Full Blood stood in his two-legged form, towering over the SUV and snarling through a mouthful of daggerlike teeth. "Don't make me ask again," Liam snarled in a voice that was barely comprehensible through his stalagmite teeth.

After circling around the rear end of the SUV, Paige could see that most of the Amriany had gotten out as well. Milosh and Nadya stood across from her, positioned at the other corner of the rear bumper and surrounded by four Half Breeds. Nadya had a MAC-10 in her hands, which must have been stashed in one of the bags they'd carried from the plane. Milosh wrapped both fists around the knives he'd been sharpening during the flight, and Gunari stood less than two paces away from the massive Full Blood. The hatchet in his hands was bigger than something that could be found at a hardware store, and the metal of its blade was smeared by the same dark coloring as a Blood Blade.

"What young one?" Gunari asked.

Paige was impressed with how well the Amriany held their ground. She'd given up on counting how many Half Breeds surrounded them, and the presence of a Full Blood was enough to tip the scales irrevocably away from their favor.

As his single, crystalline brown eye shifted in its socket, something moved beneath the scar tissue filling the hole where Liam's right eye had been. "You know goddamn well what I'm talking about. Why else would you be here?"

"We are here because you have overstepped your bounds,"

Gunari said. "Just because the Skinners allow you to roam free doesn't mean we will let you do as you please."

Liam pulled in a breath through nostrils wider than quarters and let it out through a mouth that had shifted into something better suited for forming words coated in his thick cockney accent. "Gypsies, eh? I thought I recognized that stench."

"I mean what I told you," Gunari said with a venomous tone. Taking a step closer, as if Liam wasn't one of the most destructive forces on the planet, he added, "Whatever business you have here is done. Get out now before—"

"Before *what*?" the Full Blood roared. "Before the humans see us? Too late for that, I'd say! Before the Skinners organize to put us in our place? Too late for that as well. Things ain't goin' the way they been goin'. Not anymore!" Sweeping a clawed hand toward a pair of Half Breeds that snarled through a set of curved tusks, he said, "Take a look at these wretches. When the Breaking Moon rises, this'll be *all* of your faces! Human, Skinner, Ammrianny, it won't matter." When he spoke the true name of Gunari's people, Liam let the word roll off his tongue like something he'd hacked up from the back of his throat.

"We won't let that happen."

"You won't," said the second Full Blood who approached the SUV from Paige's side like a cat slinking up to a wounded rodent. "Because you don't even know what he's talking about."

Paige's scars hadn't warned her of the other approaching Full Blood because her senses were already on fire from the pain running through her body after the crash and the heat that flooded through her palms to the point of overloading them. Although obviously possessing a Full Blood's stature, the other werewolf kept closer to the ground and moved as if her glittering violet eyes could see straight through to the truest essence of whatever was before them.

"These hunters do not know about the Breaking Moon," the second Full Blood said in a voice that was purely feminine, despite its emergence from a hellish maw. "They have come because of the commotion you have caused, Liam. Nothing more."

Since she was closest to the other Full Blood, Paige asked, "How can you be so sure?"

The female werewolf looked just as likely to pounce as she was to sit down and make herself comfortable. "Because all of your thoughts are known to us, Skinner."

"The Mind Singer is dead."

"We don't need him any longer. Do you truly think we are so primitive that we cannot think several steps ahead of a bunch of clannish brutes like you? Maybe we should thank you after all, Liam. The Skinners and Amriany alike seem to have mistaken us for common dogs that don't pay attention to the shifting world around them."

"Oh, it's about to shift, all right," Liam said.

Focusing on Paige, the female werewolf spread her paws out to plant them in a stance so firm that it seemed not even the hand of God could pry her loose. "After what the leeches did to you, there is only panic among the Skinners. I think you don't even know who I am."

"I know," Nadya said. Without taking her eyes off the Full Bloods, she nodded toward Paige and explained, "Her name is Minh. She roams the territory east of Europe."

"Knowing my name is one thing," Minh said. "When the Breaking Moon rises, you will be just as surprised and helpless as the rest of the humans."

"So you don't think they know about the young one?" Liam asked.

"I'm not sure," Minh replied while tilting her head, as if that was enough to screw Paige to a wall. "Do you know about the young one?"

Without blinking, Paige replied, "Of course we do."

"Be careful what you say, Skinner. Your history with the Amriany isn't pristine, but something tells me you might care what happens to that one."

When Minh glanced toward the windshield of the SUV, she drew Paige's focus to the body hanging out halfway through the shattered field of safety glass. Drina was covered in blood from wounds that had been opened by the crash and closed by whatever method the Amriany used to toughen their systems. Even though a Half Breed's teeth were firmly embedded in her shoulder and sunken in almost to the gum line, she maintained a grip on the side of the werewolf's neck with one hand while fumbling for her FAMAS assault rifle with the other.

"If we even suspect you're lying to us," Minh purred, "she's dead."

"We were coming to see if anyone had found her yet," Gunari said. "It looks like you haven't."

"You know the young one is a *she*?" Liam asked.

Before he could answer that, one of the Half Breeds turned to look at him with eyes that contained much more than the brutish instinct of a hungry animal. Like a cloud dissipating in a windy sky, the feral wildness cleared to show pupils the color of milk that had gone bad weeks ago. "That was just a guess," it said. Shifting into a lanky form clothed in dirty rags as if he'd simply stepped out from behind a screen, the man hung a head weighed down by a mane of shiny black hair. "More like a bluff, but a good one."

When she looked at the lean figure that climbed up to stand on two legs, Paige saw the shapeshifter that had held the police away from the warehouse in Denver long enough for the Nymar to get their dirty work done. Even worse, she'd felt the subtle power of the First Deceiver for herself. For all she knew, Rico was still suffering under it.

The pressure of Kawosa's words pushed against her ears, and his gaze pressed upon her eyes.

Judging by the strained expression on the Amriany's face, Gunari felt it as well. "It's not a bluff," he said in a voice that could have been dipped in the same alloy as Paige's machete. "We're here to make sure you didn't find a way to get to her. How else would I even know it's a her?"

"Fifty-fifty chance," Kawosa replied while crossing his arms. "You can't lie to me, human. Tell me what you know of her."

Before she could think about saying anything different, Paige told him, "I don't even know who the hell you're talking about."

"And the Breaking Moon?"

"Never heard of it." Even as she spoke, Paige couldn't believe hers was the voice that put life into those words. As much as she wanted to staple her mouth shut, she added,

"The Amriany found you, and as long as it means killing more fucking shapeshifters, I'm along for the ride. You can take the moon, the sun, and every planet spinning around it and shove them up your ass."

"Good," Liam growled as he dropped down to all fours and sprouted multiple layers of muscle beneath his sleek black coat. " 'Cause that means there ain't no reason to keep you healthy."

Chapter Ten

While the Full Bloods had been talking, the Half Breeds stayed still. For creatures ruled by instinct and driven by pain, this was no small feat. The only time they remained still on their own was to prevent the sun from burning the pasty skin beneath their fur when it was retracted during sleeping hours. If they smelled blood, Half Breeds ran. If the taste of fresh meat hit their tongues, they gnawed and tore until nothing remained.

When Liam barked, every wretch in the vicinity of the overturned SUV did what they'd been born to do.

Drina screamed as the Half Breed's teeth sank all the way into her shoulder. She pressed the muzzle of her FAMAS against its torso, but the Half Breed's fangs had already scraped against each other within her. Even though her hold on the rifle's grip was solid, it simply wasn't made to be fired one-handed. After a few shots thumped into the Half Breed's upper body, the FAMAS kicked up and sent its next several rounds into the sky.

Firepower of that caliber at that range would have been enough to put down a normal Half Breed. They were tough, but not bulletproof. The one biting Drina was hurt, but not badly enough. Whatever pain it felt was wrapped up in a bellowing howl and spat back at the Amriany as it tore her open amid a flurry of claws that quickly separated major pieces of her body from the trembling whole.

Paige tried to get around the SUV to help her. By the time she arrived, Drina's dark blond hair was slick with blood and her eyes were devoid of life. Gripping her machete with enough force to push the thorns deeper into her palms, Paige connected with a swing that buried the blade into the side of the creature's neck. From there she slid the machete in farther and dragged it back across to saw the Half Breed's head from its shoulders.

"Drina!" Paige shouted. "Can you hear me?" She'd seen the other woman move, but that was only because one of the Full Bloods had shaken the vehicle by jumping onto its roof.

Minh crouched on top of the SUV, but was suddenly distracted by the chattering gunfire of Nadya's MAC-10. When the lithe werewolf bared her teeth and lunged at her, Nadya hopped to one side without taking her finger off her trigger. As soon as her magazine was emptied, she rushed over to her fallen partner to retrieve Drina's FAMAS. Minh's paws hit the dirt, and Milosh was right there to drive both of his charmed blades into her side.

"What do you want here?"

At the first sound of Kawosa's voice, Paige raised her left hand and squeezed off three shots from her Beretta. Rather than stand and absorb the rounds like his Full Blood companions, Kawosa dropped beneath one, shifted into a smaller form to clear a path for the second, and then skittered away before the third could find him. After that, he returned to a spot no more than three feet from where he'd started.

"You have to tell me what you want here!" he demanded.

For whatever reason, Paige believed him. "I want to kill you. All of you."

Kawosa's brows lifted as the pure truth of her words sank in. "You can't kill me, Skinner."

Paige's finger had already begun to tense for another shot. Instead of pulling the trigger, she slid it out from beneath the guard and rested it along the side of her Beretta. After holstering the gun, she swung her machete in a way that would build up the greatest momentum for a downward strike when it came around.

Only a supernatural thing could have been fast enough to avoid the lightning-fast swing. Despite Kawosa's unearthly

Skinners: The Breaking

body and reflexes, even he felt the bite of her machete as it scraped his front paw and peeled away several layers of skin along his left side.

"That won't kill me either," he panted.

"One way to find out."

Kawosa's form was leaner than the Full Bloods and longer than the Half Breeds. His tapered snout was filled with thin, crooked teeth. The expression on his face wouldn't have fit anything of this earth, but had a vague hint of surprised pleasure. After rolling away from her next attack and then jumping away before she could follow it up, he perched on the edge of the SUV roof and let his head droop, as if he intended to whisper into her ear when he told her, "It's been a long time since I've had a surprise. Thank you for that."

Paige turned on the balls of her feet, leading with her eyes and twisting around until her upper body was a coiled spring. Her right arm came around next, allowing the machete to slice through air previously occupied by the gnarled shapeshifter.

"You can't kill me," Kawosa insisted. "Not with any weapon."

She believed him.

"Don't listen to him!" Gunari said.

Paige snapped her head around to find him standing beside Minh. The Full Blood wasn't as bulky as Liam, who'd moved back to direct the Half Breeds with short, huffing barks. Wrapped in a soft pelt of dark, reddish-orange fur and coated in spilt blood, Minh bared her fangs while grabbing the front of Gunari's tanned leather tunic and tossing him through the air. Milosh still hung onto her like a tick, so she reached around to knock him off.

"You can tell me if you know something regarding the young one," Kawosa insisted while taking a few cautious steps back.

Screams came from down the street as well as from the nearby airport. Cars tore past and some screeched to a halt to get a look at what was going on in the field. Paige glanced around for the closest threat and found one Half Breed circling around to get behind her. When it opened its mouth to snarl at her, she twisted around in a similar pivot she'd used to attack Kawosa. The Half Breed wasn't as quick as the wily old deceiver, so her machete sliced horizontally through the back of its mouth. Paige angled the blade downward so it reemerged from the creature's left shoulder. When the Half Breed dropped and skidded against the ground, it opened like an old Zippo lighter.

Liam must have gotten his paws on Milosh, because the Amriany landed on the roof of the SUV, slid across it on his back, and dropped off to land in front of Paige. Only a quick tuck of his head made the difference between impacting on Laim's shoulders and breaking his neck.

"If you know anyone who might be more useful," Kawosa said while Liam howled victoriously, "you should tell me."

"Shut your goddamn mouth, woman!" Milosh said. Seeing the stunned expression on Paige's face, he reached behind his back to draw a snub-nosed revolver from a holster and fire two quick shots at Kawosa. Each round hit with a hard thump that kicked up more dirt than blood from under Kawosa's fur. "He is Ktseena! Don't listen to a word he says!"

Minh got to him in a series of movements that looked like a smear of dark colors against the canvas of empty space. Milosh was able to pull back before the Full Blood's teeth clamped around his throat, but not before she caught his arm with a second snap of powerful jaws. The Amriany screamed and his eyes widened as Minh sank her fangs into his flesh. With one quick twist of her head, she pulled away his left arm and chewed it into pulp.

Heavy steps pounded against the hood of the SUV, prompting Paige to step back so she could put that area in her peripheral vision without looking away from Minh and Kawosa. Gunari bounded over the vehicle just ahead of a downward swipe of Liam's paw that flattened a portion of the driver's side.

"Fall back!" Gunari yelled. "Too many of them!"

Paige only concerned herself with the threats in her immediate line of sight, chief among them a Half Breed that crept over the front of the SUV. Having already been wounded, the creature now had to drag itself toward Gunari using long claws that curved from formerly human fingers, punching into the vehicle's dented hood as it did so. Snapping her arm forward like a whip, Paige willed her machete into a shorter and thinner shape before letting it go. The weapon sliced through the air and hit the Half Breed less than an inch from its eye. Slightly off her mark, but a good enough blow to put the creature down.

"Watch it!" Gunari shouted.

Before she could heed the warning, Paige was knocked over by something that felt like a battering ram. After hitting the dirt, she looked up to see a mass of luxurious fur and the glint of claws longer than human fingers directly above her. She tried twisting away but was pinned beneath Minh's weight. Paige reflexively raised her right arm and was just quick enough to catch the incoming slash before it removed her face from the front of her skull. Claws raked through the petrified skin of her arm but didn't go in very far. Somehow, she lifted her Beretta and pulled the trigger. Her nose filled with the scent of burnt cordite as hot brass was ejected from the pistol. Minh winced as she licked the blood from Paige's arm, and then used the side of her muzzle to bat the gun aside.

"Enjoy your Breaking, Skinner," the Full Blood said. Then she reared up and shifted into another body, taller than Gunari's but not as imposing as Liam's. Beneath the bristling dark red coat, Paige could see a rounded female body. Minh's thighs were strong and thick. Her arms were long and capped with hands that stretched out into impossible proportions. A tapered waist extended upward into a lean torso, complete with the subtle hint of curving breasts. The sight of her was almost captivating enough to keep Paige still as the Full Blood brought more Half Breeds to her side with a few huffing barks.

Paige dropped to the ground and rolled until she bumped against the SUV's front tire.

Boots thumped against the packed dirt to her right.

Gunshots blasted through the air.

Another Half Breed dropped dead, several close-range gunshot wounds still smoking in its fur.

Gunari rushed to Paige's side, reloaded the .44, and then offered a hand to her. "Back to the plane," he said. "There's no more we can do right now."

She accepted his help but wasn't happy about it. "What the

hell does that mean? We didn't come all this way just to turn around and go home!"

"Quiet and do as I say," he scolded before firing another couple of rounds into Minh's chest. The bullets thumped against the Full Blood, causing the fur to rustle as each bullet snagged within her coat. "Do you see Ktseena?"

Paige circled around Gunari so she could retrieve her weapon and then bury its blade into the shoulder of another Half Breed. After the wretch dropped, she finished it off. Kawosa was nearby, shifting into his gangly human form. "I see him. Don't you?"

"No."

"He's right there!" she said while pointing to him.

The shapeshifter was dressed in filthy rags that barely covered his human form, his face almost completely hidden by long stringy hair. Tilting his head, Kawosa showed her a sympathetic expression while gently shaking his head.

"He told me I couldn't see him, and I cannot," Gunari explained.

Since Milosh was still crawling toward her and Nadya was backing away from the SUV amid a steady spray of automatic fire, Paige didn't waste any more time before grabbing Gunari's arm and pointing his .44 at Kawosa. "Just fire, goddammit!"

He did as he was told and they both sent their last few rounds through the air toward Kawosa. The shapeshifter dropped straight down, shifting into a nightmarish equivalent of a coyote before scampering away on all fours.

"Back to the plane!" Gunari shouted.

Nadya nodded and quickened her steps through the field toward the airstrip.

"We're just gonna run for it?" Paige asked while fending off a Half Breed with her machete.

"We can make it," he replied.

"If you believe that, then you're screwed up too much to be of any use to anyone. We're only alive because that bastard's toying with us."

Gunari's eyes drifted to Liam. The Full Blood squatted on his haunches with his elbows perched upon his knees, grinning wider than a jack-o'-lantern at the Amriany.

"I'll give a five second head start," Liam snarled. "That's only sportin', eh?"

Of the Half Breeds that Paige had spotted when she first climbed out of the SUV, only one was still standing. Another was doing its best to crawl despite having caught a significant amount of gunfire. Liam's coat was slick with blood that may or may not have been his own, and Minh had already shaken off wounds given to her by Amriany steel as well as Nadya's MAC-10. In addition to that, Half Breeds crept in from farther down the street and from the far end of the field. As they drew closer, the sound of panting breaths and anxious yelps drifted upon the stagnant air.

"One . . ." Liam said.

"Head for the street," Paige snapped as she began jogging in that direction.

"Two . . ."

A few choppy commands in a foreign tongue were enough to steer Nadya toward the street. Gunari scooped up Milosh and looped the smaller man's one remaining arm across the back of his shoulders so he could be dragged away from the SUV.

"Three . . ."

As all the shapeshifters waited impatiently, Paige and the Amriany made it to the street. Paige rushed over to a car that sat just off the shoulder of the road. She circled around, pulled the driver's door open and checked inside. Judging by the shredded interior, dented door panels, and shattered glass, the driver had probably been twisted into one of the Half Breeds attacking them. She had never seen werewolves created that quickly, but now wasn't the time to think that over.

Liam's voice grew into a thundering roar that exploded from a body swollen into a mass of muscle nearly twice as large as it had been a moment ago. *"Four . . ."*

"Come on!" Paige shouted. "The keys are in the ignition. Let's *go*!" She didn't waste any more time or breath on the others. If Gunari or Nadya weren't going to get in the car she'd found, they deserved whatever they got. The Amriany piled into the Mazda by the time Paige had settled in to the driver's seat.

"Five!"

Paige started the car, slammed her foot down on the gas pedal and cranked the steering wheel to get the car pointed in the opposite direction. Packs of Half Breeds emerged from behind the few buildings along the side of the road and were quickly joined by more werewolves that tore through the little town in her rearview mirror.

"How come your Dick Jango didn't see any of *this*?" Paige asked while steering toward the building with the big garage door they'd passed on their way from the airport.

"It's Dikh Chakano. And . . . *now* you want to criticize?" Gunari roared in an accent that thickened with every agitated syllable.

She jerked the wheel to the left and sped toward a group of Half Breeds that had raced around the garage. "Where is everyone? Where's the panic? Where's the chaos?" she asked while ramming the two lead werewolves with the Mazda's front bumper "Where's the freaking cops?"

"No time to worry about that," Gunari said. "Just get us to the plane. What about your arm?"

Milosh forced a breath through gritted teeth. "My arm is all right. We can save it." His shirt was soaked through with blood. Nadya had pulled the belt from around his waist and used it to tie a tourniquet around the short stump of his left arm. There was barely enough left to fill the sleeve of a T-shirt.

"I'm talking about your arm, Paige," Gunari said. "You were attacked by the female Weshruuv."

"The Full Blood?"

"Yes. She cut you with claws that had to have gone down to the bone and then licked the wound. She wanted to turn you."

"Speaking of turning . . ." It was a clumsy transition, but served its purpose when accompanied by a hard swerve to the right so she could drive off-road and avoid a blockade of encroaching Half Breeds. Liam's massive ebon frame approached from behind and to the right, forcing her to turn sharply again.

The Full Blood trotted to the street and then alongside the Mazda.

Skinners: The Breaking

He actually trotted.

In her years of being a Skinner, Paige had never thought she'd see something like that.

"Are you listening to me?" Gunari asked.

After faking Liam out with a quick swerve to the left, she steered in the other direction and hit the gas to speed around the back side of the airport. "No!" she snapped.

"I asked you if the Weshruuv bit through to the bone. Tell me if she did or didn't."

"Save it for the plane."

"No," Gunari snapped as he lifted his .44 to point it at Paige's temple. "Tell me right now. If you've been turned, it's better for everyone if you die now."

"While I'm driving?"

"Yes."

When Paige blinked, her vision was obscured for a fraction of a second. That was enough time for her to catch a remembered glimpse of Minh's narrow snout as it formed the words, *Enjoy your Breaking, Skinner.*

"Tell me," Gunari insisted.

"She didn't get through to bone," Paige said while holding her arm out to him. "See for yourself. She did want to turn me, just like it seemed they turned the rest of this town. The only one we need to worry about now is Milosh."

She gunned the engine to power through a turn that brought the Mazda's front end all the way around to face the fenced-in corner of the little airport. The closest pack of Half Breeds made it to the car, only to be forced back by Nadya's MAC-10. Bullets thumped against their bodies while some of the rounds sparked against the pavement and ricocheted into another werewolf's face. Some of the creatures stumbled and a few of them yelped, but the pack collected itself and kept moving.

"Last reload," Nadya said as she slapped a fresh magazine into her weapon.

"We just need to make it to the plane," Gunari insisted. "There's medicine, ammunition, and bigger guns there."

"Maybe you should have brought that stuff along in the first place," Paige chided. "Could have come in handy right about now."

Firing out his window, he replied, "Now I see why your partner was so quick to hand himself over to the police. Talking to them must be much more pleasant."

The airport was close enough for them to smell the engine fumes. Behind them, Half Breeds swarmed through Atoka. The scars on Paige's palms were alive with fiery pain that she had to ignore. She'd been there when Liam laid siege to Kansas City and this was already so much worse. No matter how badly she wanted to charge into the thick of it, she knew that would only add more bodies to the pile.

As she got close enough to spot the Gulfstream, werewolves darted in from the far side of the airstrip, leapt over the chain-link fence surrounding the airport, and even stampeded through the little hangar and offices. Paige gripped the wheel and lowered her head as if she meant to butt it against the wall of thick fur and solid muscle closing ranks in front of her.

"Can you get reinforcements from the Skinners?" Gunari asked.

"I . . . don't know," Paige told him through gritted teeth. "Just get to the weapons in that plane and clear a path to get the hell out of here. We'll worry about the rest later."

Lunging from the backseat, Nadya said, "How could you **not know**? We can't let Drina die for nothing!"

"We don't even know if we will escape," Gunari cut in. He nodded toward the Gulfstream and said, "Get us as close as you can. Do you think you can fend them off long enough for at least one of us to get inside?"

A row of seven Half Breeds fanned out to block the Mazda's path. They were the newer brand of terror, displaying longer claws and tusks that curved out to frame their faces in sharpened bone.

"Sure," Paige said.

One of the bigger werewolves howled and the others sang along even as the Mazda plowed straight through them.

Paige and the Amriany were knocked against the car's interior and bounced against the roof as windows shattered and steel bent around them. The car was damaged even further when the stubborn Half Breeds hung on after being hit and shredded the Mazda as if it had been constructed from wet toilet paper. After skidding to a stop within ten yards of the private jet, Paige said, "This is as close as I can get."

"Good enough," Gunari replied. "Let's go."

"Leave me here," Milosh said.

Both passenger side doors were open. Gunari stood with his feet planted and his arms raised in a two-handed firing stance. The .44 sent a pair of blazing rounds into an approaching Half Breed before he shifted his aim and fired again.

"We're not leaving you," Nadya said. "You're wounded."

"I know. That's why I should stay to make sure the plane gets away."

"We're all getting out of here," Paige said. "But only if we stop dicking around in the car. Get to some bigger guns and get that fucking plane ready!"

Just as Milosh seemed ready to take Gunari's hand and allow himself to be pulled from the car, Nadya pointed the MAC-10 out her window at a mass of dark red fur that had leapt over the small airport building. Minh landed less than twenty yards away, bullets pounding against her coat like rain on a heavy tarp. She opened her mouth to roar angrily and then surged forward. Bullets struck her face, but none of them so much as chipped a fang. Then, less than a second before she could close the distance between herself and the Amriany, Minh was struck in the side of the neck by a blade thrown by Milosh. Charmed steel dug through the protective layers of fur and lodged into her flesh. She twisted away to bark at the closest Half Breeds, and like dutiful soldiers the smaller werewolves broke formation to circle around the Mazda from two different directions.

Knowing that the Half Breeds would take her down the moment she left the car, Paige threw the Mazda into reverse and backed away from the jet.

Gunari ran up the stairs leading to the Gulfstream's side door, opened it and stepped inside. He emerged a second later with an assault rifle braced against his shoulder and unleashed a torrent of three-round bursts at the Half Breeds. In between chattering onslaughts, he motioned for his partners to come to him.

The Mazda was still running, but plowing into so many

bodies wasn't doing it any favors. The only thing that allowed the car to keep rolling at all was the fact that the multijointed Half Breeds could bend on impact instead of taking the hit like dead weight. Smoke drifted from under the hood and the engine made a disturbing grinding sound as she circled around to the other side of the aircraft. "You guys get out and I'll draw them away."

"You are coming with us," Milosh snarled fiercely.

"None of us will go anywhere unless I lead some of these things away from here," she insisted.

"She's right," Nadya said while kicking open the door. She helped Milosh out as Gunari continued to fire at the werewolves. He even tossed an explosive at them that thumped loudly and sent several of the creatures scattering. The two Amriany moved away from the Gulfstream to circle around it from a clearer side.

Paige backed away and then pointed the front end of the car at Minh. "All right," she said under her breath. "Blaze of glory time."

She stomped the gas pedal. The Mazda lurched, coughed, and ground noisily, but jumped forward. As the tires peeled across the pavement, gunfire popped nearby and supernatural voices rose to a singular howl.

Minh had just found Nadya and Milosh, but she stopped and glanced casually over her shoulder at the approaching car. Considering her angle and speed, Paige thought she had a real good chance of using a few tons of rolling steel to ruin the Full Blood's day until another mass of fur dropped from above to land squarely on the hood of the car. Paige's head knocked against the steering wheel, but the dizzying effects were quickly wiped away by the healing serum produced in her blood.

But she couldn't see anything.

Even the sounds were muffled.

All she could feel was the rattle of the car's struggling engine and the brush of something coarse against her cheek. When she tried to look out her window, she realized that her senses weren't as dulled as she thought. There was just an air bag pressed against her face. As suddenly as the air bag had deployed, it was broken down by a set of claws that came in through the front window to swipe at her.

"Can't get away yet," Liam said while reaching into the car as if fishing for the prize inside a box of cereal. "Killin' you won't be any help unless we can do it out in the open where all your friends on the computer can see it replayed again an' again!"

Having gotten close enough to Liam's paw to taste his fur, Paige jumped across to the passenger side, shoved the door open and rolled out. Her knees and hands hit the rough cement as a load of bile gurgled up from her stomach. Forcing down the rancid liquids along with the distinct coppery taste of blood, she scrambled away from the Mazda on all fours until she gained enough momentum to get her legs beneath the rest of her body. By then Liam had all but turned the driver's side of the car inside out. Saliva ran from both corners of his mouth in an uneven stream as he looked down at Paige. "Been thinkin' about this ever since Kansas City."

Spitting out a wad of blood, she replied, "Yeah. And you still need an army to take me on."

His massive head swayed back and forth. Fur hung down from his jawline and a crystalline eye glittered menacingly from beneath the shelf of a ridged brow. His mouth opened with the start of a word but snapped shut at the sound of whining jet engines mingling with the deep thump of heavy machine-gun fire.

"I've already taken care of her," Minh said from somewhere outside of Paige's field of vision.

Liam crawled down from the roof of the car, looked at the deep bloody grooves in Paige's right arm and sniffed. When he raised his head again, he was smiling. "Right you are, luv."

Paige couldn't tell what sort of gun was being fired, but it was raising hell among the Half Breeds. Before she could become too happy about that, the sound was wiped away by snarling howls and ripping metal. More gunfire preceded the flaring of the engines.

Hunkering down as if in prayer, Liam shifted into a vaguely human form that was covered in thickly matted fur. "They're leeeavin' on a jet plane," he sang cheerfully. "Don't know when they'll be back again."

There was no more pain from getting hit in the face by the air bag. Paige felt no more panic from the ambush or the notion of being abandoned in a town that appeared to be overrun by werewolves. She simply reached for her shoulder holster, drew her Beretta, and fired two shots into the mess of scar tissue filling Liam's right eye socket.

The Full Blood recoiled and made a sound close to a shriek Paige thought she would never hear from one of his kind. She propped herself up, steadied her aim, and continued to fire. Just as she was starting to get into it, she was knocked down by something that felt like a piece of the car that had come alive to make her pay for all the reckless driving that brought her to the airport. Now that she'd stopped shooting, she could hear the other snarling voices, as well as the wet ripping of flesh being torn asunder.

The Gulfstream was moving away from the hangar and taxiing toward the runway. Half Breeds scrambled across its fuselage, some of them gnawing at the landing gear while scraping madly at the ground, others tussling with lean figures that could have been one or more of the Amriany. Gunari leaned out the side door, firing his assault rifle until it was time to pull his head inside and shut the door behind him.

Liam rolled away from the dented remains of the Mazda and pulled something off his back. It was another shapeshifter, but not a werewolf. Paige had seen enough of the feline creatures to recognize them as Mongrels. Minh was preoccupied with a cluster of blurred figures that could only be seen as a disturbance in the air surrounding her. A familiar scent caught Paige's attention then. To confirm her suspicion, she pulled in a deep breath that was thick with traces of oil secreted by certain Mongrels, which allowed them to bend light around them until they were all but invisible. Now that she knew what to look for, she spotted at least three blurred figures attacking Minh and the Half Breeds. She didn't know who they were or where they'd come from, but if Mongrels wanted to take the Full Bloods off her hands, they were more than welcome.

Skinners: The Breaking

Paige struggled to stay on her feet as she ran from the swarm of flailing claws and teeth behind her. She kept her eyes fixed upon the Gulfstream, hoping one of the Amriany would look back and find her. If the engines let up for only a moment, she knew she'd be able to catch up. Then, like a true miracle, the engine noise died down.

The jet pivoted around at the end of the runway to line up with the strip of pavement. A surge of energy flowed through Paige's body, carrying her forward until the wind whipped through her hair. Suddenly, her body was dragged to the ground as Kawosa's lean four-legged form passed directly above her. His claws had been stretched out to sink into her back, but they only caught empty space before he touched down again. Like any shapeshifter, he was more than fast enough to adjust his body for a smooth landing. The moment his paws gripped the concrete, he turned and snarled at his fallen prey.

"Stay down and she'll get to you," someone said to Paige.

The voice wasn't familiar, but she recognized the lithe feline shape as one of the Mongrels that had attacked Liam. It stalked forward, twitching a short tail and letting out a steady flow of snarling obscenities that seemed distinctly suited to its jagged, misshapen mouth. It didn't take long for Kawosa to set his sights on the Mongrel, and when he did, he was blindsided by another one that was cloaked in the oily sheen of near-invisibility. The blurred shape came at Kawosa from the right, taking him down just long enough for the Mongrel that had tackled Paige to find an opening and join the fray. Within seconds the cloaked Mongrel's fur was stained by enough blood to give it form and shape.

Paige forced herself to put the fight behind her and run. It was the only option left, apart from tackling the shapeshifters without anything more than her wooden weapon and the few more rounds of ammunition at her disposal. She wasn't against the idea of going down fighting, but suicide wasn't her style. If she could just make it to the jet, she could regroup, come up with a better plan, and fight again. If the Mongrels were so ready to help, they might even retake the town.

The Gulfstream's engines whined loudly, and the ten-seat jet began to roll.

"Hey!" Paige shouted. "I'm here!" She waved her arms frantically and staggered toward the runway. "Right here! God damn it! *Look over here!*"

Somehow, she still hoped she could catch up to the jet or even make herself seen by someone inside. When she got to the side of the runway, it rolled past her while gaining speed.

Paige stood there, slack-jawed, watching as her best chance at living longer for more than two minutes raced toward the end of the cement strip and left the ground. The entire world became quiet, as though everything connected to her was on that plane and out of reach. Even worse, according to the bone-deep agony slicing through her bleeding arm, it might not be long before she became one of the Half Breeds roaming the streets of Atoka.

"You'd better find Cole," she said to herself as she checked to make sure there was at least one last round in her Beretta. "Or I'll haunt you so bad that you'll wish you died here too."

A gust of wind moved the cropped ends of Paige's bobbed hair. It brushed against her face, reminding her of the gentle touch she'd sampled all too briefly before being separated from the man who'd given it to her. The source of that breeze ran on paws that slapped against the ground like slabs of meat, driven by a body encased in wiry black fur with one Mongrel still clinging to it.

Paige could only stand and watch as Liam bounded across the airstrip, effortlessly catching up to the Gulfstream that waggled slightly while gaining altitude. The jet was less than twenty or thirty feet off the ground when he sprung off both legs to meet it. He extended his arms while shifting his body into its upright form. Even from where Paige stood, she could hear the scrape of claws against metal as the Full Blood dug into the left wing. The jet listed dangerously to one side, skewing in the air to correct for the newly added weight. Its engines roared and so did Liam as he tore into the wing, using claws and teeth to rip it away from the rest of the plane.

"Holy shit," Paige whispered.

As soon as the wing was gone, the Gulfstream launched into a barrel roll that sent it screaming into the ground. Before it hit, Liam jumped onto its tail section and let out a bellowing howl that could be heard even over the sickening crunch of metal meeting earth. She couldn't tell if it was the fuel tanks or a supply of weapons that exploded next, but it didn't matter. Anyone on board the jet who hadn't been killed in the crash now had to contend with a fire that lit up the Oklahoma sky.

When she dropped down, Paige assumed she'd lost the strength to stand.

When she felt strong hands clamp around her ankles and the pressure of dirt closing around the lower portion of her legs, she allowed herself to be dragged underground. Too tired to fight, she figured she might as well see where this next batch of insanity would take her.

Chapter Eleven

Colorado

As much as it hurt to dig his fingernails into such tender flesh, Cole wasn't about to stop. He sat with his back to the wall, feet pressed against the frame of his bunk, and bit into his cheek to keep from making a sound while digging deeper into the portion of his palm that had become a bloody mess.

"If you don't stop picking at that, it won't never heal," Lambert said from the cell directly across from him.

"It's not so bad," Cole grunted.

Another voice said, "Yes. It is. You're sweating and bleeding. A lot."

Cole stopped what he was doing and looked toward the bars on the right side of his cage. The voice he'd heard had the texture of meat hooks being dragged over a parched desert floor. "What makes you think that?" he asked.

When the voice came again, it was closer to the side of his cell. "Because I can smell it."

Something poked around the edge of his bars at about the height of a guard's shoulder. It was the approximate size and shape of a fist, covered in light yellow and tan scales. Cole had seen the creature in the neighboring cell a few times by now and guessed he was one of the lizard men Ned had discovered in the Florida swamps. The Skinners had salvaged some pretty impressive parts from their kind, but he doubted

Skinners: The Breaking 141

that fact would go over too well with the inmate next door.

"Since you can poke your nose out that far," Cole said, "why don't you do me a favor and see about picking the lock on my door?"

His request was answered by a strong snuff that caused the flaps on the lizard man's nose to retract. "You brought something back with you."

While he could accept another species' strong sense of smell, that statement threw him for a loop. Waylon's drilling session had lasted just under three hours, and he had somehow stayed awake for all of it. When he was brought back to his cell afterward, the only thing he cared about was that they wouldn't search him before forcing him into his cage. He was covered in blood and could barely move, but felt lucky when the guards stuffed him through the doggie door, uncuffed him through the bars, and walked away. Ever since then, he'd been digging into his hand without giving anyone reason to think he might be doing anything more than fussing with one of his many wounds. The thing he'd found wedged in his hand was a sliver the size of a chipped Popsicle stick. After a few hours of poking and prodding, the sliver had finally started coming out.

Across the corridor, Lambert stood up and approached the bars of his cell. "What did you bring back with you?"

Cole did his best to silence the other prisoner with a stern, insistent glare. Although the tattooed inmate was willing to humor him, the lizard man next door wasn't so accommodating.

"It's part of a Skinner weapon," the yellowed snout declared. It opened slightly, allowing a slick tongue to graze along the edge of the closest iron bar. It wasn't as wide as a human tongue, but longer and creased down the middle. "I can smell that too."

"Where you from, my man?" Lambert asked.

Cole got back to his work, more anxious than ever to get the object he'd worked so hard to smuggle into his cell. "Judging by that tongue, my guess is the Everglades or Detroit Rock City."

"Why do you suddenly care about that?" the lizard man asked.

"Because," Lambert cut in, "you ain't said a single word since I been here. I was starting to think you reptile people couldn't even talk."

The snout pulled away from Cole's bars so it could stretch a few inches into the corridor. "Why would we talk to such ignorant murderers like you?" he snapped, flashing a single row of identical, rounded teeth that were all just under an inch long and spaced as evenly as points on a saw blade.

"Ignorant?" Lambert said. "Maybe it'd be best if you went back to shutting the fuck up."

After a few more presses of his thumb and forefinger against either side of his tender scar, Cole coaxed the splinter out from the spot where it had been stubbornly wedged. It hurt like hell but was now close to coming out. Rather than tease it anymore, he pressed his thumb hard against the bottom portion of the wound and didn't let up until the wooden sliver poked out. "Squam," he sighed while gently pulling the sliver out.

Another huffing breath came from outside the cell.

"Huh?" Lambert said while maintaining a defensive stance, with both hands gripping the bars in front of him.

Despite the fact that the wound on his palm was bleeding more than ever, the intense pain of having the sharp piece of wood lodged in there was gone. It was a blissful tradeoff. "Not reptile people," he said. "Squam . . ." What did Ned call them? Holding up the sliver as if the word he was after was burned into its side, Cole nodded and said, "Squamatosapien."

"Now you see why I talk to him and not you?" the Squam next door said.

Lambert crossed his arms and shrugged. "If he could see how ugly you are, he wouldn't mind not having one less buddy around here. What you got there, Cole?"

"Nothing," Cole said.

Pressing up against the bars as if his voice would carry better now that he was half an inch closer, Lambert whispered, "You're right. Good thinkin'. They're probably listening to us right now."

"Maybe, but we can't afford to pussy-foot anymore. We need to get the hell out of here and we need to do it quick."

Skinners: The Breaking

"And that sliver's gonna help?"

Cole approached the bars anxiously at first, but sucked in a pained breath the moment he tried to grab one with his bloody hand. Taking a moment to wipe some blood onto his pants, he went to the other side of the front wall to examine the symbols he'd found on the bars. The sliver in his hand was flat and thin on the portion that had snapped away from the stake. The other end was still worn down into the small cylindrical nub of a single thorn. "It'd better help. I went through enough shit to get this thing."

The Squam pushed its head out from between the bars of its cell. His leathery head made a rough scraping sound as he grunted and strained with the effort of getting the nubs on either side of his face clear of the metal barrier. Once his ear flaps were past the bars, he turned to look at Cole using an unblinking, dark yellow eye. "What are you doing now?"

Cole smiled as he held the sliver tightly and leaned against the front of his cell. Angling his body and lowering his arm so he could scrape the bar without being obvious about it, he said, "I'll let you know after it works. What's your name, neighbor?"

The Squam watched Cole's concentrated efforts to scratch the pointed end of the splinter against one of the runes etched into the bar. His yellow eye rolled within its socket like a ball bearing housed in an oval casing. "Why do you want to know?"

"I don't know. Why does anyone want to know someone's name? Must be a habit I fell into ever since preschool. What's your name, kid? That sort of thing."

This time, the breath that fluttered the skin covering the Squam's nostrils sounded more like a deep-throated chuckle. "Frank. My name's Frank."

"Now we're cookin'," Cole said as he continued to scrape. He paused for a moment to wipe off some of the blood that had been transferred from the sliver onto the bar. Not only did it cut through the rune, but some flecks of iron came away as well. "Are there really only three more prisoners in this section, Frank?"

"Two Half Breeds, one Nymar. But they already took the Nymar away."

Cole's scraping stopped. "Why?"

"He's dead," Lambert announced.

"You're sure?"

"Yes. Think I'm lying to you, asshole?"

Resuming his scraping, Cole grumbled, "You seemed a lot friendlier when I first got here, you know that?"

Lambert placed his arms across the bars so he could rest his forehead against them. "That's when I thought you were someone I could work with and not some swamp lover."

Hearing Frank's angry hiss gurgling nearby, Cole said, "If things go the way I think they might, we'll need to stick together to get out of here."

"You plan on getting out soon?" Lambert asked.

"Sooner rather than later. That work for you?"

"Sure. How about we swing by to get some food first? I like them ice cream sandwiches in that vending machine downstairs."

More leathery skin scraped against iron bars as the Squam strained to get a closer look at his neighbor. "What are you doing?" he asked.

Now that the wooden chunk was out of his hand and the wound was slowly healing, Cole felt as if he had his own personal sunbeam shining on his shoulders. It was the best he'd felt for days, and his mood got even better when he saw the fine job the varnished piece of wood was doing on the bar. Like the spear he'd left behind or any other Skinner weapon, the chip was harder than stone, lighter than plastic, and sharper than tempered steel. The fact that it sliced into his fingers while it was pushed against the bars worked in his favor as the splinter absorbed even more of his blood into its grain.

"I'm working on some of this graffiti," Cole said. "You know. Trying to clean up the place before we have any more visitors."

The Squam's face twisted into a strange mockery of confusion. "Are you expecting another visitor?"

"They don't seem to leave us alone for very long around here," Lambert said while squinting to try to get a better look at Cole's busy hands. "I know about them runes too. They're not the ones used to unlock the door."

"I know. I can't reach those." Suddenly, Cole stopped and

closed his eyes. "Frank," he said, hoping he wasn't about to look like the biggest moron in lockup, "can you reach those symbols on the wall?"

"The ones the guards always touch to unlock the doors?"

"Yeah."

"No."

Cole nodded and returned to his task. Gritting his teeth, he squeezed the splinter harder until the thorn sliced into his thumb. The command he recited echoed so loudly through his brain that he couldn't stop himself from mouthing the words. The wood chip didn't respond as well as his own spear, but it did shift slightly into a more angular shape that was better suited for gouging into the iron bar. He didn't want to look up from the symbol he was carving into. Every bit of willpower he could force into the task was committed to honing the tool in his hand. "How long have you been in here, Frank?"

"Long enough to know those symbols can't be scratched off."

The chip in Cole's hand was responding quicker with the thorn fully embedded in his flesh. When he wanted to saw deeper, it grew a more jagged edge. When his hold on it started to slip, it formed subtle grooves along its surface to allow his fingers to find better purchase. "Maybe not easily, but I think I can get it done."

"Do you know how they work?"

"All you need to do is know which ones are the triggers and which way you're supposed to trace the design to make them turn on or off."

"I figured out that much by watching the guards," Lambert said. "What else you got?"

"How about this?" Cole had been hoping for a dramatic snap of metal as the wedge of bar he'd cut came loose and fell to the floor. Instead, what he got was the grind of his wood chip getting stuck inside the groove it had made. There was some struggling involved, but he managed to pull his tool loose while also popping the small section of iron from the bar. He picked it up, brushed it off and examined it. Smiling proudly, he said, "Just what I thought. The runes don't go all the way down."

"Why didn't you just cut all the way through the bar?" Frank asked.

"Actually, I wasn't sure I'd be able to do this much. This wood is stronger than I thought. Anyway," Cole added while tucking the iron wedge into his shoe, "this is better."

"Was something supposed to have happened?"

Cole dropped to his knees and bent down to the little square door. "Let me ask you something, Frank. Can you see anything special from these bars? Like maybe something the rest of us can't see?"

"Yes."

"Whoa, wait," Lambert said. "How'd you know that?"

Frank's voice was like a huff of air blown over a dry slate. "Yes. How did you know about that?"

"I'm a Skinner. We know things."

The cryptic response sounded bad the moment Cole said it, and went over even worse with the other two prisoners.

"You know how to deface prison property," Lambert scoffed. "That puts you right up there with the dickhead who had this cell before me who broke the toilet."

"How do you know about what I can or cannot see?" Frank asked.

"We don't have time for this," Cole said. "Someone's gotta be coming by now."

Lambert pushed his face into the gap between two of his bars as though he expected to pull the same trick as the Squam. "*Now* you're worried about them watching?"

After seeing the cross section of the other bar, he had a better idea how far down he needed to saw on the others. His progress wasn't hampered by the sudden rattling of his cage, but the leathery fist pounding against it sure caught his attention.

"Answer me, Skinner," Frank demanded while thumping the bars with a scaly fist. "How do you know so much about us?"

Cole knew about the Squamatosapien's eyesight because of another Skinner's research. Ned Post had spent some time in the Everglades, tracked down a few of the lizard people and discovered they could operate on another visual spectrum that essentially allowed them to see scents. Thus, they could avoid the Nymar that had hunted them, along with any number of predators both natural and supernatural. Since Ned continued his research by cutting out Squam eyes and tear ducts to create the drops used to temporarily give Skinners that same ability, Cole wasn't eager to answer Frank's question.

Of all the times he'd heard the elevator doors slide open at the other end of the corridor, this was the first time he welcomed it. Guards were coming, but it also meant he didn't have to try to bluff a creature that very possibly could have smelled a lie the moment it came out of his mouth. "If you want to continue this conversation, we can do it once we're out of here," he said to the Squam. "And if you want to join us, I suggest you do your best to keep these guys off of me so I can work."

"Fine," Frank hissed, "but I will not forget to ask again."

Cole already figured as much. Considering how things had gone so far, why should anything be easy?

"I'm in too," Lambert said.

Footsteps knocked against the floor outside the elevator. Rather than say anything that might be overheard, Cole nodded and got back to work.

"What's going on in here?" a guard asked. Cole recognized the voice as belonging to the guy who brought plates of runny stew and cups of instant oatmeal as what passed for dinner and breakfast. The steps stopped near Frank's cell, punctuated by the loud clang of a club against his bars. "You trying to squeeze out of there? When'd you learn to do that?"

Cole felt like Renfield from the old Dracula movies as he squatted down and sawed away at the cell door with his little wooden chip. The big difference between him and a lunatic was that he knew exactly what he was doing and was making progress. Then again, that's probably exactly what all the lunatics thought.

"And what do you think you're trying to do?" the guard asked while swinging his gaze toward Cole. "What's in your hand? If you're cutting yourself, it won't get you—" Frank's hand shot out from his cell so quickly that the guard never had a chance of stopping it. He barely had a chance to turn around before Frank grabbed the back of his head and snapped his temple against the iron bars.

"Good," Cole said breathlessly as sweat rolled down his face. "Just a little longer and I should have this."

Lambert kept his forearms pressed against the front of his cell and his head leaning against them. "Don't know what you're getting so excited about. What the hell's supposed to happen if you cut through another one of those? Nothing happened when you cut the first one."

"Sure, nothing you can see. Ask Frank what happened."

The guard struggled a little, but his movements seemed to come from reflex instead of any earnest attempt at escaping Frank's grip. He was allowed to move away from the bars just until there was an inch or so between his face and that of the reptile man. Then Frank closed that distance with a sharp pull that momentarily subdued the guard. "The bars were smoking before," he said.

"Huh?" the other inmate asked.

Although Lambert was confused, Cole wasn't. He'd used Ned's eye drops a few times and had seen the smoky trails drifting off objects affected by active Skinner or Dryad charms. "What about now?" he asked.

Frank strained to keep the guard under control as the guy started to come around. The quick recovery meant he was probably a Skinner, Cole thought, or at least had something in his system to help with healing. "No," the Squam said. "Not anymore."

"Good."

"Get that asshole to open the door," Lambert said.

Sucking in as much air as he could, the guard, awake now, replied, "Fuck that and fuck you."

"Kinda figured you'd be that way," Cole muttered. "Which is why I thought I'd get out myself. Just hope this works the way I think it will."

Since the arrival of the first guard, Cole's senses had jumped to high alert. Every rattle he heard, every echoed voice, every creak within the walls, pounded through his ears. The sound of the elevator might as well have been claps of thunder as the car rumbled upward. He put his adrenaline to use by cutting the bar with increased vigor. Although the groove didn't meet up perfectly with the first one, he jammed the wood chip in and wiggled it back and forth until the slice of iron finally gave way. Having seen enough of the runes to recognize the simple locking designs that showed up on most of the doors in Lancroft's Philly house, he knew exactly which ones to cut. Once the sequence was interrupted, the circuit was broken and the low square door separated from the rest of the bars.

"Sweet!" Cole shouted. "About damn time something went right!"

He shoved the door open and crawled through. As soon as he was out, he climbed to his feet and looked for the runes the guards had touched to open the door properly. They were also like the designs used by Lancroft. Similar runes were on every door in the row, situated just outside any prisoner's reach. Since Lambert was closer, Cole ran to that cell and ran his finger over the one specific rune Rico had made him memorize so he wouldn't lock himself in or out of a closet or basement.

The skinny prisoner let out a whooping laugh when his door clanked once and swung open. "I gotta learn about those runes!" he said while crawling out of his cell. He then dashed across the corridor to slap a hand on Cole's shoulder and pull him away from the wall next to Frank's cell. "What're you doing?"

"Letting him out," Cole replied. "What do you think?"

"I think that's a mistake."

"The mistake is wasting time and turning away any help we can get. Now get your hand off of me."

"That thing ain't one of us," Lambert said. "If we get out of here—"

"You *won't* get out of here," Frank warned. "Not if you plan on walking past this cell."

Lambert stood as close to nose-to-nose with the Squam as the bars would allow. "Yeah? And how do you think you'll stop us, Lizard Boy?"

Before Frank could answer, the door to his cell clanked and swung open. Cole stood with his finger still on the unlocking rune and met Lambert's glare with one of his own. "He already helped us by taking care of this dipshit."

The dipshit in question tried to swing his billy club, but his arm was stopped by a block that Cole performed out of pure reflex before bending his arm back and snapping his elbow into the guard's jaw. After taking the club, he allowed Frank to leave his cell and toss the guard in to take his place.

"The elevator's almost here" Cole said while locking the door. "We need to deal with whoever's in there. Can't be a lot of them. It's not that big an elevator."

Nodding toward the Half Breeds pacing in their cage, Frank said, "Let them out. They'll tear the guards apart."

"After they're done with us," Lambert said. "Or they'll hit the guards first and then us. Either way, we won't be able to put those things down."

"He's right," Cole said. "If we want out of this, we gotta fight for it until help arrives."

"And what if we don't last that long?" Frank asked.

Perhaps Paige's teachings and attitude problem had an effect on him, because Cole replied, "Then we don't deserve to get out." Not another word needed to be said.

When the doors opened, all three of them charged the elevator, Cole at the head of the pack. The first thing he saw was the barrel of a shotgun pointed at the floor near his feet. The man holding the shotgun started to raise it, but didn't get halfway before Cole grabbed the weapon midway along its barrel and pounded the club into the guard's face to drive him back into the elevator. Waylon and two more guards were in the elevator, all them armed with either shotguns or wooden clubs. By the time the first guard went down, those clubs were shifting into deadlier, bladed forms. Lambert took the shotgun Cole tossed to him while driving his foot squarely into another man's gut, then slammed the stock into the third guard's face, knocking him cold.

Frank was last to arrive but made one hell of an entrance. He grabbed Waylon in one hand and the last guard in the other to slam both of them against the inside of the elevator. Both men kicked and struggled, prompting Frank to pull them closer while opening his mouth to expose even rows of identical teeth. Before he could chew anyone's face off, the ratcheting sound of the shotgun's pump action filled the cramped space.

Cole ejected a shell that had been ready to fire, but the

sound captured everyone's attention when he asked, "Why are we being kept here?"

"To serve your time for killing those cops."

"Don't. Fuck. With. Me." Cole had never been so close to killing someone in such a calculated, up-close, and potentially messy way. Waylon must have read that in his eyes, because he quickly dropped his attitude.

"You're here because Jonah Lancroft wanted to consolidate all of the Skinners he could trust as well as the ones he can't."

"Lancroft is dead."

"But his Vigilant aren't," Waylon said. "He wanted us to prepare for the Breaking Moon. That's when the shapeshifters have a chance to overrun our entire society. He wanted to make sure they weren't allowed to converge on common ground, but that's already been allowed to happen. Not only that, but they've been given even more power since Kawosa was allowed to escape."

Sirens wailed inside the prison as whoever was monitoring the cameras on G7 took notice of what had happened there.

"Shit," Lambert said. He pointed the weapon he'd confiscated at one guard's head. "There's gotta be a way to get out of here other than the front door. Take us to it."

"We won't need that," Cole said.

"You got a better way? I don't even know how many guards are in the shithole."

Frank pulled in a deep breath, barely taking notice of the two men in his grasp. "Something's coming."

"Some*thing*?"

"That's right, Lambert," Cole said. "That first set of runes I deactivated wasn't part of the door locking system. It was a cloak. Isn't that right, Waylon?"

The man at the other end of Cole's shotgun paled. "What have you done?"

"I broke the rune on my bars," Cole replied. "Just one, but that's enough to disrupt the entire system."

"We've got to get out of here!" Waylon said.

Frank's head bobbed as his tongue extended and flicked out to taste the air. "He's right. It's closer now."

Shots were fired just beyond the prison walls, eliciting a round of excited shouts from several different spots within the building. Cole and Lambert remained calm until the gunfire was stopped by the crunch of metal against solid concrete walls.

"By breaking that cloak, you've opened us up for God only knows what's out there," Waylon said.

Cole nodded solemnly. "I realize that."

"The authorities aren't the only ones who want to see you Skinners hang. Even the Nymar aren't your biggest threat."

"Believe me, I know that too."

The guards in the elevator had stopped squirming as the sounds of destruction grew closer. When the building itself was torn apart and then filled with a primal roar that rose into a fearsome howl, they looked to their leader for support.

Waylon's shoulders slumped and he leaned back against the wall of the elevator as if that was the only thing that could hold him up. "Those runes were for your protection as well as the rest of us."

"No. They were to keep anything from knowing this place was here. It was also to keep Skinners from being sniffed out by whatever may be hunting them. Well I've got some bad news for you, buddy. There are some big bad things hunting me, and I'm betting they'll be just as happy to get you."

Chapter Twelve

Frank knocked two of the guards out in a matter of seconds. The one that didn't stay down was finished off by Lambert with a punch he seemed to have been saving since the day of his capture. Cole kept Waylon at the end of the shotgun he'd taken from one of the fallen guards, asked him nicely for a private route out of the prison, and was told to press the button marked P1.

"Why the hell are you trusting him?" Lambert asked.

"Because it's too late for him to lie."

"I can't believe you would knowingly draw one of those creatures here," Waylon said. "Even if you had nothing to do with the policemen that were killed by the Nymar, you'll be the reason why all of these innocent men are killed here today."

Frank stood with his arms crossed and his back pressed against the rumbling wall of the moving elevator. "You call your bloodthirsty guards innocent men?"

"They aren't lambs to be slaughtered," Waylon said, staring at the Squam as if Frank had been hacked up from the gullet of an even larger swamp resident. "They, like me, are just men doing their jobs."

"You're a Lancroft disciple, right?" Cole asked.

Lifting his chin slightly, Waylon said, "He was a great man."

"He was the man who unleashed the Mud Flu to kill hundreds of people. The only reason he didn't kill thousands was because my partners and I stopped him. Lancroft himself didn't give two shits about sacrificing innocents that way."

There was a lull in the noise within the prison walls. Everyone in the elevator held their breath to see if it would last.

It didn't.

Bricks were torn loose to hit the shaft beneath them. Men shouted and something that Cole guessed was handgun fire was followed by the distinctive roar of a Full Blood.

"It's already here," Waylon said. "See what you've done?"

"It'll be coming straight for us," Cole told him. "I've seen more than a few Full Bloods in my time, and when they set their sights on something, they have a very narrow field of vision. That thing out there will probably tear after us and any other Skinner in here. Since you and most of your men fit that bill, you really should get us out of here as quickly as possible."

Waylon's eyes darted toward the panel of buttons on the wall. The next impact against the elevator shaft made the entire car shake. "It's P Two. The floor you want is P Two."

"Are you sure about that?"

"Yes, goddammit! P Two. Hit it now!"

Cole reached out to poke the button directly beneath the one that was already lit. The car stopped, sent a muted *ding* through a small speaker above them and groaned as the doors started to open.

"That's P One!" Waylon shouted, losing every bit of composure that had been his normal exterior.

Cole speculated that his initial plan had been to get him, Lambert, and Frank to stumble into an ambush set up by more of the guards from G7. Waylon's haste to abandon that idea had less to do with a change of heart than with the creature that stood just outside the doors holding a guard in each hand as if they were toys. Frank had accomplished the same basic feat not too long ago, but the Full Blood had room to spare in each fist.

The beast stood just over seven feet tall and was covered in dark brown fur. Slowly, it shifted its head to look at the elevator and open its mouth in a way that dragged its teeth

Skinners: The Breaking

even farther through the rips they'd cut into his cheeks. "There you are," it growled.

Nodding slowly, Cole took in the sight with calm acceptance. "Burkis. Took you longer than I thought it would. Or are you going by Randolph now?"

The Full Blood cast aside the guards and swatted away several others as he hunched over to avoid scraping his head on the low ceiling while stalking toward the elevator. The parking level was wide open behind him. Beyond a few cars, there was a ramp that led down to the other levels and presumably the street. Between the ramp and the cars parked behind the werewolf, there were a few metal doors along the wall and what looked to be a small office.

"P Two!" Waylon shouted hysterically.

"What's the matter?" Cole asked as he tapped the button. "Never seen a Full Blood before? What kind of Skinner are you?"

The elevator doors slid shut as slowly as if cutting off just another would-be passenger with poor timing. The Full Blood lowered his head and reached out to grab the edges of the doors with both hands. No man alive would have been quick enough to reach the elevator before those doors closed. No animal would have been able to grab them and force them open. Randolph was neither of those things, so he got to the elevator and pulled both sliding doors completely off their tracks.

"Time and again you refuse to heed my warnings," Randolph snarled. "If you are a part of what is being protected here, then I was foolish not to have killed you when we first met."

"I just want out of here," Cole said while swinging the shotgun away from Waylon to aim at the Full Blood. "Step aside and let us go and we won't have a problem."

The Full Blood stared down at the elevator, leaned in to sniff the passengers and then scowled at Waylon. "That one stinks of Lancroft's chemicals," he snarled through shrinking fangs. Nodding toward the guards, Randolph added, "As do they."

"You probably didn't know anything about this place before, right?"

Randolph said nothing to admit such a weakness, but the flaring of his nostrils told Cole he'd struck a nerve.

When he lowered his shotgun, one of the guards attempted to grab it from him. Randolph bared his fangs and reached into the elevator to grab the guard's head and hold him in place. Cole kept the shotgun down and stooped down to take something from out of his canvas shoe and toss it at the Full Blood. Randolph caught the chip of metal, growled, and closed it in a shaggy fist.

"I cut that out to interfere with the runes cloaking this place from you," Cole explained.

"You knew I was close enough to get here so quickly?" Randolph asked.

Shrugging, Cole admitted, "I didn't have a clue who or what might be in the area. I just hoped that something big and mean would be able to sniff out this place and come running to get to a bunch of Skinners."

"You would sacrifice your own kind for a slim chance of survival?"

"These assholes may or may not be Skinners, but they're not my kind," Cole said. "They're fucking parasites who took advantage of me getting framed for the deaths of a bunch of innocent cops. They're bloodthirsty assholes, and if I have to gamble with my own life to get the hell out of here and throw some real justice their way, then that's how it's got to be."

"Justice," Randolph snarled in a manner than made it unclear whether he spoke the word as a question, statement, or joke.

"If you want to level this place, go ahead and do it," Cole said. "My friends and I will gladly leave you alone."

"And what about them?" Randolph asked as he fixed his crystalline gray-blue eyes upon Waylon and his men.

"They could barely contain three prisoners," Cole said grudgingly. "What could they do to you?"

Randolph seemed to consider that until his ears pricked up and he reached in to grab Waylon's arm. Somehow, the man in the suit had gotten a cell phone in his hand and made a quick connection. "I need all firepower to converge on Parking Level One," he shouted at the phone. "The prisoners are escaping and there is a Class One Shifter on site. Repeat, Class One Shifter."

Randolph grabbed Waylon's arm and squeezed until bones broke and the phone dropped from his grasp. "Where is the other Jekhibar?"

"I don't know what you're talking about," Waylon squeaked.

"The Unity Stone," Randolph snarled. "It's here. I can smell it."

"Then you can find it yourself."

"You truly want me to tear this place apart?" After a few more sniffs, his eyes drifted toward the floor. "Below. The Jekhibar is below." He pulled in another breath. This time, he didn't like the taste. "There are more coming."

"You're damn right there are," Waylon said defiantly. "More than enough to blast you into pieces. If you know what's good for you, you'll run before—"

Randolph pulled Waylon from the elevator with such force that his arm came away from his body and blood poured down the side of his suit. Waylon was too shocked to make a sound as he dropped. Even if he could have found enough breath to scream, it would have been washed away by the Full Blood's bellowing voice.

"No human tells me to run!" Randolph bellowed. "You have survived this long only because *we* have allowed it. I thought to hinder this madness by collecting the artifacts that would lead your kind to the brink, but perhaps Liam was right. Perhaps things should be allowed to take their course even if it leads to this world being engulfed in fire and humans are all forced to endure the Breaking."

Cole picked up Waylon's cell phone and listened to the voice coming through its speaker. "Shit," he said while disconnecting the call, then tucking the phone under the front of his jumpsuit. "There's more coming this way."

"What?" Lambert asked. "Who?"

"I don't know. Sounded like soldiers."

"Guns and machines," Randolph said. "You can go if you commit yourself to one task. Protect the young one."

Lambert tried easing past the werewolf but was stopped by an open hand covered in Waylon's blood. "He's with me," Cole assured him. "And so is he," he added, indicating

Frank. Randolph let both of them move past him and into the parking garage. "What young one?" Cole asked.

"One of my kind. She is still wild, but must be hidden from the others."

"Other Full Bloods?" Cole asked as confusion threatened to suffocate him like a rising pool.

"They've come for the Breaking Moon and are seeking any way possible to get more than their share of it. Find the young one, take her far from this continent and keep her hidden." As he shifted into a hulking body that was bigger than most of the compact cars behind him, Randolph snarled, "If Skinners truly care about your species, you must prepare for war. It is too late to avoid now. Organize and find a way to keep my brethren from becoming too powerful to be contained."

"How the hell do I find a Full Blood?" Cole asked. "You guys always find *me*!"

"True Skinners find a way. That is why the warrior spirit remains alive in you and not in the rest of humanity. The only way for me to act without answering to Kawosa is for me to remain as ignorant as you in some matters. Now if you wish to survive, you must leave this place." Shifting his gaze to Waylon, he added, "If you will help me in my search, this can go much smoother."

Waylon was on the floor, bleeding out through the ragged stump of his right arm. Several guards had shoved open a door somewhere in the parking garage beyond the elevator and fired a few shots at the fleeing prisoners before catching sight of the Full Blood. Cole watched as Randolph absorbed a wave of shotgun blasts that thumped against his side and chest. The blast rippled through the Full Blood's fur like a hot wind, shredding some of the flesh directly beneath it. The charred flesh quickly solidified into a rough patch of skin that was quickly obscured by his coat. Randolph straightened up and turned to face the guards. "So be it." Looking over his shoulder, he snarled, "You have a job to do, Cole," and then charged at the guards.

Cole hurried behind the werewolf and dove behind the cover of some parked cars. Gunshots blasted around him, but none of them came anywhere close to hitting him since they'd been fired by men who were knocked aside or tossed into a wall while their fingers were clamped around their triggers. When a fully armored guard landed heavily on the car Cole was using for cover, a piercing alarm started to wail. He could see the stairwell the guards had used to enter the garage. More armed men and women rushed through the door to fire at Randolph while shouting orders to one another.

Despite what those guards had done to him, Cole couldn't help but shout, "Just get out of here! You won't be able to kill him!"

Not only weren't the guards listening, but a few of them rushed over to Randolph wearing full riot gear and carrying crudely fashioned Skinner weapons. Two were caught in a wild flurry of claws that sent limbs and blood flying. Another was about to be decapitated when he was saved by a large figure in an inmate's jumpsuit. It was Frank. Leaping in with speed that rivaled a Mongrel, he dodged a blow from the Full Blood and grabbed one guard by the shoulders to toss her back into the stairwell. When Randolph roared at him, the reptile man spat something into the werewolf's eyes that caused him to recoil and wipe at his face. Frank leapt over the creature's wildly thrashing claws to land on top of a car. By the time that alarm started to wail, the Squam had jumped away. He landed, then ran alongside Cole, who was headed toward the back of the garage.

"She was just a medical tech," Frank explained. "Waylon forces everyone to fight whether they want to or not."

"Whatever," Cole grunted. "Let's just get the hell out of here."

The Full Blood roared and launched a series of powerful swings that chopped some of the guards to pieces while others maneuvered around him to stab their sharpened wooden weapons into his back and ribs. When Randolph twisted around to sink his claws into one of those men and bite down on another, they made no attempt to block or parry an attack. The guards barely knew what they were doing. They might have wielded Skinner weapons, but were too stupid to do anything but charge ahead, and too frightened to press an advantage.

The guards with the wooden weapons were first to go. Randolph bit all the way down to the spine of one man and then spit him at the others in the stairwell as if he was something caught between the werewolf's teeth. The Full Blood backed away from the stairwell, but not in retreat. He merely repositioned himself his remaining opponents were in front of him. More gunshots rained down from a gaping hole in the ceiling to thump into his fur. The hole must have been Randolph's point of entry into the garage, and guards stood at the edge, firing at the werewolf from what should have been a superior position. All they managed to do was further anger the beast.

Not concerned with Waylon or the guards, Cole took stock of any elements that had a bearing on his chances of getting out of that prison. Lambert was crouching behind a car and slowly working his way toward the ramp that led up and out of the parking garage. Frank jumped from one car to another, hissing loudly while flexing his hands until wide, rough nails extended from his fingertips.

Suddenly, four men in tactical armor dropped into the garage through the hole, landing either on the dirty concrete or on Randolph's back. Instead of firearms, they had wooden weapons that put the guards' clubs to shame.

One of the new arrivals carrying a large wooden halberd landed on the floor beside Randolph. The long handle resembled Cole's spear, but the squared blade at the end was unlike anything he'd ever seen. It was at least ten inches wide and over a foot long, squared at three corners, with the upper corner extending up into the shape of a rhino's horn. The man holding it dug the leading edge into Randolph's side, raked it across and then spun the entire weapon around his body so it could hit the Full Blood again.

Randolph turned and stopped the next swing with one outstretched hand, closed his fist around the halberd's blade and tried to pull it away from the man who held it. His other paw reached back to grab his side and remove a guard's club as if it were no more than a large thorn, then threw it away. The club sped through the air like a bullet, smashing through the windows of one car and, after exploding through the glass, knocking into Lambert's hip.

Skinners: The Breaking 161

Keeping his head down and shotgun raised, Cole hurried to get to Lambert before he was stomped, slashed, or otherwise destroyed by the rampaging Full Blood or the growing number of guards. He tried to channel some of the power that had been in him earlier, but all that remained was the agony of broken tendrils cinching in around his stomach. Each step was harder to take than the previous one, but he somehow got to the fallen inmate and helped him to his feet. "Get up, Lambert. We gotta get out of here."

Frank's strained, hissing voice could barely be heard over the rest of the chaos as he dispatched one of the new arrivals by grabbing a gnarled quarterstaff from the guard's hands and twisting it away. "Stairs should be this way," he said while cracking the guard in the jaw with his own weapon. Then shots were fired at the Squam, forcing him to drop down and out of sight.

When Lambert looked his way, Cole told him, "Go on. I'm helping Frank."

"Ain't time for that, man. We got another minute or two at best before them guards find us."

Already breaking into a run, Cole shouted, "Just go. This won't take long."

Frank climbed to his feet and staggered toward him. By the looks of him, Cole didn't thing he had the strength to make another jump. The Squam's yellowish skin was cracked and bleeding in several places, discolored to look like mud. His narrow vertical pupils shifted toward Cole. "They are keeping the Full Blood occupied, but won't be able to kill it."

"Go on and get out of here," Cole said without sparing so much as a glance toward the battle raging a stone's throw away. "If level two is a bust, then take the ramp. Cars get in and out of here, so there's got to be a way for us to do the same."

Frank nodded and did his best to run toward the ramp Lambert was now using. He kept his upper body hunched down so low, it looked like he was running on all fours.

The heat in Cole's scars flared up until he reflexively pulled in a breath and tightened his grip around the shotgun. The club he'd taken from one of the elevator guards was tucked under one arm. Frank was almost at the top of the ramp now, but he dove off the edge to clear a path for another Full Blood that was stormed up.

It was one of the biggest werewolves Cole had seen. Normally, a Full Blood was smaller when it walked on four legs. Resembling a bear with longer limbs and a canine head, they used that form for speed or mobility and walked on two legs when fighting or climbing. This one, covered in dark gray fur, galloped like a horse and kicked up dust from the concrete as its claws scraped gouges into the cement and through the occasional speed bump. Where Randolph's teeth grew at odd angles to slice through his face, this one's were as organized as they were deadly. The creature pulled in a deep breath and barked in a deep baritone, displaying two sets of long fangs sprouting from each spot where canine incisors would grow.

After tossing the guard with the halberd over a minivan, Randolph turned toward the other creature. "Esteban!" he roared. "There is nothing for you here."

The Full Blood with the gray fur looked as if he would cross the entire parking area in one leap, but shifted into his upright form to dig his feet into a car's roof. "This place reeks of Skinners hiding treasures they do not understand," he replied in a rumbling voice colored by a Spanish accent. "It is no surprise to find you here while the others cluster around the Torva'ox like children gazing upon a shiny trinket."

Randolph charged at the other Full Blood with men attached to him by blades, hooks, or other weapons embedded in his flesh. The guards dangled from his sides and back like decorations until they were scraped against a post or brushed off against a parked car. The two Full Bloods collided like storm fronts, completely ignoring the wave of guards that had just arrived. In his upright form, Randolph was shorter than the gray werewolf, but wider in the shoulders. Once they clamped their jaws around the thick matting of fur protecting the other's neck, Cole found his opening to put that place behind him.

He ran down the ramp and quickly spotted Lambert and Frank racing across a crumbling parking lot for the safety of a wooded hillside less than a quarter mile away. It was early evening and the sun was making its descent to the western horizon. Police cars and several unmarked trucks sped toward the building, which sat by itself at the base of a tall set of hills. Wailing sirens filled the air, a helicopter roared in from the east, and more vehicles sped down the road that led to the prison's poorly tended fence line. No one, however, seemed to notice Cole and his companions working their way up the rise that led to higher ground covered by trees and dense bushes.

Above all the chaos surrounding the cement block of a building, Randolph's howl was joined by the voice of the other Full Blood. Before the armed men could leave their vehicles, the werewolves exploded from the parking garage. The few remaining men trying to hold a line in front of the building's main entrance were decimated by the gray creature's teeth and claws as Esteban tore through them.

Even when he got to the top of the rise, it was tough for Cole to make sense out of which Full Blood was winning. All he could tell from his new vantage point was that the prison would need some repairs if it was ever going to be used for anything more than a quarry. Randolph jumped down onto the gray werewolf but was grabbed in midair before he could sink his teeth into Esteban's flesh. He then found himself on the ground with the gray wolf on top of him. The group of men Cole guessed were police opened fire on the Full Bloods, unleashing a chattering wave of gunshots from everything ranging from handguns to high-powered rifles. The Full Bloods hunkered down beneath the pelting of bullets, too engrossed in their own fight to answer them. After tossing Randolph against the side of the building, Esteban grabbed his leg and lobbed him into the largest cluster of police cars.

"Well," Cole said from behind the rocks he and the other two escapees were using for cover, "they can't pin that one on me."

"They would if they knew what you did," Lambert replied. "Lowering them defenses was a stupid goddamn idea."

"We would have been dead if we'd stayed there."

"You think so?"

Cole looked over at him and said, "Yeah. If it wasn't for the Legion of Doom over there tag-teaming the entire prison, we would have been locked away, picked apart, and cut to pieces."

"He's right," Frank said. "Nobody knew we were there, and Waylon was after something important enough for him to kill to get it."

Another wave of gunfire erupted from the police encroaching on the prison. Randolph rolled to his feet and shifted into his four-legged form to charge the armed men who had tried to flank him. With bullets thumping uselessly into his fur, he scattered the humans, lowered his head and came back around to drive it into Esteban's stomach. Having flipped the other Full Blood into the air, Randolph shifted into his upright form to catch Esteban by two clumps of fur and fling him away. The werewolf clawed at empty air while snarling ferociously, but was unable to do much more than that before slamming into the side of the building with enough force to go through the outer wall. Randolph turned to face the cops then, warned them back with a primal, territorial roar, and leapt through the hole in the side of the prison to pursue his prey.

"We need to get moving," Cole said. "There won't be any better time than this."

Lambert couldn't nod fast enough as he jogged toward the top of the rise so he could put more distance between himself and the raging battle.

Frank, on the other hand, wasn't so eager. "You're just going to leave?" he asked.

"Yeah," Cole replied. "Isn't that what you're supposed to do after successfully breaking out of prison?"

"You're a Skinner, aren't you? If Skinners are good for anything, it's hunting things like them," he said while pointing a leathery hand at the howling Full Bloods. "Now you just want to leave?"

Cole stepped up so he was toe-to-toe with the Squam. Even though he had to look up into Frank's yellow eyes, he glared at him as though doing so from higher ground. Normally, he was on the receiving end of stares like that, and when he saw the hesitation in Frank's eyes, he realized why Paige used the tactic so often. "In case you haven't noticed, this isn't exactly a normal day of monster hunting. They're hunting us, and so far they're winning. Even if we did run back there to try and take on a pair of Full Bloods using nothing but a few crappily prepared sticks and foul language," he added while holding up the confiscated club, "those cops would shoot us and toss us back into a cell before we had a chance to get torn apart. Either way, we wouldn't be able to do much more hunting, and those Full Bloods would still be able to do whatever the hell they want!"

"They're doing that already," Lambert said, pausing to look back at them. "Let's just get to steppin'!"

"You want us to do something, Frank?" Cole asked without budging. "Then tell me what I should do."

The Squam's mouth remained closed so tightly it resembled a line scribbled across his face with a pencil.

"No?" Cole challenged. "Anything *you* want to do?"

Although the muscles in his face jumped beneath the scales embedded in his skin, Frank shook his head.

"Didn't think so. We're getting the hell away from here. You're welcome to try your luck on your own, but if you want to come along, then spare me the speeches." With that, Cole turned his back on Frank and the ruined prison so he could join Lambert as he headed for what looked to be a distant access road. A few cars raced by, but the drivers were too preoccupied with the werewolves tearing through a small army to notice a few figures making their way through the trees.

They ran for a mile, heading west through a patch of rocky terrain. Since the cars were coming from a highway to the north and helicopters were still flying in from the east, Cole didn't see any alternative but to press on into the hills. Never before had he so deeply regretted not being a Boy Scout when he'd had the chance to learn more about wilderness survival or navigating using the sun's position in the sky. When he thought the prison was far enough behind him to stop and catch his breath, he heard another explosion that spurred him onward.

Once they were deeply entrenched in what appeared to be some sort of park or nature reserve, Lambert slowed to a halt. "All right," he gasped. "Enough of this. Before I take one more step, I need to know who I'm runnin' with."

Frank looked at the wheezing, sweating inmate and replied, "I refuse to explain myself to—"

"You sure as hell will," Lambert cut in. "Right now."

Cole looked at the Squam and said, "He's a wanted fugitive just like the rest of us. We're in this together. If he was going to turn on us, he would've done it already."

"You can trust me or not," Frank said while hunching over so his chest was a few feet from the ground. "Rather than defend myself to you two, I'll find out if anyone's after us. You should move on, so don't wait for me. I'll find you." And with that, he scurried around a nearby cluster of trees.

Since he couldn't possibly follow the Squam, Lambert said, "Maybe we should just put a pin in this for now."

"Put a what?" Cole snapped.

"Something my ma used to say. It means it might be a good idea if we stuck this shit somewhere else for a little while until we're not so close to a bunch of wild animals and cops who want us dead." Shrugging, he added, "My ma was an interesting lady. What's your plan from here?"

Cole laughed and stooped, placing his hands on his bent knees and catching his breath. "I gotta level with you, Lam. I knew something would be coming to tear that place down, but I only kept that chunk of the bar because I thought it was charmed metal."

"And it was," Lambert said proudly.

"Right. I figured I could jam it into something's eye or . . . that sounds pretty stupid, huh?"

After a short pause filled by the thump of distant explosions and howls, Lambert said, "Yeah. That does sound pretty stupid. But no dumber than me running from the law with you and a lizard man."

Something crawled out from the trees behind Cole. Without casting more than a quick glance at the wide-shouldered figure that had crept up behind him, he asked, "What's our situation, Frank?"

"Nobody's following us yet. The cops are too busy sorting through the rubble and keeping out of the way of those two Full Bloods. Looks like plenty of people were hurt. Maybe worse. Ambulances are coming. Helicopters are hanging all around. Some are bringing wounded to the hospital and others are just trying to get a closer look."

"Reporters," Cole grunted. "Perfect."

"Nobody's after us?" Lambert asked. "You're sure?"

"I said it once," Frank hissed. "But that could change if we stay here."

The Squam's face wasn't the kind that inspired trust, but Cole decided to accept what came out of it. "All right. We need to keep moving."

Chapter Thirteen

Atoka, Oklahoma

The rumble of the exploding Gulfstream was still ringing through her ears when Paige tried to open her eyes. Something pressed against her lids along with every other inch of her body. She felt like she was falling, but suspended at the same time. Her ears, nose, and mouth were filled with dirt, which meant she hadn't been delirious when she thought she'd been pulled underground.

Panic set in.

When she felt rough hands grabbing her arms and cinching around her ankles to drag her deeper into the earth, panic became a fond memory.

She tried to shout but her muffled voice couldn't make it past her lips.

She tried to kick and actually felt her feet bust through into empty space beneath her, but the grip around her ankles tightened to prevent her from moving again. There was another sharp pull and Paige was dislodged to fall to a hard surface, landing with a jarring impact she felt all the way up into her molars. One hand pressed against the back of her head while more hands scrambled to search her and take away anything they could find.

At first she was too stunned to react. After a few seconds that feeling was replaced by an instinct honed over several years of getting jumped by any number of creatures. She hadn't liked it the first time it happened and liked it even less now. She put her left hand flat against the floor to prop herself up and balled her right fist. With a sharp twisting motion of her upper body, she brought that elbow around in a blind swing that connected with something solid.

"Hold her down!" someone grunted from the direction of where her elbow landed.

From directly behind her someone else voice replied, "I *am* holding her down."

"Use both hands, idiot!"

In the time it took for that little spat to take place, Paige had already wriggled onto her side and pulled one leg free from where it had been pinned to the floor. Even after she twisted her head around to get a look at where she was, she couldn't make out much more than a crowd of shadows cast by a dim light.

The hand on the back of her head gripped her skull like a melon, curling short, thick fingers against one ear until claws scraped against her cheek. The weight on her back shifted toward her shoulder blades as the second of the two voices told her, "Lay still and keep quiet unless you'd rather go back up to those goddamn Full Bloods."

"Let me go," she said. With every word, dirt trickled from her mouth, adding fuel to the angry fire that was already blazing inside of her.

"Only if you calm down."

"You know a great way to calm me down? Let me go."

A few silent moments passed, but Paige sensed that the other two were consulting with each other. Since they were diggers, the creatures were most likely Mongrels. Last time she checked, Mongrels weren't psychic. Whatever looks or gestures they were exchanging, she let them have a few more seconds to wrap up.

The closest voice said, "I'm going to let you go. Just remember that we dragged you away before you could be hurt."

"I remember."

"And we're not enemies here," the second voice added. "We're being pushed around just like you."

"Sure. Fine."

The sighs that came from the other two filled the hollowed space they and Paige now occupied. Once she felt the grip on her neck and ankles loosen, she scrambled away and turned to get a look at them.

Both were Mongrels, that was for sure. They had the thick limbs, long claws, leathery skin, and beaked noses that marked them as burrowers who traveled underground as if swimming through water and dug tunnels or dwellings beneath the surface for their pack. She and Cole had found one such pack beneath a suburban Nebraska neighborhood that remained hidden by tunneling between the basements of several homes. The two with Paige squatted within a space roughly the size of a closet that had been hollowed out of the earth. Hard-packed soil closed in on all sides, trickling dusty drips with every move they made. Their chests heaved with the effort of bringing her there, but instead of breathing through their mouths, their exhales caused large gill flaps on the sides of their necks to stretch out before laying flat again.

The Mongrel farthest from her squatted on his haunches and examined her with dark eyes covered by a set of vertical lids. A dented little flashlight clipped to a belt cinched around his narrow waist was the only source of illumination in the confined space. His beak moved in a constant rhythm that was only broken when he took a moment to crack the gum he was chewing. Tossing Paige's weapons to the ground near his long feet, he said, "You're a Skinner."

"And you're a Mongrel," she replied. "Next topic."

"I'm Burke. That there's Salvatore."

She nodded slowly and said, "I'm Paige."

Salvatore was on one knee, still tangled in his own limbs after tussling with her. A filthy wife-beater was stuck to his upper body by layers of wet grime. His lower section was covered by tattered old jeans. As soon as he got himself situated, he stood up so his shoulders, neck, and head were wedged against the top of the hollowed space, as though he was the sole support beam. "Them others ain't Skinners. They smell like metal and fire."

"The fire you smell is probably the plane that was brought down. Kind of hard to miss that."

"We didn't miss—" Salvatore stopped as if someone had pressed a button to pause him in mid-sentence. When he thought one of the others in the chamber with him was going to make a sound, he held up a clawed finger to pause them too.

Paige looked up but could only see dirt separating from the wall as something heavy thumped overhead. The impacts moved like footfalls but were solid enough to send little shock waves through the ground. They stopped and were soon followed by scratching sounds that sent large sections of the chamber tumbling onto Paige's head.

"Come on," Burke said as he rushed toward her. "Gotta move."

Her first impulse was to struggle before being scooped under the Mongrel's arm. Since she didn't have any weapons or backup, she decided that being dragged underground by a shapeshifter was slightly better than being torn apart by another shapeshifter above it. The instant the back of her head pressed into the loosened dirt, she drew a quick breath, held it and closed her eyes.

For the first couple of yards she knew she was going straight ahead. Burke's side and leg bumped against her, giving her a good enough handle on their orientation to know when they took a downward turn. Behind them the scraping of claws became a sound that rumbled through the earth. The Full Blood's roar was a tremor that made every muscle in Paige's body tense in preparation for claws to be dragged through her from above.

Cole had told her about the time when he was taken for a similar ride by the Mongrels in Nebraska. She'd wondered why he hadn't been able to get away or grab at something to slow them down. Now that she was the one being pulled through the dirt like the tail end of an earthworm, she knew just how helpless he'd been. She quickly lost all knowledge of where she was, how deep she'd been taken, or even if her head was pointed up or down. When the sounds of the Full Blood faded, she couldn't tell if they were too far behind them or if the lack of oxygen was causing her senses to dim.

Her chest started to ache. Soon she would have to draw

a breath. Even if that meant filling her lungs with dirt, she couldn't just suffocate without a fight. Her limbs twitched and her ears filled with the sounds of her own desperate grunts as every part of her fought back the urge to take a much-needed gulp of air.

The grip under her arms tightened.

Then her body moved forward even faster, making her think she was falling into unconsciousness. As it turned out, she was just falling.

The filthy cocoon of dirt was gone.

Her arms and legs were free to flail but weren't organized enough to soften the impact when she hit a solid earthen floor. What little wind she had left was knocked from her lungs, to be replaced by air that stank of mold and the hint of exhaust fumes. Once the ringing in her ears faded, she could hear the chugging of a nearby motor. Opening her eyes unleashed a torrent of tears to slice through the grit caking her lids. She scrambled to stand up while swiping at her watering eyes, hoping she wasn't going to knock her head against another low ceiling. Not only did she stand up without giving herself a concussion, but there were several feet to spare.

The room was supported by wooden beams lining the walls and ceiling with gaps wide enough for Salvatore to emerge from a wall like a leathery portion of sentient ground. Burke hunkered on the floor with his elbows resting on his knees and flipped the switch of his flashlight off. There was plenty of light in the room thanks to three bare bulbs hanging from the ceiling and powered by a generator against the adjacent wall. Pumps brought air in from outside through hoses that poked out of the ceiling at random intervals like headless snakes.

Paige's eyes darted back and forth, up and down, soaking up as many details as possible. She figured the room was about nine by twelve feet and must have been several yards below the surface. Apart from the two diggers, two feline Mongrels lay on the floor. Two more paced the room on either side of her, visible only as ripples in the air. She not only spotted the distortions, but could smell the oils that bent light around the shapeshifters' bodies.

"Where am I?" she asked. "Someone had better start talking!"

One of the felines lifted her head, which was somewhere between that of a tigress and a mole. A long rounded snout filled with needlelike teeth opened to form words that were colored by a buttery southern accent. "Or what, Skinner? You'll fight your way through us?"

Responding to a subtle nod from the feline, Burke tossed Paige's machete, stake, and Beretta. They hit the floor near her feet, kicking up a slight puff of dust.

"Go ahead," the feline Mongrel said. "You'll make enough of a ruckus to bring those Full Bloods straight down here, and if you make it through them after us, you'll still have to tunnel your way out."

"Before you get too cocky," Paige said, "you should know that I see those other two with the cloak. That invisibility thing is a neat trick, but I've done it a few times myself."

"Of course you have. Probably killed one of us and gathered up the fur like the morbid scavengers you are."

Although that wasn't quite the truth, it was close enough to take the wind from Paige's sails. She stooped down, holstered the pistol, and held her machete so the blade was pointing directly at the feline spokesman for the group. Sighting along the top of the weapon, she could make out a few rounded facial features. Those, combined with the pitch of the Mongrel's voice and curve of its body, gave the impression that it was female. "I've worked with Mongrels before," she said. "I helped Kayla's pack settle into Kansas City."

The feline's lips peeled back to show even more sharp teeth. "Sure. After Liam was done tearing it to pieces and every human in the place was anxious to bag themselves a gen-u-ine werewolf to mount onto their wall. How many Mongrels do you think were killed because they poked their noses into the wrong place just to find some food?"

"Not my problem," Paige replied. "Kayla was free to go or stay. Last I heard, she stayed. I've been busy since then, and it's not my job to babysit."

"Busy," one of the cloaked Mongrels snuffed. Its cloak fell away, allowing its body to be seen as if the air itself had parted like a curtain. "We all know what busy means to a Skinner."

"I didn't invite myself down here," Paige said. "I didn't even know there were Mongrels in Oklahoma."

"Excuse us if we're anxious right now," the feline said. "Things are a bit of a mess around here."

With a thought placed in the right corner of her mind, Paige willed the machete in her hand to shrink back down into a thick gnarled stick. "They're a mess everywhere. Since it looks like you're all pretty well settled, I take it you aren't happy about the Full Bloods moving in?"

"You got that right," Salvatore said. When the others glared at him, he looked to the feline spokesperson and said, "Hell, Quinn, I'm just cutting through the bull. With them monsters digging for us, we ain't got time to be cute with each other."

Quinn stood up on her hind legs, shifting into a form that wasn't quite human but was definitely female. "Tell us about the others that came with you. Until we know who we're dealing with, we don't go any further."

A rumble worked its way through the ground, followed by a howl and several feral snarls.

"That'd be the boys locking up with a Full Blood," Burke reported as he lifted his pointed beak toward the section of wall that he'd emerged from not too long ago.

"Better only be one," Salvatore said, "or we can say goodbye to them boys."

Unaffected by the noise that drew closer by the second, Quinn kept her gaze locked on Paige. "Tell me who those other hunters are," she demanded.

"We came to deal with a Full Blood," Paige said. "Instead we find two. I should be asking what the hell they're doing here. If you've set up camp in this town, then you must know what's going on above your heads."

"We know plenty. We just don't know who those others were that came in on that jet. Tell me or you're staying down here for the Full Bloods to sniff you out. If you think you have a prayer of digging your way out before they uproot this entire shelter, then you're dumber than you think."

The humorless smile on Paige's face was a gesture that

Skinners: The Breaking

showed just how resigned to her fate she truly was. "If you want to stay here talking tough with me, I'm all for it. Any cannon fodder is always welcome."

"After the Breaking Moon rises, your kind will have more cannon fodder than you'll be able to deal with."

"What the hell is the Breaking Moon?"

"Who the hell are those people that came in on that jet with you?"

"Amriany," Paige replied. "Kind of like Euro-Skinners. They're the ones that forged the Blood Blades."

Quinn's brow furrowed. "The Travelers have joined forces with you?"

"Not exactly one big family, but yeah." The next impact from aboveground was enough to make Paige unsteady on her feet. "Do you seriously have a plan to get out of here?"

When Quinn nodded, it wasn't to Paige. She turned to look at a spot just behind her and to one side. Before she could see what had caught her attention, she felt a familiar hand snake around her waist and pull her toward the wall. She held her breath and closed her eyes as she was dragged once more through the dirt.

It was a shorter trip this time. They traveled in a fairly straight line, and as they picked up speed, she heard the muffled grunts of Mongrels straining to complete the equivalent of a sprint while being buried alive. Before that thought could creep her out too badly, Paige was pushed upward and deposited into another room.

This one looked like a modern basement with a section of its cement floor stripped away to reveal dirt through which the diggers could enter. The hand that closed around her wrist to pull her up was smoother and thinner than any of the Mongrels' paws. Paige batted it away and climbed to her feet.

"Take it easy," Nadya said.

Blinking the grit from her eyes, Paige saw the Amriany woman in front of her. A stifled grunt drew her attention to a cot in a nearby corner where Milosh lay on his back gripping the stump of his left arm. It was wrapped in several towels that were soaked through with blood. "Weren't you guys on that jet?" Paige asked.

Nadya shook her head. "We were taken by these Kush-time before reaching it. Gunari tried to tell the pilot to come back, but . . ." Noticing the lost expression on Paige's face, she sighed and said, "Your Mongrels, we call them Koosheetmay." Although she slowed down to pronounce that word for her, she wasn't about to break stride any more than that. "They took us through the ground and away from the jet before the Full Bloods could get to us. Our pilot had to take off because he was being surrounded. Gunari shouted for him to stop. That was the last we heard before the explosion."

Looking over to Milosh, Paige asked, "What about him?"

Another Mongrel became visible as it shed its cloak. Reappearing next to the cot, it sniffed Milosh and said, "This one's turned."

"I can help him," Paige said. "All I need is my medical kit."

"And where's that?" Quinn asked from another part of the room.

It wasn't until Paige spun around to face her that she saw that the rest of the basement was nothing more than a simple storage space fenced off within a larger room. The last time she'd seen her medical kit was when she'd restocked it for her trip to Canada. Doubting that Burke or Salvatore were up for a run to the Great White North, she turned to Nadya and said, "You guys said you brought your own medical supplies, right?"

"We did," Nadya replied, "but they were in the plane."

"Tough luck for him," Burke said.

"What's that mean?"

Stepping forward to put herself between Paige and the digger, Quinn said, "You *know* what that means. It means he's going to turn into a Half Breed and there's nothing to do about it but put him down before he is broken."

"We're not there yet," Paige snapped. "He fought and bled right alongside me, and I won't just stand by and let a partner go when things get hard. Not again!"

"You want to go up top among those Full Bloods?" Quinn asked.

"We'll have to eventually, right?"

Skinners: The Breaking

Quinn's eyes had the glint of polished stones within the smooth, furry contours of her face. Her snout had shrunken, along with the pointed ears that sprang straight up from the top of her head. One by one she checked silently with the other Mongrels. And one by one they nodded back at her. Shifting her focus to Paige, she said, "We can help you get to what's left of your plane by distracting the Full Bloods. We can't guarantee they'll all come after us, and we sure as hell can't guarantee the Half Breeds will follow. He's got less than an hour before the process is too far along to stop. If you're not back here with that medicine or whatever it is you have, we take care of him ourselves."

Nadya placed a hand on Paige's shoulder. "Agreed."

"Once this is done," the feline Mongrel continued, "we've got some things to discuss."

Paige took a moment to check the remaining magazines for her Beretta. The one already in the pistol was half full, and there was a fresh one in her jacket pocket. "I'm sure you do," she said while slapping the magazine back in place and chambering the first round. "Every good deed's got its price."

Chapter Fourteen

What had once been a flat stretch of land surrounding a little airstrip was now a ravaged battleground. Dirt had been peeled away from the face of the earth by unforgiving claws. The SUV was a dented lump of metal and broken glass, currently good for nothing more than a perch for the ebon Full Blood to survey his newly acquired territory. Minh ripped at the ground, stopping only when she caught a scent that snapped her head up and flared her nostrils.

The Mongrels approached the field in a line and fanned out once they'd been detected. Quinn and two other felines were at the front of the group, while more shapes emerged from the shadows to join them. Two came from behind the wide building with the big garage door, and another came at a dead run from a nearby housing subdivision. By the time that one reached the front line, all of the Mongrels had launched into a charge.

"They come to us for once," Liam snarled while jumping down from the SUV. "That'll save us some digging." The moment his feet hit the ground, clawed hands stretched up from the dirt to grab him. Liam immediately pulled up the leg that had been snagged to reveal the Mongrel that snagged him. Salvatore tightened his grip on Liam's ankle while trying to drag him down, but the Full Blood was able to pull him up from the dirt. Only the Mongrel's upper body emerged, but that was more than enough of a target for the werewolf's left paw.

"Already used this trick in Kansas City," Liam said while the corner of his ravaged eye socket twitched. "There won't be a second time." With that, he sunk his claws into the Mongrel's belly and ripped him open. Blood sprayed from a gaping wound that went all the way up to Salvatore's shoulder blade, and when Liam pulled his leg up even more, the evisceration was complete.

Quinn and the other Mongrels leapt forward in unison. Chunks of grass and earth were kicked up behind them as the stampede met a wall formed by the two Full Bloods. While claws and fangs were bloodied, two more figures emerged from the low building with the wide garage door. Beneath that building was the basement where Milosh, Nadya, and eventually Paige, had been taken. The two women paused in the doorway, waiting for a chance to make a run for the airstrip.

"You ready for this?" Paige asked.

Nadya set her sights on the airstrip, pulled in a breath and nodded once.

They bolted from the side door as if the building behind them was on fire. Ahead they could see half a dozen Mongrels tangling with the Full Bloods and a few Half Breeds. When Paige veered to the right to try and skirt the eye of a bloody hurricane, Nadya stayed with her.

The sound of flesh being ripped apart hit Paige's ears like the tearing of wet canvas, filling the air beneath the victorious howl of a Full Blood. Heavy, thumping footfalls shook the ground beneath her feet. There wasn't time to stop and fight, and shouting for Nadya to keep running would only draw unwanted attention, so she kept her legs churning and hoped the Amriany woman was doing the same.

A Half Breed ran toward Paige on an intercept course. By the time she'd reflexively drawn her Beretta and aimed at the werewolf, the thing had already been taken down by Quinn. The Mongrel leader screeched at her packmates with blood still pouring from her mouth. Two more Half Breeds had their eyes fixed on the humans but were forced to contend with Quinn as the feline darted between them and raked her claws along both werewolves' ribs. Paige and Nadya leapt over the first creature to hit the ground in a heap and kept going.

Her entire world was enveloped by the pounding of her feet, the howling of nearby creatures, the constant thumping of her heart, and the powerful huffing of her labored breaths. The ground beneath her shifted from packed soil to softer earth that had been recently turned. There was still half of the field to cover before they made it to the airstrip, and Paige realized they probably wouldn't even make it if the galloping footsteps behind them caught up.

One quick glance over her shoulder was all she needed to see the smaller Full Blood coming after them. Minh's dark red fur was slicked back against the low narrow frame of her four-legged form. As her paws grabbed the dirt to propel her onward, her head pumped back and forth like a racehorse in the home stretch. Only one or two more of those strides was all that would be needed for her to get within striking distance of Nadya. A few seconds after that, Paige knew she would be the one feeling her body cut down by the Full Blood's claws.

She twisted in an attempt to take a shot with her Beretta. Before she could pull her trigger, however, something sprang up from the ground to grab onto Minh's front paw. It clamped around Minh's ankle and tightened its grip enough to be pulled almost completely from the earth by the Full Blood's momentum. The digger reached up with his free hand, grabbed Minh's shoulder and sank the pointed end of his beak into her back. That forced a yelp from her, which quickly turned into an angry snarl. As Paige turned back around to look where she was going, the blurred form of a cloaked Mongrel bolted past her to hit Minh squarely in the ribs. All three shapeshifters rolled to the side, biting and tearing amid a growing cloud of dust.

Knowing better than to waste time counting her blessings, Paige worked her aching legs harder and focused on the little buildings at the edge of the airstrip. Along the way, she and Nadya encountered several Half Breed carcasses in various mangled poses after being ripped apart by what could have either been a Mongrel or a wood chipper. Paige hurdled those and quickened her pace after making it around the edge of the closest building and getting within sight of the jet wreckage.

There was more of the Gulfstream left than she'd anticipated. The jet lay on its side with one wing reaching toward the sky and the other smashed into scrap metal beneath the bulk of its body. Fires crackled at various points along the fuselage and black smoke rolled up from the cracked tail section. As the stench of burnt plastic and charred steel hit her, Paige slowed to a jog and stopped.

"Where's the medical kit stored?" she asked.

Nadya came up alongside her and stopped, to bending down to place her hands on her knees. "There was one in the cockpit and another in the passenger cabin near the door."

"You mean the door that's flat against the cement?"

Looking up to see which side the plane was laying on, Nadya replied, "Yes. That side."

"Then we're headed to the cockpit."

Both women ran along the airstrip, doing their best to ignore the heat from the fires and the constant threat of being stricken down by a force of nature on four legs. The closer they got to the downed plane, the more it looked like a giant creature that had been frozen while stretching an arm up from a turbulent, smoky sea. The nose cone was cracked open and split against the runway, leaving the tail section several feet off the ground. Although that made it easier for Paige to get to the cockpit, the mangled frame and shattered windows provided a formidable barrier between her and the pilot's seat.

Half of the curved canopy at the front of the plane was completely gone and was mostly impassable due to the mangled structure. Using whatever footholds she could find, she climbed up the Gulfstream's nose cone.

"What do you see?" Nadya asked from ground level.

Looking through a crooked frame of shattered glass or plastic, Paige spotted a control panel that had been reduced to a tangled mess of broken, exposed wires and cracked dials. Along with the throttle and flight control levers, it was wrapped around the slumping body of a young man who looked to have been cut in half by a set of rough pincers. "Just a lot of wrecked controls," Paige said. "Where's the kit?"

"Do you see where the pilot would be sitting?"

Trying not to meet the dead man's final, desperate, pleading gaze, Paige replied, "Yeah."

"The kit should be down near his left hand."

The pilot's left hand was nowhere to be found. When she forced herself to look at the section Nadya had described, she realized that the pilot's left leg had also been sheared away by the crash, or by the Full Blood that had surely followed it. Swearing under her breath, she pulled herself up to clear the window frame, using the side of her hardened right arm. Rather than healing, her wounds on that limb had merely piled up like gouges in a cement post. There was pain, but no more than usual. She couldn't move it very well, but that was nothing new. It looked bad, but she could go on, so she continued climbing into the cockpit but made it less than a quarter of the way before her foot slipped. After sliding an inch or two along the outside of the plane, her foot was stopped by something solid.

"Got you," Nadya said while bracing Paige's foot in both of her outstretched hands.

When she let out a relieved breath, Paige fogged a jagged piece of broken window half an inch from her chin. She leaned back, failed to get a handhold on the frame, and then fell forward. Only by twisting her stomach muscles was she able to avoid impaling her throat. Once Nadya had helped her climb back up again, she found herself looking at a pile of miscellaneous debris that had collected on the co-pilot's seat almost directly beneath her.

"That medical kit," Paige grunted while shifting to get a more solid grip on the plane. "Does it look like a gray metal shoe box?"

"Yes. Did you find it?"

"I think so!"

As she stretched her arm toward the co-pilot's chair, she heard what sounded like car engines nearby. Since the street was too far away to be heard over the crackling fires and the rush of blood in her ears, she guessed the vehicles had to be pulling up to the airport or even onto the airstrip itself. "Is that the fire department?" she asked.

After a few strained breaths, Nadya turned beneath Paige's weight. "No," she replied. "Just a couple of trucks."

Skinners: The Breaking

Paige could feel heat from the fires on her hands and smell the buildup of smoky grease on her face. The medical kit was within her grasp. If she flexed her fingers, she could feel the tips brush against the heated metal of the box. Standing tiptoe on the shaky platform of Nadya's hands, she leaned forward and squirmed over the sharp edges of the twisted frame. "Almost got it," she said to herself as much as to the Amriany beneath her.

"Hurry," Nadya said. "Vitsaruuv!"

"Vitsa-what?"

"Half Breeds!" Nadya shouted in an accent that apparently thickened under duress. "They are coming!"

Too close to the medical kit to even think about leaving without it, Paige closed her eyes so she could focus on her other senses. Tires skidded against pavement, people shouted back and forth to each other, and the slap of paws approached the plane. The air reeked of blood and burning oil. The box was warm against her fingers and rattled when she managed to pry it loose from the pile of other items on and around it.

"Didn't do all that goddamn running to quit now," she grunted. "If I have to climb in there myself, I'll pull you out."

"Get back!" Nadya screamed. "Get away from here! Run!"

Since the hands beneath her were steady, Paige figured Nadya was yelling at the locals who'd pulled up in the trucks. She stretched her arm as far as it would go and kept straining until she felt her thumb slide down against the other side of the box. Pinching her fingers together, she gritted her teeth and started lifting it off the co-pilot's seat. After some struggling, straining, and what could very well have been a self-inflicted dislocated shoulder, she liberated the medical kit from the pile of junk. "How many Half Breeds?" she asked.

"Two." Nadya's hands twisted in one direction, which meant the rest of her was most likely twisting that same way to get a better look around. "No. Three!"

Gunshots were fired not far from the airstrip. Paige twitched at the sound of them and nearly dropped the medical kit onto the floor, where it would have slid completely out of her reach. "What the hell is going on out there?"

Enthusiastic hollers erupted from the airstrip, reminding Paige of a Civil War movie she'd seen where a division of Rebs sent a line of Federal troops running for the hills. From what she could hear, the local boys were packing hunting rifles and a few large caliber pistols. Suddenly, she developed a fondness for Oklahoma.

"All right," she said while sliding away from the window. "Got the kit."

Nadya helped her down and pointed toward a pair of pickup trucks idling nearby. One was a dark red model with a wide bed and a polished chrome box placed just behind the cab, which looked like it was used for secure storage. The second was a light green rust bucket with a set of lights bolted to the roof, which probably could have lit a full stage performance of "Free Bird." The red truck's bed was full of young guys who used the top of the cab to steady their arms as they fired at the Half Breeds.

The werewolves chasing after the trucks had all been hit and were bleeding, but weren't about to stop. There was too much fresh meat in front of them and the air was thick with the scents of their brethren. Whatever tiny bit of reasoning they had was overcome by those factors, fueling the Half Breeds with a rage that made them send bits of concrete flying when their claws scraped against the airstrip.

"You can't hit them," said someone from directly over Paige's head, addressing the pickup trucks.

She looked up to find a lean animal perched on top of the wreckage. Instead of a bulky Full Blood, this one looked more like the gnarled, beefier cousin of a coyote. Its dull orange eyes weren't the same as the ones she'd seen in Toronto, but Kawosa's voice struck a chord deep inside her.

"You men are too frightened to fight," he said.

The hollering faded away and the rifle shots began sparking against the concrete, when only a few moments ago they'd been thumping solidly into werewolf flesh.

A Half Breed lunged at Nadya and would have torn her face off if she hadn't been quick enough to duck straight down to let the creature sail over her head and into the side of the wrecked Gulfstream. Paige dropped to one knee, lifted her Beretta and fired at Kawosa.

"Don't listen to him!" she shouted. "You were just hitting these bastards! Keep it up!"

Nadya reached for the scabbard at her belt and drew a blade just over a foot long and shaped like a boomerang set into an intricately carved handle. Twisting her body around in a full circle, she snapped the blade out and around to catch the second Half Breed across its face as it leapt at her. The creature let out a surprised bark when the Amriany weapon lodged just beneath its eye socket. Jumping gracefully over the incoming creature's claws, Nadya dragged the blade all the way through to shear off the top of the Half Breed's skull. When that one hit the side of the jet, it slammed into the metal and slid down into a pile of twitching flesh and bone.

Paige raised her Beretta and pulled the trigger. The shots were taken quickly and without the proper amount of breathing to steady her hands. Fortunately, she barely needed to aim in order to put several rounds into a creature that was barreling straight at her. Absorbing three bullets at close range slowed the Half Breed a little, but the mindless beast threw itself at its prey and snapped wildly at Paige.

"Here, young ones," Kawosa said from his perch. "This is where you'll find them."

His barbed voice carried all the way to the edge of the battlefield where Quinn and her Mongrels struggled to keep the Full Bloods occupied. From that direction, one shrieking, straining howl was joined by another. More Half Breeds gathered, and within seconds the pounding of frenzied feet upon the earth told of their pending arrival.

"You cannot hit any of them," Kawosa announced to the men who now stood around the pickups as if they'd just woken to find themselves there. "The beasts are too fast."

"Shut the hell up!" Paige said while sending her last rounds at Kawosa.

The first bullet sparked against the fuselage, and the next might have clipped him if he hadn't darted away in the opposite direction.

"You can hit whatever you aim at," she said as she stuck the Beretta back into its holster and approached the red pickup. "But don't push it. Just get out of here."

The front line of Rebs looked at her, started to put their rifles to their shoulders and then lowered them. At the head of the group stood a man in his early to mid-forties. His beard was dark brown with a few strands of gray that came almost down to his breastbone. He wore weathered jeans, work boots, and a hooded sweatshirt from the University of Texas wrapped around his thick body. "You two need a ride?" he asked.

Nadya rushed to Paige's side. The blade in her hand still had blood dripping from it as she said, "Yes. We need to go back up the road to—"

"No," Paige cut in. "You guys need to get into those trucks and ride somewhere safer than this. We got here on our own. We can get back on our own."

Another man hopped down from the back of the green pickup, striding past the cab while notching an arrow into what looked to be a compound bow. Paige had seen one or two of the things in hunting catalogues and on a few nature shows when she'd been too lazy to change channels. The man with the bow clamped a cigarette between his teeth, which flared brightly as he inhaled and drew the arrow all the way back to his shoulder. He released the arrow and sent the pointed missile straight into the neck of a Half Breed that had attempted to circle around the group. Even with the arrow lodged so close to its shoulder, the thing barely slowed down. A trickle of blood seeped from the wound, which only made it angrier when it charged the pickup in a series of off-balance steps. The archer cursed while reaching over his shoulder for another arrow. Before he could notch it, his buddies opened fire with their hunting rifles and buried the Half Breed in a storm of lead.

The creature made it to the truck, climbed onto the hood and snapped at the driver through the windshield. Its snout cracked the glass and rivers of saliva smeared the pane.

"Get it away from there, Al!" the archer said while calmly circling the red truck.

While staring at the werewolf through the windshield, the driver of the red truck reached for the steering column and pulled the lever that sent a spray of blue fluid from the squirters. Most of the cleaning solution soaked into the Half

Breed's matted fur, but some of it splashed into its eyes and got the thing to backpedal toward the front of the hood. After shaking some of the fluid away by tossing its head from side to side, the Half Breed glared at the driver with such single-minded intensity that it took no notice of the archer until he put an arrow straight through its eye.

"Don't like that, do ya?" the archer said while rushing forward to grab the shaft protruding from the Half Breed's face. When the werewolf snapped at his hand, he gripped the arrow tight enough to hold the werewolf in place as his buddies with the shotguns surrounded him and emptied their buckshot into the creature's body.

When the Half Breed stopped twitching, the archer jerked the arrow from its eye and asked, "Now what were you ladies saying about us finding somewhere safer to be?"

"You did real good against one of those things," Paige replied. "But there's a lot more out there."

"We know," the man with the long beard said. "Town's full of the damned things."

"Which is why you should get somewhere safe."

"Ain't nowhere safe," the archer grunted as he flipped his cigarette to the ground, then stomped it out. "Didn't you hear the man just now? The whole town's full of these fucking things. Now do you have somewhere you need to be or don't you?"

Paige looked down at the medical kit she'd tucked under her arm. Then she looked at Nadya and back to the guys near the pickup. "Are you guys locals?"

"We can swap names and numbers somewhere else or we can part ways right now. You got until I make it back to my truck to decide." Without wasting another word, the archer slung his bow over one shoulder and went back to the green pickup.

The driver of the red truck, who Paige assumed was Al, stuck his head out his window and said, "Them things are crawling all over this town and it looks like they won't be leaving anytime soon. You're lucky enough to walk away from that wreck, so you might as well come along with us."

Paige didn't know what to make of them. If they were Skinners, that would explain some things. With the battle raging nearby, the only thing of which she was certain was that she didn't have the time to sit and plan out every move as much as she would have liked. "Can you get us to that garage down the road?"

"You mean the autobody place?"

Since she'd smelled motor oil and metal before rushing out of the wide building, she guessed that was it. She climbed into the back of one of the trucks and said, "Just drop us off as close as you can and then get to wherever you need to be. If things get too hairy, you can let us off wherever."

The archer slapped the side of the red truck as he headed back to the green one. "Lady, every damn thing's getting hairy around here. Whether we ride up one street or down another don't matter anymore." With that, he climbed into the green truck and told the driver to get moving.

Once Nadya was in the bed of the red vehicle with Paige, both pickups made a U-turn and jumped a curb to get back onto the street. Along the way, Paige studied the field next to the airport. It was hard to tell for certain, but it seemed the Mongrels were making some progress. Liam held up the body of a digger, threw it into another Mongrel and was attacked by two more that had been cloaked. Minh tried to jump to Liam's side and was weighed down by several felines that clung to her with every tooth and nail at their disposal. Bodies of all shapes converged on the Full Bloods. Before she could see any more than that, Paige's truck veered into a parking lot and sped around to the back of the wide building with the garage doors. Sure enough, there was a little sign on the side of the building that read SAL'S AUTOBODY.

"You gonna be okay here, ladies?" the archer asked.

Paige and Nadya jumped down from the truck. Handing the medical kit to the Amriany, Paige replied, "We'll be okay. What about you guys?"

"Made it this far. That don't mean shit when it comes to the end of days, but we should be able to make it a little longer."

Hearing that made Paige fairly certain the man wasn't a Skinner. At least, he hadn't been one for long. Most experienced werewolf hunters had already seen and killed enough to have grown comfortable with anything resembling the

Skinners: The Breaking 189

end of days. Just to be sure, she approached the green truck and extended a hand. "My name's Paige and that's Nadya. I'd ask you in, but that's not such a good idea."

Glancing to the door through which Nadya had already disappeared, he said, "John Waggoner. Ask anyone in town and they'll tell you I ain't about to hurt you. Whatever you're protecting in there, it's safe with us."

"I'm sure it is, John. I appreciate the help. Is there a way I can get in touch with you?"

"We'll swing by here in an hour or so. If that throw-down out there gets worse, it may take a little longer. There are other folks in town we need to check on. Any chance we could send some stragglers this way?"

Waggoner was no Skinner. His palms were rough and callused, but not scarred. Although she'd had her notions about the bow slung across his shoulder, that wasn't a Skinner weapon either. It was too smooth to have ever changed shape, and the handle was made for comfort instead of drawing the blood of its owner.

"Yeah," Paige said. "If anyone needs to come here, send them over. Just tell them not to be alarmed with what may greet them."

"Are you sure about that?" Nadya asked quietly.

Patting her arm, Paige watched the men in the pickups. "Just have your stragglers mention my name if you come back and they should at least get shelter. Still, we're kind of in a bad spot right now."

"Understood," Waggoner said with a nod. "Paige, right?"

"Yep."

"Appreciate the help. We'll swing by later to check in on you." With that, he slapped the side of the truck and motioned for the driver to get moving. Both vehicles rolled away, gunning their engines as they were almost immediately chased by a pair of wandering Half Breeds.

"You think we'll see them again?" Nadya asked.

"Odds of survival aren't much worse for them than they are for us. Let's just see what we can do for Milosh right now."

Nadya led the way downstairs to the cellar inhabited by the Mongrels. Stopping at the top of the stairs, Paige dug into her pocket for her phone. The device might not have been up to Cole's technical standards, but it was sturdy enough to survive all the bumps it had taken during the last several hours and still let her know she'd missed a call. The number on the caller ID was familiar, so she tapped the screen right away.

"Midwestern Ectological Group, how can—"

Paige interrupted the unfamiliar voice with a bare-bones introduction and an identification number that verified she was one of MEG's "special contacts."

"Hang on," the operator said. "I'm supposed to patch you right through to Stu."

The first voice was replaced by a very familiar one that said, "Paige! Where are you?"

"Oklahoma."

"I knew it! As soon as I heard about the town that was overrun, I knew you'd be in the middle of it! Atoka, right?"

"Yeah," she said. "It's already on the news?"

"Not the major networks, but there's plenty of reports coming in from people taking pictures and videos and whatever else. They're getting squashed by official channels that go pretty high up. Know anything about that?"

"Maybe. I need to get in touch with someone in this area. One of us. And nobody who might be a friend of Rico's."

"You worried about the Vigilant?"

Paige's stomach clenched into a knot. "Who are they?" she asked.

"We've only heard the name once, but several of you guys have been breaking off from us."

"How many?"

"It's hard to say for certain," Stu replied. "There are a few out west who don't normally check in anyways and plenty that never made it onto our list, but they aren't necessarily broken away. Lots more as you head east. We lost track of everyone from Philadelphia and that vicinity. That's about all we've got on them."

"What about anyone in the Oklahoma area? Anyone out here at all? Vigilant or not?" As she waited for Stu to look up the information, her phone beeped. It was another incoming call, but she ignored it since Stu was already pulling up results.

"Sure. There's a small group based in Oklahoma City."

"Is one of them named John Waggoner?" she asked.

"I've only got one name and it's Bill Phillips. You want his number?"

"Just send it to me. I've got to go. Thanks, Stu." Before he could say anything else, she cut the connection. Paige stood at the top of the stairs, listening to what sounded like some very uncomfortable grunts coming from Milosh. Since the noises he made weren't growls or dying breaths, that probably meant he was getting the treatment he needed. The fingers on her right hand tingled, so she flexed them. More than likely she needed to get some preventive medication herself.

The phone rattled in her hand, causing her to twitch. It buzzed once and stopped, and when she looked down she saw Stu's text message passing along Bill Phillips's phone number. That was followed by *U R welcome*.

The next call she made was to a number that wasn't listed in any directory. As far as she knew, it wasn't even supposed to be written down on anything that wasn't set on fire a minute later. After two rings the connection crackled through several layers of electronic security measures and was answered by a curt, "Adderson."

Ignoring the beep of an incoming call, she asked, "Have you heard anything about Cole yet?"

"If you know where he is, then tell me right now!"

She grinned, which was enough of a silent gap to make the man at the other end of the connection nervous.

"Paige!" Adderson barked. "I'm serious. I can't offer any assistance if you don't offer some in return."

She cut the call short with the quick poke of a button. By the time she got to the cot where Milosh was being treated, she was already getting another call. This one she answered right away.

Chapter Fifteen

Three miles north of Westcliffe, Colorado
An hour earlier

Cole and Lambert rode in an old Chevy hatchback they'd stolen not too long ago. Actually, Frank had stolen it. The Squam waited alongside County Road 255 until he spotted a solitary car with no others in sight. Bounding in a loping stride that forced him to lean forward and swat the ground with his hands, he caught up to it, pulled the passenger door open and climbed inside.

Although Cole felt bad for the petrified, twenty-something girl behind the wheel, he had to admit it was one of the coolest things he'd ever seen. He rushed over to the car, pulled the trembling little blonde out through her door and shoved her into the back with Lambert. "Who are you guys?" she screamed. "Please just let me go!"

"Can't do that, darlin'," Lambert said with a slimy grin. "What's yer name, sweetie?"

Cole, behind the wheel and about to look in the purse he'd seen on the passenger seat, snapped his eyes up to the rearview mirror. "Lay off," he said. "We're just getting what we need."

"She likes me."

"No I . . . don't," the girl muttered.

"She likes the bad boys," Lambert said. "Gangsta types. That's what she's thinkin'."

According to what Cole heard, Lambert had been locked up in G7 because he was a mind reader. Judging by the look on the girl's face, he might have struck a nerve. Even so, he told Lambert, "Just watch her. The only time you need to touch her is if she makes a wrong move."

Lambert met his eyes in the rearview mirror. "What do you think I'm gonna do to her? Just because I'm a—"

"Spare me the hurt feelings speech and just watch her!"

"What is that . . . thing?" the girl asked. "The thing that climbed into my car."

Frank was nowhere in sight, but Cole assumed he'd return on his own, as he had before. Instead, he concerned himself with the purse. He took most of the cash as well as a debit card, left the credit cards, and kept digging until he found the girl's cell phone. It was a newer model, wrapped up in a hot pink case with little fake jewels glued around the portrait of a Hollywood pretty boy who'd made a living playing even prettier vampires in a cable television series. "Great," he sighed.

"Let me go," she demanded.

"We're not going to hurt you," he assured her. Tossing the purse on the seat beside him, he put the car in gear and pulled back onto the road. "We just need the car, okay?"

She nodded and wrapped her arms around herself. Lambert stayed on his side of the seat as the car picked up speed. Thanks to the DOOR AJAR light on the dash coming on, Cole knew exactly what the inmate was doing when he lunged across at her. After grabbing her arm, Lambert pulled her away from the door that now swung open. By the time Cole pulled over, Frank had run up close enough to the car to shut the door again. As soon as she saw him, the girl yelped and pressed herself against Lambert.

"See?" the inmate said. "Told ya she liked me."

Cole twisted around and placed his arm across the back of the seat. "I know this is scary," he said to the blonde. "We aren't going to hurt you. Just bear with us and you'll have a hell of a story to tell to your friends."

"Or to the cops," Lambert said. "Or the news. That's what she's thinkin'."

"Could you always read people that easily?" Cole asked.

"Nope. Just when they ain't guarding their brains. Young ones are easier too," he added. "They think they're so smart but . . . Ooooh! That's nasty, girl!"

She scowled at him and grew pale. The combination of fear and excitement in her eyes was close to what Cole had seen on the faces of humans who'd frequented Steph's Blood Parlor and paid for Nymar to feed on them. Apparently, being the food of supernatural predators was still what all the cool kids were doing.

"Hold on to her, Lam," Cole said. "What's your name, miss?"

"Brianne."

"She don't like bein' called miss."

"Yeah," Cole said. "I figured. Okay, Brianne. Just sit tight and we'll let you off the first place we can. Sound good?"

She didn't say anything, but must have been thinking in some pretty colorful terms because Lambert chuckled and shook his head.

Cole kept driving south, simply because that was the easiest way to keep the prison behind them. On all sides there was nothing but flat land covered in dead grass. The air was getting crisper, as if blowing in straight from the top of the distant mountains. Frank bounded ahead of them, scouting for any policemen or roadblocks set up in response to the situation at the prison. Every so often the Squam would show up on the side of the road to wave them along. The next time he showed up, he pointed them toward another highway to avoid a pair of state troopers. Cole drove for another several miles until he caught sight of a billboard advertising a truck stop coming up. Pulling off to the side of the road, he asked, "Have you been able to read Frank?"

"Off and on," Lambert replied. "That's why Waylon forced me to stay so close to him for so long. He wanted to know where the rest of them lizard men were hiding."

"Lizard men?" Brianne squeaked, as if she'd convinced herself the sight of her carjacker had been a bad dream. "Oh God."

"Can he be trusted?"

Lambert screwed his face up into a distasteful frown, but shrugged and replied, "Hasn't dicked us over yet."

Since it had been a while since the last time he saw his

scaly partner, Cole kept his eyes on the shoulder until the Squam bounded into view. He reached for the shotgun he'd tucked near his feet, making sure Brianne saw it as he stepped outside. "Stay put," he told her.

She couldn't take her eyes off the weapon as she nodded meekly.

"What's wrong?" Frank asked as he approached the car. His eyes darted back and forth before focusing on a vehicle approaching from the other lane. He stood closer to Cole and lowered his head so anyone in that dark blue Camry couldn't make out more than the shapes of two men standing beside the hatchback. "We can't stop in plain sight like this."

"I know," Cole replied. "You're taking this girl into those trees and keeping an eye on her."

Frank's brow furrowed. It would have been a menacing expression for anyone his size, but on a man covered in yellow scales with gill flaps along his nose, it was downright chilling. "I won't kill her."

"Damn right you won't. I want you to keep her here while me and Lambert drive ahead to that truck stop. Give us about fifteen minutes to top off the tank and get some supplies and then point her toward the same place. It's only about a mile walk so she should be able to make it."

"And what if she doesn't?" Frank asked. "A pretty girl on her own, walking on a stretch of road, she could get into trouble."

Suddenly, Cole felt bad for bringing the shotgun along. Not only had Frank proven to be nothing but honorable this far, but he seemed more concerned for Brianne's welfare than he himself did. "Then stick with her to make sure she gets there safely. You might want to stay out of sight, though. I think you freak her out."

"I understand."

Cole opened the car and settled behind the wheel. "Hand her off to Frank."

Brianne looked outside and practically jumped into Lambert's arms. "No. No! Please don't!"

"Get out," Cole demanded.

When she looked to him, Lambert said, "You heard the man, sweet stuff."

Somehow, the endearing tone in Lambert's voice seemed more of a motivator than the shotgun in Cole's hands. She kicked the door open. Almost immediately Frank was there to take her hand and help her out. Resigned to her fate, Brianne sobbed to herself and shuffled away.

"How far away can you read someone?" Cole asked.

"Don't know. Depends on if I know them or not."

"What about her? Will you be able to read her from a mile or two down the road?"

"Hell yes. That girl's scared shitless, and not too bright anyways. Makes for a good combo."

"Just let me know if she gets hurt." Grudgingly, Cole drove away. The next time he checked his rearview mirror, Frank and the blonde were already out of sight.

About two minutes later he pulled up to the farthest pump at the truck stop that had been advertised on the billboard.

"Thank Christ," Lambert said. "I gotta take a piss."

"Hold it."

"I can't!"

"You're dressed in a freaking gray jumpsuit. You know what that makes you look like? Someone who escaped from a prison!"

"Fine," Lambert grunted as he unzipped the front of his jumpsuit and rolled down the top portion so it was gathered around his waist to reveal a sweat-stained wife beater similar to the one Frank wore. "Better?"

Cole counted up Brianne's money. She had thirty-eight bucks and the debit card. He handed the cash to Lambert and said, "Get as much food and water as you can with this. Don't attract attention. If there's trouble, run for the highway and I'll pick you up. Come to think of it, wait until I'm done pumping the gas."

"You wanna pump somethin'?" the inmate grunted. "Then follow me into the toilet." With that, he stuffed the cash into his waistband and headed for the main building of the truck stop.

Cole felt a tension in his belly that had nothing to do with the tendrils wrapped around his guts as he slid Brianne's debit card through the reader on the pump. The fact that he was probably being taped by a security camera didn't bother him, since stealing a tank of gas barely qualified as legal trouble anymore. He was more concerned that the card would be denied for some reason. It wasn't, so he topped off the tank. By the time he was done, Lambert still hadn't shown up. Cole couldn't see any signs of a commotion through the front window of the truck stop, so he pulled off to another parking space and dug out the phone from where he'd tucked it away.

Before he touched a single button, he reminded himself that it wasn't his phone. Considering what had happened, it was more than likely that the cops or somebody would be monitoring calls made on Waylon's line. Even if they didn't do so now, the records would be there if anyone decided to do it later.

"God damn it," Cole grumbled as he chucked the phone out the window.

His luck changed for the better when he found three folded ones and about four more dollars in change stuffed into Brianne's ashtray. Since Lambert still hadn't reappeared, he walked up to a bank of three pay phones outside the building. Peeking in past a faded cardboard advertisement for Ding Dongs in the window, he saw cash registers, soda machines, snack bars, showers, a metric ton of unhealthy snack foods, and a line for the restrooms. Scraping up enough cash to make a call had been fortunate. Discovering even one of those phones to be in working order was something close to a miracle. He dialed a number from memory and got an answer right away.

"Midwestern Ectological Group, this is Stu."

"Hey! I was hoping I wouldn't have to get transferred a hundred times to get ahold of you."

"Cole? Is that you?"

"Yep." Before he could say another word, the connection crackled and there were several clicks that made him wonder if he'd been disconnected. Since his legal troubles were extraordinary even for a member of a group with rampant issues at the moment, it could also have been a new MEG policy where Skinners were concerned.

When Stu's voice returned, it was a little tinnier, but twice as excited. "Can you hear me okay?"

"Yes."

"I'm using some new equipment that should make certain nobody's listening in on us."

"Are your phone lines being tapped?" Cole asked.

"I don't know, but with all that's been going on, we figured a little extra security wouldn't hurt. Where the hell are you, man?"

"Did you hear about what happened in Colorado?"

"Of course I heard!" Stu said. "It's all over the news! When they're not showing clips of those two things running away from all that wreckage, they're comparing it to archive footage from K.C. The video is still coming in. It's shaky and doesn't really show a lot as far as those creatures are concerned, but the online footage is impressive. I don't know who leaked it, but it's like a damn movie! Cops are shooting and running around a bunch of trashed cars, with the prison walls crumbling behind them and those two big guys just turn into some kind of four-legged bear things and jump completely out of the frame. Epic!"

Cole couldn't exactly hold it against Stu for getting so excited. Considering the MEG guys spent most of their time sifting through black and white footage of empty rooms or surveillance videos of supposed Bigfoot sightings, actual recordings of werewolves fleeing the scene of a major attack was bigger than a jackpot. It was hitting the cryptozoological Power Ball.

"Is that all the video there was?" Cole asked. "Just those two running away?"

Stu's voice dropped as if he was on the razor's edge of squealing with glee. "Do you have anything else for us? I mean, you were there in the middle of it, right?"

"Yeah."

"I knew that wasn't you wrapped up in that trial!"

"What trial?" Cole asked as a new urgency rushed through him.

"The trial in the news. There's reports of you being put on trial for what happened to those cops, but no footage. Just a lot of talk about court dates, testimony, and you being held in federal custody until you're put in front of a judge. That's all crap, though, right?"

"Look," Cole said impatiently, "whatever's on the news, whatever's on the Internet, whatever's being gossiped about or shown on TV, it just doesn't matter anymore. I need a favor."

"Wait a second. If you're not in prison and you're not surrounded by cops, does that mean you're running from those things that were on TV? Were those Full Bloods?"

"No, I'm not in prison, and yes, those were Full Bloods." Before Stu launched into an overexcited meltdown, Cole asked, "Do you know where Paige is?"

"Oh! I just talked to her! She's in Oklahoma! *That's* a whole other story! Wait'll you hear this!"

Cole looked inside for Lambert and found him sniffing around the snack food aisle. "No time for stories," he said. "I need to get in touch with some Skinners in the area, and since Paige isn't nearby, I need someone who's close and can get to me real fast. Can you do this now or should I give you some time?"

"I can call three more people, balance my checkbook, and play some *War Mutant* co-op online while talking to you."

"*War Mutant*?" Cole scoffed. "You're into that game? I thought you had taste."

"Just because it's not from Digital Dreamers doesn't mean it's bad. Besides, the new patch they just released fixed a lot of those matchmaking issues."

More than once Cole had entertained the idea of going back to Seattle and trying to reclaim his position at Digital Dreamers, Inc. After all that had happened recently, he'd be lucky if Jason would ever talk to him again. For now, he could only indulge in some quick geeky banter. Suddenly, even that felt strange. It was like putting on an old skin. Those things never fit right and they all stank after being left alone for too long.

As always, Stu had a knack for keeping Cole on his toes. "Did you escape from prison?"

Deciding it would save time if he didn't attempt to deflect that question, Cole said, "Yeah."

"That's so freaking cool! All right. Let me see here." From the other end of the digital connection came the tapping of frantic fingers on a keyboard. Every now and then Stu would mutter to himself, but Cole didn't interrupt the process. Before too long Stu declared, "Found a few that might be what you're after. There's someone named Maddy. Last time she checked in, she'd just flown into Arizona from Jersey."

"Who else? Someone in Colorado or close to it."

"There's some guys who used to work out of Kansas, but they dropped off the grid years ago."

"What do you mean by that?"

"Just what I said," Stu replied. "Not all of you guys report in regularly. Some are real jerks. I don't think they trust us. Anyway, those guys from Kansas aren't a very safe bet but Jessup is usually pretty reliable."

"Jessup? I think I met him in Philly."

"That's the one! He went out there to get what he could from all of that Lancroft loot." After a few more taps Stu added, "Looks like Jessup isn't available or he's outside of coverage. Could be his phone is off. If you've got stuff to do, I can keep trying and let him know you're looking."

"Can you connect me to Paige?" he asked.

"Sure, hang on." After a few seconds Stu returned to say, "Voice mail."

"Call right back. Maybe she'll pick up this time." That was the same trick he had used to get his parents to pick up the phone after they bought their first answering machine.

"I'll dial again," Stu said hesitantly, "but I don't . . . Wait. Someone picked up. Hang on."

Sometimes, even in the era of Smartphones and caller ID, the old tricks were still the best ones.

"Cole!" Paige said excitedly. "Where the hell are you?"

"I'm in Colorado, heading south on Highway 69."

Lambert stepped up to Cole, tapped him on the shoulder and said "The best place to be when you're fucked. Heh heh." When Cole snapped around to look at him, the inmate added, "You know. Fucked . . . sixty-nine. I got the snacks and some clothes." Holding up a bag containing a few Broncos T-shirts, he added, "Clearance sale."

"Hey!" Paige snapped. "Remember me?"

"Yeah. Sorry about that."

"Who's with you?"

"Long story," Cole sighed. "Before I start in on that, I want to know who you handed me over to."

She paused for several heartbeats, and when she spoke again, it was in a voice as quiet as it was tender. Knowing Paige as well as he did, Cole had no doubt the former was to cover up the latter. "I was looking for help while all of that garbage went down with the Nymar. I had to find someone to take some of the pressure off of us because we were getting set up for killing those cops, and I wound up talking to a guy named Adderson. He runs a group that's pulled together from police, feds, and some other law enforcement and media people. They're called the Inhuman Response Division. Bob Stanze hooked me up with them and they seem to know their stuff. There's not enough time to explain it all, but the IRD wants to prepare an armed strike force to be used against Nymar, shapeshifters, and all the other things that have been tearing up every other city lately. I wasn't sure about it, but Adderson said he already had a team working on curing Nymar. After almost losing you to that Shadow Spore, I couldn't pass on a chance to get you fixed up."

Listening to Paige, Cole felt ashamed for all of the terrible things he'd wished upon her when he was in custody or getting beaten to within an inch of his life.

"Adderson believes Skinners weren't killing cops," she continued. "He was supposed to get you out of prison and to someplace where you might get cured. If someone was needed to take the fall for those cop killings to put all of that shit to rest, I was going to be the one. Please believe that, Cole. After I almost—"

Rather than make her relive those moments when she'd thought her only choice was to kill him before he became a full Nymar, Cole said, "I believe you."

"What happened in prison?" Paige asked. "Why were you moved from Canon City?"

"That's another long story," he said.

"Did they cure you?"

"The guys running that place did cut me open. I think they honestly tried to get the tendrils out, but they didn't succeed."

"Damn," Paige sighed.

"They're also not who you think they are, Paige. I don't know if they're the same ones you talked to or someone else, but I wound up in some place run by followers of Jonah Lancroft. They used runes to hide themselves and were ready to cut me to pieces to learn whatever they could."

She pulled in a deep breath. When Paige spoke again, her voice was cold steel. "What did they do to you?"

"Don't worry about it."

"Tell me, God damn it!"

"The place is leveled, Paige. Two Full Bloods got to it and tore it down. One of them was Mr. Burkis. Do you think this Adderson guy knew what was going to happen?"

"No," she said, with some measure of relief in her voice. "I honestly don't. He knew you were taken from the prison in Canon City and was trying to get me to tell him anything I knew about where you'd gone. I seriously don't think he knew where you were."

"Are they Skinners?"

"The IRD?"

"Yeah," Cole said as he looked around. The fact that he'd wound up talking longer than he'd expected, combined with the subject matter, was making him increasingly uncomfortable standing in front of a busy door at a public truck stop. "Are those guys Skinners?"

"No. They barely know the first thing about us, but are plenty eager to learn."

"Well, the guys who held me at the other prison were Skinners. Old school Skinners who knew about the runes. Do you know about a group of Lancroft disciples who have the balls to take over that prison?"

"Holy shit," Paige breathed. The more she spoke, the faster Paige's words came out. "I do. Oh my God, Cole, and I handed you over to them. Oh my God, I'm so sorry." It didn't take her long to collect herself and switch back into business mode. "Do you know about what's going on in Oklahoma?"

"Stu mentioned something. Sounds serious."

"I'm in the middle of it."

"Just you?" he asked.

"No. Me and some of our European friends."

"How bad is it?"

"Bad," she told him. "Looks like this whole town is swarming with Half Breeds. There are at least two Full Bloods here and one of them is Liam. That shapeshifter we met in Denver is there too. The one the Amriany call Ktseena."

Lambert was already in the car and they were quickly approaching Frank's fifteen minute deadline. "I need to find Rico. He's got my weapon."

"Don't contact him." After giving him a brief rundown about what happened in Toronto, she said, "I don't know if he's still thinking he should kill me, but I think it's safe to say he's with the Vigilant. Do you know who they are?"

"I've heard that name before, but don't know a lot of details."

"They're some kind of Lancroft cult. Lots of Skinners looked up to that old man, and many still do. Just don't contact Rico, okay? And don't send word to MEG about where you are. There's no telling if or how far the Vigilant have infiltrated them."

When Paige stopped, there was only silence on the line.

He prayed she couldn't sense the tension that had clenched his eyes shut or caused his lips to form silent obscenities.

"Cole? You didn't already call MEG, did you?"

"Maybe."

Instead of the unholy tirade he'd expected, she only took a long, measured breath before saying, "We're on our own now. Don't call MEG again. Don't go anywhere you've used as a home base before. The Full Bloods are converging here for some reason, and I don't know how many more will be coming. There's already one that I've never seen before."

"Have you heard them talking about something called the Breaking Moon?"

Paige chuckled into the phone. Although her breath made a scratchy bit of static as it hit her speaker, he savored the moment as much as he could. It was the closest thing to touching her that he could hope for.

"All they're talking about out here," she told him, "is how badly they want to rip us up. One of the new Full Bloods did mention the Breaking. She told me to enjoy mine. Since it was after she tore the hell out of me, I'm guessing it could be what they call transforming someone into a Half Breed."

"Shit!"

"Don't worry," she said before he could get even more worked up. "I'm getting patched up right now. Our Euro pals brought supplies we needed, and by the look of things, the stuff works faster than what we whip up. I'll have to get the recipe."

Cole couldn't understand the language that drifted in from somewhere beyond Paige, but it had the same feel as the Amriany dialect. Judging by the venom in the woman's tone, she wasn't too anxious to swap medical tips with a Skinner. "I should get going," Paige said. "Lots of work to do. Do you think Tristan will follow through on her promise to help transport you somewhere safe if you needed it?"

"That was before the legal trouble, but I may be able to wrangle something. She does owe us big-time."

"You're damn right she does," she snapped. "Call her and set something up if you can. If not, just try to get someplace where you can stay alive."

"No!" The word came out of him as if it had been squeezed up from his ankles. He winced at how much noise he'd made, but continued in a determined whisper. "This is my fight too, remember?"

"You've been through more than anyone. I made the mistake of trusting someone too soon and nearly lost you. I thought you were dead," she stated in her steely tone. "I won't hand you over again."

"I was unconscious most of the time," Cole said with a forced, unconvincing chuckle. "From what I've heard about prison life, that's a good way to go. Randolph told me some things."

"Randolph, huh?" Paige grunted. "No more Mr. Burkis?"

"That's one of his names, and I'm sticking to it, okay?" In a strange way, squabbling with her again made Cole feel better than any amount of food he could smell whenever someone opened the door to the truck stop. It filled him up, heart and soul. Knowing better than to get that corny with her, he said, "You've got your thing going on in Oklahoma and there's something going on here as well. Since they've both got Full Bloods attached to them, I think our things are connected."

"Insert dirty joke here," Paige said. "Before I let you go, I think we should consider something."

"What?"

"That we may need all the help we can get," Paige said with a wince Cole could feel through the phone line. "Lancroft worshippers or not."

Cole ground his teeth together hard enough that he thought the sound might have carried through the phone line.

"If these guys are all like the ones that took me from Canon City," he said, "they pride themselves on being the ultimate Skinners or something. They were getting slaughtered when I left that place."

"But they've got to be preparing something against what's happening. At the very least, they've got more people to stand against these things."

"Cannon fodder," he said. "I like the sound of that. Too bad Rico's still got my weapon."

"You can make a new one. Are you okay?"

The change in her voice was subtle, but Cole picked up on it without a problem. For Paige, the absence of that edge to her tone was no small thing. "I'm better now that I'm out of that prison. What about you?"

"In the middle of a freaking meat grinder. Don't know if I'll live to see the next hour. Same as always."

"Good to hear it," he said with a tired laugh. "I'll call you when I can."

"Ring once and hang up, then call me right back. That way I'll know it's you."

"Old school. My grandma used that one for us to let her know we got home safe after Christmas."

"Mine too. Just sit tight, baby."

Cole was still recoiling from that last word when the connection was cut. Did Paige just call him baby or was something garbled along the line between Colorado and Oklahoma? Unable to think of any profanities that would have fit at the end of her sentence that could have been mistaken for "baby," he hung up and hurried to the car.

"Can you still read that girl?" he asked Lambert.

"Yeah. She's by herself and thinking of all the nasty things she wants to do to our balls with a hammer. Other than that, she's fine."

"I'm circling back to make sure she's all right, then we're getting out of here."

"Any way I can convince you to just drive before we're spotted or picked up?"

"Nope," Cole replied. "Buckle up."

Chapter Sixteen

There was a campsite about five miles west of Walsenburg, over twenty miles from the truck stop where Lambert had picked up their supplies and clothing. It was a nice, scenic area with two lakes nearby and plenty of spots for families to set up their tents or park their campers. Cole wanted to get farther away from Canon City, but Jessup had insisted they meet at the motel near Lake Meriam. Too tired to argue, Cole removed the license plates from the hatchback, parked on an access road, and stayed close enough to the nearby families to avoid too much suspicion. He and Lambert changed their clothes and Frank slipped into the lake itself, where he settled in like a rock and didn't come up again.

"Good," Lambert grunted. "Hope he drowns."

"Any reason for that or are you just being an asshole?"

After a brief consideration, Lambert shrugged. "Just bein' an asshole I guess."

"Fine. Pass me those beef sticks."

They changed into their new clothes, rinsed the old ones in the modest restroom facilities, and more important, Cole was able to take a shower. The stalls were basically cement closets with little hot water and a curtain that wasn't large enough to fully cover the opening, but the running water was a blessing. The only thing that felt better was being able to lay down in the backseat of the hatchback and catch some sleep. He and Lambert traded lookout duty, tapping the glass to wake the other one up if anyone official-looking came around to look at the car. It wasn't until the following morning that they had to do anything more than take a walk to avoid campground police.

"Fuck," Lambert snarled as he watched a man in a brown uniform take a notepad from his pocket. When he bent to look at the car's plates and found only empty bumper space, Lambert hissed, "We should take that guy out."

"Right. That's so much better than letting him go through the motions of reporting an abandoned car. He may not even file that report for hours. We'll be gone by then."

After the uniformed man moved on, Cole and Lambert drove a little farther down the road to a motel overlooking the modest lake. Since he didn't have any more money or anything else of value tucked away inside his dirty prison-issue clothing, his only option was to use Brianne's debit card again. He'd spotted her along the side of the road when he went back to check after leaving the truck stop the previous day, and Lambert couldn't pick up any deception when Frank made his report, so there was every reason to believe that the police had been notified about her encounter with the escaped prisoners. That was why they'd slept in the car, which didn't seem as attractive now that Jessup still hadn't showed up.

When he spotted a man in a rumpled business suit stepping out of a room on the back side of the motel, he looked over at Lambert and said, "Stay here. I'll take this guy."

"What for?" Lambert asked. "Let's just sit tight until that friend of yours gets here. Hell, we could just walk around until he gets here. Worst comes to worst, we drive away."

"No," Cole snapped. "We need another place to wait before someone starts asking too many questions. The car's been reported stolen, so we should ditch it. We need a place to stay until Jessup gets here. We take this guy's room and keep him here for no more than a day, sleep on a real bed, maybe catch up on some news."

"We're on the run, buddy," Lambert said. "That kinda means we gotta rough it."

"If this doesn't work, then drive away. Just don't bother coming back to ask for more help, and good fucking luck convincing Frank to go with you." With that, Cole stormed out of the car and headed across the parking lot. Even as he strode toward the man in the rumpled suit, he replayed Lambert's words in his head. They made sense. A lot more sense than what he was about to do. If only good sense could cause the cinching pain in his gut to subside. Either they'd burned through the blood he'd taken from Chop or they were becoming something more than just remains of a dead spore, because he could feel them slicing into his stomach and along the upper portion of his throat.

The man in the business suit looked at him suspiciously and quickened his steps toward a tan car with a sticker on its bumper bearing the name of a rental company. He had keys in hand, flipped through them and found the one that would unlock the trunk.

As Cole got closer, the pain inside his throat cut even deeper, until he could feel a jabbing ache reach up to the back of his eyes.

"Back off, guy," the man in the business suit said while taking a defensive posture near the open trunk. When Cole kept coming, the man reached in past a suitcase to a tire iron strapped to the spare.

Cole slapped the keys from his hand and grabbed him by the neck. The man had gotten to the tire iron and barely pulled it from the trunk before Cole slammed the back of his head against the edge of the trunk lid. When he placed both hands around the man's neck, he felt strong enough to push his thumbs all the way through to his spine.

"Don't have to . . . do this," the man croaked. "Take . . . car. Money. Take it."

Cole eased up for a second and looked around. The door to the guy's room was held open by another suitcase, so he dragged the man away from the car and marched inside. Like any of a hundred rooms he'd rented over the years, there was a TV on a long dresser to his right, table and chairs to the left, and a bed farther in on that same side. Directly ahead was a mirror, sink, and foldable luggage rack. The bathroom was to the left, in the rear corner of the room. While shoving the guy toward the bathroom, Cole made the mistake of letting his eyes linger on the mirror.

The reflection wasn't the one he was used to.

It wasn't inhuman, but wasn't anything he'd seen before.

What rattled him most was the hunger written across his face. A minute ago he was hurting, tired, hunted, and close to panic, but the same man he'd always been. The thing staring back at him now was ruled by a lingering presence that tightened until he thought his insides would rupture. Was this what the Nymar felt? Did it make a difference?

Someone stepped into the room. "Just stay back, Lam," Cole snarled. "I need to do this."

"What in the hell are you doing to that fella?"

The voice wasn't Lambert's and it wasn't Frank's. It came from a big man wearing a leather vest that rattled noisily as he stepped into the room and shut the door behind him. In one hand he carried a bulky revolver, and the other was wrapped around the wooden handle of a small hatchet. Cole's eyes fixated on the blood dripping from the hatchet handle. Part of his brain was relieved to see the sign of another Skinner, but the rest could only long to taste the drops that hit the carpet.

"Who the hell are you?" Cole demanded.

The man in the vest rushed up to Cole to place the edge of his tomahawk against his neck and crack the side of his pistol against the temple of the man in the suit, who'd been knocked out by a hatchet blow to the head. "Show me your hands, boy."

Cole lowered the suited man to the floor. "Jessup?"

"That's right. Ain't seen you since you threw that yard sale at the Lancroft house."

"You blew that place up, right?"

Jessup's laugh sounded like it had been dragged over broken glass and doused in Southern Comfort. "Ain't no better way to close down a yard sale. Who's that fella down there?"

The hatchet blow had opened a gash on the side of the unconscious man's head, but it wasn't anything serious.

"He's one of the Shadow Spore," Cole bluffed while dragging the guy toward the bathroom.

"Yeah," Jessup said. "I heard of them. Even took out a few dozen up in Montana, but they still wound up taking Helena and a few other cities. He must be a new one, though, since he still hasn't shown any markings yet."

Cole looked down. The unconscious businessman lay in a section of the room just dark enough to have brought out the tendrils of a true Shadow Spore. The teeth woven into the leather cords on Jessup's vest rattled as he stepped up to place the barrel of his .48 holdout revolver against the base of Cole's neck. The gun moved down just enough to lower Cole's collar and expose the jagged black lines that snaked up from where the tendrils inside him were nestled.

"Shit," Jessup growled. "You've been turned?"

Cole's jaw tensed, and when he pried it open, he found his tongue darting out to brush along the edges of his teeth. There were no fangs and no spore connected to his heart to make them grow. There were only the shredded tendrils attached to him, instinctually slicing into his digestive tract like piano wire. Instinct, much like the sudden irresistible force that had brought him to the point of terrorizing an innocent man like just another one of the bloodsucking assholes he was supposed to hunt. "I'm not a Nymar," he said.

Keeping the gun pressed against Cole's chest, Jessup raised his hatchet and said, "I heard about what happened to you."

"From who?"

"Rico."

"That asshole tried to kill Paige," Cole replied. "He's a fucking traitor!"

"At least he ain't a Nymar. Show me your scars." When he didn't get a response, Jessup thumbed his hammer back. "Don't make me ask again."

Cole recognized the look of a hunter preparing to kill its prey. Straightening up to his full height, he held up the hand that had previously been wrapped around the businessman's neck and showed his scarred palm to Jessup. Almost immediately Jessup eased the .48's hammer down and stuffed the gun into the holster clipped to his belt.

"See there?" Jessup said. "Just what I hoped. You're a Skinner."

"No I'm not," Cole sighed. "This Nymar shit's got a hold of me."

"But you're *not* a Nymar. You *can't* be turned."

Shaking his head, Cole felt the pain in his throat lessen while the cinching inside him became worse. "It's the Shadow Spore. It can take root in a Skinner."

"Sure it can. I've seen it happen to the rest of the Skinners in Helena."

Cole's head snapped up. Even though he thought he'd had a good grip on a bad situation, it had suddenly gotten worse.

Jessup nodded. "Oh yeah. It took some doing and surprised the holy hell outta me, but it happened. Some multi-seeded bitch made the rounds and infected as many of us as she could. Those other Skinners got sick, tried to fight it off, but they were lost before we could do much about it. Soon as they sprouted fangs, their scars healed up. Don't know if the spore was clearin' out what it thought was an infection or that was its way of wiping out every bit of Skinner that was in 'em, but it happened across the board. It didn't happen to you, so you still got a chance."

"But you just said I can't be turned," Cole pointed out.

"That's what you need to keep tellin' yerself the next time you get an urge like the one you got here," Jessup replied while nodding down at the unconscious businessman. "Just because those bloodsuckers infected you don't mean you need to give in to it."

"It . . . hurts," Cole said through gritted teeth. Ashamed by hearing himself say those words, he walked away from the man on the floor.

Jessup didn't miss a beat before kneeling down to the businessman. "You know what'll hurt worse? When I jam this hatchet through your chest like I did to the folks in Helena who used to be Skinners."

Before that had a chance to sink in, Lambert shouted from the parking lot. It was an excited yelp, followed by the slap of hurried footsteps that brought the inmate to the door of the motel room. "This asshole kidnapped a girl!"

"What?" Cole asked.

Jessup stomped across the room toward the door. Although Lambert steeled himself to stand in his way, he changed his mind when he saw the tomahawk clutched in Jessup's fist.

"Did she get away?" Jessup asked. After shoving Lambert aside, he started cursing in a raspy snarl.

"Check that," Lambert said. "He didn't kidnap her. Just hunted her down . . . again."

"What are you?" Jessup grunted. "Psychic?"

"Yeah."

"Then tell me which way she went."

Lambert screwed his face into a defiant, jailhouse sneer and looked to Cole. "Remember that young one the Full Blood was talking about? That's her."

"Take the car and get out of here," Cole said to the inmate.

The older man seemed to be favoring his left leg, but that turned into a more pronounced limp as Jessup circled around to the driver's seat of a pickup truck parked next to the businessman's car. "Best get out of town altogether," he said. "No tellin' if those cameras are workin' or who was watching when this one here decided to assault a paying customer."

Cole looked up and around to find a few clunky surveillance cameras mounted to the corner of the overlap of the motel's roof. Not even the painful hunger he'd been feeling was a good enough excuse for that kind of recklessness. Tossing the car keys to Lambert, he grabbed the passenger door of the pickup that was still swinging on its hinges.

"Where the hell am I supposed to go?" Lambert asked.

Before Cole could come up with something, Jessup said, "Raton. It's about two hours from here, just across the New Mexican border. Just take 69 to I-25 and head south."

Chapter Seventeen

Jessup's pickup was a Ford. If Cole had missed the emblem on the front or the back of the vehicle, he still would have gleaned that fact from the Ford mud flaps, Ford visor, and air freshener that dangled from the rearview mirror. There was a passenger seat directly behind him that was piled high with tackle boxes, tool kits, and rifle cases that Cole guessed contained much more than tackle, tools, and rifles. Because of the air freshener, he could smell a touch of pine mixed in with the pungent varnish used to treat Skinner weaponry. Ford pine.

"What's so funny?" Jessup asked from behind a wheel that was wrapped in a leather cover emblazoned with faded oval symbols.

Cole sat on the far end of the bench seat, with maps, atlases, and several spiral notebooks sandwiched between him and the other Skinner. His arm rested on the edge of the door, hanging partially out of the lowered window. It was getting dark, so the air was cooling down considerably. The more that blew across his face, the wider he smiled. "Nothing's funny," he replied. "I just never thought a Skinner could afford to be a germaphobe."

Jessup turned to look at Cole as if he didn't realize he was pushing the gas pedal down almost far enough for the truck to fly into orbit. The bottom portion of his face was covered by what looked to be an old surgical mask tied around his neck and ears by elastic bands. "Germ a what?"

"What's the deal with the mask?"

Jessup looked at the road and then leaned over to stick his face partially out the window. As soon as he leaned back in, he slammed his foot on the brake and twisted the wheel to send the truck into a controlled spin that pointed its nose back toward a dirt road leading away from Highway 69. "Here," he said while removing the mask and tossing it over to Cole. "See for yerself."

With the mask resting in the palm of his hand, the next logical thing for Cole to do was place it on the spot on his face where it was meant to go. Before it got close enough to touch his nose, his sinuses were flooded to capacity. The scents were pleasant at first. Trees, fresh air, oil from the truck, mildew from old lawn furniture that had been dumped on the side of the road about a hundred yards back, even the gritty scent of dirt—all of it washed through him like a torrent. It wasn't long before the combined odors were enough to make him pull the mask away.

"Takes some gettin' used to, don't it?" Jessup asked.

"What the hell is this thing?"

"Something I put together with a little help from a certain dead asshole we've both heard about."

"Lancroft?"

Jessup nodded. "That's one of 'em, but not the one I meant. I helped myself to plenty while we were all sifting through that house in Philadelphia, but I was more interested in the things that nobody else knew quite what to do with. I've always been a tracker. I love getting my boots dirty while everyone else taps away at their keyboards and checks phone records."

"Who do you know that could check phone records for us?" Cole asked. "That would be great!"

"Nobody. That's the point. When the power goes out or if you're too far away to get a damn signal, all of you techie dickheads are helpless. But that ain't the case for someone who knows their craft all the way down to the bone. That mask you're holding there is the best thing I ever done. The main ingredient comes from the other dead asshole with whom you're very well acquainted."

"Don't make me guess," Cole said.

"In case you don't remember Henry, he's the Full Blood

that happened to disappear on your watch, and don't tell me you don't know where that body's buried."

"Let's not get into that right now."

After taking a moment to steer around a pothole resembling a crack in the earth's crust, Jessup let the matter drop. "So I found a box Lancroft had in cold storage, locked away in that secret lab of his where he did all his cuttin'."

Just mentioning that room flooded Cole's mind with memories of stark white lighting, dissection tables, and a carcass that was pulled apart and held open by metal studs screwed into a chrome tabletop.

"Everyone already helped themselves to all the Full Blood spit, blood, fur, and what-have-you," Jessup continued, "but left some of the more interesting bits for me. At first I thought I'd found some kind of paste smeared onto a plastic sheet. Then I saw it was a membrane Lancroft had removed and preserved. Removed," he added with a wink, "from Henry's nasal cavity."

Cole held up the mask. "This is the inside of a werewolf's nose?"

"I don't know if that's exactly where it's from or if it's from deeper inside his misshapen dome, but yeah. Lancroft didn't know what to do with it, but I did. It took some tricky work with preservatives and a lot of playing around with the mixture that we use to bond our weapons to us, but I got the damn thing to do something besides make my nose burn when I breathed through it. Long story short, I dumbed down our bonding agent to bridge the gap between humans and Full Bloods, sewed what was left of the membrane into that mask, and voilà! Portable Wolf Nose! Patent pending."

Turning the mask over a few times, Cole said, "This could be huge! You bridged the gap between humans and Full Bloods? Do you know what that could mean for the ink Paige came up with?"

"You mean the stuff that screwed up her arm?" Wincing almost in time with Cole, he quickly added, "No, this was just a real simple tweak that barely worked. I wouldn't trust it on anything that actually goes inside of you or mingles with blood. What I need you to do is see if you can pick up our young one's scent."

"We've already gone a few miles," Cole pointed out. "Are you sure it was in the right direction?"

A sly grin eased onto Jessup's face. "This ain't the first time she tried to bolt. She's new to this, so she sticks to the roads. Just see if you can narrow it down for me."

Cole raised the mask to his face again but was cautious about drawing another breath. When he did, he was once more besieged by smells from every end of the spectrum, ranging from the candy bars piled on the dashboard to a mound of animal scat somewhere in the field outside. "How the hell did you use this to find anything specific? Do you mix in something to help weed everything else out?"

"Nope. Just good old-fashioned discipline. Concentrate on what you're after and focus. Helps to have a sample, but most of the stuff we're after is pretty distinctive. Turn your head that way and see for yourself."

Jessup pointed toward the road, and when Cole did as he'd been told, he was introduced to a new scent that easily superseded the others. It was a mixture of animal musk, something that might have been perfume, and another odor he couldn't identify. He pulled in a slow, deep breath and let it roll down his throat like a sip of wine. It wasn't perfume, but the flowery smell did have an artificial taint. The other scent was pungent and exotic, interesting and bitter, enticing and repellent.

"You smell her?" Jessup asked. "She's either wearing some sort of girly lotion or has been using it long enough to stick with her, but the main thing I followed was that scent of fungus and ripe fruit."

"Is that what it is?"

"That lotion or whatever smells artificial. There's something else that I don't really know how to describe. It's natural, but not like any nature I ever smelled. That's the scent of a Full Blood. From what I've heard, those eye drops Ned whipped up are better at close range, but this here mask can find scents that've been laying around for days or maybe longer."

"And you're sure it's a Full Blood?" Cole asked.

"Met up with a whole mess of Shunkaws in Kansas where that little girl out there damn near ripped my head off. Her and another Full Blood jumped me, so I got their scents up close and a little too personal. Followed it all the way to where that girl was hiding, filthy, on all fours, clawin' at the ground. And I don't mean in the good way."

"Lambert said she was just a kid."

Still wearing the fraction of a smile he'd put on for the benefit of his last joke, Jessup shook his head and told him, "He's got that right. *Was* a kid, but not anymore. That girl is wilder than the other Full Bloods I've ever seen, and lately I've seen a whole lot of them. Since she barely seems comfortable in her own skin, I tend to believe what I was told about her bein' nothin' but a pup."

Cole tentatively placed the mask to his face and drew a breath. It took a lot of effort to sift through the scents, but the task kept him busy enough to get his mind off the gnawing pain in his stomach. He leaned out the window and then settled back into his seat. Pointing ahead and to the right, he said, "I think she's headed that way."

"That's about what I thought. I made camp a few miles off-road."

"Another camp?" Cole asked.

"What's the matter? You'd rather take your chances in that small town after word spreads about the guy you attacked in that motel? Besides, cities ain't safe for us no more." He eased up on the gas and steered toward the shoulder of the dirt road. The truck clambered over the rougher terrain, causing both men to clear their seats with every other bounce. "She's still skittish about the whole transformation thing. Either that or she's bashful. Whichever it is, she don't like bein' too far away from her clothes. I think you and I might be okay with her, but I didn't want to scare her by bringin' much of anyone else. That's why I sent your friend away."

"Fine by me. I don't mind the break."

Ahead of the truck Cole saw a clearing that was barely the size of an overturned refrigerator and a camper parked amid some tall weeds. It was the smaller kind of camper that was towed instead of driven. A cooler and some duffel bags lay just outside the little clearing where a slender girl sat on something, her back hunched and her hands clasped between her knees. The burning in Cole's palms confirmed she was a Full Blood. Either that or there was another werewolf lurking nearby. Once the truck came to a stop, he asked, "Where did you find her?"

"She and another Full Blood attacked me in Kansas."

"And why is she sitting at your camp now?"

Her eyes took on a brilliant, otherworldly shine as she looked at Jessup. The older Skinner met them when he said, "The other Full Blood told me to watch out for her."

"Was he the big bastard who killed Gerald?"

"From what I heard . . . yeah. That's the one."

"And why would you listen to him?"

"I don't know. Why would you?" Smirking at the response that got from Cole, Jessup added, "I was wearing that mask when I pulled up to the motel, just to make sure you weren't part of another Nymar trap. I can smell the Full Blood on you. Were you attacked too?"

"Sort of. He told me I needed to find the young one and hide her away."

"Sounds familiar," Jessup said. "Why do you believe him?"

"First of all, because he didn't kill me. And second," Cole added as he handed the mask back to Jessup, "because he made more sense than the last batch of Skinners I met. How screwed up is that?"

"The way things are goin', it sounds about right. That girl's gettin' spooked. Let's have a word with her before she decides to run off again." Jessup pushed open the door and held up his hands to show them to the girl sitting in the small clearing.

She had long, thick hair that was blacker than charred coal. Watching both of the Skinners with crystalline hazel eyes, she said, "Don't kill me. Please. Randolph said you people could help me. I don't want it to hurt me again."

"What's your story?" Cole asked.

Rubbing her hands against her elbows, the girl lowered her head and pressed her arms against her chest. "It hurts."

"What does?"

She was quiet, so Jessup explained, "She means the transformation. It still hurts when she does it."

"Not just that," she said. "Whatever is inside me hurts. Like, all the time. And it only stops hurting when I change and hurt other people."

The tendrils wrapped around Cole's guts squeezed him a little tighter, as if to remind him of some common ground he shared with this girl. Still, no matter how badly he wanted to sympathize, every Skinner part of him thing wanted to see if a shotgun blast would do any better on a Full Blood in its human form. "At least tell me your name."

"Cecile."

She looked to be somewhere in her early teens. Her clothes were a tattered mess, but no more so than those worn by other girls who strove for a "ghetto chic" look. The muddy stains, however, looked like they'd come from being buried in a pile of dirt. Her body was lean and muscular, but she still held herself as though she was nothing more than a child who was still afraid of the dark.

"What do you want from us, Cecile?"

"She's in trouble and needs to be hid," Jessup said. "Ain't that right?"

"You're the one driving around with an arsenal, and *I'm* the one in trouble?" she scoffed.

"You're a Full Blood, girl," Jessup replied. "You can run laps around this state in the time it takes me to scratch my ass. You can go anywhere you like and chew a hole through the side of a bank vault, but you decide to stick with a pair of Skinners. You gotta know what we skin, right?"

"Yeah. Randolph told me."

"So what's your story, girl?"

When he got a questioning glance from Cole, Jessup shrugged and told him, "We made the drive all the way from Kansas, but I spent most of it either talking to myself or chasing her down when she decided to run away."

"I didn't mean to run away," she said, fatigue weighing down every syllable. Clawing at her midsection as if she wanted to tear it out, she went on, "It's hard for me to hold it back. I try, but sometimes I just can't."

Full Blood or not, Cecile was confused, shell-shocked and overwhelmed by what was going on around her. Cole knew just how she felt. "Take it easy," he said while placing one

Skinners: The Breaking

hand on the girl's trembling back. "Just take a few breaths and maybe you'll feel better."

She shook her head slowly as she said, "I'm . . . I'm a werewolf. That's not going to get any better."

"Is this a new thing?"

She looked at him with a fear in her eyes he frequently saw in other people, but wasn't supposed to be pointed at him. "You're Skinners," she said. "You kill werewolves."

"Sometimes," Cole said with a smirk. "Never a Full Blood, though. I'm not good enough for that." Before Jessup had a chance to speak for himself, he added, "Neither of us is. Besides, do you really think we want to kill you?"

"I guess not."

"So tell me how you got pulled into all of this."

Cecile's eyes glazed over as if she was looking at something else instead of the tall grass and water cooler in front of her. "I changed for the first time . . . I don't even know how long ago. He was there when I did."

"Who was?"

"He told me his name was Randolph Standing Bear." Cecile wrapped her arms even tighter around her legs and started rocking. "One night I was sleeping in my room. My brother was in the other bed. Dad was in his room. I woke up screaming. My whole body hurt. Then . . . I changed. I thought it was a nightmare, but he told me it wasn't."

"Randolph told you that?" Cole asked.

"Yeah. He was there. Watching me. He said I had to leave my home and go with him. He changed too and I went with him." Lowering her head while steeling herself, she added, "I guess I still thought it was a dream."

"What did he want from you?"

"He said he had to take me away before the others found me. Said I needed to figure out what I was before the others tried to teach me the wrong way. Said I needed to learn how to change, how to hunt, how to kill, how to do everything my instincts told me to do." Looking up at Cole with eyes that had become multifaceted jewels, she told him, "When I changed for the first time on my own, I was hungry. I chased down whatever I could find and ripped it apart." The jewels embedded in her eye sockets lost some of their luster, until they were merely the soft, wet orbs through which every human saw their world. "Or maybe that was a dream too."

"What about your family?" Cole asked. "Do you want to get back to them?"

Her eyes narrowed, and although she didn't change form, the beast rose close enough to the surface for aspects of it to be seen around the edges of her face and in subtle changes of musculature. "They're dead. Randolph told me and I believe him. Even if they weren't dead before, they wouldn't have lasted long once the others came."

Cecile pulled in a breath, placed her chin flat against the tops of her knees and stared straight ahead. Blinking once, she said, "When we killed those men in Billings, Randolph broke my arm and put something inside." Looking up at the men as if she could sense the reflexive anger that had come over them, she added, "Not like that. He never touched me that way. I mean inside as in . . . inside the wounds. Inside my bones."

"Inside your bones?" Cole asked.

"What men in Billings?" Jessup snarled.

Cecile stretched out her left arm and twisted it to display the veins running along the inside of her wrist. "He broke my arm there. Pulled it apart and . . ." She paused as if to consider if that was another of her dreams, but gave up on that right away. "It healed up right away. After I changed back again, there wasn't even a scar."

Jessup grabbed her by the shoulders and turned her to face him. "What men in Billings?" he demanded.

"They were in the back of some bar," she said. "They tried to kill us, but we tore them apart."

"What did they look like?" Jessup asked.

"They weren't like me or Randolph, but they had fangs," she said. "They fought back more than the first ones we killed."

"They had fangs? What else?"

"Fangs and . . . I don't know. It all seems so hazy." One blink was all it took for her focus to go away from him and to something else. She still faced the Skinners, but wasn't seeing him when she said, "Randolph told me I needed to hunt and I wanted to hunt. Wanted to kill. I . . . think I ate them, and I don't even know if they were animals or . . ." She pulled in a deep breath, gripped her arms and said, "I don't know what I've become, but Randolph keeps telling me it's important."

"That doesn't matter," Cole cut in. He looked at Jessup and asked, "Isn't that right?"

Reluctantly, Jessup nodded. Despite the bravado he'd shown earlier, it seemed the older Skinner was just as tired and ragged as Cole when he said, "Randolph told us to hide you from the other Full Bloods. You remember that part?"

"Yes," she replied.

Walking over to the duffel bags, he rooted through them and started pulling out spare pieces of clothes. He tossed a few shirts and a pair of faded cargo pants over to Cole. "Why haven't you talked about all of this until now?"

"Because Randolph said you might try to kill me," she explained. "Guess you would have tried to by now."

Cole held the clothes in his arms and asked, "What's this?"

"Might as well strap on a set of reflectors if you wanna wear that bright blue Broncos shirt."

"Got any more in there?"

"For that skinny friend of yers? He'll be swimming in them, but yeah."

Cole walked around to stand in the grass a few paces behind Cecile so he could change clothes.

Sitting down so he could stretch out his legs with a labored grunt, Jessup said, "Why don't you get us some food, Cecile?"

"You're sending me away?"

"No. I'm hungry. You and Cole probably are too. There's some PBJ, chips, and some old candy bars inside."

Cecile rolled her eyes, turned her back on the men and walked to the camper.

"All right, then," Jessup said in a low voice that made it clear he knew all too well that a Full Blood could still hear him if he wasn't careful. "What do you think of this?"

Cole's eyes were continually drawn to the other man's vest, partly because of the rattle that accompanied almost every one of his movements. The teeth braided into the fringe looked like melted wax and were sharp enough to double as bullets, which meant they'd been pulled from the mouth of a shapeshifter. "Seems like we should help her. If she's tricking us to get information about the rest of the Skinners, she won't find anything that the Full Bloods must not already know."

Jessup walked back to the bed of his truck and returned with a large overstuffed backpack. While talking to Cole, he removed several see-through bags stuffed with cash consisting of wadded bills and copious amounts of change. "Did you catch what she said about the thing stuffed into her arm?"

"Yeah. What was that?"

"I don't know," Cecile replied while coming out of the camper. She carried two plastic grocery bags to the clearing and set them down. "If I did, I would have told you. I could hear everything you said, by the way."

Cole and Jessup looked at each other, shrugged and sifted through the grocery bags. "Guess you're not as much of a pup as I thought," the older Skinner said.

"I would think the ears start working as soon as they grow in," Cole said as he picked a sandwich, tore open the Baggie and sniffed the crust. The bread was soggy after being in the bottom of that bag for too long, but the jelly was grape, just as God intended.

"You hungry?" Jessup asked Cecile.

"Yes."

He tossed her a sandwich, which she held up to her nose and sniffed. Not interested in whether she liked peanut butter and jelly or not, he asked, "So you don't know what that thing is in yer arm?"

"Nope. Randolph acted like it was special, though. I think it's something he just found."

"Does he ever mention something called a Jekhibar?" Cole asked.

She squinted while gnawing on the Snickers bar she'd found and replied, "I think so. It was while we were changed. so . . ." Rather than say the words, she waved her hand around her head as if she was scrambling her brain.

"Jekhibar?" Jessup asked. "That's an Amriany word."

"Are you sure about that?"

He nodded. "Hell yes. Ever since the Blood Blades came over, I thought it best to read up on the other stuff they've got. The Jekhibar is a Unity Stone."

"What's it do?"

Jessup shrugged and stuffed a quarter of a sandwich into his mouth like a hamster stuffing wadded tissue into its cheeks. "Hell if I know. Ever since these damn Full Bloods have been making their presence felt, all kinds of shit's been turning up. And don't take offense to any of this, girlie. We're talking big picture stuff here."

"You can call me a damn Full Blood all you want," Cecile replied. "Just knock off the girlie crap."

He chuckled and nodded. "Sure thing. Anyways, I thought all the Chupes and Squams and Half Breeds were coming out of the woodwork because they'd been scattered from wherever they were hiding on account of the big bad wolves coming around. Then there was the Mud Flu, which just about cut the Half Breeds down to nothin'. Now, buggers I haven't seen for years are cropping up all over the goddamn place, most likely because the whole ecosystem is out of whack."

"You mean like the food chain?" Cecile asked.

"That's exactly what I mean. Kind of like when hunters take out too many of the coyotes in a certain area or bobcats in another. That's when all the other things poke their noses out and spread all over the place."

"But the big wolves are back," Cole pointed out. "Now more than ever."

"Which don't bode well for us. These little peckers have been out long enough to find better food and bigger dens and warmer beds and greener pastures and . . . you get the point."

"Got it about five minutes ago," Cecile grumbled.

"What about the Nymar?" Cole asked. "Have you found a lot of Shadow Spore?"

"Hell no," he spat while tearing open a candy bar as though he was ripping off a small animal's head. "Why would they be out where we'd just pick 'em off? The whole point of burning out as many of us as they could was so they could set up shop all over the place. The cops are either on their side or believe them bloodsuckers are victims being stalked by folks like us."

Cecile didn't even look up from her sandwich when she asked, "Well, aren't you? Stalking them, I mean."

"Think I liked it better when she was givin' me the silent treatment," Jessup grumbled.

"So we don't have to worry about Nymar," Cole stated.

Jessup was quick to reply, "I wouldn't go that far. Just because they're not out skulking in the alleys everywhere don't mean they're not a threat. Fact is, they're a bigger threat than they realize. And you should pay close attention to this too, young lady. Those Nymar used to spread rumors and outright lies about how they ruled the cities to keep your kind out. That's no lie anymore."

"Trust me," she said. "Randolph is a lot more pissed off about that than you are."

"This is his territory," Cole explained. He stood up and turned his back to both Jessup and the girl. "And this shit is really getting hard to choke down."

"It's all I got," Jessup said. "There's tuna salad somewhere, but it might clean yer plumbing out more that you'd like."

"Not the sandwich," Cole said. "Why the hell do we care what a murdering animal like Randolph has to say? Why should we care what he wants? Have things slid too far down the crapper for us to even try to be Skinners anymore?" Shifting his eyes to Cecile, he asked, "Do you even know how many of our friends that goddamn beast has killed?"

"You think the Full Bloods are setting you up?" she asked. "Then you guys really must not know a lot about them. They don't need to set up anyone but themselves. Everyone else is just tall grass to them. When it gets in their way, they mow it down. And when it's time to mow, there's nothing that can stop them. I've only been one of them for a little while, but I can see that much already. How long have you guys been fighting them?"

Cole was still fired up. He looked to Jessup to see whether he stood alone against the wolf in a teenage girl's clothing.

"Look," she continued, "I know people are dying. I saw it on the news and on the Internet. Randolph told me about what's out there. You kill them, they kill you." Quickly raising her hands, she added, "And yes, I know it's not a game. Skinners have died, but you've got to see this from my side here. You don't just kill werewolves. You peel them and drain them and I don't even know what else. I may have eaten a human being, but you guys even give *me* the creeps."

It gave Cole the creeps to hear her talk about things so candidly. Then again, he knew from experience that it didn't help anyone's sanity to tiptoe around the truth. Sometimes it felt good to just embrace the madness and move on.

"Obviously you and Randolph aren't friends," Cecile continued. "But if the Full Bloods wanted to find you, they could. I barely know how to move around in my other body, but I feel like I can smell and hear everything there is. I think Randolph's older than all of us combined. When he talked about Skinners, he told me to see if I could trust you and then tell you the whole story about what's going on with the Breaking Moon. He said you needed to know because if anyone had a prayer of hiding me away from the others, if only for a while, it was a Skinner."

"And what can you tell us?" Cole asked.

"The Breaking Moon," she replied, as if reciting something she vaguely remembered from a dream, "is why the others are here."

Farther down the road a few cars rolled by. They were too far away for the Skinners to worry about and might as well have been in another universe than Cecile.

"There's some kind of heat inside of us," she said. "Full Bloods, I mean. Those big dogs too. Are they Half Breeds?"

"Yes."

"I remember Randolph mentioning that now." According to the look on her face, Cecile was hearing plenty of things in her mind at that moment. She winced at the screams the same way Cole had when he'd been awakened to his new world. "The heat is real. I can feel it all the time. It's some sort of power," she continued. "Randolph described it as the fuel that allows them—I guess *us*—to do what we do. I thought it sounded crazy, but I can feel it working when I change. It's like a match is always on inside me. Kind of like, you know, inside a furnace?"

"A pilot light?"

She nodded and then smiled wistfully. "I used to like watching my dad light the pilot light at the old house back in West Virginia. Sometimes I snuck down there and left the little door on the side of the furnace open so that little flame would go out. Dad would go down there with a coat hanger he'd twisted up to hold a match and I'd follow him to watch."

A semi pulling a trailer rumbled down the interstate. After it passed, a stray breeze swept across the camp. Her hair fluttered like streamers against her unmoving face. Crossing her arms and standing against the wind, she looked less like she was bracing herself against the elements and more like she was giving them silent commands to function around her.

"When my dad would light the match and stick it into the end of that bent metal hanger," she said, "he told me to stay back. Then he stuck the match into the furnace and . . . whoosh!" Even as she said that word, her eyes sparkled as if she was looking at the little spectacle that had captivated her all those years ago. "The flames just exploded in every direction. They filled the whole furnace and all these streams of fire came out of all those metal pipes or whatever was in there. You know the ones I mean?"

"Yeah," Jessup replied. "I do."

She nodded, acknowledging him, but just barely. "That's what it feels like when I change. Inside, there's this little flame in me. Always burning. When I change, though . . . whoosh. It fills me up. Kind of like sex, but more." She glanced over at him with the sly expression of a girl who'd done the deed, but not enough times for it to have lost its shock value. When Cole failed to react in kind, she rolled her eyes and nodded. "I've had sex, don't you worry about it."

She was just learning to use her sexuality as a tool. If he'd been about fifteen years younger, it would have had a lot more of an effect. Instead, he was able to see her as the young pup that she was. "So what's this got to do with the Breaking Moon?" he asked.

"All the Full Bloods—and I don't think there are a lot of them—we're like the flames shooting out of those pipes. We each have some of that fire in us and we can use it however we like. Randolph says that part just goes into living, but we get to live for a real long time."

Cole felt like a spy who'd found himself sitting at the dinner table inside an enemy's camp when he asked, "How long?"

She glanced over at him, smirking like an officer who'd just found a spy sitting at her dinner table. "A long time. That is, unless we're hunted down and murdered by some psycho with a Blood Blade. Oh yeah. He told me all about that too."

"Sounds like you werewolves do a lot of talking."

"I haven't slept since that first change. That leaves a lot more time for talking." After that, Cecile became more focused. "So anyway, we all get our share of the fire and the whole world is the furnace. Like, the ground. The earth. That sort of thing. We pull it up and draw it in to . . ."

"Recharge your batteries?" Cole asked.

Cecile snapped her fingers. "Exactly! Wherever it comes from, it's tied into the moon cycles. He told me I wouldn't be able to become all of what I can be until I pass some sort of Blood Moon trial."

"You mean a lunar eclipse?" Recognizing the puzzled and vaguely annoyed look on her face after seeing it so many times when trying to bring various girlfriends in on the whole Star Trek vs. Star Wars debate, he said, "When the moon passes between the earth and the sun, it's a lunar eclipse."

"No," she said after an impatient click of her tongue. "That's a solar eclipse. A lunar eclipse is when the earth is directly between the sun and the moon."

Before fighting back with a scathing commentary on the modern school system, Cole paused and said, "Oh. You're right. Yeah, I was thinking of the other one. But they're called Blood Moons because when there's a lunar eclipse, the moon looks all . . . you know . . . bloody."

"Done?" she asked.

Suddenly, Cole didn't miss Paige so much. If Cecile had a stick in her hand and was about to crack him upside his head, she might even make him homesick for his days at Rasa Hill. "I'm done," he said.

"The Blood Moon is different. That's something each of us needs to go through. With the Breaking Moon, we all get our fires stoked. It's supposed to come up through the earth to keep us going for the next however many years it'll be before the next one."

"You don't know how many years that is?"

"Nah," she replied with a shrug. "But I know it's a lot."

A lot of years in Full Blood terms could very well mean several of his own lifetimes, Cole thought. Rather than break her conversational stride, he let it pass.

"Whatever the fire is, it's drawn to us," she continued. "Like in physics, how air will move from one spot to another to fill a vacuum. Know what I mean?"

"Uh-huh," he said in a way he hoped was convincing.

"All the Full Bloods draw more of this fire than anything else, so they all picked their own territories and patrol them. This is Randolph's territory. I think it goes up through Canada and covers most of the States as well. That system got messed up when that friend of his came over to rip up Kansas City."

"Liam," Cole said. Finally, it seemed all the crap he'd gone through since becoming a Skinner was coalescing into something greater than chasing monsters through back alleys.

"He was here for too long," she continued. "Randolph said that two Full Bloods in the same territory will threaten the Balance."

"What balance?"

"*The* Balance." Since her stressing that word didn't have much of an effect on her audience, she shrugged and added, "That's what he told me. You've never heard of it?"

"No."

"I guess another Full Blood in someone else's territory can draw some of the fire away from where it was supposed to go," she said. "This whole system has been going for a while, and all that stuff in Kansas City ruined it. The other Full Bloods know Liam is here, drawing more energy or whatever for himself and Randolph."

"So, if more Full Bloods are in one spot, more energy is drawn to that spot?" Cole asked.

"I think so."

"Like the girl said," Jessup muttered. "Physics."

He thought for a moment until a picture formed in his head. Imagining the world as a source of energy and the Full Bloods as points scattered across its surface, he was able to make a good guess as to what that Balance was all about. If the Full Bloods positioned themselves just right, they could draw from the energy equally. Once the collection points clustered too close together, more energy would flow in that direction and get siphoned away from the others.

"That's why they're here," he said. "Those other Full Bloods can't let Randolph and Liam get stronger because it would put the rest of them at the bottom of the pile. But if they all came here, they'd draw even more of the energy, right?"

"Maybe all of it," Jessup offered.

Cecile nodded. "There will always be this wildness in us, but the Balance is supposed to help ease it."

"From what I've been hearing, you Full Bloods are a long way from being balanced," Cole said. "One of them attacked Randolph and damn near leveled that prison. Others are tearing apart some town in Oklahoma as we speak."

"Atoka?" she asked.

Jessup stepped forward. However she reacted, he wanted to see it first. "That's the place. From what I've heard, things are pretty bad there right now."

"Is Randolph a part of it?"

Unable to answer that, Jessup looked over to Cole. All Cole could say was, "I don't think so. Randolph genuinely seemed to want to do something to fix whatever's going on. Since he was attacked by another Full Blood, he may be on the outside of this whole thing. Maybe the others are looking for you."

Cecile shook her head. "No. They're going to stay there until the Breaking Moon rises. I was born there. That means it's a spot where the energy collects. That's how I was turned into . . . this."

"From what I've heard, it's a war zone and getting worse." Abruptly, Cole stopped and straightened up as if smacked in the face. "Is that why Randolph wants you hidden from them? Because you'd be drawing some of this fire or energy as well. And if you have a share of it, then that means there's less for everybody else."

When he looked at Cecile, he stared into her eyes intently. Even if she'd shifted into her full, raging form, he wouldn't have backed down, because his next questions were too important. "What happens if one of them gets it all?"

"Then however bad the Full Bloods are now," she said, "they'll get a whole lot worse."

Silence fell upon the camp.

A gentle wind drifted by, fanning the flames of the campfire and sending a much-needed chill down Cole's back.

"What about that thing in your arm?" Cole asked. She looked at him intently, but he merely waited patiently. That was enough to give her the strength to continue.

"I think it draws even more of the power to it," she explained while rubbing a spot on her arm. "It's hard to explain, but it feels like it's getting hotter. I don't think any of the power is going into me, though. It's just getting hotter like it's collecting something."

"Randolph wanted you to come to us to hide you," Cole said, more as a way to let that idea roll around inside him. "There's another one of those things somewhere. He was looking for it at the place where I was being held. Can you find it?"

"I don't even know what to look for!" she cried. "Randolph protected me, but he wants me to give in to this monster inside of me. You guys haven't tried to kill me yet, even though you probably had a chance. I don't want to be a part of any of this."

Jessup crossed his arms and studied her carefully. "So Randolph is after both of these stones to collect this energy or just to keep it away from the other Full Bloods?"

"All he told me was that the others can't be allowed to get more powerful than they already are. Once things got past a certain point, he said all of it would be wiped away."

"All of what?"

Glancing back and forth between the two Skinners, she said, "All of everything."

Chapter Eighteen

Atoka, Oklahoma

The basement beneath the autobody shop was well-insulated against the outside world. While down there, Paige felt removed from everything that had brought her to that spot. The only things left were the starkly lit room next to the storage space, a few cots, and a couple of dirt walls. The Mongrels had dispersed to scout for reinforcements and not yet returned, leaving Paige and Nadya with Milosh. Treatments from the medical kit meant none of the wounded were going to change into Half Breeds, but Milosh was still missing an arm. The remains of that appendage had been cleaned, wrapped, and tied off to stop the bleeding long enough for the Amriany healing serum to be administered. After that, he passed out. In fact, all three of them had passed out for a few hours of some of the worst sleep Paige ever experienced.

At various times throughout the night Nadya spoke to some of her people on a cell phone. Even though Paige couldn't understand the Amriany language, Nadya's tone of voice bounced between angry and desperate.

The Mongrels came and went, and the Full Bloods seemed to be doing the same. Rather than run after every shapeshifter that made a sound, Paige tended to her own business. The kit she had with her was about the size of a small cosmetics bag. It was a length of leather wide enough to carry a few simple tools, some tubes of premixed necessities, and some ingredients to mix up emergency doses of healing serum. When rolled up tightly, it fit perfectly beneath a loop that had been stitched into her belt just behind her left hip.

At the moment she was only concerned with a thin plastic tube of a pungent substance with the color and consistency of maple syrup. Holding the tube up to a light, she shook it to watch the piece of Kawosa's earlobe move around within the liquid. She'd been carrying the little bundle with her since Toronto. The little chunk of skin had been soft and moist when she cut it from Kawosa's ear, but when she fished it from the tube it felt more like a glob of coagulated tomato sauce. She squashed the earlobe into the tube and then shook it some more. It didn't take much Nymar or werewolf blood to create a good batch of varnish, but this was something different. She wasn't even sure if Kawosa's sample would have an effect when added to the varnish. No matter what had happened the last time she tested her own innovation, the potential benefits were too great to pass up.

After adding a few drops and some water, the stuff was smeared onto a rag and applied to her weapons to strengthen the coat of varnish that allowed them to bond with her and change shape. This wasn't the first time she'd whipped up something in the field or modified a weapon. Sometimes it worked. Sometimes it backfired. Sometimes nothing happened at all. She considered all of those options while looking at the little chunks of earlobe swirling around in the tube. The safe thing to do would be to add a little bit of the varnish to her weapon and see what happened. Maybe later she could add more. If she didn't run out of the sample she'd gotten, she could keep trying until she got it right.

Having dealt with Kawosa, Paige knew that something needed to be done quickly. She'd been lucky to realize he was trying to influence her, but that didn't change the fact that he'd gotten so close in the first place. He was a master deceiver and would only get better as he dealt with more Skinners. If something wasn't done to help sniff him out, the skinny bastard would have free reign.

Paige checked the tube, held it up to the light and swirled

it around again. It seemed that all of the chunks were absorbed, so she opened it.

It smelled gross, but no more so than usual.

She carefully tipped the tube until a few drops fell onto the wet cloth sitting next to her on the stack of boxes where she was seated. About three-quarters of the usual amount, just to be safe. Sliding her hand under the cloth, she folded it once, rubbed the varnish in, then drew her main weapon. She worked the varnish into the machete with the cloth in the usual ritualistic fashion. The stuff glistened on the wood grain for a few seconds before soaking in to give the weapon a slightly darker color. She then applied another coat, waited for it to dry, and set the cloth down. It didn't take long for her weapon to drink in the varnish, and when it did, she picked it up and clenched her fist around its handle.

Paige barely twitched at the pain from the thorns, but she did feel a chill at the points where they pierced her flesh. She closed her eyes, waiting for something else. It had been a while after her arm was hurt before the thorns would even puncture that hand. If anything else went wrong, she might not be able to fight at all. But she knew that if things were allowed to slide much further without somehow being put into check, no amount of fighting would do much good anyway.

The chill subsided.

When she tried to shift her weapon into a deadlier shape, it responded sluggishly. Normal for that hand, so she removed the stake from her other boot. It still felt like a poor substitute for the sickle that had been destroyed, but she started working the varnish into its handle all the same.

Her phone rang. Even though she didn't recognize the number on the caller ID, she wasn't about to take a chance on missing a call from Cole. "Hello?"

"Hey, Bloodhound. Long time no see."

"Rico?"

"That's right. Sorry about the mix-up in Canada. Where you been?"

Paige set down the cloth and fought back the impulse to reach for her Beretta. "You're sorry?" she asked. "You tried to kill me."

"That was some kind of brainwashing bullshit," Rico told her. "You know that. He got both of us with that trick."

"What about the rest of what you told me? About the Skinners branching off from the rest?"

The big man let out a tired breath that came across as harsh static through the phone. "Yeah. That part wasn't bullshit. You wanna know who introduced me to these guys first? Ned. Turns out the old guy wasn't just sitting in that house after all. Lancroft had a lot of knowledge to pass along, and them runes are only a part of it."

"You've been learning about those runes for a while," Paige said. "Does that mean you were working with these Lancroft assholes all that time?"

"Why do you think they're assholes?"

"Because Lancroft's Mud Flu got a bunch of innocent people killed! Lancroft created Henry! He was a murderer!"

"He was all about the greater good," Rico explained. "You think things are bad now? How bad do you think they would have been years ago if Lancroft hadn't done his best to hold back the tide? He's always had Skinners following him, but he wasn't stupid enough to work with just anyone. You met those pricks in Philly. What about those bastards who accepted Nymar in their ranks? *Skinner* ranks! Soon as we start handing our traditions over to the bloodsuckers, we're slitting our own throats. Now the whole damn thing is crumbling."

"So you're probably going to say that Lancroft prophesized about what's happening today?"

Rico chuckled. "There ain't no prophecies, just like there ain't no Chosen Ones. Lancroft's predictions weren't any more impressive than predicting the weather by using a *Farmers' Almanac*. You look at past trends, present climates, and you can gauge the future. Lancroft's just the only one lookin' at our almanac."

"And when did you come to these conclusions?" she asked.

"Yesterday. I've been checking on Ned's death ever since it happened. I got people who can look into these sorts of things, friends I worked with since before I met you. I kept looking until I found out what drew Ned to Lancroft in the first place. Lancroft wasn't just a Skinner. He was a pioneer. He believed in taking steps to keep things from getting out of our control. You think it's a coincidence that the world went to shit after he died?"

"That's putting a lot onto one man's shoulders."

"Maybe," Rico grunted. "But he kept some damn thorough records. You know what the Breaking Moon is?"

"Why don't you tell me?"

"When someone is turned into a Half Breed, all their bones are broken and stitched together with muscle. You and I know this because we seen it happen. We've gutted the poor bastards and taken a closer look for ourselves."

"I don't have time for this," Paige said.

"Full Bloods call that first change the Breaking. Mostly, it's a random thing when people get attacked and turned. There's a time when those Breakings spike. Lancroft coordinated with other Skinners, cross-checked some notes, and realized it happened when the Full Bloods returned to the middle of their territories and stayed there. Records were pieced together over seventy years documenting people who weren't attacked changing into Half Breeds. They were just healthy, random folks who dropped to their knees and shattered inside. According to Lancroft's journal, that time's about to happen again and the Full Bloods ain't sticking to their territories."

"So what?"

"So, there's somethin' going on, Paige. We need to be united. If we all run around half-cocked, there's fewer of us to make a stand when the time comes. The bloodsuckers already tipped the scales enough. We need to close ranks and start acting instead of *re*acting. I ain't your enemy, Bloodhound. We both got tricked in Canada. If you let that split us apart, then that skinny fuck Kawosa got what he wanted. I'm giving you a chance to put your good work to use."

She stood up and gripped the phone tighter. Somewhere along the line, she'd drawn her weapon with her other hand and held onto it with a tight enough grip to bury the thorns into her palm. "So that's why you're calling. You need the info I downloaded about Cobb38."

"What are you gonna do with it?" he asked. "Hand it over

to MEG? Too late for that. Let Daniels take a look at it? After all that's happened with the bloodsuckers, I wouldn't be surprised if all of their house-cleaning involved sweeping out the rats of their own kind. If he is still alive, he's on borrowed time and probably bein' watched even closer than ever right now. So what other choice does that leave you? How the hell are you gonna put that information to use?"

"I could give it to some allies I can trust."

"Like who? Your helicopter buddies? The Gypsies?"

"At least the Amriany are up front about where their loyalties are."

"We both fought to track down Cobb," Rico growled. "We both stormed them houses, and both of us did what needed to be done even with Kawosa fucking with our heads! You, me, and Cole, we work well together. Now's our chance to finally pull Skinners together into what they need to be instead of the splintered bunch of petty assholes that squabbled over the scraps left behind in Philly. Just think of what can be done if Lancroft stayed alive long enough to pass on how he managed to stay alive all them years."

"How can you be sure the Lancroft we killed in Philly really is that same guy?" she asked. "Did you find his formula for living to be centuries old?"

"Not the whole thing, but we're closing in on it."

The Full Bloods were still roaming outside. Paige could feel the burning in her palms intensify as one of them came closer to the autobody shop. A deep, lingering howl was answered by scratchier ones that seemed to come from all sides. Heavy footsteps rumbled down the street above, and the heat in her scars faded. She knew it wouldn't be long, however, before the freshest batch of Half Breeds would roll through the area like a storm of fangs and claws.

"Sounds like you got yer hands full there, Bloodhound," Rico mused.

"I do."

"Where are you?" When she didn't answer, he asked, "What the hell do you think I'd do to you, anyway? We both fought and bled in the same battles. I carried you and Cole out of some death traps, and you guys saved my ass plenty of times. All I wanna do is help, just like I always done."

"You want to help? Then I've got someone who needs help. He's the guy who flew me into Denver. His name's Adderson. You call him and tell him you want to help. He'll put you to work."

"You mean those guys in that helicopter?" Rico growled. "If they're cops or military, they'll just toss my ass into a cell."

"They're not cops. You said you want to be more proactive. You said you want to do more than you're doing now. Call Adderson and tell him you want to join the IRD."

"IRD?"

"Inhuman Response Division," she explained, waiting for the inevitable backlash.

"Jesus Lord Almighty," Rico lashed. "Are you kiddin' me? If you think more men in helicopters are what's needed, then just call an air strike to burn all those werewolves that are howling around you right now."

"I'm not sure how far I can trust them," Paige admitted. "Cole was almost killed when he was in their custody, but I'm not sure if that was the IRD's fault."

"You mean that place in Colorado that was leveled on the news?"

"That's the one. Cole made it out, but—"

"Where is he?" Rico asked. "If he's on the run, I can help him! I know all about keeping out of the cops' sights!"

"No. Call Adderson. Check out the IRD. Things are taking a turn, Rico. You're right about that. We do need to evolve, but Skinners aren't enough to set things right again. I know Kawosa screwed with us. He's here, Rico. If you stay away, he can't screw with us again. Check out the IRD. If you think we can work with them, we may be able to put together some heavy artillery that can be enough to drop a Full Blood."

"We were never supposed to drag the real world into this," he warned. "Remember all the times that happened before? Panic. Confusion. Mass hysteria. Any of this ringing a bell?"

"Things have gotten beyond that already," she said as she dropped back down onto the boxes where she'd been sitting. "There isn't a precedent for dealing with something like this because it's never happened. The Full Bloods are gathering, but there's only two of them here. That's all it took to tear apart this whole town."

"What town?"

"Atoka, Oklahoma." Even though she knew Rico had been tricked to cross her in Canada, it still felt like she was leaving herself open for attack when she said those words now.

"I haven't heard anything about that place in the news or anywhere else," he said. "You sure the problem's that big?"

"Yes, I'm sure. It's looking like nobody outside of here knows what's going on, and I need to figure out why that is. In the meantime, we need the big guns. Bigger than the ones we've got."

"Guns don't do shit against Full Bloods."

"I know. They can take down Half Breeds, though. Just think what could happen if Skinners worked with a big group of soldiers who not only believed us about what's out there, but had plenty of guns big enough to do that job at their disposal?"

After a pause and a long, beleaguered sigh, Rico grunted, "Inhuman Response Division, huh?"

"Yep." After rattling off a phone number, she told him, "Ask for Adderson. Tell him I sent you. Find out what you can."

"Are you sure you're not setting me up for this because you're pissed about Toronto?"

"No. You're just the only one I know who's got a chance of getting out of there if the IRD turns out to be the bastards responsible for nearly killing Cole. You know all about that kind of thing, remember?"

"Gotchya." With that, the connection died.

Outside, the howling was getting closer. Whenever there was a lull in the chorus of shredded throats, she could hear the wild barks of Half Breeds using their heightened senses to close the gap between them and their next meal.

"How's Rico?" Nadya asked.

Paige put the phone back into her pocket and started packing away her kit. "I'll find out in a while. What about Milosh?"

The Amriany woman had rarely left the side of his cot since administering treatment to him. "Our healing serums seem to be working," Nadya said, "but he still may be in too much shock to survive on a dirty cot in this basement."

Quinn walked down the stairs, shifting into a more human form by the time she reached the basement. Placing her hands flat against a wall that was an uneven surface of packed dirt, she said, "We may not be able to stay here much longer."

"Any sign from Burke?" Paige asked.

Sinking her fingertips into the wall as if that could help her feel any tremors created by an approaching digger, Quinn shook her head. "Nothing yet. He and some of the others gathered farther in town. Maybe we can make it look like we've moved our shelter there."

"So the whole town is overrun?" Paige asked.

"As far as we know. We can't stay out long enough to get a good look around. Those Full Bloods sniff us out right away and get the Half Breeds to chase after us."

"That'd be Liam pulling those strings," Paige said. "He could steer the Half Breeds in Kansas City, so he's probably doing it here." Walking over to a collection of rifles and shotguns propped in one corner she asked, "Are these all functional?"

Quinn's fur was slick with gore that could have come from any number of sources over the last several hours. It bristled as she said, "Haven't checked them all. We stole them from around town when we first arrived and have been storing them here for an emergency."

Paige grabbed a shotgun and checked to see how many shells were inside. "In case nobody's called it yet, this is an emergency. Ammo?"

"There's some in those boxes."

Two bankers' boxes sat next to each other at the foot of Milosh's cot. When Paige checked them, she found only a few small cases of shells and rifle rounds stored with supplies ranging from flashlights to shoelaces. She helped herself to a dozen shotgun shells. "Can he be moved?" she asked while looking down at Milosh.

Nadya found a hunting rifle and strapped it across her back. "He probably shouldn't, but I don't know for sure. Drina was our medic, but she's dead."

Even for Paige that seemed harsh. Still, there were only two things that could be done where fallen comrades were concerned. Nadya could mourn them or, if she didn't take action, she could join them.

"We're taking him out of here," Paige said.

Another Mongrel had found her way into the basement without making a sound to announce her presence. She simply appeared as the oil in her fur was shed. "No. I'll do it," she said. "You two don't know where you're going. As far as we know, there are more Half Breeds than people in this town. We've got alternate shelters, but we can't get there on the surface."

"She's right," Quinn added. "We can tie him to her so he'll be dragged along for the ride."

"You're not one of the tunnel makers," Nadya said.

"No, but we can all use the passages that are already made or squirm through the loose dirt as long as we know where to go."

Looking at Quinn, Paige asked, "Why can't you take him?"

"Because I lead this pack and our home is under siege. I don't have the time to crawl underground at a snail's pace just to drag one human to safety. We've been wearing ourselves to the bone to keep as much of this town alive as possible. We risked our necks to save you three because we need help to make sure everyone in this place isn't destroyed. If you'd rather take a few months to learn all the ins and outs of tunneling so you can take your friend yourself, you're welcome to it."

Nadya didn't need lessons in wriggling through Mongrel tunnels. Paige knew that much after listening to Cole's stories about the Amriany using spiked wrist braces to pull themselves through the confined spaces. That didn't mean Nadya knew how to navigate a dirt maze with her eyes closed.

Staring directly into the feline's eyes, the Amriany asked, "What is your name?"

"Gail."

"Tell me if you can keep him safe, Gail."

Sensing the importance of her words, Gail nodded once and said, "I can't promise anything for him or me, but I'm the best shot your friend has."

Nadya sized up the Mongrel in a matter of seconds. "I'll help you get him ready, but I want to know where he winds up."

Already sifting through the clutter beneath a dusty workbench, Quinn said, "She'll send word to me when she gets there and we'll tell you about it as soon as we can. Here," she added once she'd found a coil of rope. "Get him secured and then we'll get out. Those Half Breeds are closing in fast."

As Nadya helped Milosh to his feet and held him steady, Gail stood with her back pressed against his chest while Quinn tied him to her. Within a minute or two rope was looped under Gail's arms and around her waist to form a makeshift harness. The Mongrel shifted into her four-legged form, which added enough bulk to tighten the harness as well as support Milosh's weight when she crawled to the wall Quinn had been monitoring. The feline's claws extended farther out from her hands and sank into the vertical surface. Although her scraping dislodged plenty of dirt, most of it merely shifted within the wall and allowed Gail to squirm inside. There was something else keeping that wall from collapsing. When the Mongrel's head got to within an inch of the wall, the dirt compacted as if being pushed by something and even moved aside before it made contact with her fur. But Paige wasn't inclined to try and figure it out. Sometimes it was best to let the experts do their thing.

"All right," she said. "You wanted our help. Did you have something specific in mind?"

"The Full Bloods have been paying special attention to a house on Montana Avenue," Quinn said as heavy bodies charged down the street above them. Judging by the scrapes and fleeting impacts, the Half Breeds were most likely scrambling across the roof in their haste to jump over the garage. "They can't track us by scent as long as we stay underground. There are precautions we can take for you two, but the Full Bloods' senses seem to have gotten even stronger than normal. The moment we come up, they will know where we are."

"Which means you can't check out that house," Paige said.

"Right."

"As long as it involves leaving this freaking basement, count me in."

Chapter Nineteen

Atoka wasn't a large place, but traveling by foot went a long way in shifting someone's perspective. Quinn and another digger could only take them as far as West Fourth Street. As Paige and Nadya headed toward Montana Avenue, she swore the town tripled in size. Every step she took was stuffed with worry that it might be too loud. Even when her foot managed to land without kicking anything or crunching on something else, there was a legitimate concern of making a noise that could be picked up by supernatural ears. Then there was the smell. That was something new, and it bugged her most of all.

When she couldn't hold her tongue any longer, she leaned over to Nadya and asked, "What the hell is this stuff?"

"What stuff?"

"The stuff Quinn smeared on us before she left," Paige said in a voice that wanted nothing more than to lift into an aggravated snarl. "The stuff that stained my shirt and will probably stink until three Christmases from now."

"You heard the same speech I did. It's supposed to keep the Half Breeds from smelling us. But it won't do us much good if you keep talking. They have pretty good ears, you know."

"I have good ears too. That's how I can tell they're still fighting with the Mongrels on the other side of town." Paige managed to keep quiet for a few more seconds before asking, "You think this stuff really works?"

"If we get torn apart before we reach that house, we'll know it doesn't work. Happy?"

Paige sniffed her sleeve, which smelled like a strange mix of ammonia and rotten fruit. Although she did find a bit more of the Mongrel concoction spattered on her elbow, she instantly regretted the discovery. "Oh God. I think I'm gonna be sick."

"Don't you ever shut up?"

"Did you just tell me to shut up?"

"No," Nadya said as she stopped and turned to face her. "I asked if you ever shut up and that seems like a good question. Do you?"

Paige stopped as well, resisting the urge to point her shotgun at the Amriany when she said, "Fine. You want quiet? How about I just forget about the fact that we might be getting set up, bite my tongue, and quietly walk into an ambush?"

"If those Mongrels wanted to hurt us, they could have done it a hundred times by now. Why do all Skinners have to be so suspicious?"

"Why didn't she get us any closer to this house, huh? You seriously think her pack's got this whole town covered with tunnels and everything else and she couldn't have dropped us off any closer than this?"

Nadya took a moment to consider that. Then, as she narrowed her eyes and studied Paige carefully, it seemed she was considering her even more. "You don't like to be helped, do you?"

"Things generally get done better if I do them myself."

The Amriany's only response to that was to cast a lingering glance at Paige's right arm, which was still stiff and scarred. "Get done better?"

Sighing, Paige propped the shotgun barrel against her shoulder and spun around to look at the houses behind her. "See, that's why I'd rather work alone. Fewer grammar lessons. Is this the house?"

They stood on the side of the street with their toes brushing against the edge of an unkempt lawn. The house had two arches in the roof, one of which looked like a cheap add-on that had probably started leaking after its second heavy rain.

The arch on the right was actually in the middle of the structure that had what looked like a boarded-up door. Directly above that was a tall brick chimney. On the right side of the house, a porch led up to a door. One of the front windows was boarded up as well, the other covered by a sagging air-conditioning unit.

Nadya approached the house holding the FAMAS at waist level and pointed at the ground. Ever since taking the assault rifle from Drina's body, she'd all but abandoned her MAC-10. There was a broken cement path leading from the street to the lowest porch step, but she deftly avoided stepping on the trail in favor of making a silent approach through the weed-infested grass. Looking back at Paige, she nodded and pointed to the cracked frame where the front door was supposed to be. She then pointed to herself before motioning to the boarded window.

It was one of the few times Paige took orders without question. Once Nadya was in position, Paige approached the door. There was something about the house that spoke to her like an intelligent chill that knew precisely how to run up her spine before reaching out to rake icy nails along her shoulders. She gripped the shotgun, bent one knee and reached down to quickly check the holster on her boot. Her weapon was in place and ready to be drawn. All she needed was a target.

Not only had the door been broken, but the hinges were knocked clean away from the frame. Crouching to examine the frame, she immediately spotted the claw marks left behind by the creature that had torn the door from its moorings. It didn't take long for the stench of spoiled food, mold, and rotten meat to drift over her on its way to the outside. A short hiss caught her attention, and when Paige swung around to see what had made the noise, she found only Nadya.

"Anything?" the Amriany asked in a barely audible whisper.

Paige shook her head, raised her shotgun and moved inside to a living room that looked like it had never been anything but cluttered. The floor of the cramped square space was littered with broken furniture and blanketed by an uneven layer of shredded papers. For her first few steps into the building, she was forced to draw shallower breaths until she became used to the smell of spoiled meat. Another hiss came from the short hallway that led to some smaller rooms. Since Nadya was no longer at the window, Paige moved toward the hiss to meet her.

She walked through the living room, holding the shotgun at hip level. Adopting a low, crouching stance, she peeked down the hall to find two bedrooms. One of them had a single queen-sized bed with a mattress ripped open almost as badly as a scarecrow that had fallen victim to flying monkeys hired by the Wicked Witch of the West. It lay splayed out with its fluffy innards piled in a mound topped by blankets, dirty clothes, and sheets. Paige almost moved on before spotting the hand dangling out from the bottom of the pile.

"Shit," she whispered as she approached the bed. One quick tug on a finger told her two things: the hand was dead and it wasn't attached to anything. Considering those facts, she didn't bother sorting through the pile of stuffing and moved on to the next room.

The second bedroom might have been about the same size as the first, but it felt a lot smaller due to all the furniture jammed into it. There were two beds, both of which had been shoved aside and upended by whatever pulled up the floorboards to expose bare dirt in a spot roughly three feet across. The air in the room had the heavy stillness of a storm that had passed. Splintered remains of dressers and bed frames had been thrown to the sides of the room as if blown there by the same explosion that ruined the floor. Paige absorbed all of this with a single sweeping glance. The heat in her scars had spiked, making her hands reflexively tighten around the shotgun. Keeping perfectly still, she bent at the knees to put the weapon holstered in her boot within reach.

The hissing she'd heard was still present. It changed in pitch, shifting between higher and lower registers. As she inched into the room, the sound was accompanied by a grating rasp.

Not hissing, she knew then. Panting.

Light came in through a filthy window to create a mass of shadows along that wall. Taking a moment so her eyes could adjust, she spotted one shape that didn't match the jagged edges and straight lines of all the broken furniture and cracked wood. Now she could see the shape swelling and contracting in time to the rasping pants. She might not have known what was causing the electric crackle through her scars, but the heat was different than what a Half Breed projected. It wasn't intense enough to come from a Full Blood, but had the electric crackle that came from a Mongrel. Whatever the thing in the corner was, it studied her with every bit as much scrutiny as she studied it.

Cautious footsteps came from the hallway. She turned toward them using only the muscles it would take to angle her head and move a hand back to motion for Nadya to stop. The Amriany froze in her tracks and questioned her with a silent expression. Paige responded by pointing at the corner. It took a moment for Nadya to find the source of the panting, and when she did, she nodded and raised her FAMAS.

"No," Paige said in a quick whisper. "I think it's guarding something."

"We leave it?"

"Just try to keep it from calling any others." With that, Paige eased the shotgun to the floor.

The creature tensed and inched forward. When it emerged from the shadows of its corner, it showed itself to be smaller than one of the newer Half Breeds, with a leaner frame and a snout that twisted into a beak. As it opened its mouth to growl at her, the creature dug its hands into the floor, pushing curved claws through the boards. Its dark eyes fixed intently on her while blinking with flapping, vertical lids.

"I think it's a Mongrel," Paige whispered. "Or it used to be."

"That is no Kushtime," Nadya said. "Not like one I've ever seen."

"No. There's something wrong with it." Paige couldn't stop looking at its eyes. No matter how strange its body was, there was something in its eyes that brought her mind all the way back to Kansas City when Liam was dragged underground by one particular burrowing Mongrel. That creature's name snapped into her mind almost immediately.

"Max?" Paige whispered.

A flicker of recognition drifted across the creature's face, but was pushed back by something else. Its eyes darted toward a second shape in the corner of the room farthest from the door. Tucked away behind the foot of one overturned bed was a more recognizable horror. The Half Breed scraped at the floor and stared at Paige with wide bloodshot eyes. It was in its resting phase where most of its fur was still tucked away to expose pale, leathery flesh. Werewolves in that form shunned the sunlight but weren't destroyed by it. As near as Paige had been able to figure, Half Breeds transformed simply by flexing whatever muscles were required to do so. The effort made their bodies tense to the point of trembling and drove them to become wilder than the wounded creatures they were. If the trait was given to them by design, it effectively shaped them into taut killers that were always snapping their jaws and full of nervous energy. Paige didn't like to think of it that way, however, because the god she prayed to would never design such a thing.

As she reached for her boot, the Half Breed shifted its gaze to follow her hand. The creature didn't have a way of knowing what she was reaching for. Half Breeds ran on instinct and pain. This one's instincts drew it from the shadows even farther as its panting grew into a snarl. Max watched Paige as well and growled in a way that caused every other living thing in that room to take a step back. There was no doubting it now. A Full Blood had reshaped Max into this thing. Paige's scars could feel it. She just wasn't sure she could believe it.

Lowering her shotgun, she closed her hand around the grip of her machete. She felt the rush of adrenaline shoot through her as its thorns bit into her palm. The connection between herself and the weapon allowed her to make the blade narrower so she could ease it from the holster without making a sound.

The Half Breed stretched out a forepaw that looked more like the gnarled hand of an elderly man with nails that had been filed down to points. Muscles beneath its skin twitched spastically, tugging the corners of its mouth to reveal fangs coated with old blood that had caked on and dried to flaky rust. Its eyes were bloodshot and its chest swelled with the effort of hauling its body up onto all four legs. Its entire frame quaked when it leaned forward, and its eyes widened even more, as if the lids were being pulled back by fishhooks connected to the wall. Once Paige stopped moving, however, it followed suit.

"All right," she said. "It's definitely guarding something."

"Maybe it is buried in the floor."

Paige studied the floor carefully, focusing on the spot where the boards had been torn up. Easing a little flashlight from her pocket, she took a quick look at the edges of the hole. Layers of the foundation were visible, along with cement and thicker pieces of wood that had either been beneath the floor or fallen in later. That hole went all the way down to the dirt, which looked to have been turned and then piled back in. Careful not to shine the light into the faces of either shapeshifter, Paige watched both creatures for any sign that they were about to attack.

Max stayed rigid and still. His body was relaxed and his eyes were all but dead. Something was holding him in that spot. Even a wild animal had more going on inside its head than that. The Half Breed presented an opposing picture. It strained and snarled as if testing the boundaries of an uncompromising leash. Its pale skin trembled and its muscles flexed in an erratic rhythm. Only when Paige backed away from the pit in the floor did either of the creatures retreat to the spots from which they'd come.

"I'll take the Mongrel," Nadya said. "You take the Half Breed."

"No."

"You want the Mongrel? Fine."

"No," Paige repeated insistently. "They're not attacking us. They're just guarding. Have you ever seen anything like this?"

"Never."

"Maybe they're just here to raise an alarm." Looking at Max's face, Paige couldn't help but feel sorry for the Mongrel. She'd only met him once for less than a few seconds, but he played a big part in ending the Kansas City siege. Now, his body was twisted into something else, his brain was somehow on hold, and she suspected Liam had something to do with it. If that was the case, the Mongrel was most likely going through hell. "Keep watch outside," she said. "Let me know if you think anyone knows we're here."

"What are you going to do?"

Holding her weapon down so as not to pose a threatening silhouette, Paige backed through the door and into the short hall connecting the two bedrooms. From there she could watch as both of the creatures retreated into their respective corners and settled back into the shadows. Fishing her cell phone from her pocket, she said, "I'm checking to see what the hell this could be."

Nadya backed out even farther and headed out through the front door.

Once her number was dialed, Paige tapped the Call button.

"Paige?" Stu asked as soon as the connection was made.

"What, you're not going to thank me for calling?" she whispered. "What happened to phone manners and professionalism?"

"You sound tired. What happened?"

"A lot's happened," she replied. "That's why I'm calling."

"Why are you whispering?"

"What do you have in your records about Atoka, Oklahoma? And I don't mean anything from the last few days. I mean something that might be in your files about weird activity or strange energy or . . ." Pausing because she couldn't believe what she was about to say, she just spat it out instead of wasting time looking for better phrasing. "Or buried treasure."

"Buried treasure?"

"I don't know. Just buried something. You have anything like that connected to Atoka?"

There was a smirk in his voice when he replied, "Nothing jumps out at me, but I'll check." After a few seconds of tapping, he said, "Sounds like we've got some reception issues."

"I know."

"So you hear that voice?"

Paige listened for a moment but could only hear the tapping of Stu's fingers on his keyboard beneath a thin layer of static. "What voice?" she asked.

"Yeah. Sounds like another call or . . . that's gotta be on your end of things. It just mentioned your name."

"I don't hear anything."

The tapping stopped. "You didn't just hear that? Or . . . or *that*? It's talking to you. Either that or someone else named Paige who's standing outside of a bedroom."

Paige's eyes drifted toward the shadows in the other room. "Hang on," she said before lowering the phone so she could listen without the distraction of any noises coming from the call. Even when she closed her eyes and concentrated, she couldn't make out anything more than the steady panting and the scrape of branches against the house. "Let me ask you something," she said when she lifted the phone back to her ear. "Is the voice male or female?"

"It's definitely a man. Sounds like it's whispering. Did you find it? It was a lot louder when you were quiet."

"No, I didn't find anything and I still don't hear anything."

"That's really— Hang on! You know what it sounded like?"

"Still haven't heard it, but please drag this out a little more," Paige snapped.

"That sounded like an EVP!"

"You mean those voices you guys hear on tape recorders that come from ghosts?"

"Or other dimensions," Stu added. "Depends on what theory you subscribe to." He was quiet for a few seconds and returned twice as excited as she'd ever heard him on any previous phone call. "Yes! That whispering sounds like an EVP. Did you hurt your right arm?"

"You know I did."

"No. Is it scratched? Bitten?" After a pause, he asked, "Were you talking to another woman carrying a big gun who stepped outside just before you called?"

"Now you're freaking me out."

"What did you do before when you were quiet? It got louder then."

"I just lowered the phone. Look, I don't have a lot of time, but I want to ask you about . . ." As she glanced down to the floor, she realized that the paranormal investigator might not have spun off on such a bad tangent after all. "How's this?" she asked before lowering the phone and stretching her hand toward the pit in the next room.

She could hear Stu's excited reply despite the distance between her ear and the phone's speaker.

"That's it!" he said once she brought the phone back up. "Holy crap! That was the best EVP ever! What did you do?"

"All I did was hold the phone down next to the floor in this house."

"Is that where you think there's buried treasure?"

"Yes."

"Sweet! Now we're getting somewhere. Okay, I did find something that may be of use. Do you know what ley lines are?"

"Aren't those supposed to be channels of mystical energy or some crap like that?" she asked.

"Yeah," Stu replied. "But don't call it crap. According to a chart in our files, there's a convergence of ley lines beneath Oklahoma. Nowhere near Atoka, though."

"Any chance your files could be off?"

"Considering we're guessing about them using a mishmash of readings taken from too many different pieces of equipment, I'd say that's more than likely. What exactly did you find?"

Paige looked down at the floor as if she might be able to see an actual line running beneath the surface. Unfortunately, she had no such luck. "I'm looking at a pile of dirt, but there's got to be more than that. A Half Breed dug up the floor in a house and is guarding it with its life. Since it wasn't making a den or trying to get to any food, I don't know why it would have gone through so much trouble. What would ley lines mean to a bunch of shapeshifters? I thought that was just supposed to be energy used for ghosts or the Bermuda Triangle or psychics."

"There are tons of theories, but that's all they are," he explained. "Energy has been measured. It's been documented. It's been recorded, but nobody really knows exactly what it's for. Most of the time it just gets written off as the earth's normal magnetic field. Are you standing close to that spot right now?"

"Yeah."

"Just don't say anything for a moment, I'm recording this and want to get a clear sample."

Paige obliged, but only for a few seconds. "You ever hear of the Breaking Moon?"

More tapping. "We don't have anything with that exact wording on file, but I do have entries under Blood Moon, Bone Breakers, and Hunter's Moon. None of those have anything to do with shapeshifters, though. All spiritual activity. Holy crap! Did you hear that?"

"Just tell me!" she snapped in a fierce whisper.

"The voice. It mentioned you again," Stu said as his own voice trembled with excitement. "It says his name's Max."

Paige lowered her entire body until she was almost crawling toward the ruined bedroom. "Can you still hear me, Stu?"

"Yes."

"Can you still hear it? Can you or not?"

"Yes. I'm taping now. EVP lesson number one. When you ask a question, give me or the entity time to answer it." After the silence that followed, he said, "Yeah. I can still hear it."

"Fine, but if you post this on a website or anything public I'll—"

"I know. You'll mess me up in a profane and creative fashion. Are you ready to start?"

"I'm going to talk to Max and you'll translate. Okay?"

"Oh my God," Stu said anxiously. "That is so much better than okay, it's . . . all right. Calming down. Go ahead."

Paige sighed and stared into the shadows at the strange shape hiding there. "Max," she whispered. "Are you one of the Mongrels from KC?"

After a few seconds Stu replied, "Yes. He is."

"What happened to you?"

"He was . . . bitten. On purpose?" As Stu spoke, the creature guarding the pit stretched its neck out even farther. At first its eyes seemed to be twitching, but that was only because the lids closed in the wrong direction. After compensating for that, Paige could better read the concentration on his face. "Liam," Stu said in a voice that was just as strained. "Liam bit him."

"When he was being dragged down," Paige said. "Liam

said something about changing Mongrels into Full Bloods. Is that what you mean?"

The pain was written across Max's face, and one of his lips curled up to reveal part of a fang.

"Yes," Stu said. "It changed him, but not into that. Something about . . . others. Better. I can't make it out."

"There were others that were changed too," Paige said. "Made them better, but not Full Bloods."

Some of the concentration on Max's face eased up.

"Yes," Stu said. "How did you know? This is me talking, by the way."

"I can see what happened," Paige explained. "I'm looking at it. I can feel it. I'm also on borrowed time here, so could you just repeat what you hear?"

"Sure, sure. Sorry."

Looking at the Half Breed and then to Max, she asked, "Should I be worried about that one?"

"No," Stu said. "The rest sleeps. The . . . the wretch? The wretch sleeps."

"Why can't you talk to me?"

"The . . . tore box? Torba box? Can't make it out. Whatever he's saying, it's something about something else giving Liam power. Liam can control the wretches and now he can control Max because . . . shared blood. Something about shared blood. Controls his body, but not his mind."

In Kansas City, Liam had been able to guide the packs of Half Breeds he'd created with simple commands and barks that steered them in a certain direction or made them cower like any animal showing deference to an alpha male. But that control hadn't been complete. As far as shared blood, if Liam had turned Max into what he was now, it only made sense that he might be able to control him too.

"What are you doing here?" she asked. "How can he hear you?" she asked while shaking the phone. "Why?"

Stu paused for several seconds. The only reason Paige knew she hadn't been disconnected was because she could hear the tapping of a keyboard and his quick, excited breaths. Finally, he said, "Paige. I recorded this. Let me play it back so you can hear. It'll be easier that way."

"All right."

She heard a few clicks and then static. There was some feedback and a clunk, but she guessed that was just from one machine knocking against another. The voice she heard was a cross between a whisper and a distant gust of wind. Once she locked onto it, she could make out the words. It said, "Guarding the . . . Torva'ox is their power. Full Blood power. Keeps them alive. Makes them stronger. Liam could influence the wretches and now he has absolute control over them. Over me too until the Breaking Moon passes."

Paige wanted to ask questions but reminded herself she was listening to a recording.

"The Torva'ox is power," Max continued. "That's . . . we can talk like this. Liam lied to us, but more will follow him. More like me. The others will grow stronger . . . Torva'ox gives them . . . will die. They will die or be broken. Die or be broken . . ."

"That's what I got," Stu said, breaking Paige's concentration.

"What's the Torvox?" When she didn't get an answer, she looked at the phone. Then she looked at Max. Whatever was happening with him, the struggle against it was wearing him out because the Mongrel's gnarled head now rested on the floor. The Half Breed, however, never stopped twitching. "What are the Full Bloods doing here, Max? You must want to tell me or you wouldn't have called out to me!"

"I'm getting something," Stu said. "I think he's saying, split. Split apart."

"Something needs to be split apart?" Paige asked.

The Mongrel's eyes came open and immediately fixed on her. "Full Bloods . . . gathering strength . . . too much strength," Stu told her. "Want to free plane . . . no, that's not it. Sorry Paige. It's *reclaim*. Reclaim . . . territories."

"The cities," Paige whispered. "Now that the Nymar have moved to take the cities, the Full Bloods want to kick them out."

"All territory. Leeches . . . destroyed. Only . . . Jesus," Stu sighed, in a way that made it clear that last part came from him and not anything he'd heard. When he spoke again it was in a frenzied rush. "He says the Full Bloods will destroy everyone and not just in the cities. The whole territory. What's that mean?"

"Full Bloods claim entire continents as their territories. Shit," Paige sighed. "They're really doing it. Skinners have always thrown out worst case scenarios, and this is the biggest one. The one where Full Bloods get sick of living in the forests and don't allow themselves to be hunted."

"They *allowed* themselves to be hunted?"

"Think of it in terms of us getting hassled by bees. We get stung and may move somewhere else because it's easier, but when we get really sick of those things, we start swatting. If that fails, we exterminate them."

"Not just . . . theirs . . . portion. Not just their portion," Stu said, sounding more and more like he was on a game show getting pantomime clues from a B-list celebrity. "All. All. All. He keeps saying all. And something's coming. *Oh!* I just thought of something. It could be a vortex!"

"A vortex is coming?" Paige asked.

"No, it could be a vortex instead of ley lines. That would explain a lot, but not the whole cell phone thing. The other part about something coming was from him."

The heat in her scars flared up again, but this time it was a deeper burn caused by the most powerful of all shapeshifters. "See what you can find about a Torvox or whatever that was. I'll check in for a report later, and don't call me!"

Chapter Twenty

Paige wanted to run.

She wasn't a stranger to that feeling, but there was never any time to give in to it. After signaling for Nadya to come back into the first bedroom, they huddled behind the bed piled high with blankets and mattress stuffing. Paige caught a smell powerful enough to let her know the rest of the body belonging to that hand was definitely hidden within the mound.

"Are you sure about this?" Nadya whispered.

The two women kept their backs against a wall, their hands wrapped tightly around their weapons, their eyes glued to the doorway.

"Yes," Paige replied. "There's a Full Blood coming. I can feel it."

"And you're sure about hiding here? Shouldn't we run? Or at least get ready to fight?"

"There's something about that hole in the floor in the other room," Paige explained. "I think it messes with their senses somehow."

"How do you know that?"

"Those things were placed here as guards, right?"

"Looks that way," Nadya said.

"As far as we know, Full Bloods can just about smell one M&M in a pile of Reece's Pieces from three hundred miles away, so why would they need to post a guard?"

Skinners: The Breaking

"What if the Full Bloods didn't post a guard?" Nadya asked.

"No Half Breed could think straight enough to do something like that."

"Could be instinct," Nadya said in a clipped whisper.

"Whatever is here is important to the Full Bloods. We need to find out why, and this may be our only chance."

"If it smells us, we're dead."

"And it may also hear us, so be ready."

The slow, lingering groan of old floorboards combined with churning breaths to silence the women immediately. Paige crouched until her nose came within inches of a cracked bone she hadn't seen before. The stench of death had been overwhelming at first, but she'd gotten used to it enough to stay there without giving away her position by puking up her last two meals. The bed was between her and the door. Under it, apart from the newly discovered body parts, there were plenty of dust bunnies, a few mismatched socks, and a short stack of porno magazines. She gazed across the top of a crinkled set of fake jugs to stare at the doorway as the Full Blood entered the room. From her vantage point she saw a thick paw press down against the floor and flatten as the Full Blood placed its weight on it. Given the lighting in the room and the narrow slot through which she had to look, she could barely distinguish the light rusty color of its fur. When the werewolf approached the bed and sniffed it hesitantly, Paige gripped her machete tighter.

Blood trickled against her palm as the thorns bit into her flesh.

Minh pulled in a deep sniffing breath and the bed creaked as she leaned against the edge of the mattress.

Whatever the Mongrels had splashed onto Paige and Nadya was working because the Full Blood couldn't seem to smell either of them. The fresh trickle of blood could have been a danger, so Paige lifted her weapon toward the putrid mattress that was already soaked through with enough bodily fluids to mask even the bitter scent of a Skinner's weapon. At least, that's what she hoped.

The bed groaned as the Full Blood leaned even closer.

On the floor, huddled against the bed frame, Nadya tightened her grip around the FAMAS she'd inherited from her dead partner.

Paige's body was twisted into an aching knot. Her head and shoulders were angled to keep from cresting over the top of the bed. Her legs were tucked into an extreme squat and her spine felt like a length of rope that had been pulled taut and stretched over someone's knee. No matter how much the air stank, her lungs demanded to be filled. Rather than give in to any of that, she maintained her position, held her breath, clenched her lips shut and kept her hand pressed against the leaking remnants of what had once been another human being. All the while, she waited for the swipe of claws through her face or the sharp impact of fangs in her throat. Then again, when dealing with Full Bloods there was always the chance of being killed before you even knew you were hurt.

When Minh drew her next breath, she coughed it right back up. As the bed creaked back to its original position, Paige lay down to watch Minh's paws swell to accommodate her upright form. Now the only thing she had to worry about was being spotted if Minh decided to use her new height to look over the bed.

Minh turned and walked back out of the room. She paused in the hallway, took half a glance over her shoulder, then let out another hacking breath. Apparently, Paige thought with relief, a hyperkeen sense of smell wasn't always such a good thing when confined in a room with a rotting corpse.

As the Full Blood approached the next room, Paige looked over at Nadya, who was staring intently back at her, but neither woman dared make a sound. Paige pointed to the Nadya and stabbed that finger toward the spot where they were currently hiding. She then pointed at herself and waved at the door. Judging by the intensity in the Amriany woman's eyes, Nadya had no intention of staying put while she scouted ahead.

They engaged in a brief staring contest before Paige conceded with a roll of her eyes. Keeping low and close to the wall, she maneuvered around the bed while trying desperately not to bump into anything. Leaving the concealing stench behind made her nervous, but she wasn't about to miss an opportunity to find out what the hell was going on in the next room.

After leaving the room where two women had been hiding, Minh shifted into her human form for all of two seconds before deciding the house was unfit for her lean, lightly tanned nakedness. By the time she got through the doorway to the bedroom with the pit in the floor, her figure had settled somewhere between woman and beast. Her movements gave her all the grace of a drunk stumbling in after a late night, which Paige guessed was due to the ley lines or whatever sort of energy was flowing up from the exposed section of ground. Although she wasn't sure about that yet, Paige was confident that she hadn't been spotted. No Full Blood would have allowed a Skinner to see them in a state like that.

Minh dropped to her knees and reached out to the pit with both hands. Her fingers splayed apart, and when they couldn't go any farther, her hand shifted into something that allowed them to become even more of a trembling tangle. The noise she made started as a wail but slowly rose to a howl. Paige found herself transfixed by Minh's cry, almost to the point of walking into the other bedroom just to be closer to its source. Fortunately, Nadya was there to place a cautious hand on her shoulder to keep her in place. Still, from where she stood she got a good look at Minh's powerful back as the Full Blood bowed down to sink her claws into the exposed dirt. Every coarse strand of fur stood on end, then Minh's head snapped up. She was about to let out another howl but managed to choke it down.

"It's a real kick, ain't it?"

Spoken in a thick cockney accent, the question struck an immediate chord with Paige that made her want to jump up from where she was hiding and sink her weapon into the other Full Blood's neck.

Liam had strode through the front door on two legs but still wearing the pelt of a wolf. By the time he entered the smaller bedroom, he'd shifted down into a human body covered with a thinning mat of fur. He was nothing but a skinny naked man when he crouched near the pit in the next room and allowed his hands to hang between his knees in what might have been a lazy effort to conceal himself.

Minh's response was a series of grunts and growls that could have been made while she was in pain or in the middle of a vigorous copulation.

"Yeah," Liam said. "I know just how you feel. It's dangerous to be here, though. Too much for the senses to be this close to a source this pure." He stretched out both hands while fur eased out from beneath his skin and layers of muscle piled up like thick waters coming in at high tide. He'd grown a long snout by the time he lifted his head to gaze up at the ceiling. When he opened his mouth, his human teeth slowly extended into blunted spikes. "Considering how strong it is here, I'm surprised we didn't get two new pups to take Henry's place. Wouldn't that have been a riot?"

Paige made it to the edge of the doorway by the time Minh snapped her head to look over her shoulder. Since Liam had swelled up to his brawnier form, however, there might as well have been another wall between her and the other bedroom.

"Speaking of riots," he continued, "there's one going on right now. You should make the rounds and keep the wretches in line."

"I can't," she growled. After the creaking of a few bones, she was able to speak a little clearer. "I can't control them. They don't listen to me like they listen to you."

"You just have to show them who's boss," Liam replied.

"Or perhaps there's another reason. Perhaps Esteban was right when he said you've been here drinking more than your share of the Torva'ox for longer than you admitted."

"I made it no secret that I was here."

"Did Randolph know?" Minh asked.

The sound he made started as a snarl but shifted into a hacking laugh. "It's his territory. If he didn't know something like that, he would have been picked off a long time ago."

"That's not the arrangement, Liam. We've lived in our own territories so the Torva'ox would be drawn to us equally."

Now that she'd heard that strange word spoken by a physical voice instead of a recording or secondhand translation, Paige sifted once more through her mental files. She still couldn't come up with anything.

"And that won't work anymore, darlin'," Liam continued. "More humans know about us and the leeches and every other thing that's been hiding for so long. What they don't know already, they're learning about, thanks to insane fools like Misonyk or those fucking Nymar who've been making the headlines. And when the Nymar do try to tend to their business without making a spectacle, the Skinners have been stirring things up to the point where it's gotten tougher for anyone to go about their business like we used to."

From where she was standing, it was difficult for Paige to tell whether Minh's response was a laugh or a growl.

"Making a spectacle?" she said in a voice almost fully human. "The Nymar are making a spectacle? This is coming from the one who tore apart a city in front of human police, news cameras, and countless other eyes staring at him?"

"That was more than just a spectacle."

"I know," Minh sighed. "You were sending a message."

"And you got it, luv. You, Esteban, and even the old trickster that had been locked in Lancroft's cage. Have you heard from Esteban?"

"He's found another one of Lancroft's storehouses. The other Jekhibar wasn't there, but he says he's found the original Shadow Spore."

Liam grunted in what was plainly disgust. "You use the name given to it by the leeches?"

"They may have named it, but it was meant for us," she said. "It's just been lost until now. Lancroft tried to keep the source separate from the first carrier, but now they've both been found."

"Are the legends true?" Liam asked. "Can he take the forbidden form?"

Paige strained her ears but could only hear the broken floor creaking beneath the two werewolves. Finally, Minh said, "Esteban needs a Jekhibar for that. Randolph chased him away and the humans swarmed in to attack them both before it could be found."

Shrugging, Liam told her, "If you can trust him. There's more to worry about than Esteban or his legends."

Liam's feet scraped against the floor as he settled into a new position at the edge of the pit. The ebon Full Blood arched his back and sunk his hands into the dirt exposed beneath the splintered floorboards. The way his head craned back and his entire body tensed, Paige imagined his toes were curling as well. When he let out the breath that had built up inside of him, she could almost feel it against her ear.

"Don't be so troubled if you can't take as much of it in," Liam said. "It's not something meant for all of us."

"Don't give me that," Minh snapped. "You've been encroaching on Randolph's territory for longer than you've been telling any of us, soaking up more than your share of the Torva'ox for all of that time."

"You know Randolph. Maybe not as well as I do, but," Liam added in a voice that must have been accompanied by a lecherous smile, "certainly in a different way. With that kind of insight, you must also know that none of us could have done much of anything in this territory without his consent. He may not be taking part in this war, but he knows better than to stand against it. It's inevitable."

"Nobody thinks Randolph was ignorant of anything happening here. That's the problem. Why wouldn't he want his share of the Torva'ox?"

Sliding his fingers from the dirt, Liam said, "He's old and tired."

"You still have to answer for how you got away from your assigned lands and managed to trade territories with Jaden."

"Wasn't easy."

"Did you kill her?"

There was a long pause before Liam finally said, "There are other ways to solve our conflicts, luv."

This time, Paige had to fight to keep from laughing. She knew better than to make a sound or even draw too large of a breath, which didn't leave her many options as far as getting out of that room. Not far away, Nadya gripped the FAMAS and studied her surroundings carefully.

The voice that came next was smooth and silkier than any human's. "If she's not dead, then why isn't Jaden here?" Minh asked.

"It don't matter," Liam replied in an accent that seemed

to get more guttural as Minh's became more refined. "There are enough of us here to draw more of the Torva'ox than any have ever felt. The Breaking Moon will see to that. Esteban probably tried to convince you to kill me before it rose."

"Something like that," she admitted.

"And now you must see what a mistake that would be," Liam said in something close to a purr. "Nobody can command the wretches like I do. After all that's happened lately, the humans are just frazzled enough for our war to be fought and won."

"We could all go back to our territories and wait for this storm to blow over," she offered. "The humans may be worked up right now, but they are short-lived and easily distracted. In a matter of a few years they'll be back to nipping at each other instead of pestering us. And in a decade or two, these instances will be forgotten."

"No!" Liam barked with enough force to send a shockwave through the entire house. "How can you be so shortsighted? We live for centuries; observe so much in that time, and still we are *blind*!"

"What would you prefer?" Minh asked in a snarling rasp that Paige could barely hear. "Do you seriously want us to remain here and continue fighting amongst ourselves? We've always been better than that."

"Have we? How long did it take for us to figure out where the territories needed to be in order to keep any one of us from acquiring too much of the Torva'ox? The only one to acquire all of that power is still a legend among us."

"Gorren became a rampaging lunatic who nearly unmade us all! He may have become the most powerful Full Blood in our history, but he had to be hunted and killed by his own kind. Is that the legacy you want to repeat?"

Wagging a long, gnarled finger at her, Liam said, "But Gorren wasn't organized and he wasn't patient. We gather here and now with a plan, and as the Breaking stokes the fire inside of us, the Torva'ox will let us spread it to the humans with nothing more than a thought! How can you not see the beauty in that?"

"And what of the Balance?"

"The Balance that Randolph loves to spout off about? That's nothing more than a bunch of dribble spewing from the mouth of a wide-eyed child."

"Now I see why you wanted to send him so far from here," she said. "Randolph would tear you apart where you stood if he heard that kind of talk. I'm surprised he hasn't challenged you already, considering the mess you've made of his continent."

"Randolph's too busy protecting the newly awakened pup and contending with Esteban to care about what any of us do anymore." Sarcasm dripped from his voice like saliva trickling from his fangs when he said, "He's tired. All he wants to do is crawl back into his forest and run free with snow between his toes while you and I and any of the others he considers to be troublemakers kill each other like the brutes of Gorren's time."

"And what do you want, Liam?" When his eyes drifted along the front of her body, the female werewolf added, "Besides that?"

"Always time for that later, eh? Remember how well I treated you back in London?"

"I remember how well you treated those ladies in Whitechapel."

"Those weren't ladies and it was never proven that I was the only one responsible for that. Besides, what the hell does that have to do with what's going on here and now?"

"Just reminding both of us what kind of man you are," Minh said.

"The portion of me that's a man never was my best," Liam admitted. "Do you feel the power coming from this spot? It's the purest essence of what gives us our gifts. Just standing here so close to it now will allow both of us to make the Half Breeds in this town sit, roll over, and play dead. Soon the Mongrels will be put back into their places as well, just like that one right there."

Until now Minh had seemed too distracted by the power leaking up from the floor to notice Max or the Half Breed. "The Mongrels have been resisting us ever since we got here," she said.

Liam was all too anxious to reply, "Maybe, but this one

is a special creation. He's got my essence running through his bones. I've been able to make him and all the others that wanted a shot at immortality see things my way. After drinking up just a little of the Torva'ox, I've made those Mongrels my pets. This one here will keep the local burrowers away while the other ones I turned are out spreading my good word."

"You've turned the packs against each other?"

"I convinced a few of them to take the step between Mongrel and Full Blood. Apparently, they've forgotten their history lessons as well," Liam said. "I sent those few out to infect more, and now that we've uncovered this source of the Torva'ox, I can wrap ones like Max here around my little finger."

"But only from a short distance," she pointed out.

"After the Breaking Moon rises, distance won't matter."

"Why talk to me like this?"

"Because you've always been the smart one," he replied. "Between you, me, and Esteban, the Half Breeds have more chaos in their little addled minds than normal. Just think what will happen when our control over them becomes absolute."

When Minh shifted into another form, Paige could hear the soft brush of expanding muscle against stretching bones and the scrape of claws emerging from her fingers. Soon, a luxurious breath drifted through the air as the Full Blood squatted down to drive her hands into the pit. "Randolph won't stand for it," she stated.

Liam's response was spoken in a voice that sounded as if it was drawn taut between two halves of a vice. "He's abandoning this territory for another. Probably back to greener pastures in Norway or some other chunk of forest closer to his hometown."

"There are a few others who didn't respond to the message you sent. And what about the Skinners? Esteban has already found one of their strongholds. There must be more."

"Calling anything those Skinners have a stronghold is giving them a lot more credit than they deserve. They're scattered, hunted by their own police, and dividing into separate camps thanks to the scraps left behind by Jonah

Lancroft. We have the leeches to thank for that. Maybe we'll only torture them a little once we pay them a visit."

"What of Kawosa?"

"All he's ever wanted to do is toy with the humans," Liam said with absolute certainty. "That and tinkering with the newest model of Half Breed. He's got his wheels turning and I've got mine. As long as they don't grind against each other, we'll get along just fine. All I want to hear from you is that you're willing to stand with me against the humans and those goddamn leeches after we've received our dose of what lays in the ground at your feet. And if one of us gains it all, they will lay claim to the last gift that Kawosa has never passed on to his kin."

"In order for one to get all of the Torva'ox, there would have to be no others to draw it away from them," Minh said. "We're not the only ones drawing from this source. Whether they know it or not, humans drink from this well. Skinners may take more than normal, but all of them take some. Is that why you've unleashed such widespread destruction? To keep the Torva'ox from trickling even into human souls?"

"By the time the next Breaking Moon rises, we'll have thinned their herd either by turning them into wretches or killing them outright."

"And," she mused, "we'll be in control of the wretches?"

Hearing the breath coming from Liam was enough to paint the picture of his toothy smile in Paige's mind. "Now we're on the same page," he said.

"But this is not the only spot where the Torva'ox flows," Minh pointed out.

He looked down at the pit as if there was no looking away. "This is where the first Full Blood has been born in the last thirteen decades. There is no stronger source and there is no better time for us to claim it. The Skinners will collect themselves before too long, but for now they are too weak to be a threat. The Nymar are entrenched, which will only make them overconfident. The humans have always been curious, but now they have the means to scour every wooded patch of land, every cave, and every corner of the desert from space."

"If that were true, they'd be able to find their own criminals."

"Human criminals are like the leeches, themselves," he sneered. "They hide for years at a time, skulking in basements like Mongrel rats or spending every dollar they steal to purchase new names and identities. Do you want to start living like that?"

In a softer voice Minh said, "Some of us already have."

Liam pivoted around so quickly that Paige was certain she'd been spotted. Instead, he hung his head low while speaking in a voice that rumbled like a tremor through the charged soil beneath the house. "The only reason we would ever fall from the top of the pecking order on this earth would be if we allowed it, and there isn't one damned reason why we would allow such a thing."

"We used to go where we pleased," Minh said in a soft, almost comforting tone. "We avoided humans simply because they were noisy, arrogant, and stank of smoke and metal. When we were curious as to how they were living, we walked among them. The ones that stepped out of line, we wiped off the face of the planet. Then the Nymar spread like a plague and lied well enough to convince us that staying in the cities for too long was more trouble than it was worth. I think Kawosa had something to do with that. He is Ktseena. Some say he can look into the soul of any shapeshifter."

"He may have spawned us in one way or another," Liam sneered, "but he can't look into my soul any more than a father can know what's truly going on inside his son. If he knew what was goin' on inside of me, he would never have left me alone for so long."

Minh approached him in the form of a lean, finely toned human. Her long black hair hung down over smooth shoulders and pert, firm breasts. Even in the little bit of light coming through the window, her skin had the color of lightly creamed coffee. "As more power flows through us, the temptation will arise for us to thin our own herd. Esteban already met Randolph, which means the first blood has already been spilt. The last time we fought among ourselves this way, entire cities were laid to waste. Human history records them as natural disasters only because there weren't enough of them left on those battlefields to record the truth."

"I don't know about you, darlin'," Liam growled, "but I *am* a natural disaster."

A cold knot formed in Paige's stomach. For anyone else on earth, that statement would have been hot air. Hearing it spoken by a Full Blood was like finding out that a tornado was not only conscious but eager to turn the next midwestern town into a swirling cloud of splinters and screaming motorists.

"There are already precious few of us on earth," Minh continued. "and there will be even fewer after a fight like that."

"And those of us that remain will have the power we should have had all along! Do you even know what can be done by someone who wields a lion's share of the Torva'ox?"

"I know the legends, but those aren't enough to start killing our own kind and laying waste to so many humans. They may be a weaker species, but they are persistent, they are vengeful, and they have numbers on their side. We must not underestimate the backlash that will follow."

"Surely you're not frightened by their precious machines and guns and bombs," he grunted.

Minh's human face had soft, Asian features. Her hands slipped through the fur on his chest and her thin lips curled into a wide smile as she said, "Their machines are useless without anyone to operate them. Guns and bombs can't do anything if there is no human hand to fire them, and with the Torva'ox, such a thing can be arranged."

"Now *this*," Liam said while reaching around to grab her hips with both hands, "is why I've continued this conversation. You have vision, my darling."

"I do," Minh replied. "Which is why I can see where this road of yours can take us. Perhaps it is too late to hope for us to go back to quiet times when the humans were blissfully unaware of what hunted them, but we must truly know what we're starting. What do you hope to accomplish? Do you want to rule them?"

"What I want is to set things in their proper order. The strong are supposed to prosper through *strength*! Not by keeping their heads down and staying away from gnats who've survived through sheer procreation and strut like kings because they can throw lead pellets in mass quantities or burn their own cities to the ground. We know how to take the machines out of the picture. We know how to knock the humans back down to where they need to be. All we lack is the will to put this knowledge to use. I may have forced our hand, but can you honestly tell me that a part of you doesn't want to thank me for it?"

After a heavy pause, Minh sighed and said, "This will get bloody. Bloodier than it already has. Bloodier than anyone could anticipate. Bloodier, even, then you may anticipate. What will be left when all that blood is spilled? What will be left when the humans retaliate and start those fires they're so fond of? What will be left for us when the world finally stops burning?"

"I don't know," Liam said with an eagerness that Paige could feel from where she hid. "Let's find out!"

Chapter Twenty-One

*Twelve miles north of
Raton, New Mexico*

"So what now?" Cole asked.

Paige's voice came through in a rush. While telling him the basics of what she'd learned, she'd been running down side streets and hopping fences from one backyard to another. She'd listened to his update without panting more than Cole after climbing too many stairs. "Now, we get our asses to another safe house and prepare to clean this city out. I need to mix up a batch of Half Breed bait to try and draw enough of those things away from here and give the locals a chance to get out."

"Anything other than that? This sounds like some pretty big news."

"I was kinda hoping to hear a good idea or two from you," she said. "I hate to say that I'm out of my depth here, but . . ."

"Yeah," Cole sighed. "Even with your Army buddies we may be out of our depth. Have you tried calling them again yet?"

"No," she snapped. "I sent Rico to check them out and I'm leaving it at that. After what happened with you, Adderson deserves to deal with him. And what about your wolf girl?"

"We're meeting her somewhere in New Mexico."

"Jessup's idea?"

"Yep."

Although the rattling on her end of the phone had stopped, Paige's breathing was getting heavier. "He's kind of a hick, but that backwoods stuff of his may be what we need right now. Should keep you off anyone's radar. Let me know what you come up with."

"Will do." Cole tapped the front of the phone, realized it wasn't his own touch-screen beauty, and put the sparkling monstrosity away. The scenery flowing past him on the other side of the Ford's window consisted of dusty rock and shrubs that were tough enough to survive the punishment doled out by a sun that only grew fiercer as it shone farther south of Chicago. "Why the hell is your window open?" he grunted.

"Because the fresh air feels good," Jessup replied. "Don't tell me you expect there to be AC blowin' on your face no matter where you go. Besides, it's a dry heat."

"You know what else is dry heat? The middle of a freaking oven. Crank the AC."

"So what's Paige got to say?" Jessup asked without even looking at the control to raise his window.

She'd told him the highlights of what she'd gleaned from the conversation between Liam and Minh, so Cole relayed that to Jessup while staring out the window.

Finally, Jessup said, "No need to stare outside like a mooning hound. If that gal was around, we'd feel her."

Cole's scars weren't burning and he couldn't see Cecile anywhere outside. Still, he couldn't quite get himself to lower his guard. "Are you sure she's going to meet up with us?"

"If she wasn't, there ain't a lot we could do about it." Since he wasn't taking any comfort from that, Jessup added, "Sometimes you just gotta do your thing and have faith that whatever you set into motion before will keep on turning."

"You think she heard anything I said about what Paige found?"

"They can sniff out quite a lot, but I don't think it's the same for hearing. At least, not for one as inexperienced as her, especially since she'd have to hear past this damn powerful engine to put any pieces together. I still can't believe Paige heard all of that from two Full Bloods without them knowing she was there."

"There was some sort of interference. She says it messed up a little bit of everything, including cell phones. Whatever it was, it distracted the Full Bloods long enough for them to have their meeting and leave before they noticed she was there. She got away and was still running when I talked to her."

"I suppose that ain't too surprising. Considering how everything's been going, the Full Bloods don't have to worry if we hear them talking or not." When Cole stared at him, Jessup added, "Time to face up to it. We're scrambling just to see another sunrise. The quicker we wrap our heads around that, the better. We're almost in town, so I'd better tell you what I got in mind for when we get there. You do much hunting lately?"

"Do werewolves count?"

"You think I let that Full Blood girl run out on her own so we could get enough privacy to talk about hunting squirrel? Of course werewolves count! Have you been out hunting since the Mud Flu cleared up or not?"

"Actually, no," Cole admitted. "We've been busy with the Lancroft business, the Nymar, and then I was locked up. The whole prison thing happened when I was hoping for some time to rest."

"Typical Monkey's Paw scenario." Seeing the blank look on Cole's face, Jessup scolded, "Don't you ever read? 'The Monkey's Paw' is a short story about making wishes. It's this charm that grants 'em but turns them around to bite you in the ass through some loophole. You wish for a million dollars, it gives you a million that was stolen from some bank. You want time away from hunting, you wind up in prison."

"Now I see why Cecile was so quick to get the hell away from you."

"The reason I brought up hunting," Jessup said without trying to disguise the sharpness in his voice, "is because it's been getting mighty crazy out here. A lot of Skinners, me included, have been stumbling onto plenty of things that even *we* thought was bullshit or myth. Some of them were just laying low because of Half Breeds in the area. Just so you know, Half Breeds love the desert. Wide open spaces, plenty of room to run, folks living out in trailers or cabins that nobody'll hardly miss."

"Tons of little caves to use for dens?"

Jessup raised his eyebrows. "Very good. Most of the critters out here hid because they didn't have what it took to survive a pack of Half Breeds. What's so funny?"

"Did you just say critters?" Cole said through a persistent chuckle. "Why not just call them varmints, Yosemite Sam?"

"I can see why Paige likes you. Smartasses travel in packs. Anyway, after the Mud Flu cut the Half Breed population, the things that were hiding from them didn't have to hide no more. What we're after in Raton is something you ain't gonna find in any Skinner journal. At least, not one from this century. I checked."

When they passed a green sign on the side of the interstate that told them they were within ten miles of Raton, Jessup eased his foot off the gas and leaned forward to scan the horizon. "Cecile wants to hide and Randolph wants us to guard her, but we're not playing this by any Full Blood's rules. I sent her ahead to sniff out some Half Breeds in the desert. When she finds 'em, she'll have to bring me a few of their hides in one piece so I can get a few of their sweat glands and mix up something that will make her smell like one of them and not a Full Blood."

"Can we really make that?"

Jessup let out an exasperated sigh. "What the hell did Paige teach you, boy? Anyway, that won't keep her busy for too long. She should find some Half Breeds, but bringing back pieces large enough to use will be tricky."

"What if those things kill her?" Cole asked.

Stabbing a finger at Cole, Jessup said, "Just because that girl is scared and young, don't forget what she is. She's a Full Blood, so she can handle any Half Breeds. We also need to watch her to see if she's setting us up for another fall. Understand me?"

Cole nodded, but hesitantly.

"When we get to town, you'll follow my lead," Jessup said. "You'll just have to trust me on the rest because there ain't time to tell you every little thing."

"The hell there isn't," Cole said while opening the glove compartment and digging beneath the receipts, napkins, tire pressure gauges, and Handi Wipes to find a snub-nosed .38 revolver.

"How'd you know that was in there?"

"Skinners are more likely to have one of these in the glove compartment than they are a pink slip."

"So you know all about us, huh?" Jessup asked. "If you know so damn much, you should know there aren't a lot of us left out here and that we have to stick together no matter how badly we got along before. Oh yeah," he added when he saw the expression that drifted across Cole's face. "I remember what a dick you were to me in Philly."

"Actually, I remember you as the dick."

"We need to put that aside. More importantly, you need to put that gun aside."

Cole tossed the revolver back into the glove compartment and slapped the little folding door shut. "There. Now since I'm willing to go along with you, the least you can do is show me the same respect and tell me what the hell you're dragging me into. If you can't trust me that far, then I might as well get out of this truck right now."

"All right. But first I need you to tell me somethin'." Placing his hands on the steering wheel at ten and two, Jessup turned to point a cockeyed stare at Cole when he asked, "Ever seen a gargoyle?"

The road circling around Mt. Calvary Cemetery ran straight along the eastern border of a burial ground surrounded on all sides by a cement wall that angled steeply up or down to accommodate the natural flow of the terrain. Naked trees scattered among dry scrub, making the barren stretch of land look as if it had been scooped straight from the desert. Unlike the lonely outside of town, this one's graves were marked.

Jessup parked on the northern edge of the cemetery on Hillside Road. From there he led Cole around the perimeter of the cemetery like a Scout leader taking his troop on a tour of the Grand Canyon. "See there?" he said while waving his hand to a chipped stone statue erected on the cement barrier.

As he had with all the other statues he was shown, Cole nodded. "Yeah. I see it. It's a statue of a dog."

"What about that one?"

A few yards away from the knee-high statue of Man's Best Friend, there was another, much larger, statue. Those two were part of a collection were set up around the cemetery that included a few wolves and one old man whose features had been worn away by the elements. Examining the next one Jessup pointed out, Cole could only find a few hastily spray-painted words on the side of the sculpture. "It's a horse. So what?"

"So what? Take a look at those up there. Don't they strike you as peculiar?"

He looked at the row of statues scattered unevenly near the wall. The cement barrier was barely as tall as he was and seemed to be there not so much for decoration as to keep drunk drivers from interrupting the peaceful slumber of residents interred on the other side. While they weren't exactly works of art, the statues on the wall itself were of birds, and one winged creatures that had enough detail for Cole to make out ridges of skin above the claws it used to grip its perch. One wing was outstretched and the other was partially folded against its back. Its eyes were blank. A stumpy beak was partially open to reveal poorly chiseled teeth.

"It does seem kinda weird that these would be here at all," he said. "There aren't any other decorations that I can see."

"Very good. Always trust your instinct. You're a Skinner. If something feels off-kilter to you, it probably is."

"You've never been to Chicago, have you? The off-kilter alarm has to be shut off sometimes."

"Don't let the twang in my voice fool you, son. I've been to plenty of places, and when it comes to hunting the things we do, chasing them in the cities is easy. Never gets too dark. Out here," Jessup said as he placed a hand on the wall and let his eyes wander upward, "once the sun goes down, it's just you and the stars."

"I've been in the dark too," Cole said. "Are you going to tell me what I should be looking for or do we wait until Frank and Lambert get here?"

Ignoring that, the older Skinner approached the horse statue, looked it over for less than a second and slapped its flank. "See this here? No artistic value. I'm not going to say that every gargoyle on every rooftop is somethin' special, but take a look at this one. First of all, the placement. Gargoyles on buildings mean all sorts of things, from good luck to keeping bad spirits away. Those are usually up high and made to look nice or scary or whatnot. Like, for example, that one there," he added, waving at the stone creature on the wall with the birds. Turning his attention back to the spray-painted horse, he said, "These others aren't anywhere near a roof. There aren't any other decorative type things about. Even the wall looks like it took all of two minutes to build. Second, the way it's standing. Decorations are made to look nice. See how the muscles on this one's back are all swollen and straining?"

"Look at the eyes. It looks scared."

"Very good! Now touch it."

Cole looked closer and reached out to tap a finger against the spot on the statue's back that Jessup was staring at. It felt like rock.

Since Cole wasn't impressed yet, Jessup led him to the next statue. "See the way that dog is cringing? And that crow's obviously squawking at something."

At the third and forth gargoyles, Jessup pointed out how some layers of rock were thicker than others in similar spots on each sculpture's chest and ribs. They'd gone all the way back to the horse when he proudly said, "But this is the best one of them all! This is why I parked here, so you could see this one for sure. You would've scored big-time bonus points if you would've spotted this on yer own, but we'll see."

"Bonus points?"

"Yeah. You're a video game guy, right?"

At first only Stu seemed to know about his former life in Seattle. Slowly but surely, ever since he and Paige had monitored the comings and goings at Lancroft's old house in Philadelphia, more Skinners got hold of that bit of news. Needless to say, a bunch of gun-toting monster hunters weren't impressed with the multiplayer maps of *Hammer Strike*'s lava level.

Skinners: The Breaking

"Okay, I'll skip the bonus points," Cole said. "Just tell me what the hell I'm supposed to be looking at."

Jessup stepped up to the statue as if sneaking up on a sleeping cat. Pointing to its ribs, he asked, "See these scratches here and here?"

Cole didn't step right up to the statue because a car was approaching from Hillside. Already imagining how bad it looked to have the two of them lurking outside a cemetery to size up its statuary, he kept his distance and waited for the car to turn north and head farther into town.

"Stop being so squirrelly," Jessup scolded. "Look at these scratches. It's important."

"More important than a Full Blood charging into town in a matter of minutes?"

"Could be."

The scratches in question were right beneath Jessup's finger. "Let me guess," Cole grunted. "No artistic value?"

For the first time since he'd met Jessup, the grizzled Skinner looked genuinely impressed with him. "That's right! There ain't no chips along the edges and the texture is smooth, which means the scratches are part of the statue and not just wear and tear. They're in the wrong spot and go in the wrong direction to have been made by anything flying off the road. That, combined with these thick patches along the sides and back, tell me there are real gargoyles here!"

"And how did you know these statues were here at all?"

"Spotted 'em while passing through town a few months ago," Jessup told him. "Gotta keep yer eyes open for this sort of thing."

"How slow do you drive?"

"See, here's the tricky thing with gargoyles," Jessup said without paying any mind to Cole's sarcasm. "It's the same tricky thing that has to do with a lot of the smaller beasties that have been surfacing lately. Since things like these have been hidden away or sleeping or whatever the hell else, Skinners haven't seen them for years. And," he added just as Cole opened his mouth to hurry him along, "since these things ain't bloodsuckers or shapeshifters, there's no way for most Skinners to feel them in their scars anymore."

"So Skinners have seen gargoyles before?"

"Gargoyles were mentioned in almost every Skinner journal from the 1750s all the way through the 1800s. That's when a Full Blood claimed this whole continent and drove 'em underground. I spotted the first one for myself when I was scouring graveyards for more Half Breed dens or Shunkaws. Did some research and now I'm spotting them all over."

Pulling open his vest, Jessup revealed a harness that might have started off as a shoulder holster but had been modified to carry two wooden clubs that were each just under a foot long. He pulled one out by the handle, using the tips of his fingers to avoid the thorns. "Shapeshifters and Nymar are the most common things out there. Wasn't always like that, though. Full Blood's closin' in."

"I know. I can feel her."

"Can you feel the Squam?"

"No," Cole said warily. "Can you?"

When Jessup tossed him one of the clubs, Cole reflexively snatched it from the air. The thorns bit into him, sinking like needles through the toughened skin of his palm. As soon as the little spikes touched his blood, something else flowed through the scars. It was a cold tingle that felt as if he'd accidentally gotten window cleaner into his blood.

"Journals talk about there being lots more than what we see nowadays," Jessup continued. "Skinners had to adapt. Their methods were more or less the same as they are now, but were a bit more flexible. Whenever they found something new, they'd take some of its blood and add it to the mix used for the varnish on their weapons. It's a practice that's been phased out lately just because there hasn't been much need for it. Old-timers like me passed along the methods for modifying the varnish even when the young ones only wanted to fight what they could see."

The Full Blood was getting closer. Cole figured he didn't have to say as much to another Skinner, so he nervously glanced toward the edge of town, where he guessed Cecile might be approaching. Then something else came along to add itself to the growing burn caused by the werewolf. The chill beneath his scars spread like a layer of slush sandwiched somewhere in between the heat from the varnish and the warmth of his own body.

"Feel it yet?" Jessup asked.

"I think so."

"That cold is from the sample of gargoyle blood I scraped up when I found the first one a few weeks ago. It'll only last a while after you switch back to your own weapon, so we'll have to modify that one too. Didn't you carry a spear back in Philly?"

"Yeah. Mind if I use this until I get it back?"

"Sure, just don't get too jumpy."

Cole's entire hand started to shake. Everything from cold to heat and every gradient in between rushed through his fist. "I think something's wrong. Feels like I'm allergic to this one or something."

"Told you not to get jumpy. I've scraped up all kinds of new blood and added it to the varnish on that club. You need to get used to it. Finding that first gargoyle was a lucky stroke. They must've either been getting too cocky, frightened, or hungry to worry about staying hid any longer. I didn't know what the hell it was at first until a bunch of them damn near got me. Faster than you'd ever think. That's one of the things that keeps 'em from being noticed. They'll jump out and take yer head off before you even knew what was happening."

"Shit," Cole said as he hopped away from the statue. "You might want to open with that the next time you give a lesson in gargoyles."

"Relax. That thing's not gonna hurt you."

The burning in Cole's scars grew hotter, but not quickly. Cecile was either circling the town or trying to approach without being seen.

Jessup stepped up to the statue and ran his fingertips along the smooth patch on the horse's back. "See, gargoyles are lurkers. They can hide damn near anywhere and you won't ever find them unless you know exactly where to look. Just because you see a sculpture that looks creepy don't make it a gargoyle."

"This cold in my scars tells me they're here, right?"

"Yep." Drawing a hunting knife from a scabbard hanging from his belt, Jessup drove the tip into the smooth patch of rock along the horse's back and started chipping it away.

"But the tricky thing is that they're damn near impossible to chase, so you gotta make them come to you. Can you guess the one thing a gargoyle don't like more than anything else in the world?"

The club in Cole's hand grew into a short stake before the bottom end extended and split into something that resembled a thick forked tongue. Not even noticing that he'd instinctually created a smaller version of his spear, he circled around to get behind the statue and said, "I would imagine they hate it when someone comes along to jam a knife in their back."

"Well, yeah, but remember what I said about them bein' lurkers. What every lurker wants is to hide and lurk in peace. What they hate is when someone knows they're there. And this stuff right here," he said, after the tip of his blade chipped off a piece of the statue that fell away like a small section of eggshell, "is one of the things that lets them know they've been found out."

Cole tightened his grip on the club. His eyes were fixed upon the statue, waiting for it to move or balk at getting a piece of its back torn off. When that didn't happen, he inched in for a closer look at the damage Jessup had done. Whatever the thing was, it sure as hell wasn't a statue. Beneath the chipped portion was leathery muscle covered in a slimy layer of thick, pungent slime.

"Aw shit," Cole grunted as the putrid smell of rotten meat and spoiled rust hit him. "That's blood, all right."

"It sure is. What'd you expect?"

The burning in his scars was growing, but not quick enough to mean that Cecile was on her way to the cemetery using anything close to a direct route. In the distance to the north, the sound of screeching tires, honking horns, and shouting voices rolled through the air.

"God damn it," Cole said while bringing the club up to a defensive position. "You think she found Frank? What if she lost control and took out some locals?"

"She could've done that with or without us lookin' after her," Jessup mused. When a whistling shriek drifted overhead, he didn't even bother looking up.

"What the hell was that?" Cole asked.

"Just stand still and wait for them."

Cole wished he had the gun from Jessup's glove compartment. As the screeching came again, it raked all the way through his body.

The chipped statue was bleeding.

Shrieking came from several different angles in the sky. Sunlight was fading into a dull glow that gave the other statues an aura.

"I think that one just moved!" Cole said, pointing the club at a nearby dog statue.

"No it didn't."

The shrieking grew louder.

"What is that crap you dug out of that thing's back, Jessup? Is that gargoyle going to wake up or not?"

"Shut up! I told you we need to wait for them. They won't come if we're looking for them."

"Spare me the predator prey bullshit and just tell me what the fuck these statues are supposed to do for us!"

"Shut up so I can listen, dammit," Jessup barked.

"Are there more cemeteries around here?" Cole asked. "Or churches? Where else do you find gargoyle perches? Just tell me what I need to know!"

"What the hell is wrong with you, Cole?"

Cole's blood surged through his veins in a sporadic mix of fast and slow rhythms. It pumped in time to his heartbeat at first, but the longer he paid attention to it, the more he realized it was moving at a pace all its own. His first thought drifted to the tendrils still wrapped around his insides, and when he looked down, he realized he was pointing the sharpened end of the club at Jessup.

The older man's eyes were locked on Cole when he asked, "Are you strung out?"

Even with the world going to hell and what sounded like a war encroaching on the outskirts of town, Cole was surprised by the question. "I'm not on drugs!" he said.

"I don't mean drugs. I mean the healing serum. How much have you been taking?"

"A lot lately, but I've been wounded."

"What about before you were wounded? Did you take it any time you got hurt even if you didn't absolutely need it?" Jessup's eyes narrowed and he moved toward him and a distant howling gave way to a shriek that became louder and more intense. "Have you reached for a needle even before you knew how badly you were hurt? When you get cut or scraped or knocked around, do you look forward to that light-headed rush that comes with—"

"I'm not a fucking junkie!" Cole snapped.

"You didn't answer my questions."

"I've got a question for you," he said while moving the club as if trying to pass it off as something other than a weapon. "What's that screeching? It's coming from everywhere."

"No it isn't," Jessup replied while closing his eyes. "That noise is today's biggest lesson. You wanna know another lesson I learned a long time ago? Don't work with someone who's strung out on anything, even if it's something we cooked up ourselves."

"I haven't even had any of that stuff for a while."

"Which is probably why you were about to stab me a few seconds ago. Now close your eyes and listen for that screech. We need to know what direction it's coming from."

The sky was growing darker by the second. When Cole looked to the east, he saw a blur of clouds and dark purple. Looking to the west forced him to squint before catching a jabbing ray of sunlight in his eyes. "It's getting closer, whatever it is. Do you know what it is?"

"Shush up and listen," Jessup scolded. "And close yer eyes. It'll help you focus."

Cole did as he was told. The stench of rotting meat and blood was still thick in his nose, and the frantic beats of his heart showed up as pulsing blobs of light behind his eyelids. Before that became too much for him, he heard something else with his newly focused ears. The shriek started off as just one of the many that crossed back and forth above him. When something screamed directly toward him, there was no way in hell he could keep his eyes closed.

A large flap of skin sliced through the air, attached to a frame of narrow bone. It was thin enough to glide and light enough to be steered by what looked like fluttering ribbons trailing behind it. Long talons stretched from the skin flap's two front corners as it extended even more to ride a wind that rippled over its back and through its body, which produced the shriek Cole had been hearing.

As the thing in the sky angled sharply downward toward Jessup's back, several more of the narrow fliers descended like pencil lines that suddenly decided to leap off a page. They were right behind the first one, filling Cole's eyes with sunlight reflecting off smooth undulating backs and filling his ears with a shriek that now sounded more like a whistle blown with the power of a concentrated hurricane.

The closest one opened its body into a tattered flag with four talons at either end. Without opening his eyes, Jessup drew the hunting knife from its scabbard to snap it up and around toward the incoming mass of skin. Between his confident swing and the creature's own momentum, the blade cut through the upper framework of bone and shredded the flying thing's body all the way down to the tattered pieces hanging from its lower end. Its shriek turned into an agonized cry as pieces of its body fell to the ground. The others still in the air veered off before getting close enough to fall victim to the Skinner's blade.

Opening his eyes, Jessup flicked the knife down to spatter a clear, viscous fluid onto the ground and said, "It's all in the wrist."

Chapter Twenty-Two

Once he'd sheathed his knife, Jessup asked Cole to help him pick up the dead flier and run for cover. Although he was more anxious to do the latter, Cole helped with the former as well. The shredded pieces of the thing that had come screaming from the sky now looked more like a broken kite made of moist skin on a flimsy white frame. When Cole jumped into Jessup's pickup, he almost crushed the parts already on the seat.

"Careful!" Jessup said as he shoved him toward the passenger door and gathered up his part of the kite.

"What the hell are—" Cole's question was nipped in the bud by the hard slap of something against his window. Although he could still see the colors of the setting sun through the thin layer of skin now pressed against the outside of the glass, his view was impeded by what looked like a hastily drawn face with features that were nothing more than dark lines on a lighter surface. Talons scraped against the top of the truck and the face twisted as if trying to shove its way inside. The mouth that gaped open against the window had small ridges for teeth, no tongue, and no lips. Cole took the .38 from the glove compartment and pointed it at the window as more of the skin flags slapped against the outside of the truck. "What are those things? Were they after the gargoyles too?"

"Those *are* the gargoyles," Jessup replied while hastily cutting apart the one he'd brought down.

"No, you were showing me the gargoyles. They were those stone animals outside the cemetery."

Skinners: The Breaking

"Nope. Those are what these gargoyles left behind."

Now that it was clear the things outside weren't strong enough to break their way in, Cole lowered his gun and focused on what the other Skinner was doing. "Every gargoyle I've ever heard of was made of stone. I've even heard of ones that are stone during the day and come to life at night."

Jessup looked up from what he was doing to ask, "Where'd you hear about that?"

"Well . . . it was a cartoon."

Shaking his head, the other man returned to his task. "Those statues were called gargoyles because they're all folks saw after these things came through to feed or defend their nest."

"They nest?" Cole asked as a chill worked its way down his back. "Where?"

"Damn near anyplace. They like cities because they can fold themselves up to fit nicely in all those angular crevices and narrow corners between buildings or under ledges. They ain't got much by way of muscle, but they sure do have something to make up for it." Jessup twisted his blade once more and pulled open a flap of skin he'd been cutting like a trapdoor. A spray of what looked like murky water emerged from the opening, which didn't do anything to dim the smile on the Skinner's face. Holding up a flat tube the size of a long water balloon, he declared, "This was worth the trip. If we don't get a few more to use against that Full Blood friend of yours, we'll have to improvise."

"You think it would help if I knew what you were talking about?"

"Take a look at them claws," Jessup said while tapping the chunk of creature Cole had brought into the truck. "Remember them scratches on the statues?"

"Yeah."

"And the flat spots on their backs? That's from this right here. Take a look." Jessup held the tube as if he was about to decorate a cake. Instead of icing, a clear gel oozed from the end of the tube. The instant it touched the seat cushion between Jessup and Cole, the substance hardened with a soft creaking sound.

Inside the truck it was easier to block out the sounds

coming from the northern side of town. Even with the Ford's superior insulation, however, Cole could now hear the occasional chatter of automatic gunfire and the thumping bass of helicopter blades.

The bottom of the creature had an opening just like the mouth pressed against the window, except now he could see rows of tiny bristles just inside the opening. With the thing dead, a flat length of skin capped by four barbed hooks that could have been a tongue lolled from its mouth. Too much experience in handling deceased nightmares gave Cole the stomach to reach out and squeeze the tonguelike protrusion. Sure enough, it was a flattened tube that ended at the top of Jessup's incision. By now the gel squeezed onto the seat cushion had formed a thick gray shell.

More of the pieces came together, finally coalescing when Cole tapped the barrel of his gun against the gray shell. It was solid and unmoving. After feeling the shell with his bare hand, he asked, "Is that rock?"

"Near enough."

"So those statues are things that these bat-things swarmed and injected with this goo?"

"Not injected. Just coated and smeared around on the inside of their wings. Them claws sink in to keep whatever it catches from squirming away. The more they struggle, the more that stuff gets spread into a nice even coat."

"Then what?"

"Then, after the stuff hardens, the rest of the gargoyles come back to feed. We think they must eat organs and soft tissue, because they sure as hell don't got the choppers to tear off any meat. We've found little holes and slits that they could stick their tongues into and then seal up again to preserve the rest of the meal for later."

Cole looked at the flattened portions of skin that scraped the window and kissed the glass. "How come they're so quiet now?"

"Because they ain't flying," Jessup replied as he worked to tie up one end of the tube he'd extracted. "Pull off some of those talons. They're light and durable. Make for great add-ons to our weapons. See anything going on outside?"

"No. There's too many of those things on your truck. They're persistent, I'll give them that."

"It's how they've survived this long. They can hide like nothing else, and when they've been found out, they don't stop attacking until they've put down whatever stirred 'em up. Soon as one of them is injured or if a statue is cracked open enough for them to smell their own juices inside of it, they swoop in to clean things up."

"Kind of like a flying rodent ninja hit squad," Cole said.

Jessup looked up from the knot he was tying and said, "Yeah. I guess that sums it up."

"So you're thinking of turning Cecile into one of those statues?"

"That's the idea."

"She seems like a good kid," Cole sighed. "Shame to have her get taken out by these flying creeps and then get her guts sucked out."

"I doubt this'll kill her. We don't know a lot about gargoyles, but if they had that kind of punch, they would have killed one or two Full Bloods over the years. Odds are a whole lot better they can contain one. Friend of mine did some hiking over in Hungary and found some statues that looked a lot like werewolves out in the middle of nowhere. Took enough pictures to find the scratches and smooth patch on the back later on, but he didn't exactly know what he was looking at. We've always wanted to go back there, but the damn Gypsies would only chase us away again. I don't even wanna know how he smuggled his camera back to the States. From what we can piece together in some old Skinner journals, we figure gargoyles migrated over here on a boat that passed through or originated from Greece on its way to the New World."

"They're from Greece?"

Jessup nodded while checking his guns, then dug out a shotgun kept under the seat in a specially crafted rack. It held the weapon in a hollowed space that would pass all but the most extensive inspections. "You heard of the Medusa myths?"

"You mean the reptile woman with snakes in her hair?"

Cole asked. "I guess something's gotta balance out the nymphs, huh?"

"Them myths came about the way lots of them do. Misinformation. As far as we can tell, Medusa was either the woman who crafted these things or first set them loose after stumbling on a nest buried deep somewhere. As for the snakes and such, I don't know. Maybe the woman was just butt-ugly. All I can tell you is that here and now, these ugly little suckers are gonna save our butts once that Breaking Moon rises."

Cole pulled in a deep breath and let it out. "I was just getting comfortable in here. Sure you don't want to tell me some more about gargoyles and misinterpreted mythology?"

"There's more guns under the seat. Ammo too. Fill up. Sounds like we're gonna need it."

Grabbing a few pistols, some preloaded magazines, and a shotgun, Cole said, "It sounds like someone's already found Cecile."

"It's more than that," Jessup grunted. "I wasn't with that girl for long, but she's not the sort to stir up whatever the hell is goin' on out there. She would've just run away before the National Guard or whoever else is out there came for her. Besides, can't you feel it?"

"Yeah," Cole said while brushing his fingers against his scars. "There's more than one Full Blood out there."

"You ready for this?"

"Sure. There's helicopters in the air, gargoyles slapping the windows, a werewolf howling, and now," Cole added as a distinctive chatter crackled in the distance, "it sounds like there's automatic gunfire. We've got some shotguns and weapons that require us to stand toe-to-toe and swing at a meat rendering plant."

"But we got something they don't."

"Please don't say courage," Cole sighed.

Jessup held up the tube he'd tied, and showed him a smile that verged on the insane. "And there's plenty more of this to be had. More than we'll need if we play this quick enough."

"How much of that stuff did you get?"

"Not what's in here. It's what's out there we need to put to use."

Cole looked outside where the frantic, nearly transparent

flaps of skin and talons continued smearing their fluids on the truck. Since the window or hood hadn't turned to stone, he could only assume that was a whole lot of slobber. "Can we at least point them in the right direction?"

"That's the idea. Give them some live meat and they'll take it. Gargoyles survive by leaving no witnesses. The more it fights back, the more they'll try to bring it down, and nothing fights back more than a werewolf." He started the truck and placed his hands on the wheel. "I don't know what's down this road either, but it's big. We're in this fight now, so should we sit here and whine about how things are going to hell or should we roll in to lend a hand?"

More than anything, Cole wanted to say something cool to that. Part of his old job had been to come up with catch phrases that fit nicely in the digitized mouths of his video game characters. The only thing to come out of his mouth now, however, was a shaky breath as he nodded his head.

Jessup pulled away from the cemetery. He didn't gun the engine, take sharp turns, or even get the wipers going to clear a bigger spot on the windshield. He did nothing while driving up Scenic Road that could possibly upset or dislodge the creatures that had attached themselves to his windshield. The road was mostly straight and in good condition. If Cole squinted just enough he could trick himself into thinking he wasn't moving at all. Apart from a few boxy little houses on one side of the road, all there was to see between the writhing bodies affixed to the glass was tall, dry grass and bushes that were too tough to die in the harsh New Mexican climate. He had almost calmed himself into believing he was looking through a dirty window instead of one covered by layers of squirming, living flesh. Stretched out and clinging with every talon it had, the gargoyle on the passenger window looked in at him with a face that could have been hastily drawn upon a dirt canvas. "What's going on up there?" he asked.

Jessup leaned forward to look beneath the gargoyle clawing at the top of the windshield. "Don't know, but it's more than Full Bloods. Could be some Half Breeds. Just when I feel like I got a good handle on the number of them, they keep changing."

"You can tell how many there are?"

"When you've had the scars for as long as I have, you'll be able to read them better. Just take my word for it. There's plenty of them and they weren't here when we arrived."

Outside the truck, road and scenery flashed by like a movie being played at the wrong speed. Cole's brain was filled with plans of how he might deal with whatever was over the next rise, but every last strategy went out the window when a black helicopter crested the rise farther along the road, pivoted in midair and then veered toward the ground.

"Hang on!" Jessup shouted as he slammed his foot against the brake pedal.

Cole's feet were already bracing against the floor and his free hand slapped against the dash. The truck skidded into a fishtail as its tires lost their grip on the road. All this time the helicopter seemed to hang about thirty feet in the air. When that frozen moment finally passed, the helicopter slapped against the ground in a shower of sparks as metal was torn asunder.

A shock wave rolled through the air, shaking the ground and throwing enough dirt and smoke toward the truck to make it even tougher to see through the windshield. Jessup fought with the steering wheel to keep from skidding off the road or slamming into a tree. Somehow the older man kept his composure long enough to bring the Ford to a stop. "You got that weapon I gave you?" When Cole didn't answer, Jessup shouted, "You got it or not?"

"I've got it," Cole replied. Since he'd been holding the short wooden blade in the fist that he used to brace against the dash, he wondered if he'd ever be able to pry it from his hand again.

The helicopter's top rotor was still waggling after the one in the tail section had been brought to a stop by digging into the ground. Its body was shaking as well, but not just from the crash. There was movement inside the helicopter, but it was tough to make out details through the cracked canopy as well as the living stain on the truck's window.

"When we get outside," Jessup said, "we need to keep moving or else these gargoyles will take us down. If one gets close, don't waste time lining up a shot. Just swing. And don't bother shooting them. Bullets will just give them a little rip and they're used to that. We just need to point them in the right direction. Once a few of them lock up with a Full Blood, all the others should swarm in to help."

"How do we get them to leave?"

"They'll leave when they're full or dead. If there's any other way to get them to go somewhere, I don't know what it is. Take this," Jessup said while tossing the long fleshy sack he'd extracted from the gargoyle. "I'll find more out there. You just need to run fast and try to get close to something that needs to be given a dose of Magic Shell." Jessup loaded both of his pistols and removed a wooden hatchet from a set of loops on the inside of his vest. "You remember that stuff that you poured on ice cream? It hardened into a chocolate shell."

"Yeah. So?"

"So . . . I love that stuff." Without any more parting words, the older Skinner kicked open the truck door and jumped outside.

For a fraction of a second Cole considered taking the sane choice and staying inside the truck. That option was taken away as soon as a gargoyle that had been clinging to the roof dropped down and hooked its talons into the truck's frame and seat to pull itself inside. From that angle Cole could see a second set of eyes placed on the upper edge of its body. Unlike the ones on its smeared face, those eyes were narrow, unblinking black slits. They were the calmest part of the gargoyle's entire body, remaining focused intently upon their target.

Cole shoved his door open and nearly fell out of the truck in his haste to get away. He pushed the door shut at the same time the gargoyle inside launched itself at the passenger door. Both things collided, forcing the gargoyle to climb the interior of the cab and press its face against the glass.

From the outside the Ford looked as though it had grown a skin and was in the process of shedding it. Gargoyles clamped onto nearly every available bit of the truck's surface area, pulling away to look up as if they were being peeled off by an unseen hand. By the time Cole had built up some power in his strides, the gargoyles were flapping the sides of their bodies to create enough of a breeze for liftoff.

"Look for casualties!" Jessup yelled while waving toward the downed helicopter.

Cole's legs were churning to carry him away from the truck as fast as possible. When he looked back again, he couldn't see a single gargoyle. Knowing better than to stop moving, he focused on the helicopter. The canopy was cracked and smudged with oil and dirt from the impact. Once the waning sunlight caught the canopy at the right angle, it shone upon the dark red hue and viscous texture of something that coated the inside of the cockpit. After so much time as a Skinner, he'd seen more than enough of it to be certain the substance was blood.

It was a helicopter similar to the one that brought Paige into Denver. During his long sleep in wing G7, he'd dreamt of that chopper plenty of times. It had landed on retractable gear, but this one didn't have time for a proper touchdown. There were no markings. No weapons. Only a sleek fuselage and a sliding door on one side. Someone inside screamed and kicked at the canopy. As Cole drew closer to the cockpit, one foot smashed through, only to be twisted completely around as the distinctive snarl of a werewolf emerged from the craft. Before Cole reached the side door, someone from within the chopper pulled it open. He was a man cut from military cloth, complete with hardened features and a bulky frame beneath standard issue black and gray fatigues.

"Get out of there!" Cole shouted.

"No! Stand back. I can't stop it!"

"But we can! Keep the goddamn door open!"

The soldier grabbed the door as the entire helicopter rocked with the weight of a creature that worked its way out of the crumpled front section. Farther down the road gunfire erupted in bursts, followed by the haggard, tortured voices of Half Breeds. Cole thought about Kansas City while diving through the door before the soldier closed it. The main compartment looked like a metal box with a series of steel posts running down its center. Collapsible seats folded down from the posts, some facing Cole's side and others facing another side door. Toward the rear of the cabin, large windows were fitted with rigs made to hold machine guns to be mounted and fired from the helicopter. Once again he had research for

Skinners: The Breaking

a Sniper Ranger level to thank for his partial knowledge of modern armaments. "All right," he said while grabbing onto one of the steel posts so he could maneuver through a cabin that was tilted worse than the floor of a fun house. "Close the door."

The soldier had a rank insignia on one shoulder, the name BUDDIG stenciled onto a strip on his chest and a patch on the other shoulder. Since it was the most colorful thing on his uniform, the patch catch Cole's eye. It was a circle divided into red and gray quadrants surrounded by gold rope. Two assault rifles were crossed behind a row of spears, all of which were above a symbol that was half wolf's head and half skull. The red quadrant with the wolf's head had the letters I.R.D. stitched into it, and the opposite gray quadrant had U.S.A. stitched beside the skull.

When the soldier lunged for the door, Cole dropped his shotgun, grabbed the soldier by the elbow and pivoted to fling him away from the open door.

"No, we have to get out!" the soldier yelled.

Outside, a building chorus of wailing, high-pitched shrieks closed in on the wreck. Without taking the time to look for a target, Cole swung the wooden blade toward the door and was immediately rewarded by a wet ripping sound. The gargoyle he'd shredded hit the dirt in front of the door and dragged itself away. Its wound wasn't fatal, but it would have trouble getting back into the air. The other dozen or so that swooped in toward the helicopter weren't having those difficulties.

They weren't in a formation and didn't seem to expend any effort in staying aloft. The group of gargoyles merely drew close together at the apex of their ascent and dove at him. Now that he knew what their second set of narrow eyes looked like, he imagined every single one of them were fixed upon him.

He shut the side hatch as best he could and turned around just in time to spot a Half Breed slinking from the cockpit. It had shreds of material hanging from its shoulders and neck and a long string of bloody saliva dangling from bared fangs. Although the creature was as deadly as it was terrifying, at least it was familiar. "Keep back," he said to the soldier without taking his eyes off the Half Breed. The club Jessup had given him was clenched tightly in his left fist, and somewhere along the way he'd drawn the .38.

"I don't know where it came from!" the soldier said as he backed toward the rear of the cabin. As he did so, he was forced to push aside or climb over the still forms of two other soldiers who'd caught the worst of the crash.

When the Half Breed lunged, Cole reflexively pulled his trigger. The pistol bucked in his hand, spitting three quick rounds into the werewolf's head and neck. He knew better than to think that would be enough to stop it, so he fired once more and swung the wooden blade in an overhead stab that dropped straight down toward the Half Breed's face. The creature twisted its neck sharply in a way that would have snapped any natural beast's spine. This one merely dodged the incoming weapon, stared sideways at him and clamped its jaws around the blade. The Half Breed twisted its head away once the weapon sliced the inside of its mouth and staggered back. Cole knew he wasn't going to get a better chance than that, so he fired his remaining rounds into its body just to steer it away from the shotgun he'd dropped earlier. Claws scraped against the tilted metal floor of the downed helicopter as the beast scrambled to regain its footing.

Half Breeds were strong and very tough, but not bulletproof. Some of those rounds made it through, which lit an angry fire in its eyes. When Cole moved in close enough to use the wooden blade again, the werewolf turned toward him and skidded on the tilted floor. Rather than succumb to gravity, it used the countless joints created by its broken and rehinged skeleton to strike from a new angle. Even though his pistol was out of bullets, it made a hell of a good thump when he smashed it against one of the bloody spots on the werewolf's fur. The creature yelped but was still able to pull away when Cole tried to stab it with the sharpened end of the club.

"If you've got a gun, you're welcome to join in here!" Cole shouted at the soldier. He wasn't about to take his eyes away from the Half Breed, but the soldier wasn't responding with any gunfire. Outside, flat bodies thumped against the fuselage and used talons to search for a way in.

Cole swung at the Half Breed and drew some blood, but not enough to prevent the werewolf from climbing to its feet and lunging at him. Backing up until his heel knocked against the shotgun, he dropped the pistol in favor of the bigger weapon. The Half Breed circled around to snarl at the soldier.

"Hey!" Cole shouted. "Right here!"

Although the Half Breed snorted in his direction, it was more interested in the wounded man who squirmed up the slant of the downed helicopter to get to a metal locker at the back of the wreck.

"Come here!" Cole said in loud, choppy syllables that would have perked any dog's ears. Thinking along those lines, he followed it up with a quick, shrill whistle.

The Half Breed snapped its head over to him and growled as if defending its meal from a would-be scavenger. Tensing its muscles and lowering its chest to the floor, it scraped at the metal panels beneath its claws and reared back on its hind legs. The werewolf was about to attack. Cole could feel it all the way down to his bones as he reached for the door handle. Suddenly, the creature bared its fangs and leapt at the soldier instead.

The thundering roar of the shotgun filled the cabin as Cole fired it into the Half Breed's side. When the werewolf thumped against the closest wall, Cole threw himself at the beast to drive the smoking barrel of the shotgun into its body. He pumped in another shell and fired it into the werewolf before the shotgun was knocked from his hands by one of the creature's thrashing legs. By the time Cole drew the wooden blade again, the Half Breed was pulling itself to its feet. Cole stretched one arm out to grab a hunk of fur at the base of its tail, pulled it toward him and buried the blade into the biggest shotgun wound.

The Half Breed yelped in pain while folding its torso in half to snap at him. Cole was fully aware of the creature's flexibility and had already pulled the weapon away so he could jump back and chamber another shell. He fired again, cracked the shotgun against the side of the werewolf's head, then drove the sharpened end of the club into its neck. Since the creature lay on its side spilling its blood onto the floor, the sounds of scraping claws and a low, hungry snarl seemed particularly out of place. Cole turned toward the cockpit and spotted another Half Breed emerging from the front portion of the craft. The second werewolf kept its body low, planted its back paws against the floor and leapt forward.

Cole leaned toward the door, grabbed the handle and pulled it open. The Half Breed sailed past him, but still had the speed and flexibility to snap its jaws in his direction before it was outside the helicopter. It landed several feet away from the hatch, sank its claws in and came to a stop amid a shower of dirt. From there it turned to face Cole, a snarl rumbling deep within its throat.

Cole rolled onto his belly to look outside. The only thing he saw was some wreckage and a Half Breed preparing to tear at him again.

"Uhhh . . . shit."

The Half Breed coiled like a spring and leapt at the helicopter. Less than a second later it was snatched in midair by a flap of skin that swooped down to wrap around its head. The creature still had momentum on its side, but was prevented from entering the helicopter by a set of talons that reached down from above and outside the hatch to snag in its fur. The gargoyle on top of the wreck wasn't strong enough to pull the Half Breed outside, but it held onto the helicopter with a grip that kept it from being dislodged. Once the gargoyle's body was stretched out like a flap of wet leather, the Half Breed jerked to a stop and fell straight to the floor less than an inch from Cole's boots.

He came at the werewolf then like a horror movie slasher, the club gripped tightly in a hand cocked up near the side of his head. The strike intended for the Half Breed's neck sliced through empty air when the gargoyle pushed a sound from its mouth that sounded like a snake being drowned in a vat of mud. The sight of those narrow black eyes staring at him was enough to back Cole up.

The Half Breed scraped its claws against the floor and let out a strained whine as its struggles dwindled to nothing. Soon it was barely moving.

The gargoyle kept its black eyes fixed on Cole and its body wrapped tightly around the werewolf until more of the fliers slapped into place around the creature and dragged it outside. When the first gargoyle loosened its grip so it could envelop more of the beast, the bitter scent of dusty vinegar poured into Cole's nostrils. It was the same scent he'd smelled in the truck, and like the section of seat Jessup had used as a sample for his crudely fashioned icing bag, the part of the Half Breed that had been wrapped up was now stiff and gray.

High-pitched shrieks filled the air outside, but Cole heeded Jessup's advice by acting without looking for the source of the sound. He kicked the werewolf out of the helicopter, and before it hit the ground four more gargoyles darted from above to latch onto the creature. Cole shut the door and left the things to their meal.

"I can't stop it," the remaining soldier gasped.

"Don't worry. Those things won't be going anywhere."

Having pulled himself to the back section of the helicopter, the soldier sat up so he could breathe a little easier. "Not that. Whatever's inside me. It hurts."

Cole had to clamber over the body of a dead man to examine the soldier. "Did that thing bite you? Was there someone else up front? Did it bite them? How did it get in here?"

"Nothing boarded us. That Class Two just showed up and started attacking the pilot. Maybe the co-pilot."

The front section of the helicopter had been battered on impact, but most of the metal that collapsed between the main cabin and cockpit had been torn away by the werewolves. "Wait a second," he said while turning to face the soldier once more. "Did you call that thing a Class Two?"

His face was smeared with blood and what could have either been grease or black camouflage paint. "Yeah. It's one of the older ones. No tusks."

"How do you know this?"

"I'm with IRD. The In . . . human . . ."

"I know what it is. What are you guys doing here?"

After pulling in a breath and swallowing it, the soldier said, "Our scouts found two escaped prisoners who were headed here. Soon as they saw the Class Ones, our scouts called in for armed response. That's us."

"What escaped prisoners?"

The soldier started to talk but came up short. After another breath he grunted, "From Colorado."

Knowing he was referring to Lambert and Frank, Cole asked, "What's a Class One?"

"You . . . call them Full Bloods. Something's wrong."

Cole had moved away from the soldier to take a look through the window. The Half Breed was on its side and completely covered by living flaps of skin. "You're damn right something's wrong."

"No," the soldier grunted through a clenched jaw. "Something's wrong with me. It feels like . . . like I broke some—" His words became a scream as his face twisted into a nightmarish version of its former self. His body flopped against the floor while his hands reached out to grab anything within reach.

"Holy shit," Cole said as he rushed over to his side. "What's wrong?"

The first crunch could have been made by the soldier's boot stomping against some rubble or a fallen piece of equipment. The second definitely came from inside his body, but wasn't extraordinary considering how wildly he was thrashing. When the soldier came to a stop, his breath was caught in his throat and his back arched. Four or five wet pops flowed through his torso as his bones were snapped like twigs inside him.

Cole stood up and watched in disbelief as more of the soldier's bones cracked into pieces. When the man opened his mouth again, his voice was a deep-throated groan. Smaller bumps formed on his arms and face, popping open to release bundles of thick, wiry fur from his skin.

"You weren't bitten," Cole said. "I checked. You had to have been bitten for this to happen. Bitten down to the bone. Nothing got to you!"

The scream that had been building inside the soldier erupted amid a spray of blood and spit that flew from his mouth and then rained down upon his face. He slapped and kicked the slanted floor while more of his bones cracked inside his body.

"What the fuck is happening?" Cole asked, even though he already knew the answer. He'd seen the before picture

Skinners: The Breaking

and he'd seen the after, but this was the first time he'd seen one transition into the other.

"You're a Skin . . . Skinner, right?" the soldier asked when the crackling within his body subsided.

Cole nodded.

The soldier's eyes had been light brown a moment ago. Now they shifted into the dark, clouded orbs of a feral monster that was just beginning to feel its first pangs of hunger. His jaw opened as far as it could go, trembled, and then snapped with a loud, wet crunch. It was a grisly sight that captivated Cole in a way that was both unexplainable and shameful. Once he recovered from his shock, he gripped the wooden weapon Jessup had given him and drove it into the soldier's heart.

The instant the sharpened end found its new home, Cole felt sick. He should have done it sooner, before the soldier was forced to endure the Breaking. He'd put plenty of Half Breeds down, but not until they were ready, willing, and able to tear his head off. This wasn't a matter of survival. It felt like murder. Through the weapon's handle he could feel the vibration of deeper bones breaking. That's when he knew the act he'd just committed wasn't murder, but mercy. Unfortunately for both of them, this act wasn't over yet.

The soldier still squirmed and pushed air from his lungs. Cole pulled the blade out, raised it high in both hands and dropped it down into the soldier's chest. Finally, the younger man's body slumped and the final huff of air escaped through bloodied lips.

Cole couldn't bear to look at the body. He didn't even want to think about what the poor bastard had become. Instead, he thought about everything that had happened up to that point. Gunfire still chattered in the distance, probably fired by members of a genuine shadow government agency. When he looked over the rest of the men who'd been in the helicopter during the crash, he realized there was nothing he could do for them. The soldier had mentioned seeing more than one Full Blood. If that was more than just a slip of the tongue due to a whole lot of pain, he would need more than a wooden club and a few guns to deal with them. He made his way to the metal locker at the back of the helicopter, pulled it open and found a rack of assault rifles and several cases of ammunition. He slung one rifle over each shoulder, scooped some ammo into his pockets, and left the rest.

Talons scraped against the side of the helicopter, sounding close enough to all the other scraping for Cole to dismiss it after a quick look through the small square window built into the side door. On his way to the front of the cabin, he gripped the steel posts to maintain his balance while stepping over the bodies. The opening to the cockpit was bent and twisted to the point that even a multijointed Half Breed must have had trouble getting out. All he could see when he looked past that opening was shredded seats, broken equipment, and so much pulpy blood that it was impossible to say how many people had been ripped apart in there. One of the Half Breeds was probably a pilot, but the first could have been another soldier. That still didn't explain how the Half Breeds had been created or ready to attack so quickly when most of their kind needed time to curl up and recuperate from the Breaking.

The scraping against the door continued. It was the same scraping as before. Same pattern. Same loudness. Same duration.

Not scraping, Cole realized.

Knocking.

He glanced out the scratched and dirty side window to find a lot of torn-up ground and an overturned statue of a Half Breed. There wasn't a single gargoyle in the sky, which meant nothing for a species that was born to hide damn near anywhere. More than likely, Jessup was already doing his thing to point them toward the center of the nearby commotion.

The knock that tapped against the door nearly made him jump out of his skin. Cole managed to control his frazzled nerves and bladder by gripping the two automatic rifles he'd slung over his shoulders. The knocks that followed came in the same pattern and were made by a very familiar forked shape that cracked against the outside of the window directly in front of him.

It was his own spear.

Chapter Twenty-Three

Cole readied the assault rifle as best he could. He might have fired a few different kinds of guns while researching his work on the *Sniper Ranger* series, but it hadn't exactly been under field conditions. Also, those weapons weren't tricked out as much as the ones stored in the IRD locker. He found the safety and knew which end the bullets came out of, and that would have to be good enough for now.

After opening the door, he thought of several different ways he could be attacked after stepping outside. The barrel of his gun could be grabbed, he could be stabbed from above, or he might be smashed in the face. So, ready for almost anything, he jumped outside with his finger on the rifle's trigger.

"Heya, Cole."

Spinning around to face the voice, Cole aimed his rifle at a man who leaned with his back against the helicopter and the spear propped casually against the dented metal beside him.

"What are you doing with my weapon, Rico?"

"You gave it to me back in Denver, remember?"

"Yeah. That was back before I found out what a traitorous piece of shit you are."

The big man scowled, which did nothing to make his face any uglier than it already was. "You've been talkin' to Paige, huh?"

"Yes I have, which is why I should shoot you right now."

Rico stepped forward and raised both arms. He wore faded green Army surplus pants, heavy biker books with chains wrapped around the ankles, and a jacket he rarely took off. The tanned leather was made from several layers of Half Breed hide, and the strips of canvas were merely filler until he could collect and treat more dead werewolves.

"What are you doing here?"

In the distance, the chattering of gunfire was washed away by the thudding rhythm of helicopter blades and the inhuman baritone of a Full Blood's howl. Cole had to strain to hear any of that, however, since his blood was pumping through him in a quickening rush that had to be spurred on by the tendrils squeezing him from the inside.

"Didn't Paige tell you the part that doesn't make me sound like a prick?" Rico asked as an ugly smile crawled onto his face. "I joined up with her Army buddies to check 'em out. A group of them picked me up outside of Louisville and hooked up with a unit of gunships and a few truckloads of soldiers. When Bloodhound decides to sell out, at least it's with some style, huh?"

"What happened in Toronto? I want to hear it from you."

"You mean the guy I brought along who turned out to be Kawosa?" Rico's eyes shifted nervously upward as he asked, "You want to hear this story somewhere a little safer? This place seems to have some sorta big bat infestation."

"We'll talk about it here. I haven't quite decided yet if I want to keep you from being petrified and eaten."

Rico opened his jacket to reveal the Sig Sauer he always carried. "I could have pointed a gun at you too. I didn't. That's because we're partners. I'm working to earn my points back with Paige, but we don't got that kinda baggage."

"You know what would have won a lot of points with me?" Cole asked. "Getting me out of prison. Since you left me to rot in there, I don't see any reason why I should play favorites with you over Paige. At least she had a reason to do what she did."

"And we got a reason to do what we're doin'. It's the same reason we didn't drop everything to spring you outta that prison." Rico let his jacket fall shut again. "Tonight, the world as we knew it cracks wide open. It's been brewing for a long time and we all seen it comin'. On the way over here, we wiped out four packs of Half Breeds. That's just what we found when flying low in these choppers or driving down an interstate. You and I both know how much worse it is in spots we can't see. If humans ain't at the top of the food chain when the smoke clears, we'll either be slaves or dead. You've already made your choice."

"What about Toronto?"

Rico dropped his arms as if he no longer cared about the gun pointed at him. "What about Denver? When that skinny shapeshifter told you he was Paige, we believed it! I made some calls and that thing's not like anything we ever faced. He didn't even have to change into something that looked like Paige. He tells us something and humans believe him. Haven't you ever heard of trickster myths?"

"I think so. American Indian stuff, right?"

Rico smiled. "That's right. You do something other than play video games after all. In most of those myths, Coyote is the trickster. Kawosa is the coyote. He may be the closest thing to a god or demon that we've ever faced, and if you want to get pissed off because I fell for a trick thrown at me by a fucking *god*, then that's your own damn business! He came to me, told me he was an old buddy, and I believed him. He told Paige the same thing and she believed him too."

"Sounds like she woke up just before you shot her. If you were both under the same spell, how'd that happen?" Cole asked.

"I been wondering about that myself. She's never really trusted anyone all the way ever since she first laid eyes on a Nymar. Maybe that was enough to give her the edge. All I can tell you is I'm damn glad she did because if I would've killed her for no reason, I would've eaten my next bullet two seconds later."

The skies directly above them were still clear. Cole could feel the crackle in his scars that told him the gargoyles were still around, but he figured they must be preoccupied elsewhere. From the sound of it, there was plenty more werewolf meat to be had over the next ridge. As far as Rico was concerned, Cole suddenly realized he was holding the big man at gunpoint simply because he wanted to make someone, anyone, pay for driving Paige into a war zone.

What changed things around was something he had learned to trust more than anything else lately: instinct. Rico was talking sense. He knew the big man. He trusted him. Rico had proven himself when it counted the most and was trying his damnedest to do so again, even with a gun pointed at him and death on all sides. The least he could do was alleviate one of those situations. Cole lowered the gun and asked, "How did you know where to find me?"

"We picked up the trail of a Full Blood at that wrecked prison and followed it south. There was some sort of Lancroft storehouse or lab under there and we think the Full Blood got to another Shadow Spore." Looking up nervously, Rico asked, "Are those bat things coming back or what?"

Cole's scars were burning so badly from the shapeshifters nearby that he doubted he could feel the gargoyles if they were circling overhead. Fortunately, more howls in the distance were followed by gunfire and a wave of high-pitched shrieks. "They stay in flocks," he explained. "I think. Anyway, it sounds like they're over there."

"Well that's where we gotta go," Rico said. "Bloodhound's Army buddies are already here. That's one of their choppers behind you, and there's another that's about to go down further up the road."

The battle in the distance was making its way to the downed chopper. The explosions he heard before had sounded like impacts, but the next ones were definitely grenades. Judging by the bellowing roars that followed each one, the soldiers weren't making much of a dent. Considering everything going on at the moment, Cole knew he didn't have time to question Rico thoroughly. Instead, he decided to make him prove himself the hard way and handed the big man an assault rifle. Then he picked up his spear, propped against the side of the helicopter, and smiled as his hands closed around the weapon's familiar grip. Its weight was perfect. The largest spearhead gleamed with metallic varnish containing flakes of the Blood Blade. Even the thorns in the handle punctured his flesh in the spots marked by the

Skinners: The Breaking

very first scars he'd gotten as a Skinner. There was only one other homecoming he'd looked forward to this much.

"Do you know some skinny psychic dude and a Squam?" Rico asked as he started jogging toward the worst of the fighting.

"Yes! Do you know where they are?"

"The IRD picked them up in Colorado. Once I convinced them that I know you well enough to be trusted, they told us you and Jessup were headed here."

"So that's also how you found me," Cole said. "Why didn't you say that before?"

Rico looked over to him and admitted, "I wasn't sure about you yet."

Considering what had happened about a minute ago, Cole had to laugh.

"Your friends are locked up," Rico said. "I'll take you to them."

Cole kept his eyes open for any trace of Jessup. He might not have known the other Skinner for long, but he'd be damned if he would lose a partner. An explosion rolled through the air like a boulder that had been dropped into a still pond. Both Skinners looked toward the hill where several black columns of smoke rose to smear the sky. As Rico checked the rifle he'd been given, Cole pulled on the harness that Rico must have rigged to hold the spear. It wasn't much more than a large belt with two loops stitched into the leather, but it did the trick. Without another moment of hesitation, they ran toward the growing storm of gunfire and unearthly cries.

"Did you ever meet another Skinner named Jessup?" Cole asked while taking hold of the other assault rifle he'd taken from the helicopter and checked to make sure it was loaded. Now that he had more than a second to examine the weapon, he recognized it as a Heckler & Koch MP5A3 with some slight modifications made to the barrel and stock.

"Yeah, I know Jessup. Is he here?"

"Hopefully." There were still about a hundred yards to cover before they crested the hill. "Do you know when the Breaking Moon rises?"

"About an hour ago."

Cole looked up and found the moon hanging in a smoky, darkening sky, but there was nothing about it to catch his eye apart from a slight rusty hue cast upon its wide face. "Is that a Blood Moon? I've seen it redder. And the damn thing isn't even full."

"After all this time running with Paige, you still think a full moon has anything to do with werewolves?"

"No, but what's so special about this one?"

"Nothing as far as we can tell," Rico said. "But it don't matter what we see or don't see. The Breaking Moon has to do with Full Bloods, not tides."

Cole felt a pain in his gut that caused him to stumble for a few steps. The tendrils inside him had picked that moment to give him a quick, jarring squeeze to let him know they were still there and hadn't been fed for a while. Before Rico took notice, he regained his footing and came up with a quick bit of acting to try and make his stumble look natural. The sideways stepping movement was close to the one he used when trying to get a bunched-up pair of boxers out from where they'd been wedged. Unlike that awkward situation, this one had to be pulled off convincingly enough to make sure a trained killer didn't have an excuse to stab him in the chest. At the moment, however, Rico seemed to be having problems of his own.

The big man was still moving, but just barely. He gritted his teeth, hung his head low, and clamped a hand over his stomach.

"Are you all right?" Cole asked.

"Yeah. Just a cramp, that's all." Suddenly, Rico lunged at Cole like a battering ram. As soon as they hit the ground, a gargoyle sliced through the air less than two feet over both of them. Cole pressed his face against the dirt, waited until he was sure there wasn't another shrieking dive bomber behind the first, then scrambled to his feet.

"Don't worry about a thanks or anything," Rico said as he followed in Cole's wake. "There'll be plenty of time for that when you buy me a beer for saving your neck."

"Remind me if we're still alive tomorrow."

According to several of the small, rectangular green signs they'd passed along the road, they were in a park. Under

Skinners: The Breaking

normal circumstances the wide stretches of New Mexican desert would have been beautiful, but now it looked more like the dry, scabbed patch of exposed bone beneath a section of burnt flesh. Fires were scattered across a stretch of sandy rock on the downward slope of the hill to Cole's left where another helicopter had crashed. Of the four covered trucks in sight, half were overturned and burning, while the other two were being torn apart by Half Breeds. There could have been more vehicles in the convoy, but he couldn't figure out how many or what kind they were based on the scorched, twisted metal that seemed to have been dumped from a passing cargo plane. Now that he was at the top of the hill and looking down at the devastation, his ears were nearly shredded by the din of automatic gunfire and pained howls.

"Over there!" Rico said as he pointed toward one of the overturned trucks. "That's where your prison friends were being held."

Another wave of howls erupted to Cole's right and was quickly followed by paws thumping against the hardened desert floor. Once he caught sight of the Half Breeds stampeding toward him, he snapped into survival mode. Rico's Sig Sauer went off behind him to send a bullet hissing through the air. The Half Breeds were the newer models, which meant the bullets that hit them only chipped a few tusks and pissed them off even more than usual. Allowing the MP5 to hang from his shoulder by its strap, he drew his spear and dove forward as two Half Breeds launched themselves at him. Being animals of sheer instinct and brute force, the werewolves didn't waste a thought on the threat of mortal danger as they rushed head first toward the business end of the Skinner weapon. The Blood Blade coating on the spearhead allowed the sharpened point to tunnel into one creature's chest cavity, while the other Half Breed snapped at Cole's leg.

The thorns in the handle tugged at Cole's palm when he twisted the weapon down to block the second beast's attack. Its head rammed against the thorny handle and twisted to try and get at him from another angle. The more Cole pivoted the spear to prevent the second werewolf from getting to him, the more his spearhead twisted within the first one's chest cavity. Finally, he pulled the weapon out and swung it in a half circle so the forked end raked through the second Half Breed's throat.

Rico yelled with a haggard voice as he fired a shot into the eye of a third werewolf and jumped aside to let the fourth one sail past him. When that one hit the ground and turned around to face him, he stepped up to it and punched it in the mouth. Cole had read about Rico's wooden version of brass knuckles in Paige's journal but hadn't actually seen them in action. He sure as hell hadn't seen the big man slip them on before delivering that last blow. Spikes sprouted from a ridge of varnished wood that covered the top of his hand and wrapped around to dig into his palm. The punch shredded the beast's face, and the multiple joints in its neck allowed its head to turn almost a full 180 degrees before snapping around amid the chatter of gnashing teeth. Before it had a chance to regain its bearings, Rico drove his fist into its jaw two more times. When the third Half Breed rushed at him, Rico pulled his fist back and willed a short blade to emerge from the outer edge of his weapon. Swinging as if gripping a dagger, Rico drove the blade into the Half Breed's eye. It howled in pain and slumped straight down to spit its last breath into the dirt.

The Half Breed that Cole had impaled was losing steam, but not its will to fight. Even after being forced onto its side, it continued to scrape at the ground. Removing the spear with a straight pull, Cole flipped it around and dropped the forked end to trap the creature's head. His palms were slick with blood and the thorns burrowed into him as he willed the inside of the fork to sharpen into blades. The spear shifted into a tool that nearly decapitated the creature with a few downward thrusts.

Holding the last Half Breed at arm's length, Rico placed the barrel of the Sig Sauer against its temple and pulled the trigger. After three muffled shots the werewolf dropped for good. "God *damn* those new ones are tough," he said while reloading the handgun.

"This one's wearing a uniform," Cole said. After looking at the other two, he added, "What the hell's going on here?"

"Probably one of the IRD soldiers. The rest might have been bitten or came here to follow the Full Bloods."

Judging by the way Jessup, several soldiers, and many more Half Breeds converged at the truck Rico had pointed out earlier, the escaped prisoners inside were probably dreading the day they'd left their cells. Cole took a deep breath and started running. The uphill climb had been steep, but the terrain sloped much more gradually on the other side. Dry scrub and exposed rocks covered what looked to be a wide basin surrounded by some trees and a tall fence on the far side. It was next to impossible to judge any distances since every one of his senses were overloaded with the chatter and smoke from automatic gunfire, the stench of burning fuel, and the overwhelming presence of the unnatural. That last part may have come from what some might call a sixth sense. Cole couldn't see it or taste it, but was overcome by the uneasiness of having the real world turned upside down.

Half Breeds ran wild across the desert.

Gargoyles swarmed the sky, dropping onto the wildest prey they could find.

Cole had to hurdle dead bodies while swinging his spear to deflect incoming claws or swat a snarling face before it ripped his throat out. When his foot touched down again, it became wedged under something heavy enough to break his momentum and drop him onto his face. His ears rang when he hit the ground in a crumpled heap.

The Sig Sauer went off several times at close range, followed by the grinding rattle of assault rifles. "Get up," Rico said. "We're almost there."

"I think I broke my ankle."

The big man dropped to one knee and unceremoniously twisted the foot in question.

"Holy shit!" Cole gasped.

"It's not broken."

"What are you talking about? That hurt like hell!"

"If it was broken, you'd be passed out right now," Rico explained.

"And if I would have passed out, *then what*?"

"I would've left. You wouldn't do anyone any good with a broken ankle. Carrying you would just get me killed too.

The serum in your bloodstream will kick in and I'll get an injection for you ASAP. Until then you're just gonna have to rock through this shit."

Cole drove his spear into the ground so he could use it to prop himself up. "Rock through this shit? What's that supposed to mean?"

"It means you'll get up and keep movin' or I'll crack you over the head with this rock."

When Cole looked up, he saw that Rico indeed had a rock in his hand. Suddenly, he seemed more like the ugly asshole who'd fought and bled alongside of him in Philadelphia and Denver. He tried pulling himself up but his foot was trapped under something. Whatever had ensnared it was solid and unmoving. At first it looked like a thick, dirty root emerging from the ground. The more he tried to pull it loose, the more certain he became that it wasn't going to budge. It only took one touch for him to realize what it was.

"This is stone," Cole said. Grabbing hold of it, he added, "I think it's an arm."

Rico was already helping him up, so he placed the toe of his boot on the gray protrusion from the ground and pushed against it. "It's really in there. Looks like a gargoyle got to it, but they usually stay aboveground. Of course, I ain't seen a flock of them this big before."

"You've seen gargoyles?"

"Yeah, they've been popping up in big cities, wedged in between buildings or under rain gutters. You know when you're driving and you see all that shit hanging from trees that looks like moss or spiderwebs or that kind of thing? It's usually more gargoyle than moss."

"Aw, Christ. First goth girls and now road trips. Any other simple pleasures this job wants to spoil for me?"

Cole and Rico scraped at the ground to uncover the stone structure he'd found. Shots were fired from all directions and more soldiers were carried in by a truck at the bottom of the hill about a hundred yards away. When Cole uncovered a foot at the end of the stony arch, he stopped digging. Seeing that put the rest of it in context, and the knee at the top of the arch became clear.

"It's a Mongrel," he said after he took a closer look at the curved claws and structure of the foot. Pointing to a flat, smooth patch on the back of its knee, he said, "Looks like a gargoyle got it on the way down. Maybe it burrowed this deep before the shell hardened."

"Damn," Rico said. "It actually sounds like you know what you're talking about."

"Is that such a surprise?"

Answering the question with a noncommittal shrug, Rico patted him on the shoulder and pointed toward the overturned trucks. Since there wasn't anything he could do for the Mongrel, and had healed enough to support his weight on his twisted ankle, Cole followed him even further into the storm.

When he heard the shrieking in the air behind him, he shouted, "Drop!"

Both he and Rico hit the dirt and felt a gust of wind as gargoyles passed above them and veered upward. The pain in his ankle spiked as he climbed to his feet, but he continued running toward the trucks. When the howling started again, it blasted through his head like a wave of napalm. One of the overturned trucks rolled onto its back and was shoved aside by a gray Full Blood who stood on its rear legs and roared up at the sky. It was Esteban, and he faced the soldiers and covered his face with both hands as all of them opened fire.

"Shit," Rico grunted as he pressed his back to another truck. "You feel that?"

Cole took cover alongside him and willed his spear to collapse so he could tuck it into the harness and grab the MP5. "Feel what?"

"It's like my stomach's compressing. Makes me wanna tear through this whole goddamn field."

"You feel that too?"

They looked at each other long enough to wince as the next wave of pressure rolled through them. This time Cole couldn't blame his discomfort on the shredded Nymar tendrils inside him. Before they could take any time to come up with an explanation, their attention was diverted by another howl followed by a familiar voice.

"Don't waste your ammo!" the distant voice shouted. "Just keep them offa me so I can get closer!"

"That's Jessup!" Cole said. "Sounds like he's with some of those soldiers."

"Then what the hell are we waitin' for?" Rico snarled as he swapped his Sig Sauer for the assault rifle Cole had given him. "Let's lend him a hand."

At the first lull in gunfire, they bolted from their cover and ran toward the overturned truck that was now swarming with men in bloodied fatigues. Every step Cole took was accompanied by a stabbing pain that began at his twisted ankle and lanced all the way up to his knee. That was shoved to the back of his mind, however, when the earth began to churn on either side of him.

Exploding from the ground in a shower of dry dirt and gravel, two burrowing Mongrels emerged from beneath the surface, hit the ground running and fell into step with the Skinners. One of them was so lean that it looked more like an overgrown weasel. The other was larger, covered in smooth scales, and kept his belly low to the ground so he could move in a quick series of slithering steps. That one glanced up and said, "Been a long time, Cole. Looks like you need help with another Full Blood."

As soon as he saw that the Mongrel was missing its left leg below the knee, Cole recognized him. "Ben?"

"All the way from KC. We heard there was going to be a meeting here."

"Where'd you hear that?"

"Max and Lyssa split off from our pack after you and Paige left Kansas City." Flattening his body against the ground without breaking his stride, Ben allowed a Half Breed to sail over him and then carried on as if he'd simply ducked under a low branch. "They've been recruiting other Mongrel packs to Liam's cause and were supposed to meet in Oklahoma for the Breaking Moon. Instead, me and some others tracked Lyssa until she met up with a Full Blood and he brought us here."

Esteban straightened up, grabbed the closest soldier and threw the screaming man at the Skinners. Rico took the brunt of the attack when the flying man's legs caught him across the chest and sent him to his back. Cole hopped away to avoid getting hit, but Rico was already climbing back to his feet before he could lend the big man a hand. They got to the overturned truck, circled around and put it between them and the Full Blood. Looking to Ben, Cole asked, "How many of you are here?"

"There were five, but two of us were taken out by gargoyles. I thought those things were extinct."

"Think you can gang up on this one like you did with Liam back in KC?"

"We can try, but we'll need to get in position around her."

"Her?" Cole asked.

Ben backed into the ground as if simply easing down a ladder into the dirt. "We saw her outside of town. Looks like a young one. Never seen her before."

Through the cracked glass of the truck's side windows, Cole could make out the sandy brown fur covering Cecile's left side. She stood apart from Esteban and swiped wildly at soldiers who fired shots at her as though prodding her with a stick. She dropped to all fours to point her hazel eyes at Cole and bared her fangs with a savage roar.

"I've seen her," he told the Mongrel while ducking away from the window. "But she was a lot nicer then."

"All of the werewolves are going wild," Ben said. "Their blood is boiling. Even our kind who were tainted by them have responded to the Breaking Moon."

"Great," Rico grunted as he jogged over to them. "Shewolves gone wild. I think I saw a late night ad for that video."

"Ben, I need you to bring that Full Blood to me," Cole said. "The young one. Rico, we need to get Lambert and Frank away from here and help these soldiers bring down that other Full Blood."

"You want fries with that?" Rico snarled as he braced his elbow on the front end of the overturned truck, then fired three-round bursts from his assault rifle. Several nearby soldiers took that as a call to arms and added their weapons to the mix.

"Just don't shoot her when she gets to me."

"Should I let her rip you in half?"

"If it comes to that," Cole said, "there won't be much you can do to stop her."

"Fair enough."

"God damn! How many times do I gotta tell you that your bullets are only pissing that thing off?"

Cole followed that voice to its source and saw Jessup rush around to put his back against the truck. Patting the Skinner on his shoulder, Cole said, "You can run fast for an old guy."

Jessup looked once at him and then took a quick glance around the truck. "Where the hell have you been?"

"I was gonna ask the same thing. Haven't seen you since I ducked into that helicopter."

"Find anyone?"

"Yeah," Cole said in a voice haunted enough to tell a good portion of the tale on its own. "They're gone. One of them turned into a Half Breed right in front of me, and I don't think it was from a bite."

"That's what caused the crash," Rico said. "Men have just been randomly doubling over with their bones breaking inside of them. None of the ones I saw were bitten, but they just started to change. Some of those were driving trucks or flying helicopters and, well . . . there you go."

"We need to do something about the Breaking Moon," Jessup said. "If they can make Half Breeds without attacking anyone, it'll only get worse as their power grows."

"It's rising whether we like it or not," Rico told them. "Are you gonna make that call to Tristan or not?"

Something heavy landed behind Cole. When he spun around to get a look at it, he found himself within inches of a face that had haunted his nightmares ever since the bloody night in Canada when he was introduced to the power of a Full Blood. The man once known as Mr. Burkis crouched amid the swirl of dust from his landing. The structure of his face shifted slightly, pulling in his fangs and reshaping his jaw so he could say, "This is her first Blood Moon trial. You'll need my help if you want to control the girl."

Cole's instinct was to take a swing at him. As if to prevent him from following through on that desire, the pain inside him hit like a sharp jab to the solar plexus. When he winced and crumbled under the jolt, so did Jessup.

"Ahh," Randolph snarled while looking at both Skinners. "I see you're enduring your first trial as well."

Chapter Twenty-Four

Cole couldn't take another second of hearing Randolph speak like a human. The Full Blood stood on two legs and even had the nerve to watch him as if he was so much better than all the humans he'd ripped to pieces with his bare hands. When he felt the next stabbing pain through his innards, Cole swung his spear with every intention of driving it through Randolph's face.

The Full Blood merely leaned back and stepped away as if he'd been told years in advance that the attack would come. "The wildness of the Torva'ox is in you Skinners as well. Harness it and you may survive the war that is just now showing its face." While coiling like a spring, Randolph shifted back into his four-legged body. His legs bent under his weight and fangs stretched out to rip through his cheeks. The claws at the tips of his fingers scraped against the side of the truck as he leapt straight up and over the vehicle.

"Let the soldiers deal with that thing!" Jessup said while squaring off with the rear door of the truck. "Your friends are in here. You want 'em out? Help me get this goddamn door open!"

Cole hurried to the other Skinner's side while Rico laid down a steady barrage of cover fire. Since Ben and a few other Mongrels had convinced Cecile to move away from the IRD, the dwindling number of soldiers shifted their fire to Esteban. In a matter of seconds the Full Blood shouted

Randolph's name and the two werewolves locked horns with even more force than when they'd met in Colorado.

"Fucking useless grunts!" Jessup snarled. "No wonder they're getting hacked to pieces."

"Take it easy! They're doing their best."

When Jessup swung, it was with full force. His fist thumped against Cole's chest and sent a shock wave through the upper part of his body. Although it forced him back a step, the impact wasn't nearly enough to put him down.

"Get to the driver!" Jessup said. There was a tremor in his voice that let Cole know he was struggling just as hard to keep the stabbing pains from overtaking him.

Cole ran to the front end of the truck and heard the all-too-familiar sound of flesh being torn from bone. Two Half Breeds feasted on the bodies of two dead soldiers, shredding their flesh as if it was made from wet cardboard. Cole fired his assault rifle until every last round had been spent. He didn't know how much damage he'd done before swinging the rifle like a club to smash a Half Breed in the face. Letting the rifle slide through his fingers, he pulled his spear out from behind his back and drove the metallic end into another creature's chest.

No matter how much his body hurt, he couldn't stop fighting until both of the Half Breeds were down. He didn't black out. Something simply took over to complete the task. Cole wasn't just in the zone, he was happier than he'd been in a long time. The rush didn't end until two howls filled the air. Randolph and Esteban tore at each other with a vengeance, giving the soldiers a chance to regroup at another one of the trucks.

Since his truck was on its side, Cole was able to reach in through a hole that had been ripped through the roof. The driver lay with her arms entangled in the steering wheel and her throat slashed open. After taking the keys from the ignition, he searched her pockets and found another set of keys in her jacket.

Racing around to the back of the truck, he handed the keys to Jessup. "Are these what you needed?"

The older man tried the ones on the ring that had been hanging from the steering column and quickly dismissed them in favor of the next set. The second one on that ring fit inside the lock of the door, and when he turned the handle, there was a satisfying clank and the doors swung apart. Jessup hopped back before the lower one knocked against his shins.

Inside, two narrow benches were bolted to the floor. Frank sat on what was supposed to be the side wall of the compartment. His wrists and legs were shackled and a chain ran through both sets of restraints, securing them to a metal ring embedded in the bench. Lambert was shackled in a similar manner, but because he was chained to the bench on the wall that was now a ceiling, he hung down like a tattooed and very pissed off chandelier. The scowl on his face instantly turned into a sloppy grin when he looked at who stood in the doorway.

"Cole! We been looking all over for you!"

Frank tried to stand up but was immediately brought down by his restraints. "Get me out of these fucking chains and put a weapon in my hand," he said.

Going to the Squam first, Cole said, "I know just how you feel. Jessup, toss me the keys for these shackles."

"Here," snapped the older Skinner. "Find 'em yourself." After he tossed both rings at him, Cole ran toward the closest group of Half Breeds.

Narrowing his search down to keys small enough to fit the locks on the shackles, he quickly found the one he needed.

"What?" Lambert whined. "Lizard Boy gets out before me?"

"Just shut up and try to keep your head down," Cole told him. "You'll probably just want to stay in here anyway."

"Keep him chained," Frank said.

Lambert waggled his head back and forth so much that his body swung from the iron ring. "See? That's the thanks I get for swinging by to pick him up at that lake and *then* getting him past those cops at the state line! You crocodile-looking, pus-colored motherfucker!"

"The scent of Half Breed is coming from him," Frank whispered.

"Was he bitten?" Cole asked.

"No, but he's still turning."

Even though Frank's eyes were yellow and lidless, the sincerity in them was easy to read. Cole looked over to Lambert and approached him with spear in hand. When Lambert tried to explain himself or spit insults at either of them, Cole didn't listen. When the skinny inmate winced at the sound of a crunching bone inside him, Cole knew that Frank had been right.

Tearing at Lambert's clothes and turning him like a slab of beef on a hook, Cole said, "I don't see any wounds big enough to infect him as a Half Breed. There's barely any scratches on him! I just don't see how they're doing this!"

"We weren't attacked by Half Breeds until we got here," Frank insisted. "They swarmed us and tipped the truck, but none got in here. I've never seen someone turn without being wounded. Usually, they're hurt so badly they can't even move."

Every inch of Lambert's body trembled, and he clenched his teeth with so much force that bubbles of spit were forced out between his lips. "The Full Blood's doing it! I can hear him sending that shit to me!"

"What shit?"

"Whatever is doing this! Just distract him! He needs to concentrate. *Hurry*!"

Outside, the howling of the Half Breeds grew to a wailing crescendo. Something about it was different than the sounds that filled the air before. Their voices had more substance than any sound that had ripped across that battlefield so far. Automatic fire erupted from several different sources, but not even an artillery strike could have prevented Cole from stepping out of the overturned truck to get a look at what was happening.

Although there were considerably fewer soldiers on their feet, every one of them had weapons to their shoulders and was unleashing a steady stream of gunfire at the remaining Half Breeds in their sights. Those creatures had become the easiest targets since they'd set their paws firmly against the ground and craned their necks to point their heads at the sky. As the clouds continued to sail to the east, moonlight filtered through to rain down upon the furry backs of all the shapeshifters singing up to them. Away from the soldiers, Cecile was in her four-legged form, rearing up like a frightened horse and churning her front paws in the air while Ben and another Mongrel attempted to herd her away from the others.

Randolph gripped the dark gray Full Blood by the neck and roared directly into his face. Suddenly, his head snapped upward, but not to gaze at the moon. As Esteban stood, he brought Randolph with him, lifting the other Full Blood by the claws that he'd sunk into his belly. Randolph squirmed but was quickly stilled when Esteban clamped a hand around his throat. Pulling him closer, Esteban growled, "Picked the wrong side, Burkis." Maintaining a firm grasp beneath Randolph's chin, he pulled his other hand out to open the Full Blood's stomach. He dropped Randolph like so much garbage, raised his face to the moon and howled.

Lambert's screaming became louder. Without wasting another moment, Cole slung his assault rifle over his shoulder and charged.

"Focus on the smaller ones!" Jessup shouted to the remaining soldiers. "We've got the big ones!"

Without anyone else to give them orders, the handful of soldiers kept their guns pointed at the Half Breeds.

Hearing the quick slap of wide feet against the ground beside him, Cole looked over to the Squam and said, "We've got to distract that Full Blood from whatever it's doing."

"Draw its attention and I'll get behind him." Without another word, Frank dropped to all fours and sprang forward in a loping charge that allowed him to cross from one end of the park to the other in a few powerful strides.

Standing up to his full height, Esteban was the biggest werewolf Cole had ever seen. His gray fur seemed to absorb the moonlight and the muscles of his body swelled with every breath. "You're needed elsewhere, Skinner," he snarled.

Cole screamed as if it was the last sound he would ever make. Gripping his spear in two bloody hands, he charged across what felt like a dozen miles of open ground, and when he reached the towering Full Blood, he was swatted aside like a bug.

"Here's one for you, Randolph!" Esteban said. Before his solid white eyes found his brethren, Frank was on him.

The Squam threw himself at the Full Blood as if he was somehow impervious to the creature's deadly claws or fangs. Judging by the blood that sprayed from him when the two creatures met, he wasn't.

When Cole hit the ground on his side, he lost the wind from his lungs in a single pained gasp. He put his hand on his ribs, ignored the agony of aching bones and cinching tendrils, and crawled toward the two creatures. Frank was putting up a fight, clinging to Esteban's fur but unable to do much damage. Even so, the Squam bit and clawed while avoiding the werewolf's slashing claws. It wasn't long, however, before one of those swings connected and Frank was sent flying through the air.

Between Jessup, Rico, and the soldiers, all but one or two of the Half Breeds had been dispatched. Cole ignored those few desperate barking voices as he dragged himself up to one knee and stuck a hand into his pocket.

Leering down at him, Esteban growled, "There's nothing left for you to do, Skinner. It's over for you and every other human. But don't worry," he added with a Spanish accent that became silkier with every word. "The war that begins tonight will be mercifully short." He closed his eyes, exhaled, and shifted part of his body in a way that somehow caused Frank to drop off him as though his nails simply had nothing left to grab.

"It's all right," Rico said as he strode forward with the Sig Sauer in hand. "I got this. Remember those rounds Daniels made with the Blood Blade chips bonded to them?"

"Yeah!"

Rico sighted along the pistol and fired two rounds at Esteban. The Full Blood twitched as the bullets thumped against his chest, but didn't go down. When he placed his hand against the spot that had been hit, he snarled and brushed several gleaming fragments from his fur.

Rico fired until every round was spent, but each bullet only put a metallic glaze on the werewolf's coat. "Fuck!"

"I thought you made those special rounds to—"

"So did I!" the big man growled. "Guess they didn't work."

"Well that was anticlimactic."

Although the Blood Blade fragments caused Esteban to

pause for a moment, the novelty had already worn off and the Full Blood howled louder than ever.

"Let's go back to Plan A," Cole said, and with one sharp squeeze punctured the sides of the rubbery membrane Jessup had removed from the gargoyle, which released the clear, bitter fluid inside. Like the rising wail of crickets on a summer evening, the shriek of gargoyles filled the sky. Cole threw the long sack at Esteban and jumped away. After hitting the ground face first, he could only listen as the shrieks swooped in behind him and leathery bodies flapped against his back. Rico dashed away before he was consumed, swearing venomously.

Esteban roared and slashed several of the fliers, but that only caused more of them to swarm to him. Without any other prey to distract them, the gargoyles hit the Full Blood as a unified force. They surrounded him in a tornado of bony limbs and curved talons to envelop the werewolf completely. Cole made a cautious retreat, and with such a big meal to tackle, none of the gargoyles seemed interested in giving up their share to come after him.

"Could have . . . warned me about that," Frank said from nearby.

Unable to look away from the mass of gargoyles grabbing onto the Full Blood, Cole asked, "You all right?"

Frank cradled his right arm against his chest and allowed Cole to take his left hand and help him up. "Yes. I don't hear Lambert's voice. We should check on him."

They went back to the truck to find the skinny inmate hanging quietly from his chains. Cole approached, carefully extended a hand toward his chin and raised Lambert's head so he could get a look at his face.

"I think my bones are broken," the inmate grunted.

"Which ones?"

"All of them. Is that possible?"

"Yeah, it is." Unable to think of a quick way to humanely check Lambert's claim, Cole used the forked end of his weapon to prod his ribs. When he didn't get a reaction, he repeated the procedure on an arm and leg.

"Knock it off!" Lambert screeched.

"Just checking to see if your bones are broken."

"What the hell is poking me with a stick gonna do?"

"If your bones were broken, you'd be screaming a lot louder than that."

"Maybe I have a high pain threshold," Lambert said. "What about that, huh?"

Cole prodded him once more, this time with the sharp end delivered to a tender spot beneath one of the inmate's arms. When Lambert twisted away and yelped like a scalded dog, Cole said, "So much for the high threshold theory."

"Fine, so the pain from before stopped while you were out there. What about getting me down from here?"

Cole used his key to unlock the shackles around Lambert's ankles. When those around his wrists were removed, the inmate dropped like the proverbial sack of rocks. His legs held him up for a second, and when they buckled, Cole was there to prop him up.

"Are you all right to walk?"

Although he wheezed with every inhale, Lambert replied, "If it means getting the hell away from here, I'm ready to sprint the goddamn hundred and fifty yard dash. Are there any other trucks in good enough condition to drive? From in here, it sounded like most of them got taken apart."

"They did," Rico said as he stepped up to the rear of the truck. "The Half Breeds are either dead or turned to stone. Wanna know what I like best about this job? I get to say crazy shit like that."

"Where's the other Full Blood?"

"The Mongrels dragged her down before she got away. Guess she didn't get the memo about what happened to Liam in KC."

When Cole tried to use the sparkly phone he'd stolen, all he got was dead air. Actually, it had taken Brianne longer than expected to deactivate it. "You got a phone, Rico?"

"Yeah."

"Hand it over."

The big man did and asked, "Who are you calling?"

"Information. Just give me a second." Cole lifted the phone to his ear before pressing the button to make his call. The clearing in front of him was a mess of broken vehicles, smoking metal, dead werewolves, and mangled soldiers.

The ground glistened like mud after a long rain, due to moonlight reflecting off so many shredded gargoyles. He'd barely noticed them during the fight because their fragile bones and paper-thin bodies had been trampled into paste.

Although Lambert was happy to be out of his chains so he could rub the raw spots on his ankles and wrists, Cole didn't have more than a few seconds of quiet time before Jessup walked around the overturned truck and asked, "What are you dicking around with this time?"

"Making a call. Have the Mongrels showed up yet?"

"One's right here. Says he needs to talk to you."

Cole spotted Ben's head and shoulders emerging from the dirt. It was in a clearing well away from where Rico now tended to a few of the fallen soldiers. Injuries there ranged from serious bite wounds to a woman in bloodied fatigues with a leg that was half encrusted by stone. He left the other Skinner to his task and approached the Mongrel to ask, "Is Cecile down there with you?"

"We pulled her under just long enough to get her to stop attacking soldiers, but then she got away. Sorry."

"Got away? That's it?"

Ben crawled out from the dirt to show his hands were empty. "If we could get rid of Full Bloods that easily, we wouldn't have to worry so much when they got too close to our homes. In Kansas City, you and Paige wore Liam down after how much fighting and running all over the place?"

"Where did she go?"

Since Ben's face was dominated by a large, hooked beak, and the lids of his black eyes were vertical instead of horizontal, it was tough to read his expression. The movement of his bony shoulders, however, was most definitely a shrug.

"Thanks for getting her away from here," Cole said. "Do you think you can find out where she went?"

"We do our best to track the Full Bloods. We'll let you know what we find."

"Bring her back here," he ordered. "Just find a way."

Ben disappeared beneath the dirt like a Whack-A-Mole barely escaping a giant padded mallet. Cole allowed himself a few tired laughs while tapping the touch screen of his phone. Since he wasn't getting a good enough connection to log on to the Internet via Rico's device, he did things the old-fashioned way. "Madison, Wisconsin," he said to the operator after dialing 411. "Shimmy's."

"What did you say?" Jessup asked as he walked over to him.

Cole twisted his wrist so the phone receiver wasn't directly in front of his mouth. "I'm calling information. Shimmy's is a strip bar in Wisconsin."

"People are dead here and dying somewhere else and you're calling tittie bars?"

"Not just a tittie bar. It's one of the Dryad temples. You used the damn portals to get to the Lancroft house in Philly, remember?"

"Yeah."

"We need to separate those Full Bloods from whatever it is they found in Oklahoma," Cole said. "From what Cecile was telling us about the pilot light and that energy those things are after, the worst thing going right now is that so many Full Bloods are in one place."

"You think the nymphs can zap them back to their territories if we could lure them to one of them bars?" After thinking it over, Jessup cringed. "Even if we could get them there, I doubt the girls would go for that. They don't want much to do with Skinners, with all the police looking for us." He stared at the statue of Esteban and scratched his cheek. "I just wish I knew what the hell he found beneath that prison of yours."

"What about the gargoyles? Are they still here?"

"Circling," the older Skinner replied. "With this much blood bein' spilled and plenty of their own kind gettin' shredded by werewolves, they won't be goin' anywhere anytime soon."

"Tell me if you can— Yeah, connect me . . . Yes, I'll pay the extra fee . . . Sorry, that was Information again. If you can get those gargoyles to— Yeah, is Tristan there?"

Wiping his hands on the front of his jeans, Rico approached the other two Skinners. "Need something better than dirty rags to patch these guys up."

Jessup shoved past the big man and grumbled, "Headin' back to the truck. Gotta get my medical kit to treat these wounded soldiers proper."

"Somehow," Cole said to Rico, "the Breaking Moon is allowing Full Bloods to turn people into Half Breeds without biting them."

"Kinda found that out the hard way, didn't we?" the big man scoffed.

"Yes, but if that gets any worse, it could be what Paige heard Liam talking about in Oklahoma. He said something about taking our guns and machines out of the picture. It they're able to turn anyone just by— Yes I'm a friend of Tristan's! Just tell her Cole Warnecki is calling. She'll know who I am!"

"Get back into the truck, guy," Rico said to the skinny fellow who tried to sneak past him.

Lambert stared intently at the Skinners, bouncing his eyes back and forth between them fast enough to make it look like a facial tic. "He's right about what the Full Bloods can do," he said to Rico while jabbing a finger at Cole. "I heard its thoughts. I'm psychic."

"So you've been saying ever since we picked you up."

"Why doesn't anyone believe me?"

"Because," Rico snapped, "you talk like a nut job and you're givin' me a headache. You got something to say, just say it and stop with the crazy eyes."

"Crazy eyes?"

"Yeah. Was that something you did in prison or did you freak out yer mama with them things too?"

When Lambert tried to screw his expression into something he felt was more normal, he only succeeded in creeping Rico out even more. Finally, he let his squint and twitch return as he told the Skinner, "I was kept in that place to spy on people's thoughts, and the ones who used me for that were like you. Skinners. They believed me and they were pricks. You and Cole aren't pricks, so why the hell can't you just listen to me?"

"I'm listening," Cole said.

Letting out a relieved sigh, Lambert said, "I heard the Full Blood's thoughts. It was something I ain't never heard before. It wasn't even words. It was just some kind of wild . . . static. It's the same thing I heard in all of those Half Breeds tonight, but it wasn't inside the ones back in Colorado."

"These Half Breeds are different," Rico said. "Normally, they got to ferment before they're ready to run. These just popped and were good to go."

"It's the Breaking Moon," Lambert insisted. "It's all the Full Bloods have been thinking about since we left G7. The gray one, the brown one, even the girl. Tonight, everything for them is sped up. They're getting stronger every second. Even that one."

Cole followed Lambert's trembling finger and was directed to the statue of Esteban. "He's still alive in there?" he asked.

Lambert nodded. "And he's pissed."

Cole was about to shove the phone back into his pocket when a voice came through that was almost sweet enough to make him forget about everything else. "Cole?" she said. "Is that you?"

"Yeah, Tristan. It's me."

"I was so worried." She sighed in a way that Cole savored like a guilty pleasure. "You were all over the news when you were brought in for those murders and now there's nothing anywhere. No pictures, no reports. Just nothing. Where are you?"

"New Mexico. Is there any way for you to get out here?"

"There are clubs in New Mexico, but that depends on where you are."

"What I really need to know is—"

"Are you in Raton?" she asked.

Cole did a mental checklist of all the powers he knew the nymphs possessed. They could appeal to senses most humans didn't even know they had. Dryads were powerful enough to channel the energies given off by human lust and desire into temples scattered throughout the country, but as far as he knew, there was no mind reading involved. Finally, he asked, "How'd you know that?"

"Because I've always got at least one of our TVs turned to the news and it says the National Guard was attacked by creatures or something there." Beneath the thrumming bass and pounding rhythms of Joan Jett's "Heartbreaker," Cole could hear the voice of a newscaster anxiously relaying some information he couldn't quite make out. "It looks like there are more soldiers flying in."

"You need to get here and it's got to be now," he said. "Is there any possible way you can reach me using only one temple?"

After a short, unusually quiet pause on her end of the call, Tristan replied, "Yes. We've done it before. It just requires more energy and a Skipping Temple, but we still can't get involved with known criminals."

"It's too late to worry about that. This is about survival."

"You want to talk survival?" she asked in a voice that was severe and still sultry. "The Nymar have more connections than ever with the police. They also view Dryad blood as the most valuable substance in existence. We can't afford to draw police attention by becoming Skinner accomplices."

"The Breaking Moon is rising. Do you know what that is?"

"I've heard some things, but just a few vague legends."

"The Full Bloods are gathering and they no longer give a rat's ass about being seen or anything else," Cole said in a voice that became fiercer with every syllable. "They're tearing through entire towns and are drawing on some kind of power that allows them to change humans into Half Breeds without biting them. Now here's the big question. Can you make a bridge between two spots where neither end has a temple?"

"Why do you want to do that?"

Resisting the urge to snap at her, he said, "Just tell me if it's possible."

"I may be able to act as a Skipping Temple, but it depends on how far you're going."

"There's going to be more than one that needs to be moved," he explained. "Some can just go a few hundred miles, but others will have to go across the world."

She laughed without a speck of humor in her tone before saying, "Sometimes I can't tell if you're joking."

"I'm not."

At the beginning of the call, her side of the connection had been filled with the usual mixture of loud music, catcalls, and DJ ramblings one might expect from a strip club. Now, she'd moved to a place where her voice was clearer and everything else had been relegated to the background.

"What is it you want me to do, Cole?" Tristan asked in an intensely sober tone.

"First of all, I need you to get me to Atoka, Oklahoma. After that, I'll signal you, and that's when I need you to open another bridge." From there, he proceeded to tell her what he needed, with as many of the details as he'd been able to put together.

After he finished, Tristan let out a deep breath and said, "That's a tall order."

"Is it possible?"

"It's been done before, but that was a long time ago when we had a lot more power at our disposal. I'm talking about daily visits to our temples by true worshippers."

"I've seen the way those guys look at you when you're in that hot little outfit with the veils," Cole said. "You're being truly worshipped."

"Lust and desire are different and much shallower than reverence," she pointed out. "If we're going to do this, we need to tap into a deeper well."

"Tristan, we need to make this happen. The Breaking Moon has just come up, and every Full Blood may be getting the power to turn humans into Half Breeds just by looking at them. I've seen it and it's only getting worse. These soldiers have already been killed or turned. Paige says it's worse in Oklahoma, and when more troops are sent here, they'll be turned too. The people in this town still may be changed by this Breaking Moon or could get torn apart by any Half Breeds that got away from us and turned the old-fashioned way. We need to make sure this doesn't spread to other towns, other cities, and possibly other countries."

"Oh my Lord," Tristan sighed.

"Yeah, so what've you got for me on this Skipping Temple thing?"

"Are you sure this is the only way to get this job done?"

"If you've got a better idea, I'm open for it. Just be quick because Paige is in the worst of it right now."

Tristan drew a deep breath and let it out in a measured voice. "Our temples and bridges use emotion as fuel. Pleasure, desire, and reverence are the purest sources, but what you need is a quick burn, and the only way to get that is to tap into a darker source. Channeling these emotions can taint even the best of us and possibly destroy the Dryad who attempts to put them to use."

"What do you need from me?"

"Fear."

Cole chuckled and closed his eyes as a chorus of Half Breed snarls rose in the distance. "I should be able to accommodate you on that one."

Chapter Twenty-Five

Atoka, Oklahoma

When Paige's phone vibrated against her hip, she was sitting in the back of a hardware store on a stretch of East Court Street that had been destroyed by roaming packs of Half Breeds. She'd gotten there in Waggoner's green pickup. He waited near the broken front window, watching for more shapeshifters while Jesse and Bill Phillips dragged in the bodies of Half Breeds that had either been killed by Skinner weapons or shredded by copious amounts of gunfire. Al drove out to collect more carcasses, leaving Bill to gut the creature with quick, efficient movements. "You gonna get that?" he asked.

Paige straightened up from where she'd been hunching over a large plastic bucket. It contained a pungent mixture that she stirred using flat sticks meant for mixing paint. She dug her humming phone out, checked the screen, and answered the call. "Cole! This had better be good. Things have taken a turn out here."

"Things aren't much better here." After filling her in on what he'd discovered, he added, "But whatever they're doing to force the change doesn't seem to work on Skinners. Something's going on with us, though."

"I know. I hooked up with a few Skinners who have dealt

with the mess since this town was overrun," she explained. "Once the Breaking Moon rose, they've been getting bouts of crankiness that are bad enough to rip each other's faces off. They say it feels like something stabbing them in the gut."

"Same here. What about you?" Cole asked. "Have you felt a tension that makes you want to rip something apart?"

"No more than usual. Why did you call?"

"I need you to get as many of those things together as possible because Tristan will be trying to zap me right to them."

Paige gave him a tired laugh. "I'm on the front lines and you're talking to strippers. Typical."

"Just call me when you know where they are or where they might be headed."

"The Full Bloods won't be going anywhere anytime soon, I can tell you that much. There's a source of power here, and from what I've heard, they intend on keeping this place as some sort of stronghold." She felt a warm smile grace her lips. "It'd be nice to see you again at least once more before—"

"Just stop right there," he interrupted. "It'll take a little while for Jessup to find enough gargoyles to chase after me, but I'm on my way."

"Why get them to chase you?"

"Because seeing those things dive straight at me, staring with those black little eyes, freaks me out, and that's what Tristan needs to open the . . . forget it. Just do what I asked and we've got a chance at keeping this thing from getting any worse."

"We've got at least five Full Bloods to kill," Paige said, "and maybe hundreds of Half Breeds to put down while we're being watched by a clueless public and a whole lot of smug Nymar making themselves comfortable in the cities they've kicked us out of. I don't see how things could get much worse."

"Some of the Full Bloods are fighting each other," Cole said. "That's something."

"Any casualties?" she asked hopefully.

"Randolph was nearly gutted, but don't get too excited. He's gone."

"What?"

"I saw him get his ass handed to him by a gray Full Blood named Esteban, and when we went to salvage the body before I made this call, we couldn't find him."

Although Paige didn't like hearing that, she wasn't too surprised. Werewolves like Randolph and Liam didn't survive for hundreds of years by being easy to kill. "The Full Bloods have waited to make a move like this for centuries," she said. "They've got more planned than taking over a few towns or nipping at each other."

"According to MEG, the Breaking Moon won't be fully risen until about three in the morning."

"The Witching Hour?" Paige asked.

"They called it the Dead Hour, but yeah. Three a.m. is when the Breaking Moon will give all it's got. From everything we've seen so far, I don't think we want to let that happen or be there when it does."

"Well, if there's a big bomb that's gonna go off, I'd prefer to be two inches away from it. Quick and painless. Same goes for this."

"You're a scary lady sometimes."

"Just sometimes?" she mused. "Must be slipping."

In the distance a muffled explosion ripped through one end of town. The ground beneath her feet trembled with the passing of digging Mongrels. A few gunshots from directly outside the store silenced a pair of snarling Half Breeds. She closed her eyes for a second, savored the relative calm that followed, and tried to imagine the face at the other end of the phone connection.

"How bad is it over there?" Cole asked.

"Bad enough that this town's pretty much gonna have to be written off. Kansas City was brutal, but this . . ."

"Don't think about that, Paige. We need to keep this craziness from spreading any farther, *then* we'll worry about the big picture."

"It's already spreading," she said, as if admitting to a terrible wrong she'd personally committed. "From what we can tell, at least two nearby towns in this county were hit by Half Breeds. Could be worse already by now."

"Well, the cops are already sealing this place off," Cole reported. "Your IRD buddies have come in to quarantine the spot where all the fighting took place, but Raton, New Mexico, is all over the news. Why the hell isn't anyone taking notice of Oklahoma?"

"That's what I plan on finding out, but I have my suspicions. How long before you can get here?"

"I'm still waiting for Tristan to get herself prepared for what she needs to do," Cole said. "It sounds like this could take a lot out of her. I just hope it's worth it. This would go a whole lot smoother if we knew exactly where to find you, but if I don't hear from you in an hour, we'll try to get as close as possible."

She nodded and steeled herself as a low howl crept through town. Everytime she heard that sound, it reached deeper inside her. "You said the IRD is there. What about Rico?"

"He came with the helicopters and soldiers. Seems to be back to his old self."

"Keep an eye on him."

She heard another explosion, followed by a howl and what sounded like grating interference over the digital connection. This time, all of it came from Cole's side. "Just try to stay alive long enough for me to see you again, okay?" he said.

"I will."

The next two seconds were heavy with sentiments that neither one of them bothered to express. They knew they could not afford to drift away from the mind-set required to kill or die if the opportunity presented itself. After some bare-bones farewells that slipped from Paige's mind the moment she said them, the connection was cut and she was on her own once more.

After handing over the plastic bucket to Bill, she stepped outside through a shattered window and surveyed the street while her concoction was loaded onto the green truck and driven away. Cars were situated at odd angles on the curb, in parking lots or on lawns where they'd stopped after hitting a tree that was solid enough to do the job. The smoky air reeked of burning oil, gasoline, and charred wood. Sections of concrete were cracked after too many Mongrels had tunneled beneath it, and nearly every pane of glass in sight had been smashed to pieces.

Paige looked through the remnants of the shop's front window as the ever-present heat in her hands flared up. Two Half Breeds approached the green pickup, drawn by the scents drifting out from the paint store. Bill had gone out the back and Jesse was next door checking to see if any supplies could be salvaged from a discount bakery thrift shop. When one of the werewolves stared directly at her and perked its ears, Paige gripped her machete in one hand and her Beretta in the other. Rather than take cover inside the paint store, she stood just inside the shattered front window where the Half Breeds would have to come at her head-on.

The first one sprung forward, and as soon as it left its feet, she responded with a clubbing downward swing. The flat of the machete's blade thumped against fur-covered muscle, sending the creature down onto a jagged landscape of broken glass sticking up from the bottom of the window frame. The glass didn't go in far after being snagged in the natural armor of the creature's furry hide, but it was enough to hold it there so she could get in a few uncontested shots with the Beretta. The shots were still ringing in her ears when she swung her machete again. The steel coated edge hacked through the Half Breed's neck and lodged in its spine. Rather than remove the blade, she used the gun in her hand like a hammer to hit the machete and drive it the rest of the way through.

Then she turned toward the other Half Breed. No sooner had it set its sights on her than the creature was stuck by an arrow. It entered its right ear and carved a tunnel through the middle of its skull. Staggering like a drunk, the Half Breed tried to look for the whoever had fired the arrow, and meanwhile caught another one in the mouth. Waggoner stepped up and notched a third arrow. When the Half Breed dropped and began convulsing, he slung the bow over one shoulder.

"Now that," he said, snapping a photo of the Half Breed with the arrows through its skull, "was one hell of a shot. Reminds me of that guy with the white hair and the arrow through his head."

"Steve Martin?" Paige offered, looking down the street.

"No. That's not the one."

"Yes it is. He's the one who wore the arrow through his head back in the seventies."

Waggoner pocketed his phone and reached down to retrieve the arrow protruding from the Half Breed's ear. "You know. He was the wild and crazy guy. I think that was George Carlin."

"It's not, but whatever. The others are headed back to Al's house, right?"

"Should be."

Satisfied that the street was clear for the moment, she said, "There's got to be a reason why this town isn't crawling with cops, news crews, and at least a few soldiers by now. Have your guys been calling for help?"

"We called the county sheriff. That's his office down the block. Didn't do any good, though. Al tried calling the National Guard and even the damn United States Marine Corps, but they didn't listen to him. Of course, Al calls them about plenty of stupid shit. He's probably on some kinda list by now."

"That doesn't explain all of the calls that have got to be coming from here." Paige said. "You said that's the county sheriff down the street?"

Waggoner nodded. "It's the building with all the benches and the flagpole in front of it. I still don't see how the hell someone didn't get help using their own damn phone by now."

"They probably made the call," Paige replied. "But if the military is going to take it seriously, they'll try to verify with someone official. With everything else that's going on now, they're probably swamped with crank calls that sound just as crazy as the real ones. How about we check out a hunch of mine. You ready to make a run for it?"

"Let's do this."

They vaulted through the window and landed on the sidewalk outside the paint store, then headed toward the corner of East Court Street and North Delaware Avenue. In the silence between attacks, the sound of Paige's steps echoed in her ears, and her breath sounded like a windstorm being pulled back and forth through her head. Distant howls mixed with everything from screams to shotgun blasts.

The county sheriff's office was a tan brick building with a large wavy shelf of black stone protruding from the upper floor, supported by round posts. A few marked cars were parked in front, but were just as empty and ravaged as the building itself. Waggoner led her toward the corner of the building, down a sidewalk and to a side entrance. She followed him while taking a moment to make sure they hadn't picked up any four-legged followers.

Paige couldn't feel any additional heat in her scars, so she ducked into the door that Waggoner held open without bothering to check the street behind her. It didn't take much of a detective to realize that a pack of Half Breeds had spent extra time inside the building. Not only was the floor covered with broken glass and splintered wood, but the walls were covered with claw marks and bullet holes. Drawing her machete, she stepped through a door hanging partially off its hinges and into a room with a desk and several metal lockers bolted to the wall adjacent to a caged window. A broken metal detector crackling with electricity marked the entrance to a hallway leading farther inside the building.

Behind her, Waggoner notched an arrow into his bow and pulled it halfway back. She motioned down the hall toward three more rooms. From one of them a man's voice could be heard engaging in an urgent conversation. Waggoner acknowledged Paige's signal with a nod and shifted his stance so he could watch the area behind them while slowly following her down the hall.

"There are no werewolves in Atoka. I don't care what you're being told," the voice in the other room said. "Whatever you heard didn't come through official channels. It's probably just a bunch of kids trying to pull some sick joke in light of the crap they're seeing on the news."

Paige moved along the hall with her weapon held at the ready. Now that she'd pinpointed the source of the voice as coming from the second door from the end of the hall, she put her back to the wall and watched it intently. Her scars gave off the same prickly cold that she'd felt at the site where the Amriany plane had gone down.

Metal springs creaked in the room in front of her. "There are some problems, a few disturbances and such, but they're small fires and we can put them out. You should do your best to keep any armed response from being sent to the state of

Oklahoma . . . Yes, sir. I will, sir. Thank you." A heavy sigh followed the distinct sound of a phone being slapped onto its cradle. Then Paige heard, "Hello, this is the Atoka County Sheriff's Department." Clearly, another call had been made. "Yes, sir I'm the sheriff . . . Yes, sir, I've seen the news . . . Really? Someone said that was happening here? Who would say such a thing?"

The voice was like smooth metal being dragged over a wet stone, but Paige was certain that's not what the people on the other end of the phone calls were hearing. They heard whatever they were told to hear and believed it without question. With the grating chill beneath her scars provided her with a warning, she steeled herself to deal with a being that could change the way she perceived her world with nothing more than a carefully worded statement.

"Whatever you've been told about what's going on in Atoka," Kawosa carefully stated, "it's wrong. Everything here is under control, so you should focus your efforts where they're needed elsewhere . . . Sounds good to me . . . That's right."

As he wrapped up his bundle of lies regarding this latest pleas from a cowering citizen or someone driving close enough to town to hear the howls, Paige made her way down the hall. When she got close enough to see the shadow he cast while shifting in his spot, she fought the impulse to rush into the room and chop his head off. Behind her, Waggoner's bowstring creaked as he drew it back in preparation to take whatever shot he might be given.

Kawosa hung up and dialed a number in a quick series of taps.

Paige stood still and signaled for Waggoner to do the same. Once that rasping voice emerged from the next room again, she inched toward the door.

"Hello, Associated Press? I'm the duly appointed spokesperson for the state of Oklahoma. You need to connect me to whoever is in charge of reports regarding recent attacks made on cities by these creatures in or near my state . . . Yes, I'll hold."

When she was aligned with the doorway so she could take a look inside, Paige recalled the first words she'd heard coming from that room. *There are no werewolves in Atoka.* Somehow, even though he hadn't been addressing her directly, Kawosa's lies had their intended effect. The heat inside her flared up again as she closed her eyes and reminded herself that every word Kawosa spoke was a lie. Then the warning in her scars returned.

Opening her eyes again, she stared almost directly into the bloodshot eyes of a Half Breed who sat just within the door, its twisted snout pointed at her, its muscles tensed in the same manner as the sentry who had been posted in the house with the hole dug into its floor. As with any simple animal, the werewolf's emotions were clearly painted on its face. It wanted to run. It wanted to howl along with all of the other shapeshifters that had claimed the town for their own. And when it saw her in the hallway, its entire body trembled with the desire to lunge at her and taste the delicate meat just beneath her skin. Judging by the twitching of its nose, it had smelled her coming for some time.

"You must spread this same news to any official channels and prevent any more resources from being wasted by investigating Atoka," Kawosa said from where he sat with his feet propped up on a desk. "I have to do the same, so you have to give me the contact information of anyone in the government who might be able to get this news to the military . . . Yes, I'll hold."

With a subtle wrinkling of his brow, Kawosa sent a command to the beast guarding the door. The Half Breed slumped as if an invisible chain around its neck had finally been allowed to drop. When it charged at her, Paige stepped aside so Waggoner could put an arrow through the creature's eye. Instead, the other man ran past her while gripping an arrow in each fist to hit the werewolf at the apex of its jump. The two of them met like feuding stags, their chests thumping solidly against each other with an impact that brought both of them to the floor. Not only was Paige shocked by the reckless intensity of Waggoner's attack, but she would have been hard pressed to say which of the two was hunter and which was prey.

Both of them had the same glassiness in their eyes as they fought. Although the Half Breed was able to contort its body to snap at him with a minimum amount of wasted time, Waggoner thumped his fists against the werewolf's sides, driving both arrows between its ribs. Somehow, Waggoner's muscles were strong enough to flip the Half Breed onto its side and pound both arrows into its chest cavity. Paige finished it off with a stabbing blow from her machete that cut straight up into its heart. When she pulled the weapon out, there were enough barbs protruding from the sides of the machete to pull a sizable portion of the creature's innards out along with it.

"Come in," Kawosa said as he tapped a button on the phone. "And don't worry. There isn't—"

Before he could finish, Paige rushed forward to look inside the room. A second Half Breed sat on the other side of the doorway, looking even more tortured by its inability to move.

Swinging his feet down from the desk, Kawosa leaned forward in his chair and clasped his hands. Long stringy hair hung on either side of his face, plastered to his forehead and parted like a curtain to reveal angular features that looked as if they'd been drawn onto him with chalk. Studying her carefully, he said, "There isn't another Half Breed guarding that door."

"I'm looking straight at it," she said with what little bit of confidence she could dredge up.

"No. Your partner did away with the only guard I posted. There wasn't enough time for me to find another. There is no other Half Breed guarding that door."

Even though she could see for herself that Kawosa was lying, his words were still tunneling into her brain. Paige kept her eyes focused on the second Half Breed, holding onto its image as if it was about to fade from her sight. And no matter how hard she tried, that's exactly what it did.

The Half Breed strained against its instinct to run and destroy.

Paige fought to keep hold of the knowledge and vision that set her apart from every other schmuck who didn't know any better than to believe monsters didn't exist.

None of that struggling helped either one of them.

The Half Breed remained where it was, and Paige's sight

was clouded until she saw nothing but empty floor space where the bestial guard had been.

Kawosa allowed his fingers to slide together so he could clasp his hands. Although he was still watching the door, he relaxed when Paige's gaze wandered away from where it had been anchored a moment ago. "So, Skinner, how did you find me?"

Unsure whether she could sneak a bluff past Kawosa, she told him, "There's a distinct lack of authority figures around here for a town being overrun by werewolves. This seemed like a good place to look for an explanation."

Kawosa's features might have shifted, but not so a mortal's eyes would notice. "That makes sense."

"They'll still come, you know."

"Who will?"

In the hallway behind her, Waggoner was just finishing with the Half Breed that had jumped him and took no notice of the one still by the door. He held his ground to catch his breath in a series of wheezing gasps.

"The military," Paige said. "The police. Local gun nuts. More of us. It doesn't matter. What you're doing here won't go unnoticed for long. The Full Bloods in New Mexico are already cleared out, and if we can't do the same here tonight, you'll get obliterated by some good old-fashioned American firepower sooner or later."

"I thought you Skinners shunned the spotlight. Isn't that why your Dr. Lancroft had me caged in a dungeon beneath a basement for all those years?" Kawosa studied Waggoner's sweaty face and tensed muscular frame as if the man was pressed between glass slides beneath a microscope. "So the wildness truly is inside you," he mused.

"You're damn right it is," Waggoner said while holding out a bloody arrow to point at the shapeshifter. "And you're about to get a taste of it firsthand."

"What wildness?" Paige asked.

Almost immediately Waggoner moved forward. He'd already forgotten about the prone Half Breed at his feet and had his sights set upon the scrawny man sitting next to a phone that blinked wildly with incoming calls. Paige stretched out an arm to prevent him from getting past her, which prompted him to push against her as if he didn't even realize there was something in his way.

"The same wildness my kin are feeling," Kawosa said while observing Waggoner's frustration. "It's the spark inside those of you who find yourselves in the role of warrior, whether that be soldier, Skinner, criminal, or beast. Surely you've known humans who've tried to pick up a Skinner weapon and didn't have the spirit to swing it?"

"Yeah," Paige scoffed. "And there are people who wash out of the Police Academy. Are you saying they're missing some mystical energy?"

"There's nothing mystical about it," Kawosa replied. "Just because you don't know how to measure something with one of your meters or devices doesn't mean it's not there. You know the difference between someone like me and a species like you?"

"If you say enlightenment, I'll save you the trouble of killing me by laughing myself to death."

Kawosa didn't laugh, but he did smile at her. The expression on his face was similar to a grandparent wondering how the beautiful little girl he once knew could turn into such a fine young woman. "Acceptance. That's the difference. I've stopped questioning why things are and accept what I know is here. When I was locked in Lancroft's cage, I had to accept that there was no way for me to escape. When you and the rest of the Skinners killed him, I had to accept that the humans had become a force to be reckoned with. Now, you humans should do yourselves a favor and accept that all of your petty concerns, the society you've built and the world you think you've shaped, is all about to be brought down. Other species had to accept that fact when you started spreading like a plague and now it's your turn." Placing his hands flat upon the desk, Kawosa stood up and looked at Paige and Waggoner. "You've got no other choice but to set your weapons aside and accept it."

"He's right," Waggoner sighed. "There's no other choice." Then he calmly set his arrows on the floor.

Paige's scars were so cold that she could barely think of anything else. A jabbing, arthritic pain shot through her fingers as she placed her machete on the floor.

Chapter Twenty-Six

Kawosa stood in front of them. "Here's what you must do," he said. "Meet Lancroft's favored ones called the Vigilant. If you don't already know who they are, you'll need to poke around until you find out. I can tell you most of them are based in Louisville, Kentucky. When you find them, it's essential for you to kill as many as possible. They are dangerous to your cause and to humanity in general."

Waggoner nodded and Paige followed suit. She could feel his words sinking in without the slightest touch of invasion that accompanied the lesser psychic manipulations pulled off by Nymar or even the Mind Singer himself. Kawosa's words were wrapped in something that made them feel as if they'd been spoken by a loving parent who only wanted the best for his precious little babies.

"Now," Kawosa said, "you have to go back to the other Skinners and tell them you found nothing here because there is nothing in this building. There is no reason for them to risk themselves and they just need to find somewhere to hide because the authorities must surely be on their way."

"Right," Paige said as she looked up to finally meet his gaze. "The cops or Army have to be on their way."

"Exactly."

"Because I'm gonna call them." With that, she drew her Beretta using the hand that began creeping toward her holster while Kawosa had been talking. She removed the pistol in one fluid motion and fired a round at his head.

Skinners: The Breaking

In the fraction of a second between taking aim and pulling the trigger, Paige got a look into Kawosa's eyes. They began as light blue and shifted into a dark violet while widening with genuine surprise. Surprised or not, he had just enough time to pull his head to one side and avoid the nine millimeter rounds that were fired at him. By the time she pulled her aim to track him, Kawosa was shifting into a form that drew the mass of his body into a more compact frame. His hands shifted into paws and he dropped to all fours. His ears stretched into long points and his face tapered to a narrow snout.

Kawosa barked at the other Half Breed while jumping toward the door. Waggoner was there to catch him and managed to wrap both arms around the shapeshifter's midsection.

"Hold him steady!" Paige said as she scooped up her machete. She tried to swing at the Half Breed, but the werewolf was more than quick enough to evade the weapon.

Kawosa squirmed, kicked, and thrashed in Wagoner's grasp, but didn't have the multiple breaks in his skeleton that would allow him to twist free or attack like a Half Breed. The other werewolf in the room lunged at Waggoner and sank its teeth into his hip. Waggoner dropped to one knee, screaming in agony. When his grip loosened, Kawosa broke free. The shapeshifter took less than two steps before Paige's machete cut into his back.

Paige pointed her Beretta at the Half Breed and started firing. It shook its head furiously, as if trying to turn away from the gunfire while simultaneously ripping off a portion of Waggoner's body. Her machete had become embedded less than half an inch into Kawosa's flesh and couldn't be driven any further. Instead of trying to fight a losing battle, she twisted the blade until it was angled to slice a piece off Kawosa's back the way a butcher might carve off a thick slice of ham. She managed to draw the blade through his flesh for about an inch or two before Kawosa flailed too much to be held. Once he sank his claws into the floor and dragged himself toward the door, he pulled forward and tore off the piece of him Paige had been cutting. Then he bolted from the room, leaving them to contend with the remaining Half Breed. Paige flipped her bloody prize off the machete and onto the floor, then drove the blade straight down through the back of the creature's neck to sever its spine.

Waggoner wanted to go after Kawosa but couldn't take one step before he crumpled to the floor. "Son of a bitch! What got me?"

"There was another Half Breed waiting in here for us. That one," Paige said, jabbing a finger at the twitching werewolf. "Right there!"

"That wasn't there before . . . was it?"

"Yeah. It was. That thing that ran out of here just told you it wasn't."

"And I believed him?" Waggoner asked.

"Yep. That's his shtick." Paige picked up the meat she'd carved from Kawosa and turned it over to examine both sides. "But not anymore. At least not if I can get this wrapped up before it dries out. Where's a grocery store around here?"

"There's a Town and Country back down on Court Street and a few other places along Mississippi Avenue."

"Which one's closer?"

"Mississippi Avenue is pretty torn up and there's lots of folks taking refuge there. That means there'll be those wolf things prowling around."

"Half Breeds," Paige corrected. "Let me see your palm."

Grudgingly, Waggoner leaned back and stretched out his wounded leg to show his callused but relatively scar-free hands. "That's right," he said. "Half Breeds. That's what Bill and Jesse call them. You looking for scars like they have?"

"You're not a Skinner," Paige mused. "If we get out of this town in one piece, we'll have to talk about offering you a membership. Now which way to Mississippi Avenue? We should check on some survivors and see if any of them have some plastic wrap."

After spending so much time in Atoka, there weren't many medical supplies left in the green truck. Still winded from running back to the pickup, Paige sifted through the supplies to find a baby bottle filled with a few squirts of the light blue fluid used to sterilize Half Breed wounds. The bottle was from Jesse and Bill's supply, and there was barely enough left to drizzle on Waggoner's hip. From what she could see, the creature's teeth hadn't gotten down to the bone, but it was better to be safe than sorry. If they were closer to the spot where the Amriany were hiding, she would have raided their medical kit to heal him up even better.

After dressing his wound as best they could, Waggoner was feeling good enough to support his weight on a hastily bandaged leg. Paige didn't need to examine the wound to know it was bad. When they arrived at a small ranch style house on South Mississippi Avenue, Waggoner refused to stay in the truck.

"You'll need me," he told Paige. "Last time I checked, there were three families in there, and they ain't about to open the door for a stranger."

"We just need to grab a few supplies and make sure they're alive."

"And they need to protect their loved ones. Besides," he added while pulling himself from the truck, "I told them we'd come along to look in on them, and that's what I'll do."

"Are they protected in there?"

"They got one of them panic rooms in the master bedroom. Bet they didn't think it would come in so handy, huh?"

He knocked on the door to announce their presence as they entered the house, shouted through a reinforced wall and mentioned four people by name, but still he and Paige found themselves looking down a trio of shotgun barrels when the panic room door swung open.

"You guys need to come up with a secret knock," Paige said as she helped Waggoner sit down inside the cramped secret room. "That would cut down on a lot of grief."

"You don't know what grief is, lady," said a man in his late fifties with a salt and pepper beard and skin tanned to a dark bronze. "For all we know, you could turn into one of those things."

Barely taking notice of the guns pointed at her, Paige looked at the people in the room and focused on what she could feel in her scars. "Seriously, a secret knock isn't that hard. Two quick followed by three slow. Or what about the ol' shave and a haircut?"

One of the people not holding a shotgun was a short

woman with cropped red hair and a kind, soft face. "Shave and a haircut?" she asked with a distinct New Jersey accent.

"You know . . ." Paige stretched out a hand to strike the first part on the wall. *Knock . . . knock knock-knock knock.* Before she could get to the last two, something rumbled beneath their feet.

All of the shotguns were pointed at her as the man with the beard snapped, "Don't make a goddamn sound!"

She knew it was Mongrels passing nearby, but still waited another couple of seconds before saying, "Two bits. You guys have any Tupperware?"

The panic room was roughly half the size of the adjacent bedroom. Fourteen people were crammed inside, along with boxes of food, crates of bottled water, two flashlights, three cots, four shotguns, and a small television set. There was barely enough room for anyone to move, and nobody wanted to speak loud enough to be heard over the chugging of the air circulation system. The bearded man broke the uneasy silence with a single question.

"What the hell did you just say?"

"I need Tupperware," Paige told him. "Or any container with a sealed lid. I know that seems strange, but—"

"I have Tupperware," the redheaded woman said. "In the kitchen. I can show you."

"You're not leaving this room, Ginger," the bearded man said.

She leaned over to look around the man's bulky frame so she could make eye contact with Paige. "Far right cabinet in the kitchen. You can't miss it."

"Thanks. What about some water, something to drink, maybe some food?"

Before anyone could object, the redhead held a hand out to the man and said, "These people are out there fighting those things, they can take whatever they can find." To Paige, she said, "Anything."

"Thanks. Is there room for one more in here?"

Waggoner looked at Paige. "You ain't abandoning me!"

"And you aren't about to run anywhere with that leg. If you come with us, you'll either slow us down or die alone. If you stay here, you'll be safe until we can get you patched up

Skinners: The Breaking

for real. Besides, it you're going to join the big leagues, you need to stay alive and healthy through this."

Returning her wary smile with one of his own, Waggoner looked over to the bearded man and asked, "So you got room for one more or not?"

Looking down at Waggoner's bandaged leg, the bearded man grunted and stepped aside. "I suppose, since it's you."

"Yeah. Thanks." With that, Waggoner eased back and stretched his wounded leg out in front of him. "I'll just need a little time to heal up," he told Paige. "Then I can be right with you again."

"You've got a phone?"

"Of course. And now," Waggoner said, and tossed his keys to her, "you've got a truck. Don't bust it up too bad."

Paige went into the kitchen to look for the Tupperware. The redhead was right, she couldn't miss it. At least four piles of the colorful plastic containers were piled high in the far right cabinets with lids stacked neatly beneath them. After she found a piece that was just the right size to hold the pound of flesh she'd extracted from Kawosa, she popped the lid shut and said, "I've got to get me some of this stuff."

Collecting some bottled water, chips, and snack cakes to stuff into her pockets, she returned to the panic room just as the bearded man was closing the door. "Here," she said, handing the container to Waggoner. "Keep this for me. It's important."

"I ain't out of this fight yet and I sure as hell ain't sitting it out just to guard some leftovers."

Crouching down so he could hear her whisper, she tapped the container and asked, "Do you know why you believed what Kawosa told you and I didn't?"

Although obviously not proud of that instance, he replied, "No, but I was wondering about that."

"It's because I finally made something that works." She held up her hand and showed him her scarred palm. "I met up with that coyote before and he almost got me and my partner to kill each other. I clipped him back in Canada. It wasn't a bad wound, but it drew blood. Have you seen Bill's weapons and what they can do?"

Shooting a cautious glance to the others in the room with him, Waggoner nodded.

"We can use those weapons to sniff out things like these werewolves," she explained.

"I know. I've seen that too."

"Well, I got enough blood to modify my weapon to sniff out that lying shapeshifter. Maybe it's because I trusted that more than anything else, but when he spoke to me, I didn't buy what he was selling."

"If we can put this stuff to use—"

She silenced him with a hand placed gently on his shoulder. "All I got was a warning, and even then it was tough to fight it when he tried to manipulate me. We need his blood to do the trick, and this," she said while placing her hand reverently on the orange plastic container, "won't even be enough to treat everybody's weapons. When you're feeling better, I think we should see about getting a weapon for you. A real one."

"I don't know," Waggoner sighed. "I like my bow. But I'll watch this for you. That skinny prick is just a lying little scumbag who cuts and runs."

"He's survived worse than us, so there's got to be more than one trick up his sleeve. This'll help, though."

Waggoner's arms closed around the Tupperware container until it disappeared within his grasp. If anything was going to get to it, they would have one hell of a fight on their hands. "Where are you headed?"

"There's still a little bit of time to get things prepared. Remember that stuff I was working on at the paint shop? I'll need a lot more of that."

"How long will that take?"

"The Breaking Moon won't be at full strength until around three in the morning. At least, that's what our sources say."

"You mean MEG?" Waggoner asked.

"Yeah. You've heard about them?"

"Bill told us about MEG. Kinda had to. After hearing him mention that name a few times, we thought he was cheatin' on his wife with some girl who he called all the time."

Two of the women from one of the families huddled in the back of the room perked up. Judging by the similarity of their features and age difference, they were most likely mother and daughter. "You mean those ghost guys on TV?" the daughter asked, having overheard the whispered conversation. "We love them! They really know their stuff."

Paige rolled her eyes and in a normal voice said, "The MEG guys are the rock stars now? Dark days indeed."

"What?" the mother asked, since she didn't know the history between Skinners and the paranormal research group. "They're really smart?"

"They sure are," Waggoner said. "Let's just hope they're more on the ball about this than the Bigfoot that was supposed to be stomping around northern Indiana."

After pulling in a deep breath and letting it out, Paige stood up and checked to make sure her Beretta was loaded. "I should get going."

"What you should do is get an hour's sleep," Waggoner said. "How long's it been since you rested?"

"I caught a few hours on the plane over here. Feels like a week ago."

"Then take an hour. What can it hurt?"

"If my partner's plan is going to work, we'll need to move those Full Bloods and any other shapeshifters away from town in a matter of a few seconds," she explained. "Have you ever herded werewolves, cowboy?"

"No, ma'am. But it might not be a bad idea to sit tight and pick a better spot for a fight," Waggoner offered.

Paige flexed the arm that required constant movement to keep from petrifying into a stump. "Believe me, I know all about rushing in. The problem here is that we already let the Full Bloods get too far. They can turn people into Half Breeds without biting them. Isn't that right?" she asked the families huddled against the walls. Some nodded back and others were too frightened to move a muscle.

"I saw people drop to their knees in the parking lot of a gas station," the bearded man said. "They were fine one minute, and the next, their bones were snapping until they became monsters. Werewolves," he said, as if the whole situation was just sinking in. "Jesus Christ."

Paige was all too familiar with the look on his face. "Since there are humans still left in this town, that must mean the

Full Bloods have some sort of range or limit to this thing they can do. If they make it all the way through the Breaking Moon, that could change for the worse, and we can't allow that to happen. I won't let that happen. Stay in here until someone comes for you. That goes for everybody."

"What if nobody comes for us?" the bearded man asked.

"Then you might as well get comfortable inside this room because there won't be much of an outside waiting for you."

That sent a wave of frightened sobs through the little space, but also served to push the families back against the walls with no sign of moving. Paige resisted the urge to reassure the youngest children and turned her back to the group. At certain times, a dose of justified fear served a good purpose, and if her words kept those people locked away for the next few hours, that was just fine.

"When I'm feeling better, I'll come help you," Waggoner said.

"No. Stay here and protect these people."

"There are others locked up in other houses that need help too, you know," he said.

"Yeah, and there's only so much we can do. We either protect a few or lose them all."

He grunted. "Now there's one of the shittiest choices I've ever heard."

"You obviously haven't been around Skinners for very long," she told him.

Chapter Twenty-Seven

Finding the Full Bloods wasn't difficult. Even a blind man would have been able to follow the growing crescendo of howls drifting from the east end of town. Paige met Al and Jesse outside a convenience store that had been all but gutted by shapeshifters or looters. While filling the tanks of both pickups at a set of pumps, she slapped the window behind Al's head until Jesse slid it open. "Any word from Milosh or Nadya?"

"We don't need them Gypsies," the Skinner replied.

"We need everyone we can get. We'll swing by to pick them up."

"For all we know, that poor bastard's dead."

"Then we'll pick Nadya up. Besides, we need to check in with the Mongrels too."

"They've been getting their asses handed to them since we got here," Bill said. "I don't know what you Chicago guys do, but we don't work with animals."

"Fine. I'll let them know to pass you by if you need any help. In case you're blind, though, I should remind you that these Mongrels have been fighting the Full Bloods just like we have. Since I'm not quite ready for the ol' blaze of glory, let's just work with whoever we can."

"I'm with her," Al said.

Bill's narrow face twisted into a disapproving sneer, but he kept the rest of his comments to himself. The group piled into their vehicles, and Paige checked in one more time with Cole as she drove north into a residential area.

By the time they got to the house where the Amriany had been taken after leaving the autobody shop, the sky was dark enough for the stars to shine brightly overhead. The sight was even more breathtaking thanks to the pale glow of a mostly full moon and no competition from the darkened town. Al pulled up to a two-car garage and Paige parked the green truck directly behind him. The garage door was already on its way up, so she hunched over and walked beneath the door. When she stood up straight again, Nadya was staring at her over the top of her FAMAS.

"How's Milosh?" Paige asked.

"He won't turn into a Vitsaruuv, but some of the others in these houses weren't so lucky. I could hear their screams. The Breaking Moon must be allowing Full Bloods—"

"I know. Ready to do something about it?"

"Yes!"

But it wasn't Nadya who answered her question. Hobbling down two wooden steps that connected the garage to the house with the remains of his left arm bound in bandages and towels, Milosh gritted his teeth and shuffled across the cracked, oil-stained garage floor.

"You're barely conscious," Nadya scolded. "What do you think you'll do in this fight?"

"He made it this far," Paige pointed out. "Can he fire a gun?"

"You're damn right he can," Milosh replied. "And if I fall over or bleed out, go on without me. I'd rather get picked off out in the thick of it instead of hiding and waiting for the fucking axe to fall."

"Has Quinn been here?"

"She has been gone for a while, but another Kushtime remains in the basement to watch us." Picking up steam with every step he took, Milosh continued his arduous journey to the driveway. "Get me to the plane. We've got some more weapons that might help us."

"No time for that. Unless you've got another Blood Blade stashed in that wreck, we have to make do with what we've got." Raising her eyebrows, Paige asked, "You don't have another Blood Blade stashed in that wreck, do you?"

"We won't have any more of those for at least another month, but there's guns and some blades that were charmed to do some damage."

"Forget it," Paige sighed. "We need to stick together if we're going to cover as much of this town as possible."

Someone else walked up from the basement. Because of all the dirt caked into his fur, it was impossible to make out Burke's features until the Mongrel shook some of the grit from his coat. "I can cover a lot more ground than you. What do you need?"

"Can you tell me about any Mongrels working with the Full Bloods?" Paige asked.

After a pause, Burke said, "There are some of us who have decided that joining the Full Bloods is the best way to end our troubles. Most of those have been tempted by the Full Bloods' twisted promise that they can change us into their kind. Even the thought that some of the Full Blood longevity can be passed on has been enough to draw entire packs to their banner. What's happened recently only sped the process along."

"So why should we trust that you would want to fight on our side?" Paige asked.

"My pack and I are not under any Full Blood control because we haven't allowed ourselves to be tainted by their bite. If you don't believe that, then you can go to hell. Just know that we've been in contact with Kayla and Ben from Kansas City and they say you're good for your word. You fight against the Full Bloods and so do we. If we survive this war, we think we can trust you to work out an amicable arrangement."

"War?" Nadya asked. "Has it come to that?"

"Better here than in our country," Milosh grunted.

"Yes it has come to that," Burke said. He shifted his slitted eyes to Milosh. "And it has only started in this country because this is where the biggest source of Torva'ox is to be found. The Full Bloods will not stay put once they have gathered their power. They will either return to their territories or try to acquire new ones. Either way, no place is safe."

"I've heard some news myself from New Mexico," Paige said. "The Full Bloods are fighting among themselves."

"If they whittle their numbers down far enough, the survivor will be the most powerful creature on the planet and will be able to shift all humans into Half Breeds or possibly something worse. Our legends are filled with these warnings, which is why we fight when we could just as easily hide to let the storm pass us by."

"There's more than legends and old grudges on the table," Paige said. "Now that the military is involved, there's little things like air strikes and nukes to worry about."

"Nukes?" Milosh said. "It would come to that?"

"I've spoken with men who represent the military, even if it may be on a sketchy basis. They're willing to work with Skinners, but only because they want to get rid of the things that are tearing apart our cities. If we don't step up and do our job, they'll fall back to the best way they know to kill big things as quickly as possible. I'm doing my best to keep them in line, but if things keep escalating like they have been, I wouldn't be surprised if the fingers over those big red buttons start getting twitchy."

The unearthly howls outside were becoming more musical and jubilant, as opposed to the wild, hungry sounds earlier. Ironically, that strangely beautiful sound sparked genuine fear inside all of those gathered in the garage.

"We can sit here talking doomsday scenarios all night long," Paige said. "It doesn't matter if I'm blowing things out of proportion or not. Things have already gotten way out of hand and we're the only ones that can do anything about it. Kawosa's taken the authorities out of the picture for now, but help is on the way. What we need to do is draw the Full Bloods to a spot where Cole, my partner, can meet us."

"Where's that?" Milosh asked.

"About five or six miles north of here at the Atoka Reservoir. Water acts as a natural booster for supernatural energies, and the Dryads who will transport him here need all the help they can get to do their part. Finally something the MEG guys got right." She smirked at the memory of days when a call to the ghost hunters was all she needed for her and Cole to know what to do next. "Plus there's fewer civilians out there. Drawing as many shapeshifters away from here gives the survivors here a bigger chance to see tomorrow."

"We don't owe them nothing," Milosh snarled as he rubbed the stump of his left arm.

"Miro," Nadya snapped in her native tongue, followed by a string of words. Since Milosh clamped his mouth shut reflexively, Paige assumed that's pretty much what she'd just told him to do. Looking to Paige, she said, "Among our people, we are known as both cursed and chosen. Above either of those things, we are protectors and so are Skinners. No matter what the quarrel is between our peoples in the past, this is a problem that will affect us all. But there must be an understanding."

"Be quick about it," Paige said as the howls outside grew more ecstatic.

"Us helping you now means the start of a true joining of Amriany and Skinner. We fight on your soil tonight and you must fight on ours in the future."

"This thing is gonna go on for longer than one night," Paige warned.

"Your fight becomes our fight, just as ours becomes yours. However long it takes."

Paige extended her hand and Nadya shook it. "Fair enough, but I can't guarantee all of us will be crazy about setting the past aside. I'll vouch for you, which will go a long way with some. Then we'll talk sense into the rest."

"As will I. It is decided then. Right, Milosh?"

The wounded Amriany muttered in his own tongue, but nodded.

Bill walked into the garage carrying a shotgun. "Are we doing this or not?"

And that was that.

When Paige walked away from the garage, the only thing in her world was the fight that lay ahead. Even though there was no target for her machete, she tightened her grip around its handle until the thorns punctured her palm. The wood creaked and the weapon shifted. After climbing into the back of the red pickup, she noticed a more familiar sickle in her grasp.

Paige stared at the weapon as the truck's engine roared to life and the vehicle rattled down the road. Unlike the sickle she'd forged throughout the course of her training, it was more like what that weapon would have aspired to become once it grew up. The handle was thicker and shorter, which allowed the blade to become wider and longer. Until now, the fact that she'd been unable to shift the weapon's cutting edge had been attributed to the coat of metallic glaze added to the varnish. The edge was still there and its shape was mostly the same, but it was bent around the crescent edge of the sickle. Even as she marveled at the feat she'd been unable to perform ever since the injury to her arm, she could feel the potential for more. Looking up at the moon, feeling the wildness Kawosa had promised, she wanted to howl.

Chapter Twenty-Eight

Every time she looked up from the back of the red pickup, Paige felt as if she was farther from civilization. Atoka was still there, but its buildings were husks. Some were on fire. Most were broken to one degree or another. Claw marks had been scratched onto just about every surface and the only things that moved were being pushed around by the wind.

"Take a look around," Burke said while running alongside the pickup. "This is what every city will look like if the Full Bloods have their way."

"Why would they want things to be like this?" Milosh asked.

Paige flipped her sickle in her hand. Although her fingers weren't as nimble as they'd been before her injury, they compensated by closing around the handle with an even stronger grip than before. "If we live until tomorrow, we can ask them."

"If there's any of those Full Blood assholes left to ask," the Amriany snarled.

"That's the spirit."

They drove to the paint store to pick up the bait mixture that had been mixed up earlier. It was stored in all the containers they could scrounge from nearby houses and garbage cans, ranging from plastic water bottles to canteens and an insulated iced tea jug. Anything that could hold the viscous mixture without spilling it or allowing its scent to sully the air before it was needed was put to use. As they piled back into both trucks, those containers were divvied out to Skinner and Amriany alike.

"Come here, mole man!" Bill shouted.

Sighing reluctantly, Burke approached the passenger side of the red truck. The closer the Mongrel got, the more the bristly hairs along his back stood up. When he was within a few feet of the window, he was splashed with a slimy load of the pungent bait mixture. He bared his teeth, which only allowed some of the rancid gel to trickle into his mouth. "That shit's gonna make me puke!"

"Don't get your panties in a twist," Bill said. "Run around town and find as many Half Breeds as you can. Shouldn't be hard with that stuff. Get them to follow you, and bring them to us. When it looks like we can't handle any more, take them to the reservoir. Got it?"

The Mongrel grunted. "Could have warned me before splashing that shit on me."

"Would that have made it smell any better? Just don't do any tunneling or you'll wipe it off."

Paige unscrewed a plastic container she'd taken from Ginger's kitchen that had been used to hold the pretzel sticks she and the other Skinners had devoured. "And tell Quinn to send any of the others over to us so they can do the same." When she saw the resistant look on the Mongrel's face, she added, "You said you guys wanted to help. This is what needs to be done." Some of the howling in the vicinity stopped and was replaced by excited, panting breaths. "I'd be quick about it too. Sounds like someone's already picked up our scent." With that, Paige turned the container over and dumped its contents onto the side of the truck.

"You're not getting that shit on my baby, are you?" Al said from the driver's seat.

"Not at all," Paige told him. "Get moving."

The truck lurched forward, forcing her to sit down and brace herself with her feet against the interior of the bed. As they picked up speed, she let the large empty container roll around near the tailgate so she could pick up the water bottles. She tossed one to Milosh, who was in the back with her, and handed another to Bill through the little sliding window that opened into the cab. He took it and jammed it into the cup holder so he could tend to his hunting rifle. It was a large caliber model that Paige didn't recognize, although she was certain Cole would have known it just by the scope. The sickle was trapped beneath her foot like a long-lost friend.

On the edge of the parking lot, Quinn threw a fit as Jesse doused her in more of the bait mixture. Nadya waved to Paige and climbed into the green pickup. By the time Al rounded the next corner, Jesse was gunning the other truck's engine and heading for the opposite end of town.

Gail ran up to the red truck on Paige's side, moving on all fours with every bit of the feline grace that her form suggested. When she looked up, she snarled in a voice that was barely understandable through her needlelike fangs. "Bait," was all she said.

Paige obliged her by squirting some of the stuff onto the Mongrel. Farther down East Court Street, larger paws scraped against the cement. She drew her Beretta and braced herself against a pipe that had been welded into the bed to be used as a handle. "All of you, go!"

Gail scampered past the truck to rush headlong into the approaching Half Breeds. The werewolves barked at her and bared their fangs, allowing strings of drool to trail from their mouths as they lowered their heads and quickened their pace. Even with her unnatural speed, Gail was barely able to veer away from the creatures before being clipped by greedy, snapping jaws. Three of the five Half Breeds veered off to chase her, while the others charged at the truck. Once they got a healthier whiff of the bait Paige had applied to the pickup, they became so anxious to chase it that their paws slid against the gritty street in their haste to circle around it.

By the time they made it to South Kentucky Avenue, Al had quite the following. Half Breeds relentlessly pursued the pickup, sideswiping telephone poles and streetlights in their haste to try and keep up with his erratic driving. More werewolves joined them as the main group fanned out and put some real steam into their strides in an effort to catch up.

"I think maybe you didn't think this through," Milosh said.

Paige held her Beretta in one hand and one of Bill's .45s in the other. "Then why did you follow me?"

"At this point," he said while waving his stump at her, "there's not much else to lose."

She waved her scarred and nearly petrified right arm at him and said, "I know how you feel. Since you seem to be doing just fine, stop your bitching and start shooting some of these things." Leading by example, she turned to point both pistols over the side of the truck and pulled the triggers.

Milosh's left stump had been cleaned and redressed by one of the Mongrels. There was always a medic in their packs, along with other vital members of a traveling community, including trackers and diggers. The only reason he was up and conscious was because of the Amriany healing serums that had been pumped into him. Paige knew he was going to crash and crash hard when the initial buzz wore off. If they were alive for that moment, she would be more than happy to crash along with him. For now, Milosh gripped one of Al's hunting rifles and used his stump to steady the barrel. The Covid Accura .50 caliber fit snugly against his shoulder and made a satisfying crack as it went off. Even more satisfying was the sight of a Half Breed stumbling and rolling into the werewolf beside it as the round caught it low in its chest.

"Feeling better now?" Paige asked while pressing her side against the truck bed in order to fire three quick shots from the Beretta.

The Amriany nodded and showed her a wide, toothy grin. "This is the perfect cure. A little hair of the dog that bit me, no?"

"And then some. Watch your right."

Milosh shifted his aim in that direction to find another group of Half Breeds charging down Sixth Street and skidding around the corner to fall into step with some of the others. His rifle sent a few carefully placed .50 caliber rounds into the front of the group. Between thundering shots he shouted, "I like this gun!"

Paige chuckled at his enthusiasm and took a few shots of her own. When the Beretta ran dry, she placed it under her foot and switched the .45 into her right hand. Half Breeds were closing in, despite the gunfire being thrown at them.

They were only prevented from overtaking the truck by the sharp turns Al took and their own tendency to get in each other's way in their haste to follow the malodorous bait. Once the Half Breeds had the scent in their nostrils, they would keep coming at them even if they lost a limb or two.

When her .45 ran dry, Paige reloaded both guns using spare magazines she'd prepared and tucked into her pockets back at the paint store. On many occasions, she and Cole had argued about gripping a pistol in each hand and firing away. He called it dual-wielding. She called it a great way to waste a lot of ammo without hitting much of anything. His defense boiled down to how cool it looked. Paige had to admit, when she fired both pistols at the werewolves that were now close enough to scrape their tusks against the side of the truck, she did feel pretty cool.

The guns bucked against her burning palms, spitting point-blank fire at the werewolves. When one Half Breed took a round in the face, it fell behind so another could charge forward and take its place. The motion of the truck and the constantly changing field of targets made it difficult to hit her mark every time, but even the misses did some damage as they ricocheted off the street and into another warm body. But somehow, no matter how many hits she scored, the werewolves were even closer by the time her pistols ran dry again.

"Milosh!" she shouted while ejecting the empty magazines one at a time.

The Amriany glanced over at her, spotted the pair of Half Breeds that had climbed onto the side of the truck and swung his rifle in that direction. Paige lay down and was forced to look up at the werewolves that in turn were looking down at her after scaling the side of the truck. Drool spattered against her face, dripping from their anxious jaws. When one of them hiked a third paw over the side of the truck, a .50 caliber round exploded from Milosh's rifle and hit it like a sledgehammer. That werewolf collided with the other one, sending both of them to the street, to be swallowed by a growing wave of creatures.

Al steered onto Dickerson Avenue and headed south. His route would bring them to Route 3, through the main stretch of town, and back north to complete their circuit. More Half Breeds following them meant fewer of the creatures hunting the human survivors of Atoka. "There's more of them than I thought!" Paige shouted.

Milosh fired another round at a Half Breed that had leapt forward to grab the tailgate with both front paws. The bullet chipped its tusk and snapped its head to one side, but didn't knock it down. The werewolf set one paw inside the truck before the next .50 caliber round knocked it back into the street. "We took too much time preparing," he said.

"We needed that time or else we couldn't have done much of anything about these things."

"Then follow your own advice," he said while clumsily fitting fresh rounds into the rifle he balanced against his knees. "Stop bitching."

No matter how much she wanted to, Paige couldn't argue with that logic. Once her pistols were reloaded, she holstered the Beretta so she could grab the sickle she'd kept trapped beneath her foot. She braced herself to keep from sliding across the bed as the pickup took a hard right onto Route 3. The sudden swerve caused the Half Breeds climbing Milosh's side of the truck to either drop off or fall into the bed. Paige shouted for him to drop, and he tucked himself into a fetal ball as she leaned forward to sweep the curved blade in a deadly arc. Even though she'd managed to log some impressive hours with the machete, the shape and balance of the weapon was finally restored to its former glory. The sickle blade sliced across the eyes of one Half Breed and dug a deep trench across the chest of another. As those two yelped and recoiled, a third pulled itself forward until all four paws were in the bed of the truck.

Paige swung the sickle until her arm was bent across her face. Gritting her teeth, she sent the curved blade on a return path that drove its tip into the Half Breed's shoulder. The edge that had been treated with fragments of the Blood Blade allowed the weapon to burrow several inches down, and the thorns in its handle kept the weapon in her grasp as the creature tried to attack Milosh. Its claws flailed wildly, scraping the Amriany's shoulders and back to tear away layers of clothing before reaching his battered tactical vest. The wounds Milosh sustained were ugly, but nothing that the healing serums in his system couldn't handle. Paige grabbed her weapon with both hands and leaned back, pulling at the Half Breed. The creature snapped its mouth shut within an inch of its meal before a charmed dagger punctured its forehead and scraped against the sickle blade within its skull. Milosh swore at it, twisted his dagger and then pulled it out.

"Al!" Paige shouted. "See if you can shake these things off. They're scratching your paint job!"

She wasn't sure which part of her warning ticked Al off the most: mortal danger to his partners or the damage to his truck. He shouted a string of obscenities while sending the pickup into a lurching series of turns that brought them careening up South Dunbar, around a tight corner, down Lincoln Street, and back onto Route 3. Since she and Milosh were already laying flat inside the truck bed, they were able to stay there while the Half Breeds were forced to struggle just to maintain their grip. Even with claws that could dig through metal, most of them were tossed to the street. The few creatures that tried to run in front of the truck were turned into living speed bumps that jostled Paige and Milosh even more.

Paige had kept hold of the Half Breed she'd impaled with her sickle. After twisting the weapon to make sure the werewolf was dead, she finally let go with her left hand so she could grab one of the squeeze bottles. "Get ready on that tailgate," she said.

Milosh slid his knife back into its scabbard and scooted toward the rear of the truck until one foot was propped against the edge of the frame and the other was flat against the back.

Paige dumped a good portion of bait mixture onto the dead Half Breed and then pulled the sickle free. "Hit it!"

Milosh popped the latch and opened the tailgate with a solid kick. Then he pulled himself against the side of the truck bed so his body pinned the rifle in place and a path was cleared for her to shove the Half Breed out. She didn't know where she got the strength to move the heavy creature, but her muscles barely protested as she pushed the carcass toward the back of the truck. The vehicle's momentum and erratic movement went a long way in sending the dead werewolf into the anxious faces of the creatures running directly behind them. Knowing that some of the Half Breeds might try to jump up into the truck while it was open, she unscrewed the squeeze bottle and tossed it at the ravaging crowd so the rest of the mixture was sprayed across as many of the creatures as possible.

Propping herself onto her knees, she swung her sickle out and down to hook the tailgate beneath its curved blade. All she needed to do then was fall back to lock it into place. Since Al was constantly checking his rearview mirror, he knew when to steady his course so as not to throw her out along with the carcass they'd just unloaded. She grabbed the side of the bed and watched chaos unfold among the Half Breeds.

Most of the creatures swarmed the baited carcass. Others splintered into smaller groups to chase creatures with the mixture spattered on their coats. The newer breed definitely had a keener sense of smell than the previous generation and were driven beyond frenzy as they got closer to the mixture. One of the Half Breeds that had been sprayed by the water bottle ran in circles and flopped on its back like a dog trying to grind an itchy spot against the floor. It twisted itself into a pretzel in its attempt to gnaw at the bait and was quickly overtaken by its brethren as the overzealous werewolves ripped it to pieces. As the green pickup carrying Nadya and Jesse sped down a nearby street, more Half Breeds followed it onto northbound I-69 and led a couple dozen others in that direction.

Even with the road momentarily cleared, Paige knew better than to celebrate. She flipped the sickle into the bed and trapped it once again beneath her foot. "Where are we headed, Al?"

"Straight through town on Mississippi Avenue. Don't know how far we'll make it before one of those damn things shreds a tire."

Paige winced. She hadn't thought of that. While making a suicide drive through a town infested by shapeshifters, getting a flat tire seemed almost too common a problem to consider. Even so, anything that brought the truck to a halt would be one hell of a serious situation. "How far is the reservoir?" she asked.

"Just a few miles north of town. Getting there is still pretty sketchy considering how much we'll have to plow through."

"Don't think about that," she told him while popping the top off another squeeze bottle. She sent it pinwheeling into some trees at the intersection where Liberty Road met Mississippi Avenue. Some of the Half Breeds peeled away from chasing the truck, but the ones that remained had their sights set on her and would not be diverted. To make matters worse, some creatures emerged from those same trees to either attack the container of bait mixture or replace the Half Breeds that had broken off their pursuit.

Al turned to look over his shoulder. There was a maniacal glint in his eye when he said, "Give the gimp something to hang onto."

"What?" Before Milosh could fire back with anything more than that, he was tossed from one side of the bed to another. He and Paige rattled around as the pickup tore through a tight series of turns that sent it between groups of Half Breeds, over refuse scattered in the road, into the dirt beside the road, over a set of low bumps, and finally back onto northbound Mississippi Avenue. Once there, Al slammed his foot onto the accelerator and cranked the knob of his stereo. If he was going to drive into hell, there wasn't any reason why he shouldn't hear some Tom Petty along the way.

It took a few seconds for her to reorient herself, and then Paige sat upright and grabbed onto the side of the bed. Most of the light in Atoka came from whatever spilled down from the moon. Even though it wasn't full, the pale glow was especially dazzling. To many people in other parts of the world, it must have been a beautiful sight. From where she was sitting, however, the moon made Atoka look like death frozen over. Many of the town's lights were off and an overwhelming percentage of those that did shine were sputtering to stay that way. Smoke rose from fires in a few different locations, and whenever she spotted another human being in the distance, that person was cut down by the rampaging beasts that had overtaken the town. In some houses or beneath a few darkened stores, people were huddled just like the ones jammed into Waggoner's panic room. For all she knew, the redhead with the Tupperware, those families, and even Waggoner were already dead. Even worse, they could have been among the Half Breeds being led to the reservoir.

Paige reached over to help Milosh get back into a seated position with his back braced against the wheel well. Unlike the other times she'd tried to help him, the Amriany accepted her efforts. "We shouldn't be leaving this place," she said in a voice she thought would be too quiet to be heard over the truck's engine and the snarling of her countless shapeshifter pursuers.

Having reloaded the rifle and steadied himself so he could sight effectively along its barrel, he replied, "We aren't going far."

"But there's people who can still be saved. The Mongrels probably need our help."

"Plenty of people need help. There will always be someone to save. When you watch the news on television, all you see are those in need, and people like us are always thinking of ways to help them. You know what we have to do?"

"What?"

Milosh shifted and grunted as the heavy hunting rifle weighed down the tender stump of his left arm. "We need to stop watching the news."

She would have chuckled at that if she hadn't been forced to hang on for dear life as Al swerved to avoid running into a wall of Half Breeds. The truck took the corner and headed north.

"Did you ever hear of a village called Bruusk?" Milosh asked.

Since the green pickup had helped take some of the pressure off them, Paige said, "No."

"They were being terrorized by Nymar, and three good Amriany refused to leave even when more and more of the villagers were turned."

"This had better be a quick story," Paige said. "We're getting close to the Full Bloods."

"All three Amriany, along with every last villager, died because none of them knew when to leave. How's that for a short story? This is the case now. It is time to leave, and if we don't, we die."

Paige hadn't allowed herself to feel guilty over decisions she'd made for a long time. There were things that needed to be done, and she did them as best as she could. That's all there was to it, and that was usually enough to get her through the night.

It was going to take a lot more than that to get her through this night.

Chapter Twenty-Nine

Nadya, Jesse, and Quinn waited for them alongside I-69, waving at the red pickup like a pair of pushy hitchhikers. Farther back on the road, the green pickup was completely covered in a writhing mass of knotted muscle, wiry fur, and gnashing teeth. Al skidded to a halt and Paige crawled across the bed of the truck to lean over Milosh's side. "How many are left?" she asked.

"We killed many of the Vitsaruuv, but there will be more coming once those get finished lapping up all of the bait we poured onto that truck."

"Waggoner's going to be pissed," Paige said.

"I've got something to show you that might make up for it." Nadya accepted her partner's help in climbing up into the bed of the red truck. Although Milosh was working with only one arm, he'd offered it to her gladly and now allowed his body to be wedged against the metal wall as she pulled herself in.

"Get in!" Paige said to Jesse.

The man in the U of Texas shirt shook his head strongly enough to waggle his long beard. "I'm headed back into town. With you all dragging these things along, it shouldn't be too hard."

"It only takes one to bring you down," Paige warned.

"If that's all it takes, then I won't do no good to you in that truck," he snapped. With that, he held his rifle at hip level and dashed away from the road, disappearing into the trees.

Milosh growled something in their native tongue when he saw the object in Nadya's hand. She quickly silenced him and then looked at Paige to show her a long steel tube that resembled an ornate bicycle pump. "This is one of our tools that we guard closely. It's charmed to attract the Weshruuv."

"Bait specific to Full Bloods?" Paige asked. "Nice. How does it work?"

Gripping the middle of the tube, Nadya tapped the pump handle with her other hand and said, "Pull back to load the spring. Push forward to shoot."

"How many rounds?"

"Just one. Make it count."

"Are we ready to go?" Al asked. "I don't like sitting still this long unless we're piling out to make our stand."

Quinn stayed on the ground and nervously watched the huge pack of Half Breeds. The dirt encrusted in her fur was thick enough to add some bulk to her frame and slick her ears back against her head. "My pack is keeping the Full Bloods occupied. Some of the wretches were diverted to deal with them, but that also means more of my kind will die this night. If those deaths prove to be in vain, you had better hope I'm counted among them."

"I speak for all of us," Nadya replied. "They won't be in vain. Thank you for helping to see us through this hell."

Bill watched them shake hands and let out a low, disgusted grunt from the back of his throat.

"Tell your pack to bring those Full Bloods to us," Paige said. "After that, you can all find the deepest hole you've got and hide in it until the howling stops."

Quinn nodded and then disappeared underground with an ease that made it seem more like she'd been absorbed into the earth itself. Everyone in the pickup took a moment to reload their guns in preparation for the thundering wave of shapeshifters that had taken a renewed interest in them. Inside the truck, Bill spoke in a tersely guarded voice that wasn't loud enough for Paige to hear. Al responded only with an occasional nod as he gripped the steering wheel and stared at a little sign along the side of the road about seventy yards ahead. Paige stomped her heel against the bed of the truck and shouted, "Let's *go*!"

The truck's engine roared, causing the vehicle's frame to shake. Paige's eyes were fixed on the road behind her, waiting for any sign of the Full Bloods. Dumping the last of the bait onto the side of the truck, she scooted back until her shoulders bumped against the cab, then drew her pistols. By the time the truck built up some speed, heavier paws thumped against the ground. Trees alongside I-69 shook, shedding their leaves in a slow tumble toward the ground as they were assaulted by heavily muscled bodies. Quinn and another Mongrel exploded from the woods, keeping low to the ground and their heads held high. Seeing the truck, they split up to race past either side of the vehicle while Minh charged after them.

Now it was Nadya who told the driver to wait as she lifted the gleaming metal tube to point it over the tailgate. She drew back the pump handle, causing the mechanism inside to clatter and snap into place. Her feet pressed against the interior of the truck bed and her back stiffened as the Full Blood charged forward. Paige wanted to fire at the creature but choked back that instinct so the Amriany could do her thing.

As soon as Minh came within twenty feet of the pickup, Nadya pushed the pump handle back into the tube. An oiled piston within the device shot a gleaming projectile out to trace a shimmering path through the air that ended somewhere between Minh's left shoulder and upper chest. The Full Blood grunted, staggered, and then recovered while slowing to a trot. She snarled and nipped at the spot on her coat that was now stained with blood, but was unable to remove the thing that had been shot into her. In the distance, Liam's distinctive howl rose above all the others. Minh's crystalline eyes snapped at the truck, found Nadya, and then narrowed.

"Go faster," the Amriany said. "Go, *go*!"

Al nearly jammed the gas pedal through the floor, causing the pickup to lurch forward in a burst of speed that sent all three of the passengers in the bed toward the tailgate. Bill reached out to slap the top of the cab gleefully while hollering as if to compete with the baying Full Bloods.

Hanging on with one hand while using the other to tuck the engraved tube under her arm, Nadya said, "Now that the bolt has made contact with the blood of a Weshruuv, they will follow whoever carries this."

"How long will that last?"

"Long enough. I also dipped the bolt into some of your bait, so she'll have plenty to keep her busy."

Al steered toward a small access road on the left that led toward the reservoir. The exit was overgrown and barely seemed large enough for the truck. Paige could only hang on and watch as Minh tore up the road in her haste to keep up. Although she had the same frenzied look in her eyes as the Half Breeds, there was enough intelligence there to keep her from devolving into a mass of flailing limbs like her twisted brethren. Fortunately, that twisted mass was snapping at her, latching onto her coat and forcing her to slow down and periodically swipe at the Half Breeds clinging to her back.

"Now that's some damn fine teamwork!" Paige said.

"Arvah," Milosh said with a nod. "This is good."

Once she'd rid herself of enough Half Breeds to once again face the right direction, Minh caught up to the truck with only a few powerful strides.

"This," Milosh said with chilling calm, "is not so good."

Nadya fumbled with the FAMAS strapped across her back. Before she could swing the assault rifle around to use it, the entire truck was jostled by a nudge from the side of Minh's head. The next impact lifted the truck off its back tires and dropped it down again with a powerful jolt that knocked the small of Nadya's back against the wheel well and sent the pickup into a fishtail.

Rather than risk being thrown into an uncontrolled skid, Al worked the brakes while wrestling with the steering wheel. The man beside him leaned out the passenger window and fired his rifle at the werewolf.

Bullets from several different weapons thumped against Minh's hide without penetrating her fur. One knocked against her temple, snapping her head to the side, and when she looked back at Nadya, there was a hellish glint in her eyes. As the pickup gained speed, Minh leapt with both front paws stretched out to snag the vehicle as if to grab a wildcat by the tail. After digging one set of claws into the rear corner of the frame, she roared at the Amriany.

Nadya rattled around the back of the truck like a pinball, struggling to get a better grip on her FAMAS. A rough hand slapped against her shoulder and pulled the strap hard enough to drag her to the other side of the bed less than a second before Minh's claws sparked against the lining. Paige threw Nadya toward the cab using a right arm that felt stronger than it had in months. Gripping the sickle in her left hand, she put everything she had into a swing that carved a trench across Minh's chest. The sickle would have opened the Full Blood's throat if not for a last second defensive movement from the werewolf.

When Minh retreated, Paige surged forward to swing again. The metallic edge of the sickle caught the light from a moon that seemed to glow brighter as the combat intensified. Everything from the weapon's distribution of weight to the shape of the grip was familiar to her, allowing each motion to flow more fluidly than the one before it. Minh attempted to get closer to the truck, but pulled away from the Skinner's attacks as though her snout was threatened by a rotary saw.

"Hang on!" Al shouted while powering into a rough stretch of access road. "There's a clearing that butts right up to the water! We used to come here to get high back in the day." The truck's tires kicked up a spray of gravel and dug into the rough terrain well enough to regain some speed.

Keeping her eyes on the Full Blood that now loped behind the vehicle, Paige asked, "How far is it?"

"Less than a mile."

Although the words were spoken with confidence, Paige didn't take any comfort from them. She switched out her sickle for the pistols, and when she pulled her triggers, she wasn't alone. Nadya had the FAMAS against her shoulder and fired in a quick series of three-shot bursts. Weathering the storm of lead, Minh planted her front paws and crouched down in preparation for a leap that would surely overtake the truck. Just as her muscles were tensing for the jump, a .50 caliber round thumped against her front left knee to take that leg out from under her.

Glancing over to Milosh, Paige asked, "Why the hell haven't you been covering us with that thing until now?"

He pulled the lever to move the rifle's slide back and then dropped the weapon. "That was my last bullet. Hope we can trust that partner of yours to pull his weight."

"He's been pulling his weight long enough to be trusted," Paige replied fiercely. "You just be sure to do the same."

Milosh smirked, which curved the scars on his face even more. "For Amriany, the fight doesn't stop until we are dead. Even then there's a chance of us taking a few more good swings at whatever needs to be killed."

Behind the truck, Minh hobbled and licked her leg where it had been shot. Even though the ammunition was treated with a coating that would have allowed it to punch through a Kevlar vest, it wasn't enough to do more than cause a Full Blood some discomfort. A few seconds later Minh was up and moving again. When Nadya held the metal tube up high enough for it to be spotted, the creature broke into a run.

A rasping howl tore through the night. It only lasted a few seconds, but that was long enough for Paige to be certain the werewolf was less than two hundred yards away and closing in fast. Al followed the road as it turned sharply to the right. When he cranked the wheel to point the truck in the direction of the lake, his headlights illuminated a massive beast covered in thick ebon fur. It shifted to face the truck and then rammed its shoulder into the pickup's grill.

"Son of a bitch!"

The first two words had escaped Al's mouth as the truck wrapped around Liam's body, the last word expelled in a grunt that came when the back tires bounced against the ground. In the rear of the vehicle, Paige, Nadya, and Milosh hung onto whatever they could to keep from being tossed out. They might have stayed inside, but the beating they took in the process made it feel like anything but a victory. Al slammed the truck into reverse and was greeted by a discouraging rattle from beneath the hood.

"Forget it," Bill said, kicking his door open. "We walk from here!"

"Walk?"

"You're right," Bill said, tossing his rifle to the driver so he could take a shotgun from the rack above the rear window. "We should probably run."

Minh was on her way, but slowed to a walk when the humans began piling out of the truck. She lowered her chest, bared her teeth, and dug her claws in deep enough to create jagged scars in the earth.

Liam shifted into his two-legged form and watched the Skinners with his one gleaming eye. "Where you off to, eh?" When Bill fired his shotgun, Liam turned toward the thump of lead against his shoulder and took half a step in that direction. Al circled around to flank the Full Blood, but Liam intercepted him by lunging and raking his paw along the ground to scoop him up several feet into the air. The werewolf clamped his jaws around the Skinner's right arm, shoulder, and a good portion of his chest so he could shake the screaming man until Al's body went limp. All the while, he took no notice of the bullets that thumped against his chest and stomach. When he was done, he spat out the corpse like a piece of unwanted gristle.

The reservoir wasn't far away, and it took every bit of restraint Paige had to lead Milosh and Nadya into the trees instead of standing her ground to take the Full Bloods on. Even the certainty of that being a death sentence didn't make the retreat any easier to swallow. Bill, it seemed, was having an even more difficult time restraining himself.

"Fuck you!" he shouted while firing his shotgun again.

Liam walked over to Al's body and nudged it with his foot. The shotgun rounds ruffled him slightly, but didn't do much more than that. Once he was satisfied that Al was dead, Liam picked him up and sniffed his bloody torso. "Randolph was right. It *is* in them!"

Minh tore apart the last of the Half Breeds to come after her and then leapt over the truck in order to take off after Paige.

When Liam looked toward the retreating humans, he caught sight of the polished steel in Nadya's hand. "Gypsy trickery!" he snarled while dropping to all fours and exploding into a bounding run. "You want me to follow you? I'm happy to oblige!"

"Come on," Paige said, running toward the large body of nearby water. "We've got to keep moving!"

Nadya held the metal tube in one hand, which she extended as far in front of her as her arm would allow. Now that she had both Full Bloods' attention, she turned her back to the werewolves and ran at full speed to keep up with Paige and Bill. The only problem was that neither of the creatures was running directly after them. Both had split away from the path to circle around on either side.

"You'd better have a real good plan, lady," Bill grunted once they broke through the tree line to find themselves facing a wide expanse of standing water. "We're lucky to have made it this far and we sure as hell can't swim fast enough to get away."

"We won't be swimming," Paige said.

Liam emerged from the trees and stopped so his hind legs were still lost in the shadows. "You got that right," he snarled in a voice that could barely be heard through the fangs that prevented his mouth from closing all the way.

Minh was nearby as well. Paige couldn't be certain where, exactly, but the burning in her scars was intense enough so that she knew it was coming from two sources. Now that she'd calmed down enough to focus on what the scars were telling her, she could feel a cold prickly moving beneath the heat like an underlying current of jagged ice.

As if sensing he'd been detected, Kawosa spoke in a voice that drifted through the air like another wandering breeze. "Now this is interesting," he said.

Despite being able to hear him, Paige couldn't pin down the shapeshifter's location. Judging by the way Nadya, Milosh, and Bill looked wildly around at the trees as well as the standing water, they weren't having any better luck.

"Watch your step, young ones," Kawosa said. "The hunters have set a trap for you."

Liam bared his fangs and retreated just far enough into the trees so his single eye was the only thing that could be seen. As he clawed and snarled, he shifted into a shape that raised his face up several feet. When he leaned forward again, he was in his hulking two-legged form. "There is no trap they can set that will do them any good," he growled.

"Can you be so sure? Why are you holding the others back?"

Liam glanced in the direction of the low growls emanating from the Half Breeds that had followed them this far. Shifting his eye to Paige, he growled, "Because they've had all the fun tonight."

A rustling of branches announced Minh's arrival. Unlike the other two, she wasn't content to remain hidden. She exploded from the trees and landed about ten paces from where Bill stood with his shotgun. The Skinner reflexively fired a shot at her when Minh leapt at him. At the apex of her jump, the Full Blood was intercepted by a lean figure that barely disturbed a leaf when it pounced to wrap his arms around her upper body. Both of them landed in a heap, and Minh scrambled back up to all fours to knock Kawosa aside. He hit the ground, stopped his slide with an outstretched leg, and then used his other leg to push forward so he could clamp his jaws around her throat. Minh grunted with surprise, and by the time she swiped a paw at the elder shapeshifter, Kawosa had already moved out of her reach.

Unlike the Full Bloods who shifted to stand upon two legs, Kawosa seemed more comfortable on four. He scampered away from Minh, planted his paws so his chest was lower than his hindquarters and turned his head toward Nadya, to spit something petulantly in her direction. The charmed metal projectile, still smeared with Minh's blood, hit the dirt and rolled until some of the Amriany markings glinted in the moonlight.

"Feel better, girl?" Kawosa asked.

Minh shook her head to clear whatever had compelled her to blindly chase the charmed device gripped tightly in Nadya's hand. Although she wasn't about to recklessly throw herself at Nadya anymore, the promise in her glare was sharp and spiteful.

"Even while I was locked beneath Lancroft's floor, I knew what our biggest weakness had become." Kawosa snapped his eyes toward Liam and said, "You are all too damn loud."

"You want peace and quiet, trickster?" Liam grunted. "You can crawl right back into that hole where you were caged and forgotten."

Paige glanced at her companions. Although they weren't

Skinners: The Breaking

fighting for their lives at the moment, there wasn't anywhere for them to go that didn't require passing dangerously close to one of the werewolves. In fact, as more seconds ticked by, the panting breaths of encroaching Half Breeds from the nearby town drew closer.

"I gave you a gift," Kawosa said. "And I passed on knowledge of how to use it. Instead, you either disappear into the forests or bay at the moon like common dogs. Pathetic."

This time Minh was the one to step forward. "Pathetic? The Torva'ox moves through our veins like never before. You must feel it as well."

"I do."

"And you have us to thank for it. Without taking steps like the ones we've taken here, we would have simply watched another Breaking Moon rise above cities infested with humans and leeches, above mountains that look down upon lands that are being torn apart by machines. We bay at the moon because we are choking on air that sticks in our throats while the old ones like you are either too far removed to notice or buried too deep to care."

Kawosa settled into a seated position, looking like a twisted version of a large dog waiting calmly for its supper. While the Full Bloods needed to change their physical shape to speak clearer, his voice was smooth and slippery regardless of the mouth that formed the words. "Interesting that you should mention the leeches. While the human armies now mass to strike against you, the Nymar have taken residence in comfortable businesses and homes after dispatching with the Skinners. Isn't that right, Paige?"

Having been content to fly under the shapeshifters' radar, Paige felt her nerves clench when one of them called her by name. Before she could respond to the challenge, Bill stepped forward and said, "We aren't letting the bloodsuckers get away with what they've done. There's more goin' on than anyone here knows about."

"So," Kawosa said, "there is more than anyone knows. More than, I assume, your so-called friends here even know? Go on, you must tell me."

When those words slid from the coyote's mouth, Paige

could feel the chill beneath her scars slice even deeper. She turned to Bill and said, "No, you don't have to tell him anything!"

But the other Skinner shoved her aside in his haste to step forward. "I don't take orders from fuckin' Gypsies and I sure as hell don't take them from someone who favors working with bloodsuckers and Mongrels over her own kind. When the Full Bloods get cleaned out, so will you."

"You've come this far," Kawosa urged. "Might as well go all the way."

Nadya drew a breath and stood by Paige's side. Milosh stopped her from going any further by grabbing her arm and shaking his head. Whatever information Kawosa was pulling out of Bill, he wanted to hear it as well.

"The Vigilant will take it all the way, asshole!" Bill roared. "What was started by locking your ass in Dr. Lancroft's cell will be finished once we collect our own piece of this pie."

"What pie?" Kawosa asked as his brow furrowed and the smug look on his bestial face drifted away.

"He means the Breaking Moon," Liam said. "They know."

Bill nodded triumphantly. "Hell yes, we know. Some of that juice that flows through your veins goes through Skinners as well. The difference between Vigilant and the rest is that we ain't gonna squander what we're given, like the Skinners that have been stepping up to get killed over the last year."

Kawosa nodded and smiled. His eyes shifted from unnaturally clear silver orbs into things that looked to have been stolen from the skull of a mischievous child. "Go on."

Behind her, Paige could hear water lapping against the shore. It hit the land, rolled back, and was hit by another wave too impatient to wait for the first one to recede. The reservoir churned, and when she turned to look, she could see the first hint of a green glow emanating from just beneath the most turbulent spot on its surface.

"Is this all you're after, old man?" Liam asked while stalking forward in a two-legged form that easily towered over all the humans. "Talk, talk, and more talk?"

"The Breaking Moon is almost fully risen," Kawosa replied. "What better way to pass the time with our Skinner friends than calmly standing here and waiting for the Torva'ox to visit us?" Looking over to Paige, he added, "See what I mean about taking the quieter path? These hunters have been pacified with some talk, just as the rest of the humans can be diverted with words instead of actions that endanger us all. Now they can all see what we've become before being torn to pieces by the legion that surrounds them."

Half Breeds snarled from the shadows cast by the trees surrounding the reservoir.

Paige had no vehicle to get her out of that untenable position, no time to get to the survivors huddled in the basements and panic rooms of Atoka, and no way of knowing if any of Quinn's pack remained. From what she'd heard, the only Skinner in sight didn't care if she lived or died. Milosh was wounded and Nadya seemed to be out of tricks.

"What's troubling you, cutie?" Liam asked as he stepped forward and locked his eye on her. "Waiting for that nymph magic to sweep you away?" He drew in a deep breath, craned his neck and licked his lips. "Yes, the nymphs do make good allies. Still, you gotta be quick enough to cross their bridge before I can get to you. Think you're up to it?"

By the time the scent of freshly cut timber and pine hit Paige's nose, all three of the shapeshifters were coiled like springs and ready to launch themselves at the first one to take a step in the wrong direction.

Paige took a sideways stance so she could glance back and forth between the Full Bloods and the reservoir without letting either out of her peripheral vision.

The water churned until it began spraying up from the rippling surface. Instead of the shimmering glow she was used to seeing through the beaded curtain of a Dryad temple, Paige watched as droplets of water froze several feet above the surface of the water, as if they'd spattered against a window suspended in midair behind her.

Liam smiled. "Better run, Skinners. Just to keep it sporting."

The crackle that came from the glistening smudge in the air sounded like a static charge preceding a lightning strike. Cole emerged from the dim green glow as if he'd been thrown through it. He grunted in agony and dropped straight down into the cold waters beneath his feet.

Liam drifted between an amused smirk and a surprised grimace.

Minh raised the hackles on her back, preparing for whatever came next.

Kawosa sat calmly and watched.

Paige turned to the closest Full Blood and snapped her arm like a whip to throw her sickle before the diversion Cole had provided was wasted.

Without even bothering to shift his weight to dodge the incoming weapon, Liam caught the spinning sickle less than an inch from his nose. He flipped it around to grip the weapon by its handle, cocked it back next to his ear, and threw it into Bill's head, where it landed with a solid *thunk*. Before Bill could drop, Liam's ears pricked as another shrieking wave of hooked talons and flattened skin poured through the shimmering opening hanging above the water.

Chapter Thirty

Though she'd heard Cole's rushed explanation of what he'd found in New Mexico, there was no way for Paige to prepare for being in the middle of a gargoyle hurricane. They emerged from the dripping bridge between two states, veering off to either cut straight up into the air or out to either side before curling back in to dive-bomb those who stood below them. When Liam reflexively swiped at one of the fliers and cut it into ribbons, the rest descended upon him and every other living thing on that shoreline.

Screaming from above, the leathery things swept down to scratch at her face and wrap bony arms around her body, putting even her steely nerves to the test. She, Milosh, and Nadya wrapped their arms around their heads and tried to duck beneath the incoming swarm. Bill, on the other hand, lifted his shotgun to aim at a cluster of the things diving at him and pulled the trigger. The shotgun blast was all but washed out by the grating wail of air passing through the gargoyles' bodies. The powerful blast obliterated most of that group, spraying their clear blood and fluids across the entire shoreline.

Once the rest of the gargoyles caught that scent, the swarm of flapping bodies drew even closer, to wrap around him and latch on using their long, curved talons. Paige had almost made it to the water when she was slammed down by a gargoyle that dropped onto her like a wet leathery towel.

It covered the back of her head, scraping at her shoulders and convulsing against her hair while sucking air through a wide, toothless mouth. A warm dampness spread between her shoulders, and before she could wonder if the thing had pissed on her, that spot began to tense and twist as if an invisible fist was clenched around her flesh and drawing it in. The sensation spread through her body, accompanied by a feeling of dry numbness.

"No, no, no!" she shouted while rolling over and swinging both arms at the creature. She saw, then, a muddled, sloppy attempt at a face that reminded her of a stingray's underbelly. It gazed blankly at her until the gargoyle was sent hurtling away from its meal. Scraping its talons against the dirt, the thing popped itself less than a foot off the ground, drifted forward, then swung back at her. Paige watched it gain altitude like a piece of paper fluttering back up to a spot from which it had been dropped. More of them descended from a whirling cloud circling the shoreline, separating to glide away and adjust their flight path to find her. Even as she staggered toward the water, Paige doubted she'd be able to dive in before at least one of those things wrapped around her. The substance that had been poured onto her back was still hardening, making it difficult to remain upright. Suddenly, the water erupted and a large figure rose from the reservoir to charge at her. Her arms came up reflexively to defend herself, and by the time she spotted Cole's face, her punch was already on its way to his chin.

Cole ducked under the swing, thanks to a familiarity with her that came in no small part from getting his ass kicked throughout months of sparring. Keeping his head down, he pressed his shoulder against Paige's torso and wrapped an arm around her so he could drag her into the water. "Did they get any of that stone juice on you?" he asked.

Paige knew what he meant. "Yeah, but—" Before she could say another word, he shoved her into the water and held her there. As soon as the pressure on her eased, she stood up and sputtered, "I have to breathe, you know!"

"That crap dissolves in water before it hardens," Cole said. "Just stay in there until it comes off." After that he was forced to swing his spear at a group of the creatures that flapped over his head. The spearhead tore a few of them open badly enough for one to do a flat spin into the water and another to wind up hanging on the end of the weapon like a flag made of pale skin. Cole kept his spear upright and charged onto the shore.

Paige dropped below the water as three gargoyles screamed down at her. Their muddled, stingray faces gaped into the reservoir as the fliers swooped above water that was still reflecting pale glows emanating from the moon and the nearby portal. Pushing up with both legs, she broke the surface of the water to find the Amriany standing their ground no more than ten feet away.

"Milosh! Nadya!" she shouted. "Get in the water!"

Milosh turned while Nadya fired up at a cluster of the gargoyles without hitting a single one. "You hide there and we will keep them away," he replied.

"You've got to come in the water or they'll poison you!"

"Turn you to stone is more like it, but not if you scare them away. Takes loud noises," Milosh said. Both he and Nadya stood their ground as two of the shrieking gargoyles swooped in from opposite sides to try and close in on them. Nadya waited for them to get close enough to see the black slits of their second pair of eyes before firing a short burst of automatic fire directly above them. The gargoyles parted and flapped away, getting close enough to the humans to slap the Amriany's heads with the tattered tails at the ends of their bodies.

"Noises," Milosh said with a crooked smile, "and a set of cast iron balls!"

Not far from the Amriany, Liam and Minh had their hands full. While Liam roared and swiped at the gargoyles, Minh kept her head down and did her best to avoid getting hit. As Paige watched, Liam turned one gargoyle into wet ribbons while another clamped onto his back. The Full Blood reached over both shoulders, grabbed the fleshy creature and ripped it away before howling with a pain Paige could actually recognize. He turned to bite another one in midair, giving her a good look at a strip of his back that had turned from a dirty white to light gray. Liam howled louder, arched his back and cracked the substance off him in what looked to be chunks of freshly dried cement.

Paige smiled and reached around for the spot where she'd been hit. The substance was still on her but had the consistency of paste. When she examined her fingers, she could feel it solidifying around their tips. The stuff broke away in a thick crust, taking a layer of skin along with it.

The Half Breeds weren't content to stay within the trees. As Liam thrashed and fought with the gargoyles, the wretches surged out from hiding to attack the creatures that filled the air directly above the shoreline. Some leapt at the fliers, only to get their heads, shoulders, and upper bodies wrapped up. Others were brought down by several that enveloped them and didn't let go until the solidifying paste was smeared over their bodies. Liam might have attracted more of the things, but was slashing too wildly to destroy very many of them.

In stark contrast to Liam, Minh kept her chest low to the ground and moved in slow, slinking steps. The gargoyles wound up either skidding along her back like stones across a pond or ignoring her completely. That stretch of good fortune ended when Cole rushed up to her and drove his spearhead into her side as if he'd finally chosen the perfect spot to plant his flag. Minh stood up and roared loudly, lifting him off his feet.

Paige stood up in the water, wiped off as much of the stuff from her back as she could and sloshed toward the shore. She was stopped by a gentle hand placed upon her back. Twisting around, she saw Tristan reaching out to her while crouching on the surface of the water as if the rippling reservoir had frozen beneath her feet.

"Let him go," the Dryad said. "He knows what he's doing."

"Cole never fully knows what he's doing," Paige snapped. "And are you walking on water?"

"Yes," Tristan said in a calm that seemed as out of place in the midst of battle as a woman did perched upon the surface of a lake, "and yes."

Minh's bellowing roar filled the air as the green glow in the water faded and died off completely. Tristan rose to her full height, displaying a perfect figure wrapped in veils of dark green and bright purple. With the water sprayed onto her flawless skin and the wind blowing around her, she became the spitting image of a siren lovingly depicted by the sailors who'd almost drifted to their deaths in pursuit of them.

It hadn't taken long for Cole to regain his bearings. Still holding onto his spear with both hands, he curled his legs up to press both feet against Minh's body. The spear came loose and he hit the ground on his side, leaving the wet stain of gargoyle innards smeared upon her fur. Almost immediately several of the gargoyles diverted their path to encircle her. Even though Minh slashed and roared at the flying creatures, she turned her gaze to Cole and bared her fangs.

"That's it," Tristan whispered as she closed her eyes.

Cole struggled to get to his feet and stood with his spear held in front of him. Paige could only watch for a second before she once again sloshed toward the shore.

"No!" Tristan told her. "Stay where you are! I need to feel his fear."

Paige had every intention of ignoring the command until the air popped and hissed in front of her. Beneath the shrieking, howling, screaming, and gunfire, the pure tone of Tristan's singing voice ran like the current flowing along the deepest ocean trench. As Cole faced the possibility of being torn apart by Minh, the Dryad's voice rose in pitch and the disturbance in the air ripped apart to become another glowing green portal like the one that had brought him into Oklahoma.

Since the portal was between her and Cole, Paige walked around it in knee-deep water toward the Amriany. Once half a dozen gargoyles latched onto Minh's fur, Cole backed toward the shimmering gateway. He waved his spear in the air to attract the next wave of fliers and was just quick enough to lay flat so they could streak over his head and disappear through the Dryad bridge.

Liam stared in utter disbelief. Minh swatted at the gargoyles around her but was losing her battle as more and more of them clamped on. She looked at him and roared for help, which Liam sent in the form of more Half Breeds. The wretches ran at her as well as the humans seeking shelter in the water, but were covered in so much of the gargoyle juices that the other flying creatures were drawn to them like magnets.

Paige stepped into the little area cleared by the Amriany and cupped her hand to her mouth. "On the ground at your feet, Cole! The silver thing! Pick it up!"

Cole turned and started walking toward her.

"No!" Paige shouted. "On the ground! Look on the ground!"

He looked down, spotted the discarded Amriany projectile, and stooped to pick it up as a gargoyle sliced through the air where his head had just been.

"Throw it over here, Cole!" she said.

She couldn't be certain he'd heard everything she'd said, but there was no way Cole could miss the angry growl that rolled out of Liam's throat like the engine of a rumbling semi. Cole's fist tightened around the gleaming little cylinder before he tossed it to Paige. The object was passed to Nadya, who stuffed it into the engraved tube, pulled back the handle and shot it at Liam.

"It's Full Blood bait!" Paige shouted.

Nadya threw the tube into the portal. Although Liam moved toward the glowing opening, he resisted with every powerful muscle and shred of willpower at his disposal. He ignored the gargoyles diving at him, shook off the ones that had sunk their talons into his fur, and dropped to all fours to run at Cole like a man that had suddenly become wild. His steps were clunky and off-kilter. Every time he stretched out his hands to claw at the earth, more of the rocky crust that had been poured onto his back cracked away. Rather than run at the portal, however, he charged Cole. By the time the splash of his steps reached Paige's ears, the Full Blood, Cole, and several of the gargoyles disappeared through the green portal, which then flickered from existence.

"Where are they?" Paige demanded as she turned to face Tristan. "Where did you send them?"

She blinked, drew a breath, and quickly collected herself. "Hush."

"Did you just tell me to—"

Paige was cut off by the crackle of one bridge closing and another being shredded into the air. This time the pale green light emerged in the vicinity of Minh and a group of Half Breeds. "We brought those gargoyles to deal with the Full Bloods, and I'm here to send them away. If that doesn't happen now, it won't happen at all."

Minh was making her way to the trees, her movements slow as she kept a low profile, in contrast to the Half Breeds that barked and climbed over each other to wildly attack the gargoyles flapping around her. Paige could see that Tristan was right. And after all that had happened to get things this far along, she wasn't about to let Cole's plan go to waste.

"Can you herd those things?" Paige asked while making her way to the spot being held by the Amriany.

Nadya swapped the empty magazine in the FAMAS for a full one. "I may be able to steer them a little, but that's all."

"Then steer them toward me." Without another word of explanation, Paige ran to Bill's body and removed her sickle from his head. Tightening her grip on the weapon, she drew the stake from the holster in her boot and rushed toward Minh.

Now that Nadya's bait had disappeared, Minh didn't have to struggle to maintain her focus amid the swirling storm of predators. She turned her back on the reservoir and crouched in preparation for a leap that would carry her into the trees when a stabbing pain lanced all the way through her lower right side. She howled and tried to take a step, which only aggravated the wound created by the sickle blade now wedged into her thigh.

"You wanna run?" Paige asked as she raced to Minh's side so she could grab the weapon she'd thrown and turn it like a crank within the meaty portion of the Full Blood's leg. "Too late!"

Minh's growl rose into a wailing howl as the metal-encrusted blade rotated within her. After pulling the weapon out, Paige dropped her other fist like a hammer to drive the pointed end of her wooden stake into the bloody gash she'd created. Minh's flesh pinched together around the weapon, healing from what should have been a crippling injury. As the Full Blood straightened its back and looked down at her with fierce, crystalline eyes, Paige willed the stake to stretch deep within Minh's thigh, where it branched into a sharp network of thorns.

Charmed wooden needles burrowed inside Minh's lower body. When her knee hit the dirt, wooden points sprang from beneath her flesh, while others ripped her from within. The howl that she offered to the Breaking Moon was matched only by Paige's war cry as she swung her sickle toward the Full Blood's chest. Moving with a speed impressive even for a Full Blood, Minh blocked the sickle using her own forearm. But though she prevented that strike from landing, the wooden lattice still burrowed inside her leg.

The chatter of Nadya's FAMAS remained on the outer edge of Paige's awareness. Even the screaming gargoyles were demoted to background noise as one of the most powerful creatures in existence was held prone by the stake in her hand. Locking eyes with the Skinner, Minh planted her other foot and began to pull the sickle away from her. Unwilling to let the weapon go, Paige could only grit her teeth as her elbow strained to the point of popping out of joint.

Her ears were filled with the rush of blood pulsing through her body. Desperate thoughts raced through her mind, most of which were in expectation of losing a limb that she'd become very fond of throughout the years. The werewolf grinned widely, lifting her off the ground until the thorns snaking through Minh's leg were twisted at a sharp angle. Paige willed as much of the weapon as she could to stretch into the Full Blood's thigh and expand in every direction until more of the thorns emerged from her flesh. Minh narrowed her eyes into slits, bared her teeth and pulled Paige's arms in opposite directions.

The Amriany were shouting and firing wildly behind her, but Paige was fading. When her elbows and shoulders crunched before snapping out of joint, she was hard-pressed to remember anything but the single face that had driven her this far.

Paige's fist remained locked around the handle of her weapon. Coppery blood washed over her hands and shrieking cries mixed with the deafening chatter of assault rifle fire as she stared into the face of death itself. The glow of the moon that had played across Minh's fur was suddenly splayed over the leathery back of a gargoyle that wrapped around the Full Blood's face. It was followed by another and another, all of which sank their talons into Minh's body to draw themselves tightly against her in a desperate, suffocating embrace. The only part of the Full Blood protected from the gargoyles was the section of her thigh where Paige's stake protruded.

Abruptly, Paige fell to the ground. Not only had Minh released her to try and fight off the gargoyles, but Paige had somehow maintained her grip on the sickle. The Full Blood was unable to move quickly enough to shred all of the gargoyles that descended upon her, and the more of them she ripped apart, the more creatures showed up to take their place. A pair of hands grabbed Paige by the shoulder and dragged her away. She screamed as her dislocated arm was tugged with a crack that reverberated inside her head. When she was set down again, the pain from that shoulder had lessened significantly.

Now that the remaining gargoyles had their meal, the only sound they made was the brush of one leathery body against another and the scrape of talons against flesh. Every so often one of their gaping mouths sucked like a baby trying to latch onto a nipple.

Tristan's voice filled the air, and the pale green glow flared up to an almost blinding flash. When it was gone, so was Minh and all the gargoyles attached to her.

"What happened?" Paige asked.

"This nymph would not let us help you!" Milosh roared.

Tristan stepped onto the shore and lowered herself to sit with both legs tucked beneath her. "I needed to use what you could gave me. The pain. The fear. It was strong enough to open a bridge and send her away."

"Away to where?"

"Deep into a Japanese bamboo forest where one of our temples was built," Tristan replied. "The gargoyles should have plenty of space to hide themselves when they're through, and Minh should be disoriented enough to let them finish what they started. Someone should check to make sure she was contained, though. Also, some Half Breeds were sent with her as well, and the ones who don't fall prey to the gargoyles will make trouble if they catch the scent of civilization."

Blinking as if none of that had sunken in, Paige gasped, "Did you say Japan?"

"Cole will explain. We just needed to separate the Full Bloods before they got too powerful."

"You mean return them to their territories?"

"Exactly," the Dryad said. "Didn't Cole warn you?"

Rubbing her shoulder, Paige winced and looked around. "It's a lot quieter now. Can't figure out if that's a good or bad thing." She watched as sections of the sky sprang to life with gargoyles gliding up and down to attack the remaining Half Breeds. "You seem to know a lot about those things," she said to Tristan.

"Yes. We have many gargoyles back home. Dangerous, but merely pests if you know how to handle them. After feeding this much in one night, they will find a place to hibernate for a few months."

"Will they kill her?"

They all looked toward the spot where Minh had stood.

"No," Milosh sighed. "They will not be able to kill a Full Blood."

"But can one be contained?" Tristan asked. Now that she'd gotten to her feet, she took on a presence that made her seem somehow beyond human. The sight of her supple body encased in wet veils and moonlight was enough to calm even the most raging soul.

Milosh looked at her with the same mix of awe and arousal that showed up on everyone's face the first time they gazed upon a Dryad. "I think so, but not for long."

"How long?" Paige asked. When she didn't get an answer or even a glance in response, she reached out to snap her fingers in front of his face. "Hey! How long?"

"I don't know! Maybe a few days or weeks."

Placing a hand gingerly upon Paige's shoulder, Nadya asked, "Do you need a sling?"

"No," she replied while gently flexing her arm. "You must've popped it back into place when you dragged me away. It's already healing. At least something went better than expected tonight."

"Where is the trickster?" Tristan asked.

Paige's head drooped forward. "There goes the better than expected thing. How the hell could I have forgotten about him?"

"The same way your civilization has forgotten him throughout every human era. The First Deceiver survives through lies and being able to slip away after telling them. All he needs to do is distract someone long enough and the memory of him will fall to the wayside."

"And there," Paige said while cautiously approaching one of the many Half Breed statues, "is one hell of a distraction."

"What do we do now?" Nadya asked.

Tristan placed a hand on Paige's shoulder, but not in a comforting manner. Using the Skinner to keep her upright, the Dryad said, "Cole is alone with Liam. That animal cannot be allowed to claim his prize from this night."

Paige felt a surge of adrenaline rush through her that was the instantaneous equivalent of two nights of sleep followed by a cold shower. "Where are they?"

"Finland."

"Finland?"

"The Torva'ox will be drawn to the Full Bloods more than any other creature on this earth," Tristan replied. "Now that they are spread out, the power they seek is unfocused. I can't take you to him without the energy to open another bridge."

"Tell me where the closest strip club is and—"

"No," Tristan snapped. "We don't have time for that. We need more power than a local temple can provide. Cole and I tapped into darker energies before, and I'm willing to do that again."

"How dark are we talking here?"

Before Tristan could answer, the distant howl of a few Half Breeds drifted through the air and a lithe body separated from the shadows within the nearby trees. It bounded toward the reservoir in swift, agile steps. Judging from the shape of its head and body, along with the fact that it stopped when it caught sight of the humans, Paige guessed it wasn't a Half Breed. The creature trotted closer, favoring one of its forepaws. When it shifted to walk on two legs, it became a naked woman who held one arm across her chest for reasons that had nothing to do with modesty.

"The remaining Half Breeds are scattered," Quinn confirmed. "My pack is almost completely destroyed, but we should be able to get you to safety if you come along with us now."

Tristan lowered her head and closed her eyes. "Let them come."

"They're stronger than we've ever seen," the Mongrel said. "Perhaps they are drawing from the Breaking Moon, but the fewer there are, the worse they get."

"Take him to shelter," Paige said while nodding to Milosh. "He's wounded."

"To hell with that!" he said. "If we are to die here, then we all die."

"Bring the wretches to us," Tristan said, ignoring the Amriany. "They can produce the energy I need."

"You can draw strength from Half Breeds?" Paige asked.

"A little," Tristan replied, "but I need a pure source that only comes from humans. We take our power from your spirits, which is heightened by emotion. There is no time to collect in our normal way, so I must draw from your fear."

Paige had heard about wicked forest sprites and beautiful witches who drained humans of their essences and souls, but hadn't connected them to Dryads until now. "There's one problem," she said while driving the thorns of her weapon handles into her palms. "I'm not afraid."

"That is not the only darkness within the human soul," Tristan replied. "Stand your ground and don't fight the wretches. Let them overtake you."

"There are maybe two or three Half Breeds left," Quinn said. "Even if they were anywhere close, we couldn't bring them back here." When several gargoyles shrieked in the distance, she added, "I think you see why."

Tristan's eyes were closed, and even in the moonlight, the subtle shading of her skin and the smooth texture of her flesh was plain to see. The fact that she was still wet from the water spray coming from the reservoir only added to her sensuality. "There's nothing I can do for you."

"What?"

"There's not enough in you for me to use. I won't be able to do this."

"*Now* you tell us? What about Cole's plan?"

The Dryad shrugged and turned her back on the Skinner and Amriany. "You're right. It was a stupid plan. Sorry."

"You're sorry?" Paige bellowed as the Half Breeds thundered toward her. "And now you're leaving?" The air around her started to crackle, but Paige was too fired up to notice.

Tristan propped a hand casually on her hip and said, "Sorry, sweetie. Guess we have to leave Cole on his own. But that's nothing new for you, is it?"

"*What* did you just say to me?"

Nadya and Milosh spoke to each other in clipped phrases pulled from their own language. For once they truly didn't seem to know what to do.

"Fuck you, lady!" Paige roared. "If the world's going to hell right now, then that's the last thing I want to say! *Fuck you!*"

"There we go," Tristan sighed as the crackling in the air turned into a spark that blinded every human eye in the vicinity.

The green glow was brighter than the other Dryad bridges she'd used, but Paige recognized the tumbling feeling that came along with it. Instead of having to step through a curtain set up at a temple to mark the spot where the mystical opening would appear, the ground simply opened up beneath her feet and she fell just over five thousand miles in the span of a few minutes.

Chapter Thirty-One

Hailuoto, Finland
A few minutes earlier

There was an explosion, after which Cole thought he fell for an eternity. He'd traveled through Dryad bridges before, but those were jumps between cities, no more impressive than stepping from one room and landing in another. The trips had been more difficult after he acquired the broken, hungry tendrils that wrapped around his insides, but only in a dizzying, disoriented way. This was beyond any of that.

The bridge was wild and unfocused, filled with power that could only flow from one of nature's opened arteries and set alight by raw human emotion. Plummeting through that was like being dropped down an elevator shaft. After a while, his brain didn't expect his body to survive the impact of landing. Instead of slapping against terra firma, however, he reached the other side of the bridge and was spat into existence two feet above a patch of cold, desolate ground.

He hit the hard-packed dirt on his side, his arms jerking at an odd angle because of the spear he still gripped in both hands. The tug of thorns within his palms brought back his combat reflexes as well as recent memories of what was following him from Oklahoma. A fraction of a second after he rolled clear of the landing spot, the Full Blood impacted against the earth. The gargoyles hit the ground next, like wet blankets tossed out of a passing car. Before the creatures could flap into the air, Liam was shredding them and scattering their bodies. Once the others caught the scent of their decimated companions, they scraped their hooked talons against the ground and convulsed until they were able to get some air beneath them. The trip had been dizzying to human and flier alike, but Liam seemed energized by the voyage. He looked up, clear juices dripping from his claws, and let out a breath he might have been holding for the last thousand miles.

Cole gripped his spear as a harsh wind tore across his face. Tristan had told him they'd land on Finnish soil, but the sudden time difference was still jarring. The sky was colored with light purples and reds. The wind felt as if it had claws that tried to shred his skin off. That alone reminded him of dawn. Only mornings were that cruel.

"You're not leaving this spot," Cole promised the Full Blood.

Liam crouched down and roared loud enough for his voice to rip across the landscape in every direction. The grass beneath their feet was brittle and thin. In the pale colors reflected from the sky, every green blade seemed washed out and tired.

Hearing shrieks in the distance, Cole held his spear so the metallic end was pointed like a bayonet at the end of a soldier's musket. He charged the Full Blood, unmindful of how badly the odds were stacked against him or how slim the chances that he would live to regret it. Liam's eye caught light from the clear sky and shone it back at the Skinner in an excited gleam. When their bodies collided, it was accompanied by the revelry of dive-bombing gargoyles.

Cole's weapon drilled into Liam's chest, but was stopped by a steely, unmoving rib. The Full Blood splayed his arms out, reared his head back and howled at a moon that could still be seen in the early morning sky. When he was out of breath, he gripped Cole's hand along with the spear and snarled, "That all you got?"

"Nope."

Remembering his lesson, Cole didn't bother looking over his shoulder or checking to see where the gargoyles might be. When he heard their cries clearly, he simply let go of the spear and jumped away. His chest hit the ground and he covered his head with both hands, as if expecting a bomb to go off. The fliers, attracted to the blood on Liam's coat and claws, swooped down with their bodies outstretched so they could immediately sink their talons in.

The gargoyles clawed Liam's arms, their excretion making it harder for him to move. In his haste to peel the creatures from his shoulder and back, he left the spear where it was. Cole seized the opportunity to grab the spear again and grind it within Liam's torso until he could feel it slide against the Full Blood's rib cage. After ripping one gargoyle away and cracking the stony crust that had begun to form on his upper arm, Liam clapped a hand over Cole's face.

"All I gotta do is think it and I can put a human through the Breaking," Liam snarled. "You can't take that away from me or any of the others. The power we've soaked up tonight is part of us now. You may have stopped the flow, but you won't be able to stop what we started."

It took all of Cole's strength along with some supernatural reserves, but he managed to grab Liam's hand and pull it away from his face. But no matter how good it felt to gain less than an inch of breathing room, he knew he was only getting what the Full Blood gave to him.

"You . . . can't break me," he said. "I know you've tried but you just . . . can't do it."

"You're going to tell *me* what I can do? You think you even know what I *can't* do?"

Liam's hand shifted within Cole's grasp. The muscles beneath his skin swelled and expanded like boiling paste. Bones creaked and stretched until his fingers were things that could wrap around Cole's head and grip it even tighter. Watching a shapeshifter's body reform was one thing, but feeling the grisly mechanics at work was something that brought the Skinner closer to his prey than he'd thought possible. By the time calcified claws scraped behind Cole's ears, he couldn't decide whether to feel panic or awe.

"I don't know where you dug up these bats," Liam said in his guttural cockney brogue while slapping down the last gargoyle that had followed them through the bridge, "but they won't be enough. And even if you kill me, the gears are already turnin'. The humans that don't feel the Breaking will watch as the rest of the world is pulled over to our side of the fence . . . just the way it should be." Pulling Cole closer, he moved his hand so he could see more of his reaction when he added, "God created his finest creatures in his image. Who's to say the man upstairs don't 'ave claws and a snout?"

Cole pulled in a breath while he had a chance. The coppery scent of blood filled his nose, but it wasn't his. When Liam had grabbed the spear to remove it from his chest, the thorns must have ripped the Full Blood's palm. Blood trickled from the werewolf's hand thanks to a wound he probably didn't notice. Cole took notice, however, as did the tendrils wrapped around his innards. Rather than fight the impulse that came next, he grabbed Liam's wrist and sank his teeth into the minor wounds.

If he'd had fangs, he would have gotten much more than a trickle of Liam's blood. He turned his head and wedged his canine teeth into the Full Blood's palm as the wounds tried to close around him. The thirst wasn't something his entire body craved, but the part that felt it most was determined to make the rest pay for being denied.

"Ain't this a sight?" Liam mused while waving his free hand to keep the gargoyles at bay. His movements had become sluggish and were now accompanied by the dry crunch of stone being chipped or cracked. "I could smell the leech in you, but thought it was just from that shit you Skinners pump into yourselves. Gonna try to bite me now? That's just precious."

Cole had tasted more blood than he cared to admit. He'd tasted his own during fights both practiced and genuine. He'd tasted splashes of Nymar blood in Denver and even human blood in G7. Now he tasted the blood of a werewolf. It was sweet and alive, shifting into something that stung and burned as it went down.

"You're feeding?" Liam gasped, finally noticing.

Although Cole could only feel the occasional drop on his lips, the tendrils were more than eager for more. He didn't know how they were getting the blood, didn't want to think about how they could be slicing into his digestive tract or poking into his throat so they could absorb what he drank. All he knew was that the pain of their clenching grasp was a constant thing, and when it faded, the absence was pure bliss.

Liam grabbed the back of Cole's head with his other hand, the gargoyles still attached to him, sinking their talons in deeper and drawing tight against his body and limbs. "What is that? What are you doing?"

The same question had flashed through Cole's mind when he felt the tickle deep in his throat as wet tendrils reached up like hungry, eager hands. When Liam pulled back, it was a cautious, tentative movement that drew the tendrils out far enough to make it feel like his intestines were being drawn out by a string. A crystalline eye shifted within the Full Blood's skull as he tossed Cole aside, forcing the tendrils to snap back into him like juicy rubber bands.

"So Kawosa was right," Liam growled as more gargoyles settled on his back. "The leeches truly have gotten a foothold into the Skinners. Perhaps we should have just left you to them."

"You're an arrogant bastard who doesn't know when to run away."

Struggling to stand up proudly while purposely leaving the gargoyles in place, Liam raised his chin and howled to the fading moon. That bellowing roar was still drifting across the Finnish landscape when he proclaimed, "Humans may have weathered the Black Plague, but that was nothing compared to what I've started! Even if you unleash your best weapons and set your finest machines upon us, you will only succeed in killing yourselves. Even these bats you've dredged up are useless!"

In the light of dawn, Cole could see the rocky shell forming around Liam's body. Every move he made caused pieces of it to shatter and fall away. The gargoyles, either too focused or too ignorant to stop, quietly gnawed on him while continuing their attempts to grind him to a halt.

Before Liam grew tired of reveling in his dominion over lesser things, Cole dove for his spear and then stuck it into his abdomen after piercing the gargoyle that had attached itself there. Light blazed from over the Full Blood's shoulders, illuminating Cole's features. Wincing as the spearhead was driven deeper, Liam reached down to remove it. Unlike a few moments ago, he couldn't take the weapon out so easily. Cole held on to the thorny grip with every ounce of strength at his disposal, and now that the tendrils had fed, he was stronger. He leaned against the weapon to push it between Liam's grasping fingers.

The Full Blood tightened his grip until Cole's hand felt like it was trapped within a vise. "You didn't bring enough bats," Liam said.

Gargoyles lay scattered on the ground like skins shed by a truckload of giant snakes.

"Don't need them," Cole said through gritted teeth.

Liam's eyes widened, absorbing the sight of the Skinner before him as though witnessing the birth of a new species. The glow behind him shifted from brilliant white to green. "I can feel the humans nearby," he wheezed. "Now . . . one of them feels me."

The Breaking.

Even as Cole tried not to think about it, he swore he could hear the shocked cries of whatever random person was unlucky enough to receive the gift of Liam's mental touch. Bones would snap, muscles would unravel, a Half Breed would be born. After that, a spot on the globe chosen for its relative calm would be dragged into the war.

Liam suddenly grunted and dropped to one knee. Cole could see the top of Paige's head behind him. She swung her sickle again to cut the tendons behind Liam's other knee with the same stroke she'd just used to sever the others. Knowing it wouldn't take long for a Full Blood to recover, Cole pulled his spear back and drove it into Liam's chest. Once again the fragment of the Blood Blade that had been melted into the spearhead's metallic coating allowed it to puncture the werewolf's hide, though it didn't have the power inherent to the genuine Amriany artifact. Sacrificing quality for quantity, Cole stuck Liam again and again until he'd dug all the way down to a breastplate that felt more like the hull of a battleship.

Coughing up enough blood to make the tendrils inside of

Cole shiver with anticipation, the Full Blood looked up at him and smiled. "You . . . don't got what it takes to finish me, Skinner."

Cole silenced him by jamming the spear through Liam's throat. It went in easier than he'd thought, and emerged from the other side without making a mess. He grinned as he attempted to reshape the spearhead into something that could extend within the werewolf's skull and pierce his brain. The smirk lasted until he realized the embedded portion of the weapon was coated in the metallic varnish that kept it from shifting so drastically. Realizing he was on borrowed time, Cole pulled the spear out.

Liam slumped over and grasped his throat. When the forked end of the spear came toward his neck again, the Full Blood batted it aside and swung at Cole's face. Cole ducked under the claws, but just barely. Liam tried to slash him again, but his arm was restrained by the sickle blade that now snaked around his wrist like a meat hook.

Most of the Full Blood's wounds had stopped bleeding. Not only did Liam have to contend with both Skinners, but the fluid the gargoyles had secreted was now hardening into stone on his body. Cole stuck both wooden ends of his spear into the Full Blood's chest, focusing all of his will through his hands and into the weapon. The wood creaked in response, so he commanded it to snake within Liam's chest to find the werewolf's heart. First one tine scraped against solid bone and then the other hit a similar barrier. Even after he narrowed the wooden tendrils down to burrow deeper into Liam's chest, he was unable to pierce his heart. The beast's skeletal structure was moving to protect the thick, solid muscle that was strong and durable enough to fuel a force of nature through what some believed to be an eternity.

"He's right, Cole," Paige said while pulling Liam's arm back. "We don't have what we need to kill him."

Peeling his eyes away from the point where he'd hit the Full Blood, Cole looked at a sight that he thought he'd never see. Liam was driven to his knees, silent. The werewolf's powerful arms hung limply from his shoulders and his body twitched with every impact, internal and external, of the Skinners' weapons. Still, the creature drew breath and the petulant spark in him refused to be dimmed. "We came too far to stop now!"

"The real Blood Blade could kill him, but this isn't doing it. He's slowed down for now, so we need to contain him with the gargoyles before we lose our chance."

Clearly, the only thing holding Liam upright was the spear embedded in his chest. As sweat rolled down his twisted face, he glared at Cole with one crystalline eye as well as a bloody, partially formed orb at the bottom of the scarred pit of his right socket. Just as Cole's pain allowed him to remain standing for this long, so too did Liam's agony allow him to replace what was taken from him when Paige's sickle had pierced his eye in Kansas City.

"Don't feel bad, Skinner," Liam wheezed. "This was never . . . your battle to lose." When he pulled in another breath, it was even more labored than the last one.

Cole looked down to see some of the gargoyle fluid trickling down the Full Blood's chest and entering the wound. He tried to pull the spear out but realized it was wedged in by a thin layer of rock that cracked like sandstone. The only reason he could move it at all was because the Full Blood's healing process was slowed by the stone barrier forming inside him. When Cole jerked the spear from where it had been lodged, he made certain to do it in the most painful and messy way possible. Liam's eye widened, his mouth opened, and his body fell.

"Keep hitting him, Paige," he said. "This is the best chance we've ever had!"

As soon as Liam's back hit the ground, she dropped her sickle blade into the gory pit in his chest. Cole dipped the metallic spearhead into some of the gargoyle fluids that had yet to solidify in Liam's fur and waited for Paige to remove her sickle blade. Now that the gargoyle fluids coated the metallic end of his weapon, he gripped the spear in both hands and drove it straight down into Liam's chest. A few seconds after the weapon had once again scraped against his breastbone, the Full Blood's eye snapped open and he clawed at the ground. The gargoyle substance had formed a thicker layer that went deeper inside to hold muscle tissue back and prevent the wound from healing. Liam convulsed as his body responded to the toxic substance within him.

As soon as Cole withdrew the spear to reapply more of the stuff, Paige drove her sickle into the wound, placed her foot on the blunt end of the blade and stepped down on it to drive the metal-infused weapon in even farther. Tightening her grip with both hands, she leaned back and pulled the multiple shifting layers of the Full Blood's muscle aside. Although Liam's body struggled to heal or shift into another shape, the edges of the wound that had been petrified by the gargoyle fluid were too solid to respond to the werewolf's desperate commands.

Cole gazed down at the gaping, horrific injury. After so many direct hits from weapons modified by the Blood Blade, a chipped, scraped, and ultimately cracked breastplate had been revealed. He looked into Liam's eye, expecting to find fear. Instead, the Full Blood stared back at him with raw, unmerciful hate.

"Only . . . gets worse . . . from here," Liam wheezed.

Unable to deny those words, Cole drove his weapon straight through the last bit of armor protecting the Full Blood's heart. The spearhead stopped less than an inch past the layer of bone, Liam's body becoming rigid, his claws sinking into the earth. Using every bit of muscle he'd built during Paige's rigorous training sessions, as well as the jolt of power the tendrils in his body had given him, Cole forced the spear down still farther, until it drilled all the way out of Liam's back.

The Full Blood's mouth gaped open to allow his last breath to bellow outward like a curse dredged up from the deepest chasm of primordial bedrock. As bright as the fire in his eye might have been, Liam simply didn't have anything left to back it up. More of the gargoyle substance dripped into the chest wound and was absorbed in the deeper layers of his body, to seal off even more layers of muscle and prevent vital arteries from resealing. He reached up to grab the spear and barely got his fingers to close before he lost his grip and the back of his head thumped against the ground.

Paige had to fight to retrieve her weapon but eventually pried it from the shifting layers of petrified muscle that had closed around the blade. She looked cautiously into Liam's eye, nudged him with the sickle, and then dropped to one knee. When she stretched a hand out to his face, Cole said, "Be careful!"

Instead of touching the werewolf, she merely held her palm out to him. Slowly, the expression on her face shifted from battle-hardened intensity to disbelief. "He's gone." She looked up at Cole and jumped to her feet so she could grab his wrist. Holding his arm toward Liam, she said, "Feel for yourself, Cole!"

Cole's scars were lukewarm but slowly cooling. "He's dead?"

Paige nodded as a tired smile drifted onto her face. "We did it!"

Cole dropped his spear and wrapped both arms around her. She hopped up to wrap her legs around him and gleefully squirmed in his embrace. Before they could get too wrapped up in their celebration, however, Cole's foot bumped against Liam's arm. As soon as he looked down, the spell was broken.

"We have to find a way back home," Paige said as she separated herself from him. "Tristan could barely get me here."

Still looking down at Liam, Cole asked, "We've got to bring him with us, right? Do we need to . . . preserve him or anything?"

"I don't know. First time I've ever killed one." She smiled and shook her head. "I still can't believe you pulled this off."

"I know," Cole sighed. "I'm pretty great."

For the first and most likely only time, Paige didn't say anything sarcastic in response. Instead, she started picking up the largest pieces of shredded gargoyle. "Let's wrap him in this stuff and crack it open later. At least that way he won't make such a mess during transport."

Still reeling from what had just happened, Cole half expected the werewolf to sit up or laugh at them before bounding away. Whether that fear was real or just the product of too many Schwarzenegger movies, he was quick to lend a hand with the task Paige had assigned.

It wasn't an easy job. Although there were plenty of gargoyle remains to be found, there were barely any in good enough shape to be of any use. Cole explained what Jessup had told him about the creatures as the two of them collected more bodies. They wrapped the partial gargoyle bodies around Liam and squeezed as much of the petrifying solution as they could from the tubes they'd collected. Once the gargoyles were in place and there was no more of the petrifying substance to be found, the Skinners had only to stand back and watch the magic shell harden.

Liam had shifted halfway between his upright werewolf form and human body. His fur was thick and his musculature thicker, giving him a primitive quality offset by the distinctly canine features of his face. His claws had the smooth texture of granite, while his coat, ears, and face looked more like clay that had been fired in a kiln for weeks on end.

Cole dropped to one knee and tapped the Full Blood's snout, venturing so far as to slide his fingers along the points of Liam's teeth. "What if he's still alive?" he asked. "He survived KC."

Placing her hands on her hips, Paige replied, "According to every animal expert or scientist out there, most of the things we fight shouldn't even exist, so I don't know how he survived KC. I've become an expert in dead things, though, and this thing's definitely dead. All we need now is a ride back to the States."

Cole reached into his pocket for his cell phone. When he tried to make a call, he cursed and shoved the device back into his pocket.

"Can't get a signal?" she asked. "I told you not to keep splurging on those new ones before all the kinks are ironed out."

"Okay, smartass. You try to call this number and ask for Tristan." She punched in the number he gave, listened to the recording that followed, and calmly deactivated her phone. "Let me guess," he said smugly. "No international calling plan?"

Paige nodded toward a pair of headlights that bounced through the tall, swaying grass. "Maybe we could use this guy's phone."

Following her line of sight, Cole picked out the headlights in the distance. The sound of the vehicle engine mingled with gusts of salty air brushing leisurely against the barren field. He closed his eyes, sampled the fragrances that had been carried in from the Gulf of Bothnia and smiled as he heard the distinctive creak of fur hardening into stone. After less than a minute the single live gargoyle flapped away from Liam's shoulder and the others fell off like wet cloths sliding down a wall.

"I've read journal entries on gargoyles," Paige said while bending down to take a closer look at one of the thin leathery bodies, "but never saw a real one. I thought they were wiped out."

"So did Jessup. He said lots of things are getting flushed out from where they've been hiding. Gargoyles, Shunkaws, more Chupacabra. All sorts of good stuff like that."

She shook her head and turned to watch the vehicle that ambled straight toward them. "It was bound to happen. Things had been balanced so precariously for so long that we got used to it being that way. Half Breeds sprouted up here and there and we hunted them down. Full Bloods were kept in check by thinking Nymar controlled the cities, and Nymar were kept in check by thinking we could enforce every law we laid down. Once Misonyk and Henry came along to upset that balance, it all crumbled."

"We lived through this," Cole pointed out. "That's saying a lot."

"We did more than live through it. We actually won. But the Breaking Moon hasn't even fully risen yet," she said while standing up and brushing off her hands. "What's left in New Mexico?"

"Esteban is wrapped up but not dead. Randolph was wounded but he and Cecile got away."

"You talk about her like she's still the girl she pretends to be when she's not covered in fur. That's not smart," Paige warned. "There's a long way to go, and even though we're short one Full Blood, the others are stronger than before."

Since the sight of Liam's petrified body had already lost its luster, Cole focused on Paige's face. That was good enough for the moment.

The vehicle that had driven out to them was now arriving with the noisy rattle of an outdated engine. Cole allowed himself to catch his breath. He plastered on a friendly smile and returned the wave thrown at them by a skinny man with a round face who drove a strange little thing that looked like the front half of a compact car welded onto the flatbed of an old farmer's truck.

"Hello?" the man said in a thick accent while climbing out of his vehicle. "You look like you are in trouble, yes?"

"You speak English?" Paige asked.

He nodded and squinted in the sunlight that had grown bright enough for him to kill his headlights. "Just a little. You are Americans?"

"Yeah," Cole replied. "Does it show?"

"Oh yes, for certain. Americans come out to see the water and they like to wander. I saw the lights and heard the loud noises and knew more Americans were throwing a party. I come to tell you to stop. Now I see there is no party."

"Not yet."

Now that he didn't have to run off a bunch of kids from his field, the man's face creased into a tired smile. That faded when he got a look at the mess of shredded gargoyle bodies scattered around the petrified werewolf. "What . . . is this?" he asked.

"We're artists," Paige told him. "Sculptors."

He leaned toward the werewolf, rubbed his chin and studied the roughly hewn rock while sniffing air that smelled of guano and bird guts.

Cole stepped on his spear to make sure it was hidden within the grass when he announced, "It's called, 'Beast Who Crawls Out to Sea.' What do you think?"

"It is troubling. Will you be moving it?"

"Of course," Paige said. "Just as soon as we can call some friends of ours. Do you think you could take us to a phone?"

"You have no phone?" the man asked. "Or car?"

"It was a beautiful night," Cole said as he looked up at the sky. "The muse struck and we answered her call."

"Ahh," the man grumbled. "Artists. Come. I will take you to my lighthouse."

"I'm Cole," he said while extending a hand. "And this is Paige."

"Vihtori," the man replied while shaking Cole's hand.

After collecting their weapons and quickly tucking them

out of sight, Cole and Paige followed Vihtori back to his truck. Since the flatbed portion was barely large enough to hold a pair of duffel bags, Paige sat with her back against the cab, Cole with his legs dangling off the side and his hands locked onto the side of the vehicle.

"Should we leave him here?" Cole whispered as the man settled in behind his wheel.

"He should stay fresh for at least a week and maybe up to a few months. This is a first for me, so I'm kinda winging it here. All I know is that we need to get to a phone." As the vehicle began trundling along, she asked, "So the whole gargoyle thing was your idea?"

"I didn't find them, but yeah."

"And Tristan?"

"She wanted to help and this is what she could do. She said there may be side effects with having to tap into the darker emotions, so we should probably keep an eye on her for a while. That was quite a jolt flying through a fear portal, huh? Lots of falling and tumbling through dark, empty space. Freaky."

Paige's trip across the Norwegian Sea had felt like she'd been tied to the back of an F-14. Screams filled her ears and there had been so much light that she wondered if she would be blind when she finally arrived at her destination. "Yeah. Freaky, but worth it."

They watched each other without saying much of anything else for the remainder of their ride. Vihtori's lighthouse was situated at the farthest edge of the field. Tall grass gave way to flat rock. The rustling of wind was soon overridden by the sound of water crashing against the shore. Cole's pulse returned to something close to normal and hundreds of questions rolled through his head, but he kept his mouth shut. If one thing had become clear in his time as a Skinner, it was that he needed to enjoy the quiet moments when he could because they didn't come around too often.

Hailuoto was much cooler than New Mexico and Oklahoma. Even though he'd never been to Finland before, there was something different in the air that made it clear he was far from where he'd started. The scents were different. The automobiles were different. The road was rougher. The fields were cleaner. Whatever it was, Cole liked it. Before he could settle into thoughts of early retirement, Vihtori turned onto a gravel road that led straight up to a silvery gray lighthouse. He parked the car/truck combo, hopped out and motioned for them to follow.

"If you make expensive call, I will know," he warned. "I have food and water inside. Also, some bandages, yes?"

Cole was about to insist he was all right, but one glance down at himself was enough for him to realize he looked as if he'd been dropped from a plane and into a trash compactor. His clothes were ripped. His skin was dirty and scarred. He even smelled like war, which clung to the back of his nose as a mix of blood and fire. "Thank you," he said. "I appreciate it."

"Was there trouble?"

"No," he said. "It was just a really rough night."

Vihtori obviously didn't believe him, but wasn't suspicious enough to call the authorities. At least, that was his read on the man. If he did call the cops, Cole hoped the other man had the decency to let him sit down and have a glass of water first.

"We wrecked our car," Paige said while climbing down. "We're still fuzzy on the insurance, so . . . you know."

Vihtori didn't know, didn't believe her or didn't care. He unlocked the lighthouse and showed them to a room. "He will wait here," he said to Cole. "She and I will go to a phone."

"Sounds fair," Paige replied.

Cole was left alone in a small room that had a few chairs, a beat-up little desk, and a black and white television set he would have sworn was just as extinct as a Brontosaurus. Sitting on that chair, listening to nothing other than the breeze and the waves, he felt better than he could have thought possible. He started drifting to sleep and snapped awake again when Paige came back.

"Feeling better?" she asked as he stood up and approached her.

He nodded and reached past her shoulder to shut the door. Remaining in his spot, he pressed his body against hers and looked down into Paige's deep brown eyes.

"I talked to Jessup," she said. "He said Cecile was gone but that he could track her. Can he really do that?"

Cole nodded.

"Esteban is still a statue. Randolph is in the wind and probably won't come back to that place, since a couple tanks and a few gunships arrived to lock it down. Let's just hope those guys are IRD. I've gotta call Adderson, but not until I can get to a safer . . . what are you doing?"

"Touching you," Cole said as he ran one hand along the side of her face and the other against her hip. "It's been a while since I was this close to you."

"Yeah, but maybe this isn't the best time."

"I don't care."

"What was that?" she asked as her eyebrows perked up and she backed against the door. "Just because your blood's running hot and you were locked up for a while, you think you can pull the whole macho hero thing on me?"

"Yeah. Pretty much."

Paige meant to shoot something back at him, but was genuinely surprised when he kissed her. The moment their lips met, she embraced him and kissed him with as much aggression as she'd used to chop Minh or Liam down to size.

"I missed you, Paige."

"Shut up. You're spoiling the macho thing."

Cole tugged at the straps holding the remains of her tactical vest in place and then pulled at the clothing underneath. When his hands finally found the smooth surface of her skin, he felt all his terror, hopelessness, and uncertainty drain away.

She smiled and unbuckled his pants with almost enough force to rip his belt in half. His hands continued to fumble with buttons and zippers before finally pulling her shirt open and working her jeans off her hips. She wriggled out of them and slid one leg up along his thigh. All he had to do from there was reach down to cup her backside in both hands and lift her when she hopped into his grasp. Paige's legs wrapped around him and her shoulders knocked against the door. Their breaths were short and choppy until he finally entered her. Once he'd buried himself between her legs, both Skinners let out easy, relaxed sighs.

Cole stayed put for a few moments as everything else in his world faded away. It didn't matter what country they were in, how they'd gotten there, or what remained for them to do. All he cared about was the smooth, familiar touch of her cheek resting against his and the miraculously gentle touch of Paige's lips drifting along his neck. When he thrust into her, she sucked in a quick breath and held onto him tightly. There were no words to express how good it felt to be inside her again.

None were necessary.

"Pardon me, in there," Vihtori said while tapping on the other side of the door.

Cole pushed all the way inside her and stopped. Judging by the faraway expression on her face, she wasn't anywhere close to formulating an answer for their host. "Yeah?" he grunted. "What is it?"

"Someone called back for you. They say they are Meg somebody."

Keeping her eyes closed, Paige started to laugh. It was barely a chuckle, but tensed her muscles in a way Cole could feel intimately. "Well?" she whispered while grinding her hips against him and digging her nails into his back. "Aren't you going to answer him?"

"Okay to call them back?" he asked the door.

Judging by its voice, the door wasn't happy. "They are on the phone now."

Having laced her fingers behind his neck, Paige stared at him with a hungry, mischievous smile. Once again Cole's entire world boiled down to one person. The tight curves of her bottom felt supremely perfect in his hands, and with just a little prompting, she pumped her hips as if riding him. Pressing his lips against hers in a hungry, desperate kiss, he pounded into her until her back thumped against the door. Paige leaned her head back and let out a long, contented moan.

"Artists," Vihtori muttered before shuffling away.

Chapter Thirty-Two

Raton, New Mexico
Eighteen hours later

The hill where Cole and Jessup had met Rico was now completely cordoned off by the military. In fact, most of the town had become a base inhabited by men wearing fatigues adorned with a mix of Army and Marine Corps insignias. The only thing those uniforms had in common was a patch on the shoulder bearing the wolf and skull insignia of the IRD. Helicopters roared through the air. Armored vehicles rattled down the streets. Command centers had been set up in spots that were formerly in the quiet section of town.

"Well," Cole said as he and Paige were escorted by Adderson and three soldiers carrying large caliber machine guns, "at least we don't have to worry about news choppers getting too close."

Dressed in simple khakis that could have been lifted from any Middle East conflict over the last couple of decades, Adderson displayed nothing but the IRD insignia and a colonel's eagle pinned to his shirt. "You obviously haven't been watching the news," he said.

"No. We've been busy."

"I'm sure you have, but it's all out there. These creatures have taken over entire towns, which has made our jobs that much more difficult. What happened in Atoka is still under review. In the last twelve hours several Class Two shifters have been spotted throughout the country."

"Half Breeds," Paige said to Cole.

Grimacing as if her use of such common terminology hurt his ears, Adderson continued, "There have also been several reports of spontaneous transformations occurring in neighboring states."

"Do we really have to go through all this official talk?" Cole asked. "You're just adding syllables and wasting time."

"You want me to cut down on the syllables? Fine. How's this? FBI. Manhunt. Escaped prisoner. Oh, sorry. Was that last one too long for you?"

"Nope," Cole replied. "Point taken. Continue."

"You're taking care of that escaped prisoner thing, right?" Paige asked.

Adderson nodded. "Already done. Just try to steer clear of Colorado for a while."

They'd reached the center of the IRD barricades, which put them within eyeshot of a crude stone statue. Esteban still crouched on all fours and snarled at something roughly at Cole's eye level. The Full Blood's stone covering was a little dusty but mostly intact.

"We want to contract your services on a regular basis until this crisis is dealt with," Adderson said to her.

Paige looked around at the uniformed soldiers. "Don't you have enough bullets to throw at these things?"

"Bullets don't help. I don't need to tell you that. Since you and your associates are the only ones to have hurt these creatures, I've been authorized to make an offer. You'll be compensated for your efforts, but trust me when I tell you we can't afford to take no for an answer. Things have gone way past the point of people like you sneaking around and covering up vampire raids as gang fights, or werewolf sieges as wild dog attacks. We've already been covering those tracks and now our entire unit has been forced into action, so you might as well come along for the ride. It's either that or get rolled over by the machine you see around you."

Paige closed her eyes, unable to think back to simpler days when changing a license plate or laying low for a while was enough to shake unwanted attention from the authorities. "I'll have to contact some of the others to see what they think about this."

"You could always give us their information so the IRD could—"

"Or," she cut in, "I could do it myself. Nice try, though."

"I'll give you time to think it over, but don't take long. We're launching an offensive within seventy-two hours, with or without your help. Between you and me, your help could save a lot of soldiers' lives."

"Or you could just stick to lying to the media and keeping the cameras away from us while we do our job."

Adderson shook his head. "Too late for that. And before you tell me about how tough it is being a Skinner, just know that I've got an appointment with several highly ranked officials to try and convince them not to carpet-bomb areas that show signs of getting half this bad."

"So there really have been Half Breeds sighted?"

"In six different states. There are unconfirmed reports of sightings escalating internationally as well. Canada, the Czech Republic, and Finland have all made reports that coincide with Class—" Recognizing the exasperated look on Paige's face, Adderson crossed his arms and said, "—Half Breeds, and at least one Full Blood was spotted. That's just the first wave of intelligence, with more coming. We need expert help. We've got resources you could never match, and it's not like you people could deal with this problem on your own anyway. Shouldn't be much to think about, but I'll let you talk to your partner."

"Where's Rico?"

Adderson pointed to a tent that had been constructed near a portable toilet and said, "Right over there getting medical attention, not that he seems to need much. That's a trick that could do my men a lot of good, you know." When he didn't get a response to that, he added, "Naturally this offer extends to him as well. He was a definite asset to us here. Take a few minutes and talk it over. You know where to find me." He walked away and took his escort with him, leaving Paige and Cole mostly alone at the top of the hill.

She got to Cole's side as quickly as she could and leaned in to whisper fiercely at him. "I don't like this!"

"I hit that point when we were met at the Casa Bonita Club by G.I. Joe and a freaking tank," Cole snapped as he ran his hand over Esteban's petrified back. "So does that mean you told them about the nymphs as well?"

"No," she said. "I just told them we were calling from a strip bar and to come pick us up. They're already in this and would have been dragged in sooner or later anyway. This way, we've got some say over what goes on."

"You really think so?" Cole scoffed.

Paige turned away from the pair of modified AH-1 Cobra helicopter gunships being tended by a crew and said if a low voice, "It's not like we could just wash our hands of this and take a vacation in Finland."

"At least they could have let us get something to eat while we were at that club."

"Didn't you take anything from that buffet in Sven's Viking Lounge?"

"Is that what that strip bar was called?" Cole asked.

"I don't know! I can't read Norwegian or Swedish or whatever the hell was on the signs in that place. It was creepy enough that all those girls knew Vihtori on sight. So . . . what do you think about Adderson's offer?"

"First things first. I want my coat back from Canon City's lockup."

"Sure," Paige said. "Let's push our luck with that. What will you say when they ask about the other prisoners that got away?"

"I have no clue what you're talking about." Since she obviously wasn't buying that, Cole added, "You could fire back by asking where to find Esteban."

"What do you mean?" she asked while slapping the Full Blood statue. "He's right here."

"Right. Too bad it's hollow."

She cringed, glanced at the group of soldiers clustered around Adderson, and then peeled her hand away from the statue to touch her palms. Cole knew damn well that she wasn't feeling any heat in her scars either. When she slapped the statue again, it was hard enough for the sound to reverberate beneath the stone surface. "Did they take him somewhere?"

Circling the statue, Cole found the scratches along Esteban's midsection as well as the multiple smooth spots where the petrifying substance had been administered. "This is the real thing," he said, placing his palm against the stone.

"Well you're the expert," she said in a low, insistent voice. "How did he get out? Is that even possible?"

Cole dug out his phone and tapped a few icons on the screen. "I don't know, but Jessup may know." He didn't get an answer, so he called the next number on his list.

"MEG Branch 40, this is—"

Cutting him off with a hastily whispered identification number, Cole asked, "Where's Jessup? Have you heard from him?"

"Are you kidding?" Stu replied. "I'm surprised to hear from you! Every other Skinner has dropped off the grid. Nobody's answering our calls, but a few have left messages."

"Is Jessup one of them?"

After some tapping on a keyboard, Stu said, "Yes, but he didn't give a location. The message he left is for you or Paige."

"Could have started off with that part," he growled.

"I didn't take the message. Abby did. Anyway, there's a phone number."

"Give it to me."

Stu rattled off the digits, which Cole committed to memory. Suddenly feeling very nervous with continuing the call around so much military communications equipment, he was about to wrap up the call with a quick goodbye.

"Wait!" Stu pleaded.

"What is it?"

"There's chatter all over the place about what's happening. People are getting killed and werewolves are showing up on the news. Reporters aren't even bothering to call them anything other than werewolves, for Christ's sake! What the hell, man?"

"I don't know what you want me to say, Stu."

"Tell me this isn't as bad as it seems."

It was a simple request, but one Cole knew he couldn't fulfill. "Just stay safe and keep your eyes open. Don't give out any information unless you get an ID number. On second thought, we need to change the ID numbers."

Happy to have something to do that fell within his area of expertise, Stu said, "On it."

Cole hung up and dialed the number that was already fading from his memory. The call was answered on the first ring by a familiar scratchy rasp. "Jessup?"

"Cole, thank God. Where are you?"

"Back in New Mexico. Where the hell are you?"

"About six miles outside of Louisville, Kentucky. I've been driving all damn day tracking Cecile. What happened with you?"

"Never mind that. The military's got this place and us locked down tight. Where's Esteban?"

There was a pause, followed by the rattle of an engine winding down. Knowing the older tracker, it had to be another Ford. "I stayed as long as I could. That thing just walked out and ran away."

"What do you mean he walked out?"

"Stepped out of that stone shell like he was a ghost. I made some calls and found out what he was doin' at that Colorado prison where you were being held. He was after some of them Nymar Shadow Spore collected by other Skinners. There were other samples down beneath that place. Older samples."

Cole could still feel the Nymar hand clamped around his throat while he was strapped to a hospital bed, and could still hear the hungry rasp of the vampire's voice taunting him when his body was almost too drugged to move. Shaking off those memories like so much cold water, he asked, "The IRD has been collecting Nymar?"

"No. It's one of us. That prison has been there since 1868, but portions of it shifted into private ownership in 1904. The deal was made as part of an experiment in corrections philosophy but basically gave one man free access to prisoners to be used for his own research."

"God damn," Cole sighed. "Lancroft?"

"We knew Jonah Lancroft ran more than just his reformatory. He had labs and hidden facilities like this prison all over the country. Probably all over the world."

Although Adderson and the soldiers were keeping their distance, Paige was becoming increasingly anxious. "Did you say something about Lancroft?" she asked.

"Wait a second," Cole said while going through the potentially painful motions of waving Paige away. "You said we knew. Who's 'we'?"

"It's not as sinister as it may sound. Your friend Ned Post was a Lancroft historian. Lots of us are. We could all learn a lot from a man like that. Now that his journals are being unearthed, he's getting an even bigger following than he had when he was alive."

"Lancroft was a murderer. He *killed* Ned," Cole said while stabbing a finger into the air as if jabbing it through Jessup's chest.

"What's he saying about Ned?" Paige asked.

The harsh crackle that came through Jessup's end of the phone connection was either static or a heavy sigh. "Ned may have had a falling out with the old man, but Lancroft had plenty of supporters, and after everything that's happened, he's got even more. The Full Bloods aren't dead. Now that the Breaking Moon has risen, the Army won't be able to do a damn thing against them. The Nymar are sitting pretty. Lancroft's ideas may have been radical, but they may also be the only ones that make any sense. If we would have listened to him before, things may not have gotten this bad. At least one saving grace is that we got the cargo Cecile was carrying."

It took Cole a moment, but he recalled it and asked, "The Jekhibar?"

"Poor girl was more than happy to get that thing out of her arm."

"And what happened to her then?"

"She'll find somewhere to hide, and stay there if she knows what's good for her. You want to hear more, then come find me when you've learned some damned respect. I've got to go. There's work to be done."

With that, the connection was cut. Cole jammed the phone into his pocket and stormed over to the entrance of the tent where Rico stood sipping from a steaming paper cup. Paige tried to follow but veered away in order to keep Adderson busy before he joined the party.

Stepping up close enough to Rico to smell the vanilla almond cream in his coffee, he said, "I just talked to Jessup."

"Really?" Rico replied as he grinned widely. "How's that old cowboy doin'?"

"He says Ned was tight with Jonah Lancroft and that the prison I was in was one of Lancroft's facilities. Since you're the one who was close enough to Ned to inherit his house, I'd like to know what you think of that."

"I gotta be honest with you, Cole. The man may have been a cocksucker, but Lancroft made a lot of sense back before the cheese fell off his cracker."

"So he's still alive?"

"Not unless you believe in all that ghost shit or the philosophical 'He's with us right here' garbage," Rico chided while tapping his chest. "I'm talkin' about his ideas. Lancroft knew this shit was brewin'. All you gotta do is read his journals."

"I have."

"Really? I know some Skinners who'd love to have a look at those things."

Cole nodded and glanced toward Paige. It was obvious he wouldn't have much more time to himself, so he asked, "Have you been setting us up? Is that the real reason you tried to kill Paige?"

"You think I'd cover my tracks by making me look like a punk bitch who got his brain twisted around by shapeshifter? I would've come up with somethin' better than that." He sipped his coffee and then tapped the rim of the cup against Cole as he said, "You need to get your priorities straight. All the tiptoeing bullshit is over. Lancroft used to track Half Breeds down, poison them, and set 'em loose. Did some innocent townsfolk get killed? Maybe, but the whole den was destroyed with a minimum amount of fuss. There ain't many of us left, Cole, so we gotta do things like that. You wanna hear about effective tactics? In some of the earliest journals—and I'm talkin' books that date back to the 1700s—Lancroft's followers talk about how the old man used to take Nymar that stepped out of line and stake them to the ground outside of the spot where all their buddies hung out. He'd wait for dawn so everyone could see what had happened to the bloodsucking little shits who'd been talking so tough and then douse them in kerosene. Once he was sure all the other Nymar were watching, he set their asses on fire."

After pausing to sip his flavored coffee, Rico shrugged. "Some might see that as extreme. Maybe some wrong ideas were put into a few storytellers' heads, but it sent a message that convinced the Nymar not to fuck with us. Those messages are gone, my friend. The bloodsuckers know no fear and the shapeshifters are out of control. Don't you think now's the time for some good old-fashioned barbarism?"

"Who are you talking about?" Cole asked, thinking back to his conversation with Jessup. "The people who'd be interested in those Lancroft journals? The ones who run that prison in Colorado? The ones who you've obviously already signed on with? Who are they?"

"Lancroft used to say the only difference between a Skinner and any other human being is vigilance. That's who we are. And now that we've found what could be the source of the Full Bloods' power, we may be able to unlock the one last juicy tidbit he didn't get to pass along." Leaning in closer, Rico dropped his voice to a snarl that rivaled a Half Breed's. "There's been one big question on everyone's mind since the Mud Flu. It's just been too far out of our reach to really ask it. If that truly was Jonah Lancroft—*the* Jonah fuckin' Lancroft—then how the hell did he live that long? Maybe the Torva'ox that all them Full Bloods were yappin' about had something to do with it."

Paige, Adderson, and a group of soldiers were approaching, but Cole wasn't going to stop short just because of them. "You think Lancroft was immortal because of what we found in Atoka?"

"Not immortal, since you did kill the old guy, but yeah. If that power's in us, then we could live long enough to do what needs ta be done. That is, if we know how to use it." Rico snapped his head forward so he was close enough to speak to Cole using words that could barely be heard over his rasping breath. "Nymar, shapeshifters, you name it. We can't fuck around with these things no more. We need to take them out before the human race is either wiped out or runnin' around on four legs."

"And now that you've got the Jekhibar, you think you can just put everything back to the way it was?" Cole asked. "You think you'll make us all live for hundreds of years like some twisted old man who may be just another freak like the ones we hunt down and kill?"

"Maybe, maybe not," Rico replied. "It's something better than the bullshit we've been doin' lately."

"We did some good work. One Full Blood's still contained, another one's dead, and the rest are scattered. The last thing we need is to make them worse by tearing each other apart. Our system works. It just—"

"Our system is in pieces! Open yer fuckin' eyes and take a look. The goddamn *Army* is here tryin' to shoot Full Bloods! How do you think that's gonna end?" With that, Rico turned on his heels and stomped away without spilling his coffee.

"Everything all right here?" Adderson asked.

"Sure," Cole replied.

Some of the soldiers had moved in to flank Rico, but were dispersed by a quick shake of Adderson's head. When Cole fell into step with her, Paige steered them back to the Full Blood statue. "We need to find out what the hell happened with Esteban," she said. "I know the Breaking Moon made them stronger, but Full Bloods can't just start walking through rock. What if Minh pulls the same crap?"

"She's gone."

"What?"

"That Lancroft cult or whoever they are," Cole said. "I think they got her already. If Esteban found something that Lancroft was hiding away, I don't know how much help a bunch of helicopters will be in tracking him down."

"Esteban isn't the only other Full Blood out there. Finding the gargoyles worked out this time, but if we don't find some more tricks pretty soon, this little war will go on for a long time."

"So this is a war now?" he asked.

"What else would you call it?" She moved in closer beside him, but only to give them some more privacy as she said, "We're the only ones that couldn't be forced into the Breaking. When these guys figure that out, we may both be headed straight back to a prison."

"Don't forget the Amriany. They didn't change either. Are they around here too?"

"I couldn't say much of a goodbye to Nadya and Milosh before I was zapped to Finland, but they said they'd mention us to their clan leaders when they got back. We've got an in with the Amriany now, and they could prove to be even more valuable than the IRD."

He pulled in a breath but couldn't bear to hold it for more than a fraction of a second. "What in the hell are we supposed to do now, Paige?"

"We take advantage of the breathing room we've earned and gear up for the next round."

Rico shoved past some more soldiers on his way to a beat-up Toyota parked at the end of the road.

Military personnel snapped pictures and took measurements of Esteban's statue without getting too close to fangs that were still caked in flaking blood.

Helicopters roared over Raton, New Mexico.

Paige's hand closed around Cole's.

He smiled at her.

Things could have been worse.

Epilogue

North Yorkshire Moors, UK
Later

The old territory felt cool and familiar beneath Randolph's paws. Perhaps it had been selfish for him to return when there were so many wheels in motion back in his old territory. Or perhaps it was foolish of him to think he could leave those things behind to indulge in comforting surroundings while his wounds healed into yet another set of scars on his ancient body. If he stretched his senses out far enough, sniffed the breezes that blew across the oceans or simply bothered listening to enough human chatter, he could piece together what was left after the debacle that Liam had started.

None of that mattered now.

Liam was gone. The Full Blood pacts had broken down and the humans dragged into immortal affairs. Those things were unavoidable. Randolph knew as much because he'd spent too many years trying to avoid them. The only task remaining was to try and steer things so they fell in the most beneficial direction.

Beneficial to the humans? That was no longer a concern. Liam might have been right in thinking they had to be put back in line before the Skinners got even better at their craft.

Beneficial for the Full Bloods? He thought he'd known what was best for his brethren for all of these years, but perhaps he was wrong about that, like he'd been wrong about so many other things.

Beneficial for himself? That brought a smile to Randolph's long snout and a sparkle to his multifaceted eyes. He might have fooled himself into thinking he was sitting out while the rest of the world turned and everyone played their games without him, but that was absurd. It was inevitable that Cecile's Jekhibar would be taken from her. But since that had been such a battle in itself, perhaps the second Unity Stone would be forgotten for a while. Randolph clasped his prize in a fist that could feel the Torva'ox seeping from the perfect little trinket hidden away by Lancroft for centuries. All of the machinations, all of the fighting, even help from the First Deceiver himself had been necessary to shake things up enough for not one but both of the Jekhibar to rattle loose. As his reward, Randolph played the part of expatriate for a few glorious days.

Or had it been weeks?

Even if it had been for an hour, a few precious seconds, his time in the familiar moors was worth the trouble of getting there. Some Full Bloods spoke ill of short spans of time, as if seconds didn't matter simply because they had so many of them. After over a thousand years of life, however, time hadn't lost its meaning for Randolph Standing Bear. He knew only too well how different one moment was from the next and how valuable each minute could be. The others wouldn't see that. There was no way to speak sense to closed ears and no way to show truth to eye sockets filled with nothing but scar tissue. Sooner or later this terrible moment would have come, and he felt no shame in wanting to be far away when it finally arrived.

The Breaking had come and gone. Randolph was sure of it. He'd sensed its passing just as he could feel the fog drift through his fur and smell the humid day turn into a damp night. Moving in slow, deliberate steps that allowed his claws to sink into the same soil that had once squished through sandals wrapped around the feet of a young Celtic boy, Randolph headed back toward civilization. His pace quickened until the moors were behind him and a new tumultuous world lay ahead.

There was no more time to be bought.
No way to hold the Skinners back.
No way to rein in the other Full Bloods.
Too late to stall the fight between us and the humans, Liam's memory whispered into his ear, *but not too late to win it.*

A special preview of the final book of the Skinners saga:

EXTINCTION AGENDA

Available Fall 2011

This wasn't the first time Kansas City had fallen beneath the cruel whims of a monster. Unlike the days when Liam had climbed its towers to claim the city, there was no denying what was happening and nobody trying to paint a prettier face upon a siege. As in the rest of the country, the first packs had claimed their victims within two days after the incident in Atoka, Oklahoma. Those wretches were born hungry and they fed to create more. Unlike many cities in America, this one had its protectors.

I-29 was covered with snow. Although it had been plowed well enough to reveal the surface of the concrete, there were drifts on the side of the road that had empty cars and pickups embedded in them like peanuts wedged into a candy bar. Most of the wrecks were tagged and all of them were empty. A few still blinked their hazard lights onto the pristine surface of the white layers that had collected on the vehicles. In the morning, patrols would come along to check the freshest of the accidents to see if someone either needed to be brought to shelter or shot before they turned. Those unlucky enough to have wiped out between patrols would have to stay inside their cars for the night, lock their doors and pray the only thing to gnaw at their faces was the cold.

As if responding to the panicked thoughts of those stranded motorists, three Half Breeds trotted along the side of the Interstate, sniffing wildly at each car. Their gnarled faces twitched with every flake of snow that came to rest upon their snouts or ears. Half Breeds didn't need a reason to flinch because they were always in pain. Having been born to the sounds of the breaking of their bones before their muscles could stretch out to hold them together, the werewolves were in a constant state of wincing, whining or snarling. The cold, it seemed, only made them worse.

A man and woman sat huddled inside a blue Dodge with its two right tires buried hopelessly in the slush. Their faces were pressed together and their eyes widened when frightened breaths drifted from their lips to smear against the glass. That hint of movement was enough to catch one Half Breed's eye a second before its companions caught the humans' scent. The trio of werewolves lowered their chests to the snowy ground and stalked toward the car.

Both of the people inside wore glasses. Their lenses were fogged, but not thickly enough to keep them from seeing what was coming. As the unexplainable terrors spread across the country, people had no choice but to either hide or carry on as best they could. Judging by the tears streaming down both sets of reddened cheeks, these two were reconsidering their choice.

As the Half Breeds approached the car, they bared their teeth along with two sets of tusks curving down from one row of teeth and up from another. The tusks were thicker than the rest of their teeth, but thin enough to scrape against each other like scissor blades as the werewolves opened and closed their mouths to sample the frigid, late night air. Once they'd spread out to form a semi-circle around the vehicle, the creatures planted their feet and fixed their eyes upon the trembling humans. After hunkering down for a moment, the Half Breed in the middle of the group lunged forward to ram its head against the car's door. It made a dent, but could tell it wasn't going to get inside like that so it reared up and began scraping at the window.

From within the car, muffled voices wrapped around each other in much the same way the people's bodies clung together for warmth. When something moved beneath the car and scraped directly below the passenger compartment, the couple began to scream.

By now, all three of the Half Breeds were doing their best to find a way inside the car. Thick paws slapped against the frame. Twisted faces pushed against the doors and windows before the weight of a heavy body caused the entire vehicle to groan. The thing that scraped against the bottom of the car quickened its pace toward the side being attacked by the Half Breeds. As soon as it reached the driver's door, the scraping against the window stopped. Soon, the other two Half Breeds were pulled away from the car as well.

When the man wiped the frost away off the window to get a look outside, he found several shaggy bodies wrestling in the snow. Blood sprayed through the air in a fine mist, cast from fangs and claws. It was impossible to tell which creatures were winning or even where one ended and another began, so the man eased away from the window before he was noticed.

"I think we should make a run for it," he told the trembling woman.

"Where are we going to go?"

"I don't know. Just away from here!"

And, as suddenly as the creatures had appeared, the fight was over.

The wind scraped against the car's exterior, its slow rustle the loudest thing in the world at that given moment. Glass creaked and bits of ice rapped against the side of the car as if the winter itself had sprouted claws.

"Should . . . we still run?" the woman asked.

Two sets of claws wedged into the driver's side door; one at the base of the window and another near the handle. With a minimum amount of effort, the door was separated from its frame and tossed aside. Outside, a tall creature stood wearing a thick coat of light blond fur peppered with streaks of darker brown and encrusted with chunks of snow. Blood was already frozen where it had been spilled. Kayla had presided over Kansas City since her pack had taken part in ending Liam's siege. Although the Mongrels under her command had been thinned out due to treachery within her ranks or combat with the encroaching werewolves, she wasn't about to step aside so any invader could have their way with her territory.

"Yes," she snarled through a snout that seemed just a bit too long for her feline facial structure. "You should run."

The couple within the car pressed themselves against the opposite window and nearly jumped from their sweat-stained coats when another Mongrel appeared outside the passenger window. Ben's appearance was even more disturbing than Kayla's. Being a digger who could practically swim underground, he was accustomed to remaining out of sight. Gill flaps along his neck stretched out and immediately snapped shut after drawing in too much freezing air instead of the soil they were meant to process. Blood and ice stuck to the beak that dominated his face and his black eyes remained calm beneath their vertical lids as they studied the people within the vehicle. His fingers slipped beneath the door's handle and were strong enough to force it open despite the ice that had sealed it shut. "There is another car further up the road," he said. "White four-door just past a minivan facing the wrong way."

Dazed by the words that came from the Mongrel's beak, the woman stammered, "We can't just . . . steal a car."

"Get away from us!" the man snapped as he tried his best to squirm in the cramped confines to put himself between her and the Mongrel.

Ben merely stepped back, allowing the man to play his role as protector without reacting to the threatening tone in his voice or the way he grabbed a long flashlight and wielded it like a club. "It's not stealing," he told them both. "The owners of that car were killed by the same creatures we just chased away. My advice is to take that car and get to somewhere safer. Also," he added while dropping to all fours and scraping away the top layers of snowy earth using long, curved claws, "don't look too hard at the mess in the ditch."

When the man turned to where Kayla had been standing, he found only the bloody remains of two Half Breeds. The third had already bounded down the Interstate chasing after a lean figure that slid gracefully into another lane.

"I think we should go," the woman said.

Taking his eyes from the sight of the chase toward the row of lonely abandoned vehicles on the side of the road, the man swallowed hard and zipped up his coat. "Right. Do you have our suitcase?"

"Just move!"

He followed her order and bolted from the car. Along the way, he thought about the fire that had all but consumed Topeka after the werewolves had sprung up in the autumn. Only during the drive to KC had he asked his fiancé why they might have been spared. The conversation had lasted until they pulled over to fill the gas tank and their stomachs at a place that had a Subway sandwich shop and Pizza Hut tacked onto it. Every seat was filled with people of all ages, genders and nationalities. Each stunned face was focused intently on their meals. The terror implied within their features was all too familiar to the man from Topeka. He'd been wearing it ever since he'd abandoned his hometown.

It hadn't been an easy decision. When the first werewolves showed up, everyone he knew wanted to fight them. A call to arms swept throughout the entire country at about that same time, encouraging everyone to buy a gun and defend their homes from the animals that meant to do them harm. Explanations would wait for later. Now was the time to fight.

That lasted for a few weeks.

When the angry voices died down, it wasn't because of victory or fatigue. The people who'd bought their guns and started firing at the wild animals in their yards had been torn to shreds. It wasn't pretty and it wasn't spectacular. Even the few who'd rigged explosives with some degree of success barely managed to do any damage. After that, the wolves had swept in to kill them all.

The police were just more men with guns.

The military was taking a stand, but not in Topeka.

Soon, like most other cities, Topeka burned. Whether the fires had been started by accident or as a last-ditch effort to kill the werewolves didn't matter. The flames rose and the people who tried to put them out were set upon by another pack of ravenous beasts. The firefighters that lived to crawl away only howled in pain as their bodies were twisted into one of those things that set out to hunt for food. Like the rest of his family, the man who now clung to his fiancé to keep from slipping on a patch of ice on I-29 hadn't wanted to leave Topeka.

His natural instinct was to stay. For the first several weeks of the crisis, people barricaded themselves indoors to fight for survival. They watched their televisions for news about how far the insanity had spread and what was being done to stop it. Before long, people stopped watching the news and just focused on living for another day. Then, as things got worse, the highways became crowded with cars on their way to someplace better. The people behind the wheels may or may not have known where they were headed, but it was time to go.

The man from Topeka stayed until his friends and family were consumed. That's what people started calling it, since there often wasn't a way to know if they were truly dead. At least that word was better than the thought of seeing a parent, child or neighbor broken down into a screaming heap to be re-forged into something with fangs and wild, pain-filled eyes. The last possible good he could do was take his fiancé away before her pretty face was twisted into something cruel and hungry. They'd made it as far as KC and he was determined to keep going. When she slipped, he was there to pull her to her feet and urge her onward. They'd passed the minivan which had spun one hundred and eighty degrees before plowing into a drift. The four-door was directly ahead of them, cleared off and waiting for them like a freshly unwrapped present.

"Stay here and I'll check it out," he said.

The door was unlocked and the keys were on the dash. After fidgeting with fingers that were almost too numbed to feel the keys, he slipped the right one into the ignition and started the car. "Come on, honey!"

The woman cautiously stuck her feet into the snow. Tracks that were too large and spaced too far apart to be set down by humans surrounded the car. They converged a bit further away from the road near a pile of crimson pulp that had been covered by a fine layer of snow. Heeding Ben's advice, she turned her eyes away from the mess and fumbled with the handle of the passenger side door. After she'd gotten in, but before she'd gotten a chance to pull the door shut, the car lurched forward.

"Where are we going?" she asked while frantically tugging at her safety belt.

"I've got some old friends in Saint Louis. We'll go there."

"Can we make it all that way? How far is it?"

Blinking furiously as a Half Breed leapt out from a hole on the side of the road, only to be overtaken by a beaked

Mongrel, he sputtered. "I don't know, but we're going. We came this far, we won't stop now." He looked over to her and saw nothing but determination on her trembling features. She swiped some tears from her eyes, nodded and placed her hand in his.

MARCUS PELEGRIMAS's
SKINNERS

HUMANKIND'S LAST DEFENSE AGAINST THE DARKNESS

BLOOD BLADE
978-0-06-146305-1

There is a world inhabited by supernatural creatures of the darkness—all manner of savage, impossible beasts that live for terror and slaughter and blood. They are all around us but you cannot see them, and for centuries a special breed of hunter called Skinners has kept the monsters at bay, preventing them from breaking through the increasingly fragile barriers protecting our mortal realm. But beware…for there are very few of them left.

HOWLING LEGION
978-0-06-146306-8

TEETH OF BEASTS
978-0-06-146307-5

VAMPIRE UPRISING
978-0-06-198633-8

THE BREAKING
978-0-06-198634-5

Visit www.AuthorTracker.com for exclusive information on your favorite HarperCollins authors.

Available wherever books are sold or please call 1-800-331-3761 to order.

JOCELYNN DRAKE'S
NEW YORK TIMES BESTSELLING
DARK DAYS NOVELS

NIGHTWALKER
978-0-06-154277-0

For centuries Mira has been a nightwalker—an unstoppable enforcer for a mysterious organization that manipulates earth-shaking events from the darkest shadows. But the foe she now faces is human: the vampire hunter called Danaus, who has already destroyed so many undead.

DAYHUNTER
978-0-06-154283-1

Mira and her unlikely ally Danaus have come to Venice, home of the nightwalker rulers. But there is no safety in the ancient city and Danaus, the only creature she dares trust, is something more than the man he claims to be...

DAWNBREAKER
978-0-06-154288-6

Destiny draws Mira and Danaus toward an apocalyptic confrontation with the *naturi* at Machu Picchu. Once the *naturi* are unchained, blood, chaos, and horror will reign supreme on Earth. But all is not lost as a rogue enemy princess can change the balance of power and turn the dread tide.

PRAY FOR DAWN
978-0-06-185180-3

Mira and Danaus—vampire and vampire slayer—must unite to prevent the annihilation of their separate races when the slaying of a senator's daughter threatens to expose Mira to the light of day.

Visit www.AuthorTracker.com for exclusive information on your favorite HarperCollins authors.

Available wherever books are sold or please call 1-800-331-3761 to order.

DARK AND STEAMY ADVENTURE WITH
VAMPIRE PRIVATE EYE FELIX GOMEZ FROM
MARIO ACEVEDO

THE NYMPHOS OF ROCKY FLATS
978-0-06-143888-2

Felix Gomez went to Iraq a soldier. He came back a vampire. Back home in the States the undead former infantryman makes a living as a private detective as he investigates a bizarre outbreak of nymphomania.

X-RATED BLOODSUCKERS
978-0-06-143887-5

Gomez is approached by sexy porn star Katz Meow, who wants him to investigate the murder of her once-equally agile friend and fellow toiler in the video sex biz, Roxy Bronze.

THE UNDEAD KAMA SUTRA
978-0-06-166746-6

The dying words of an alien interloper are thrusting the immortal P.I. Felix Gomez into a seamy mess of otherworldly abductions, shady military irregularities, and unexplained murder.

JAILBAIT ZOMBIE
978-0-06-156717-9

It's vamps versus zombies and Felix's only hope of stopping the stinking, hungry horde is a precocious teenager who wants to become immortal.

WEREWOLF SMACKDOWN
978-0-06-156720-9

There's a civil war brewing between two vicious lycanthrope factions that threatens to engulf *all* creatures, living and undead.

Visit www.AuthorTracker.com for exclusive information on your favorite HarperCollins authors.

Available wherever books are sold or please call 1-800-331-3761 to order.

HARPER VOYAGER TRADE PAPERBACKS

HARPER Voyager
An Imprint of HarperCollins*Publishers*

www.harpervoyagerbooks.com

THE GREAT BOOK OF AMBER
by Roger Zelazny
978-0-380-80906-6

BRAINS
by Robin Becker
978-0-06-197405-2

SWORDS & DARK MAGIC
Edited by Jonathan Strahan and Lou Anders
978-0-06-172381-0

THE CHILD THIEF
by Brom
978-0-06-167134-0

Z IS FOR ZOMBIE
An Illustrated Guide to the End of the World
by Adam-Troy Castro and Johnny Atomic
978-0-06-199185-1

THE INHERITANCE
and Other Stories
by Robin Hobb
978-0-06-156164-1

V IS FOR VAMPIRE
An Illustrated Alphabet of the Undead
by Adam-Troy Castro
978-0-06-199186-8

Visit www.AuthorTracker.com for exclusive information on your favorite HarperCollins authors.

Available wherever books are sold or please call 1-800-331-3761 to order.